The Potter.

The Potters of Halberton

by

Sarah Caundle

HOLLYLODGE BOOKS

Distributed by Gardners Books

1 Whittle Drive, Eastbourne, East Sussex, BN23 6QH

Tel: +44(0)1323 521555 | Fax: +44(0)1323 521666

British Library Cataloguing in Publication Data

A catalogue record for this book is available from the British Library

ISBN 978-0-9954575-0-8

Typeset by Amolibros, Milverton, Somerset

www.amolibros.com

This book production has been managed by Amolibros

Printed and bound by T J International Ltd, Padstow, Cornwall, UK

In memory of my great-uncles Frank Potter (1887 – 1915) and Edward Potter (1886 – 1918)

Part One

One

---

*L*ilian Potter looked at her husband over the remains of their breakfast. She adored picnics and today was perfect for one, but Edmund, usually so amenable, was being mulish.

'It's such heavenly weather,' she pouted. 'Why can't we go to the coast?'

'It isn't possible today, my dear. I have to go to Bradcombe. Father's expecting me. Things are pretty busy at the moment.'

'Surely he can spare you for a day.'

'Of course he can, but not today. We're due to meet with Pendergast.'

Lilian sighed as she thought of the family solicitor. They would talk for hours.

'You do realise it's the bank holiday weekend tomorrow?' she said. 'You know how busy it gets. It would be far better to go today.'

Before Edmund could reply the maid showed Hugh Brodrick into the room. Edmund and Hugh had been at school and Oxford together and were close friends.

'I'm on my way to Tiverton so I thought I'd call in and say hello,' he said, looking from one to the other. 'I didn't realise I was so early. Sorry if I'm disturbing your breakfast.'

'That's all right, we've finished,' said Lilian. 'I'm glad you've come. You can help me persuade Edmund that we should go to the coast for a picnic. He's being obstinate.'

Hugh looked from one to the other. 'It's fine weather. It'd be a pity not to take advantage of it,' he said.

Edmund laughed. 'Of course we'll go, but not today, that's all. I tell you what, why don't you join us, Hugh? We'll go on Sunday and have a picnic on the beach at Sidmouth. What do you say?'

'Thanks, that's a splendid idea. I could do with a day by the sea. I'll drive us.'

'What do you say, Lily? It's only three days to wait and the weather should hold,' Edmund said.

She would much rather that Edmund had not invited Hugh, who bored her, but there was no getting out of it so she accepted with good grace.

Hugh left shortly afterwards and Edmund went to saddle up Claudius, his chestnut gelding, for the ride to Bradcombe Rogus. He owned three hunters but Claudius was his favourite. They seemed to have an intuitive understanding of each other.

★

Two years earlier, shortly after their marriage, Hugh had been the subject of the Potters' first significant disagreement.

'Edmund, I do wish you and Hugh wouldn't talk in Latin,' Lilian complained one day after Hugh had left them. The youngest of three children and the only girl, she had been educated at home by a series of governesses and although she had been instructed in Latin it had failed to capture her interest. She had therefore forgotten most of it as soon as she had learned it.

'*Sponte sua carmen numeros veniebat ad aptos, et quod temptabam dicere versus erat,*' Edmund replied with a laugh, 'I'm sorry, darling, that was a quote from Ovid – "Of its own accord my song would come in the right rhythms, and what I was trying to say was poetry". It's second nature for us to speak Latin. We've done it since we were at school. It was a good way of learning it then and the habit stuck. You should have interrupted us.'

Lilian twitched her foot, as was her habit when she was bottling things up. Edmund moved to behind her chair and leaned down to kiss her hair.

'I'm afraid we sometimes forget that you don't always understand.'

She had no intention of being placated that easily.

'I know that with *you* it's only forgetfulness but I wonder whether Hugh doesn't deliberately start gabbling in Latin.'

'Why on earth would he do that?'

'I don't know. I expect he's bored now that you're married. Perhaps he's jealous that I've taken away his playmate.'

'I wish you wouldn't say things like that, Lily,' he said, straightening up. 'Hugh's a rock. He's the best friend I'll ever have.'

'I know.'

Edmund walked across to the mantelpiece and fiddled with a porcelain vase. 'I wish you could like him a bit more. If you try to be more friendly I expect he'll open up towards you. I know he can come across as rather diffident sometimes, but that's only because he's more reserved than either of us. Believe me, it's worth making the effort to get to know him.'

'But how can anyone like him? He's so – so grey. He reminds me of winter.'

'He's not at all grey. He's decidedly dark.'

'You know what I mean. His character, not his features. He's so *negative*.'

'You're the only person who thinks so. I find him good company and so do plenty of others. No airs or graces, no fuss or bother.'

'But he's so serious. You can't deny that.'

'Well, that's only to be expected after he inherited Netherculme so young – he should be having fun and enjoying himself with no more to worry about than his next painting. It's a damned shame because he's a good artist.'

'But he –'

'He's had to learn about running Netherculme the hard way, unlike me,' Edmund continued. 'My father's idea of a gentle handover for a couple of years is child's play compared with what Hugh has had to do. It makes me quite embarrassed. You can't blame him if he's more serious than our other friends. I know he doesn't shine in large social gatherings but what does that matter?'

Lilian understood the sense of Edmund's argument but, as usual, she had to get in one last shot. 'You like him so much because you're illuminated by his greyness. You show up all the better in his company. In other words, he feeds your vanity. Why not admit it?'

'I'll admit no such thing.'

Lilian pursed her lips and looked thoughtfully at her husband. 'All right,' she conceded. 'I'll give him the benefit of the doubt. As you said, he's had a lot to deal with and must be frustrated that he can't spend as much time painting as he'd like.'

Neither of them reflected with satisfaction on this conversation. Edmund was piqued by Lilian's comment about his vanity, which he was loath to admit even to himself, though there was a certain truth in it. As for Lilian, slowly she began to acknowledge that she might perhaps be a little jealous of Hugh. She tried to overcome it and to make more of an effort to befriend him for Edmund's sake. At length he responded by being more at ease with her and shedding at least some of his diffidence. Edmund had been right, as usual.

She was gratified to hear Latin spoken less frequently.

Two

The weather held and, as arranged, on Sunday August 2nd Hugh's sleek blue Daimler pulled up outside Sydling, the Potters' house in the village of Halberton. Edmund and Lilian were ready and waiting.

Lilian had swept her blond hair back à la Pompadour. She wore a soft linen dress the colour of cornflowers, which she knew became her well.

Hugh was a good driver, fast but safe. Their journey took them along roads that were still relatively immune from motor vehicles and, apart from having to negotiate a dozen hens, a pig and a couple of herds of cows, they made good time. The powerful car made easy work of the climb beyond Cullompton, then the exhilarating descent to Honiton and on to Sidmouth. Here things changed. This was no backwater: the motor car had arrived good and proper, bringing a traffic-jam populated by red-faced, frustrated drivers. Their progress was slow as they dodged cars, horses and traps, and men, women and children laden with picnic and bathing paraphernalia who seemed oblivious to the perils of stepping out in front of vehicles. At length they reached the eastern end of the town near fishing boats that had been winched up the beach because there was no harbour. Hugh parked the car and switched off the engine.

'She should be safe enough here,' he said. 'It was too crowded nearer the centre. I don't want her to get scratched or bumped. These people don't seem to care what they do.'

'You and your car,' laughed Edmund. 'I swear the woman doesn't exist who you'd treat half so well as this car.'

Hugh looked embarrassed. 'You may be right. She'd have to be exceptional.'

'We won't be able to smell fish, will we?' asked Lilian, screwing up her nose and looking dubiously towards a stall selling what was left of the day's catch.

'Of course not,' replied Edmund. 'I should think most of it's been sold by now anyway.'

'We could always try to get some shrimps for the picnic, if they have any left,' suggested Hugh.

'That's an excellent idea. Why don't you go and buy some and we'll find a nice spot and settle ourselves on the beach.' said Lilian.

'Right ho,' said Hugh and he ambled off, hands in pockets.

Edmund lifted down the rugs and the pair made their way towards the steps that led down to the beach from the Esplanade.

'Shame there's no sand here. Can you manage on these pebbles?' he asked.

'Yes, I think so. At least we haven't far to go.'

Lilian stepped cautiously from one large pebble to another. She teetered for a moment, her parasol waving drunkenly overhead. She wished she had put on her walking shoes instead of the fashionable pair she had bought the previous week. With a sheepish look she offered her arm to Edmund for assistance. He duly obliged. Having found a suitable spot that was relatively uncrowded – although it was impossible to avoid everyone on such a busy beach – near enough to the water that going across the pebbles for a paddle would only be a mild inconvenience and far enough to avoid embarrassment when the tide turned, they arranged the rugs. Lilian settled herself while Edmund went back to the vehicle for the hamper. When he returned Hugh was with him, a smile splitting his face.

'We're in luck, Lilian. There weren't any shrimps but I bagged the last two cooked lobsters.'

'That's marvellous, but have we anything to open them with?'

'I'm pretty sure we have,' Edmund said. 'If not, we'll have to improvise.'

He took off his blazer, rolled up his sleeves and delved into the hamper. Soon most of the contents were scattered over the rug.

'Ah. This will do – I think we'll manage without too much difficulty,' he announced delightedly as he held up a sharp knife. 'And if we have any trouble with the claws we can bash 'em with a spanner from the car.'

While Edmund prepared the lobsters Lilian arranged the rest of the feast and Hugh poured fresh lemonade that had more or less remained chilled in spite of the heat. They were all hungry after the drive and the stimulus of sea air and they ate and drank in a comfortable silence, broken only by murmurs of appreciation.

'I love picnics,' said Hugh, reaching out for another chicken drumstick. 'I don't know why but food always seems to taste better out of doors, even in winter. Perhaps it's the air.'

'Mm,' agreed Edmund, as he carefully scraped out a lobster shell.

A short distance away a solitary fisherman sat in the shade of his boat, head bent in concentration while he mended his net. Overhead, gulls wheeled and mewed and the sun shone from a sky which, although still cobalt, was tending towards haziness. The gentlest of breezes played about them. The sea unfurled itself on the shore with curls so small that they could hardly be called waves.

Lilian felt warm and drowsy and closed her eyes. The men lit their pipes and stretched out comfortably.

'I could stay here for ever,' said Edmund.

'Me too. It's heavenly. We must come back next week if the weather holds,' said Lilian.

'But we can't, though, can we,' Hugh blurted.

The vehemence of his words make Lilian open her eyes and look at him in surprise.

'Why ever not?'

'Because it's odds on that we'll soon be at war.' He picked up a pebble and tossed it into the water.

'At war! Do you believe in all that? It's only a rumour, surely.'

'No, my dear. I'm afraid it's much more than rumour,' said Edmund, sitting up. 'This week, next week, the week after, some time soon anyway, Great Britain will be at war with Germany.'

'Oh.' Lilian could think of nothing else to say. She had heard the rumours, of course – the possibility of war had been talked about everywhere for the last few days but she adamantly refused to believe it.

'We'll have to enlist, of course,' said Hugh, 'I doubt it will be for long, though – a few months, possibly.'

Lilian shivered.

'When you said "we", to whom were you referring?' she asked stiffly, though she knew the answer.

There was an uncomfortable silence.

'I seem to have dropped a brick,' Hugh said at last. 'Forgive me. I assumed you'd have discussed it.'

'Not quite up to your usual tact, old man,' Edmund said.

Lilian was torn between loyalty to Edmund on the one hand, and anger with him for not being open with her on the other. 'No, we haven't. We've talked about war in general terms, of course, but Edmund must have thought that the possibility of his enlisting was so inconsequential that he forgot to mention it.'

She threw him a challenging glance. He looked away.

Hugh began to apologise again.

'Better not say anything, old man,' Edmund intervened. It's

my fault entirely. I never got round to it.' He turned to Lilian. 'Truth to tell, I knew you wouldn't want me to go, my dear, and there didn't seem to be any point in counting chickens before anything was definite. I didn't want you to worry needlessly.'

'I see. All the same, I would have preferred to hear of your plans from you, not from – someone else.'

★

Hugh was embarrassed by his *faux pas*. He clambered to his feet and strolled down to the water's edge where he stooped to pick up pebbles to skim over the sea. He was mortified that he had provoked a row between Edmund and Lilian. He could hear their voices rise behind him. He shuffled his feet on the shingle to drown them out and concentrated on skimming the pebbles.

After a few minutes he became aware of silence behind him and then the sound of feet crunching on shingle. Edmund was calling to him and he turned round. Edmund's face was flushed and taut, which was unusual for him.

'We thought we might go for a stroll along the front before going home, if you're agreeable,' he said.

'Yes, of course. Good idea.'

Hugh watched Lilian walking towards the car and marvelled at the expressiveness of her slim back. 'I'm so sorry, old soul. I shouldn't have assumed. War's been on my mind so much in the last couple of days that it just popped out.'

'Don't worry, Hugh. You know Lilian. She only acknowledges what is charming and elegant, as a rule. An admirable trait in peacetime but I'm afraid we'll all have to face a different reality soon. I just couldn't bring myself to break the spell. Anyway, I think I succeeded in making her see the bright side – jolly officers, team spirit, medals on my chest. She's swung right round now and wants me to go as soon as possible so that she can boast of her hero to her less fortunate friends.'

Hugh laughed. 'She's right. If there are any medals going, you're sure to have one.'

'Course I shall. Can't let her down. Come on, let's stretch our legs.'

When they had stowed their belongings in the car they turned and strolled along the Esplanade. Lilian took Edmund's arm, her free hand holding her parasol. Walking on the other side of her, Hugh was conscious that he ought to atone for his tactlessness. He was relieved to see that she and Edmund now appeared to be on amicable terms again but, as so often happened in her company, he found himself struggling to find the right words. Moreover, her parasol was an effective barrier between them. It seemed that he would have to walk the whole length of the Esplanade without talking to her.

It was Lilian who broke the silence.

'Are you serious about enlisting, Hugh? What will you do about Netherculme?'

Yes, I believe I must. It's the only possible course for a single man like myself. The OTC training I did at school should be a help. As for Netherculme, that's a difficult one. I think I'll have to have it moth-balled, and just keep a skeleton staff. It's a shame, as I've just about got it shipshape and was looking forward to being able to devote more time to painting. I've got woefully out of practice.'

'But do you really have to enlist? There are plenty of other men who can go. Men who don't have your responsibilities.'

'Are there? There are lots of men who don't have the running of an estate, it's true, but many will have wives and families who depend on them.'

'Like Edmund.'

'Well, yes, but I was thinking more of households where the sole source of income is the weekly wage. Those families will be hardest hit.'

Lilian looked at him.

'Edmund will make a fine officer, Lilian.'

'I dare say.'

'Anyway, it probably won't be for long.'

'That's what he said.'

They lapsed into silence.

A short distance away a lively crowd was gathered and soon they found themselves at a Punch and Judy booth. The crocodile was attacking Mr Punch, who was defending himself for all he was worth. Excited children, seated cross-legged on the beach, egged on the crocodile at the tops of their voices while their parents and other assorted adults, some equally raucous, stood around the fringes. Edmund, Lilian and Hugh soon joined in. There seemed to be a tension in the air, a heightened mood, a determination to enjoy it to the utmost. When the show was over a hush fell over the scene and people dispersed in their various directions. The trio retraced their steps to the car. Perhaps it was the sea air, perhaps it was the prospect of war, but as they travelled home none of them felt inclined to chat, each privately feeling that they couldn't reach home too soon.

Three

The following day the Potters held a tennis party.

To her chagrin Lilian found that not only was war the major topic of conversation but it was considered inevitable. She sat between her mother and mother-in-law while she rested after a vigorously contested couple of sets. Maud Potter was a homely woman whose face had become enhanced over the years by the laughter lines around her eyes. Edmund had inherited her hair which still retained its rich chestnut tone and which tended to curls.

Lilian looked at her mother. Some people thought that Lilian was a younger version of May Franklin but she herself couldn't see the resemblance. They were more or less the same height and build but she thought their features were not at all alike. She didn't have the advantage, as others did, of being able to compare herself with her mother in profile.

'Don't you think the boys will look good in uniform, May?' Maud Potter said, indicating Edmund and his younger brother Noel with a nod of the head.

'Simply splendid. What do you say, my dear?'

'They would certainly look well,' agreed Lilian, 'but I still don't see why they should think of enlisting at all.'

'My dear,' exclaimed Mrs Potter. 'Of course they should. It's their duty.'

'Really, Lilian, how can you say such a thing?' said her mother.

'But why should they? Edmund tells me that it will all be over soon anyway, so what's the point? He might as well stay here and be useful. After all, Arthur's depending on him to take over Bradcombe.'

Both women frowned at her and pursed their lips.

'Of course, there's no reason why Noel shouldn't go,' she continued. 'He has no attachments. He can easily be spared from his job for a few months, I dare say, like Hugh Brodrick. But it's different for a married man. You must agree that Arthur can't spare Edmund, Maud.'

'Naturally, Arthur was hoping to hand over Bradcombe to him but he knows where his duty lies, and I'm happy to say that Edmund does too. You mustn't be selfish, you know, Lilian. What about John and Walter, May? Are they going to enlist?'

'Naturally they are. John's determined to enlist as soon as war's declared, with the full blessing of Annie, I'm happy to say.' Lilian caught her mother's forthright look. 'Walter wants to enlist too, but being a cautious sort of soul he's going to wait for a month or two and see how things are going first. Vicky wants him to join up now. She says it'll be embarrassing to have a civilian husband when all the other men are in khaki.'

'Surely not,' said Lilian. 'What about the children?'

As she spoke, John's two boys came running up to them.

'Granny, Granny. Daddy's going to be a soldier,' they shouted together.

'Is he now? How exciting.'

'Yes. He said he's going to fight the Germans as soon as he can,' said Tommy, the older boy.

'And he's going to win more medals than Uncle Edmund,' said three-year-old Roly.

'That will be very difficult,' said Lilian. 'I expect Uncle Edmund will win lots.'

'Daddy will win lots too.'

The conversation descended into pantomime banter and

after many hugs and tickles with the boys Lilian got up and went to see her other guests. But whichever group she joined, the talk was of war and bravado. She moved on as soon as she could without being rude and applied herself to the tennis, at which at which she knew she was both competent and elegant.

By the time the party broke up the sun was dipping, huge and red, behind nearby elms while beyond the garden to the east the red sandstone tower of the village church glowed as though alive in the sun's deep light, the whole effect enhanced by the churchyard yews, so dark that they seemed almost black. House martins wheeled and dived in the sky, chattering incessantly. Edmund was the last player left outside. Glancing through a window, Lilian noticed him standing motionless, facing the church. She wondered what was going through his mind to make him linger like that. Then he picked up his racquet, tossed his blazer over one shoulder, and strode purposefully towards the house.

★

The next day Germany's intention of invading Belgium was confirmed. Great Britain sent an ultimatum demanding German compliance with Belgian neutrality. There was no reply. War was declared. When Edmund had read *The Times* after breakfast the following morning his first thought was to talk to Lilian. He had broached the subject several times since Sidmouth but on every occasion the conversation broke down in heated words, leaving them both in the enjoyment of righteous indignation. He was frustrated by her wilful inability to accept the truth about what was happening and to recognise his sense of duty, while she, who had barely been crossed in her life before now, could not understand why he should be so selfish and inconsiderate.

He looked for her around the house and eventually tracked

her down outside, where she was feeding her hens. There was no point in beating about the bush.

'Lily, my dear,' he said gently. 'We're at war with Germany. It's official.'

She bit her lip and looked away.

'You know what I'm going to say. I must enlist. I know it won't be easy for you but I couldn't live with myself if I didn't.'

'But darling, can't you wait? It may be a storm in a teacup – just a threat. The government might change their minds, then you'll have done it for nothing. Can't you wait and see what happens first? Mother told me that Walter's going to do just that. Why can't you?'

'That's his decision. I believe it's more serious than that. I feel that I must go now. As I've said before, it will probably mean my being away from home for no more than a few months in any case. I'll be home by spring almost certainly. The declaration of war can't be withdrawn but nobody believes the war will last long.'

'Spring! But that's an age. What shall I do without you? I can't imagine it.'

'You have all your friends, and our families. You won't be alone, my dear.'

'I learned yesterday that John and Noel are planning to go now as well. I'll never understand it. And your mother said that your father wants you to go. I'd have thought he of all people would want you to stay and take on Bradcombe but it seems not.'

'I've discussed it with Father at length. He would do the same in my position; in fact, he's rather envious of Noel and me. It will mean more work for him, of course, but he'll manage as he did before I started helping him. It's all settled. Come, let's go inside.'

'Edmund.'

'Yes?'

'I want you to know I consider it beastly of you to have discussed the war and made your plans with everyone except me. My opinion – my needs – our marriage – all seem to count for nothing.'

'My dear, we've been over this. I held back from discussing it with you because we're so close. I knew you wouldn't want me to go. I wanted to spare you needless worry in case it all came to nothing. Unhappily, the Germans didn't consider our feelings. What I'm going to do in no way reflects badly on our marriage. You mustn't think that for a moment. I love you as dearly as the day we were married and nothing's going to change that.'

'Nevertheless, I feel that you don't trust me. I used to think I knew you but now I'm not sure.' She sighed in the particular way she had when she wanted to get round him.

'It isn't a question of trust. I'm sorry, Lily. My mind's made up. It's my duty to go. I wish I could have your support. It would mean so much to me.'

Lilian did not reply at once. She looked at the hens that were busy scrabbling around her feet. 'Of course you'll have it if it comes to it,' she said at length. 'But I can't lie and tell you it will be easy. And I shan't give up trying to persuade you to stay until you go.'

★

Lilian was true to her word. She coaxed, she cried, she threatened, but Edmund was steadfast. She could think of little to cheer her. War was all very well for a *man*, it gave him something exciting to do, a chance to live again in a schoolboy atmosphere – *esprit de corps*. But for a woman the picture was altogether more insipid. She would miss him dreadfully. She was not given to introspection. Seven years younger than her brothers, she had enjoyed an indulgent childhood and had been led to believe that she could do little wrong. She had a mild

18

nature most of the time but any shows of petulance were, in her girlhood, found to amuse rather than to invite correction. Now, for the first time in her life, she found herself playing second fiddle and unable to get her way. She was baffled.

She shuddered at the thought of Edmund being away, perhaps for months. Of not being the centre of his world. She was not afraid of his being wounded or killed because she knew he would only receive a light wound, and action would give him an opportunity to win a decoration, which of all men he was the most likely to achieve. After all, hadn't he always been top in his class at school and Oxford, and led the field in the many sports he enjoyed?

At last the fractious day drew to a close, none too soon for either of them. What should have been a final day of peace and understanding had left them both drained. Still cross with Edmund, Lilian retired early to bed, pleading a headache.

★

After she left him, Edmund called his greyhounds Castor and Pollux and went out into the garden. The air was warm and heavy with the scent of honeysuckle and stock. He stood still and silent, savouring the moment. The sky was teeming with stars. An owl glided overhead and disappeared behind the church tower. Bats darted about, sometimes almost brushing his head. A cow lowed in a distant field.

Eventually he roused himself and went round to the stable. With sentimentality that he refused to acknowledge he opened Claudius's stable door and went inside. The horse nuzzled him as if in empathy. When he judged that Lilian would be asleep Edmund made his way back to the house.

★

Lying in bed, Lilian's mind was revolving over the injustice with growing resentment when she heard Edmund enter the bedroom. She feigned sleep and was relieved that he did not speak. Before long she heard him breathing smoothly and rhythmically and soon she too drifted off.

When she woke, dawn was only just starting to streak the sky. Edmund was already up. She turned and lay on her back, looking out through the open curtains. Her temper and resentment had been quieted by sleep, and she reflected on the previous day. She flushed with shame at her own selfishness, and tried to think more charitably of Edmund's desire to enlist. She made a vow not to argue with him today.

He intended to go with Hugh to the hastily arranged recruiting office in Tiverton immediately after breakfast as they wanted to be sure of training together. Lilian heard Hugh arrive while she was still dressing. Breakfast was peaceful. They made a determined effort to talk about any subject except the one uppermost in their minds. The meal over, Lilian was soon waving them off. On impulse, she ran down to the Jubilee Tree, an oak planted to commemorate Queen Victoria's diamond jubilee which marked the junction of the lower village with the Tiverton road. She did not take her eyes off their retreating backs until they crested a bridge and disappeared from sight.

She need not have feared a long wait to see Edmund again. He returned alone later in the day. She was on the lawn, reading in the shade of a tree. Flinging the book aside she jumped to her feet when she saw him.

'They're totally unprepared,' he said. 'No rifles, no uniforms, no quarters. They sent us home tonight in the hope that things will be more organised tomorrow. Hugh's gone back to Netherculme.'

'You must be ... disappointed.'

'Of course I am. If I could see the war coming, so could the army. I can't understand it.'

'Well, never mind, darling.' She paused. 'I behaved shamefully yesterday. It was unforgiveable of me. All day I've been thinking of you going off to war with my ridiculous words and moods to remember me by. I'm so sorry. You must do what you need to do. I know your heart's set on it. Forget my selfishness. I shall support you to the utmost, no matter what.'

'There's nothing to forgive,' Edmund said, hugging her.

Four

The following days and weeks found the army more in control. Edmund and Hugh joined a newly formed battalion of the Devonshire Regiment. It was lucky to have a core of officers and NCOs transferred from the First Devons, a regular battalion. The new service battalion initially had no uniforms and weapons for training but at least they had unlimited enthusiasm. At first the men squeezed into overcrowded barracks and billets in Exeter; then they moved under canvas in Hampshire. It would have been fun if the men had not been desperate to get to France before it was too late. Officers were in short supply and, as Edmund had guessed, those with OTC training like himself and Hugh were quickly gazetted. Their fellow subalterns included undergraduates and boys straight from public school. At the age of twenty-five, Edmund felt rather grand and old.

The battalion's first parade was held at the end of September after which blue uniforms arrived. Khaki would have been better but at least it was some progress.

Wherever he went when he was able to get away from his billets, Edmund saw more and more men who had obviously been at the front, their uniforms having a more worn appearance and their faces less smiling than those of the men who had yet to go out. Some were on leave and others recovering from wounds. He envied them and had to bite his tongue to hide his impatience. Training, marching and musketry drill were all very necessary but were no substitute for the real thing.

One thing grieved him more than not going to France and that was having to part with Claudius. Horses had been commandeered across the country and Edmund willingly offered up two of his in the hope that he would be able to keep Claudius but he had been obliged to let him go as well. He knew he was being selfish and if he had kept Claudius he would have gone to fat with no one to ride him, but it was still a wrench. In idle moments he wondered where he was, who was riding him. Was he in France? Was he still alive?

Of course he missed Lilian, but that was different: she was at home and would always be there for him.

★

Lilian found herself swept up in the pervading enthusiasm for the war effort. She formed a knitting circle with some friends. She did not knit well but Edmund had asked for a scarf and mittens for the colder days ahead and she had not wanted to disappoint him. After he had enlisted and she knew that further resistance was futile, Lilian became philosophical, doing all she could to make his life as comfortable as possible. She wrote to him every day and sent him weekly parcels.

From a scarf and mittens it was a short step to knitting socks and comforters for Tommies at the front.

One day in December the circle met in the drawing room at Sydling. The room was well lit and a fire burned brightly in contrast to the gloom outside.

'Edmund's asked me to send him *Far From the Madding Crowd*. Honestly, I don't know what they do for their so-called training. He simply devours books,' she said as she finished a left-hand mitten. She held it against a right-hand one.

'Why is it that my left hands always turn out smaller than my right hands? No matter how much I try, it always happens.'

Dolly Tranter looked up. 'With me it's socks,' she said. 'But at least they don't come in left and right pairs, so I can more or less match one with another eventually.'

'Same here. I hope the men have got big feet,' said Madge Eliot.

'Well, at least we're all using the same wool, so we should be able to find some pairs between us,' offered Violet Hawkes, her tongue protruding slightly as she concentrated on a difficult thumb.

The needles clicked silently for a few minutes.

'Freddie's got a couple of days' leave next week,' said Madge.

The others looked up enviously.

'What will you do?' asked Violet.

'I expect he'll want to party. He usually does.'

'There aren't so many people to party with now,' said Dolly with a sigh.

'True enough. When's Edmund coming home, Lilian? He hasn't been here for an age,' said Madge.

'I'm not sure. When he can get a couple of days together. As you know, when he thinks he can only get a few hours we meet in London. It's rather fun, like being courted again. We go to a show or to a restaurant or sometimes just wander around the shops. He always buys me flowers.' She raised her head and looked dreamily out of the window, remembering how he always attached a flower to her dress. It was a small gesture but it had become a symbol of their snatched time together.

'Still, I wish he had more time and could come home properly,' she added.

They fell silent, thinking of their men.

'They'd better hurry up if it's going to be over by Christmas. I can't see any sign of it, can you? It's going to be strange without Leo,' said Dolly.

'Christopher has asked for a soldier's uniform for Christmas.

Molly wants him to have a sailor suit. They had a fight about it. I had to send them to their rooms,' Violet said fondly.

'Winifred wants a nurse's uniform,' laughed Madge. 'Time you got on and started a family, Lilian.' Her famous want of tact was usually endearing but on the subject of children it only made Lilian bridle.

'Bother. I've dropped a stitch,' she said.

If only she and Edmund had had a child before now. They had wanted one from the beginning of their marriage but so far it had eluded them. There was still plenty of time, she kept telling herself, but deep down she wondered if he was as disappointed as she was.

'I think it's time we had some refreshment,' she said, laying aside her knitting after she recovered the stitch. 'I'll ring for Mary.' She jumped to her feet and rang the bell.

'Oh, I must show you. Hugh Brodrick – Edmund's friend – they're in the same battalion and training together – he's by way of being an artist, went to the Slade after Oxford before his father died and he inherited Netherculme – he did a wonderful sketch of Edmund when they were at the camp. Edmund sent it to me. The idiot's sprawled lengthwise reading, with his pipe in his mouth, just like he sprawls about here sometimes. It captures him perfectly.' She lifted the framed chalk drawing from the mantelpiece and handed it to Dolly, who passed it around.

'He's captured Edmund to the life!' said Madge, who was a competent amateur watercolourist. 'Has he exhibited? I don't know his name.'

'I really don't know. I don't think so,' replied Lilian, who had never been interested enough in Hugh to ask about his art. 'He and Edmund are great friends and he comes here lots so you must have met him, though he isn't the sort of person anyone remembers.'

'I know him,' said Dolly. 'A quiet, thoughtful man. Very good looking.'

'I don't know how I could have missed him, then,' said Madge, and they all laughed.

At that moment Mary brought in the tea. Lilian was pleased to drop the subject of Hugh. Fancy Dolly thinking him good looking. Her taste was unaccountable.

Five

The war was not over by Christmas. Instead it seemed to be settling into a stalemate. The war of movement was over and trenches were dug from the North Sea to Switzerland.

Lilian's life carried on in the routine established before Christmas. One day towards the end of April 1915 the knitting circle met at Lowgate, Violet's home. Dolly was in mourning for Leo, who had died two months earlier. It was the first time she had ventured out since receiving the news. The group was naturally subdued. There had been other deaths but Leo's was the first one to touch their intimate circle.

'You don't have to speak in hushed voices,' Dolly had said when she arrived.

'My dear Dolly,' said Violet, unsure what else to say.

They settled down in comfortable chairs, pulled out their needles and wool and knitted in silence for a while.

'I wrote to Leo's chaplain who was one of his friends out there, and asked him what happened,' Dolly said.

The others paused, their hands in mid-stitch, and raised their eyes inquiringly.

'As you know, his CO wrote to me and said that he'd been shot by a sniper while out on night patrol. I asked Mr Timpson – the chaplain – if he could tell me any more. Somehow the CO's letter wasn't enough.

'As the CO said, Leo had been leading a routine night patrol in no-man's-land. The Germans spotted them and opened fire. Leo was hit but his men managed to bring him back to our trench. He was evacuated immediately but he had been hit in the face.'

Her voice quavered. She closed her eyes to compose herself before continuing. 'He lost one eye and the sight of the other. If he had recovered he would have been blind and ... dreadfully disfigured. He died peacefully – I mean, he was unconscious and unable to feel pain or be aware of his injuries. There. Now you know. Now let's talk about something else. I hear Agatha Jones-Fewing is working at the munitions factory. I call that noble of her.'

The needles started clacking again.

'I agree. It's splendid. I couldn't bear to do it,' said Madge.

'I've been thinking –' Lilian said, hesitantly.

'Yes?' said Violet, raising her eyes.

'I've been thinking that I ought to do something else. More than knitting, I mean.'

'Are you going to the factory too?' asked Madge, surprised. Everyone knew how fastidious Lilian was.

'I know it's important work but I'm sure I couldn't tolerate the dirt and the noise. No, I thought I might do nursing.'

'My dear Lilian, you're impatient with anyone who so much as catches a cold,' said Dolly.

'I know. But that's just normal things like colds. If I were to nurse soldiers I should be doing something for the war effort. Anyway, I haven't decided for definite. I thought I'd wait until Edmund goes to France, if he ever does.'

'And it isn't exactly clean work, Lilian. Think of the blood and other things,' said Madge. 'Oh! Darling Dolly, I'm so sorry. Forgive me. I'm the most tactless person alive.'

Dolly smiled at her. 'It's a fact of war, Madge. It can't be avoided, much as I'd prefer not to think about it.'

'Anyway,' Lilian continued. 'I haven't made up my mind and

I haven't discussed it with Edmund, so please don't mention it.'

Two days later Violet received a telegram informing her that Piers had been killed. Less robust than Dolly, her world crumbled and for several weeks she was barely able to rouse herself, even for the children. A letter from his CO followed the day after the telegram, informing her that they had been in a quiet sector of the trenches and that he was killed instantaneously by a sniper's bullet.

★

Edmund grew increasingly frustrated at still being in England. His consolation was that he could still see Lilian from time to time but, precious though that was, he wished he could be at the Front doing something useful instead of constant training in the security of England. He looked with envy at soldiers who were home on leave or who wore wound stripes, and even at the increasing number in hospital blue. Of course, there had already been deaths among men he knew but somehow that added to the mystique of war. Like so many men of his generation and class he had been brought up on the classics and was imbued with the heroic view of battle. When he talked to men who had been at the Front they said nothing to dispel his view. In fact they said very little about their experience.

One day in July 1915, when days were long and garden, hedgerow and field were a tapestry of colour, Lilian received a postcard from him preparing her for several days' leave. She was overjoyed.

Halberton was served by a Halt, a tiny station modestly secluded below a road bridge, on the five-mile branch line between Tiverton and Tiverton Junction where it linked with the main line that connected Devon and Cornwall with London.

Edmund's train was due at the Halt in the late afternoon so she had all day to make herself beautiful and check that the house was scrupulously elegant. She placed great bowls of flowers in every room. She asked Mrs Barton, their cook, to prepare a special dinner. Satisfied that everything was in order, she was driven the short distance to the station by Jacks, the elderly gardener who now doubled up as chauffeur. They arrived in good time. Lilian was too impatient to sit waiting in the car so she climbed out and paced up and down on the platform. As the train approached she saw Edmund leaning out of a window to catch the earliest possible sight of her. They saw each other and waved simultaneously. Edmund alighted, kissed her and held her tightly. A couple of farmers' wives on their way to Tiverton looked out at them and smiled indulgently, then the train, with a whoosh and a whistle, puffed wheezily on. Lilian was proud of Edmund and thought she had never seen khaki so becoming or so handsome an officer. They left the platform and when they reached the bridge over the station they turned and watched the ribbon of smoke disappear behind a distant copse.

Edmund lowered his head to kiss Lilian again. 'It's wonderful to see you again.'

'And you, darling. And for so long too. I can hardly believe it.'

'It's true enough. I'm on embarkation leave. I'm going to France next week. I can't tell you how happy that makes me after all this time.'

She hesitated. 'That's wonderful news, Edmund. You've had to wait so long.'

'Almost a year. I'd just about given up hope of getting there, to tell you the truth. Do you remember Peter Henry from Oxford? He was out within a month, lucky blighter. Came home wounded last month, so he's seen it all. Now I won't be ashamed to meet him.'

He picked up his valise, threw it into the waiting car and noticed Jacks for the first time. 'Why, hello Jacks. Are you driving us?'

'Ar, sir. Young Billy's gone off now, so I be the only one left to drive this contraption. They don't want me for the war yet, ha ha.' He grinned, displaying toothless gums.

'Mrs Potter will have to drive the car if you go, Jacks,' said Edmund.

Lilian looked horrified. 'I'm sure that will never happen. I couldn't possibly spare you, Jacks.'

'Never yew worry, ma'am. They'll be in mortal trouble if they needs the likes o' me.'

That evening was the only one of his leave that Edmund spent alone with Lilian, she was so keen to show him off to the world. He willingly went along with her scheme. It had been months since he had seen their families and friends, though Noel, and Lilian's brothers, and many of his contemporary male friends were absent. Some, like Leo Tranter and Piers Hawkes, would not be coming back. He was happy to catch up with the local news and the comforting trivialities of village life.

'Darling Lily. Tell me the news,' he said to her when he had made himself comfortable.

'I've told you everything in my letters, I think. Where to begin? You'll soon see for yourself how few men there are around now, though quite a few farmers have hung onto their men. They say they can't spare them and I dare say that's true.'

'Quite so. Who'd work the land, bring in the crops and do the milking otherwise?'

'True. And there are some wounded ex-soldiers around. I sometimes see a man without an arm and another without a leg in Tiverton.'

'Poor things,' said Edmund. 'But at least they've seen action.'

Lilian thought it was a high price to pay for seeing action but forbore to argue with him.

'I told you in one of my letters that Rogers behaved outrageously and lied about his age so that he could join up with Micky.' Rogers was their groom and Micky his only son. 'I considered it disloyal of him and told him so.'

'Oh dear. What did he say to that?'

'He said that as we don't have horses any more we don't need him. I pointed out that his duties also include acting as chauffeur. As you saw, Jacks has had to take that on, which means that I'm so short-handed in the garden, with Billy having gone as well. I'm afraid the garden's growing quite wild.'

'Any news of Walter and John, my dear?' After waiting to see if the war was going to be over as quickly as every had at first expected, Walter Franklin had decided to enlist in February.

'I'm anxious for Walter.'

'At the time I thought it was a strange decision of his to join the ranks. He said it was so that he could see action quickly. If I'd known how long it would take me to get to the Front I might have done the same. How's he getting on?'

'I had a letter from him yesterday. I think he's in Gallipoli. He couldn't be specific because of the censor but that was what he implied. He'd definitely been on a long sea voyage and is somewhere hot.'

'Is he, by George?'

'Vicky's frantic with worry. So's Mama. The papers don't say much but we don't seem to be achieving any sort of victory against the Turks.'

'No, I'm afraid we don't. Never mind though, my dear. Walter's tough. He's your brother, after all. How about John? He's quite an old hand now. He must have enjoyed his leave.'

'Yes, I believe he did. Edmund, he told me about the gas attacks near Ypres. He said it was like swimming through a yellow sea. He nearly choked inside his respirator, it felt so claustrophobic. After the gas dispersed, everything was coloured yellow. What a dirty trick for the Germans to use.'

'I couldn't agree more, though I expect we'll use it too, given the chance.'

'Surely not. It isn't – isn't –'

'Cricket? I'm afraid war isn't like that, Lily. Even from where I've been, I can see that.'

'When will it end? All the talk last year of it being over in a few months was quite wrong.'

'Yes, it was. I don't know when it will end and that's the truth. Both sides have well and truly dug in. I don't know how either one will force a way through.'

'It isn't what you expected, is it?'

'No, it isn't. But I'll be better informed when I've been in France. I can't wait to see for myself.'

Lilian was deeply troubled by the thought of Edmund going to France. She could not help but think about Violet and Dolly but she was determined not to let her anxiety spoil Edmund's leave and tried to be at her liveliest the whole time. It was a strain but she could see that he was happy to be kept occupied.

The need to make conversation with the stream of visitors to Sydling or on visits to others helped mask the nervousness that had never quite left Edmund since he had learned that he was going to France. He wasn't worried. Such nervousness was natural, he told himself; he had always done his best when he felt butterflies before examinations or sport. It gave him an extra edge. Nevertheless he would rather die than admit his apprehension to anyone, Lilian included. Especially Lilian. He was not quite sure that she would understand.

On the final day of his leave he rose early, while it was still dark. Lilian was asleep. He bent over her and kissed her gently on the cheek before creeping silently out of the room and down the stairs. She had wanted to go with him to Tiverton Junction (it was too early for the trains on the branch line) but Edmund was resolutely against the idea.

'I hate goodbyes, and railway stations are the most depressing places of all for that,' he had argued as they were going to bed the previous night. 'You say goodbye and the train doesn't move, so you say it over and over again. I loathe it. I'd rather leave you here, knowing that you were warm and comfortable.'

She too hated the lingering, awkward farewells of railway stations but she nevertheless wanted every last second of his company.

'What do I care for being warm and comfortable while you're alone at the station?'

'Dearest, *I* care. I really would like you to stay here.'

'But we would have a few more precious minutes together. And this time it's different. You're going to France. Who knows when we'll see each other again.'

'I know, but it hurts me so badly when I have to leave you. Saying goodbye is like losing a limb. Let's try to make it as painless as we can.'

Edmund had his way.

★

When Lilian woke the next morning his side of the bed had already grown cold. She rose and dressed like an automaton, and spent much of the day at her piano.

The following day she received a hurriedly scribbled postcard from Folkestone, followed twenty-four hours later by a slightly more legible one from Etaples. She could hardly believe that he was in France at last, having been impatient to go there for so long. She tried to imagine what he was doing, who he was talking to, what his platoon was like, when he would go into the line, but she was unequal to the task of summoning such alien images to her mind. She hoped she would have a letter from him before long describing everything and everyone.

While she was waiting to hear from him news arrived that Rogers had been killed by shell-fire while on sentry duty in a trench.

Six

After he enlisted Edmund suggested that Lilian might do something to help the war effort, such as joining the Red Cross. She would be making a useful contribution and it would provide a focus for her life while he was away. She, still not believing in a conflict of any length, dismissed the idea and had instead formed the knitting circle with Dolly, Madge and Violet. But as winter wore on she slowly became reconciled to the notion that the war would not be over as quickly as everyone had believed.

By the time winter started to ease into spring the idea of nursing forced itself on her attention again. Several large houses in the district were converted to hospitals or convalescent homes. She learned from Edmund that Hugh Brodrick had offered Netherculme as a convalescent hospital. It was an elegant Georgian house and although not as grand as most of the new temporary hospitals it nevertheless could provide reasonable accommodation for twenty officers. Lilian was not surprised when she heard the news. It was exactly the sort of thing Hugh would do. Anyway, it was not as though he had a wife or family. The house would only have been shut up otherwise. It was an excellent idea – for him. Fortunately Sydling, though comfortable enough for herself and Edmund and three or four children and their servants, was too small for such a drastic measure to be contemplated.

The opening of these new hospitals caused Lilian to notice something else: several women she knew had volunteered for nursing. Then news came of Leo Tranter's death, closely followed by that of Piers Hawkes. That decided her.

A week after Edmund left for France she took her first instruction as a VAD at the local cottage hospital, conveniently less than two miles away. Being the junior recruit she was naturally assigned the most menial tasks. She worked a morning shift from six o'clock, returned home for the afternoon, and worked again until nine-thirty at night, when she went home and collapsed into bed.

On her first full day off she met Dolly for lunch in Tiverton.

'Well, how's it going, Lilian? We're all dying to hear. Is it what you expected?'

'I'm exhausted. I never knew what tiredness was until now.'

'I can see that you're tired. Tell me about it.'

'The men haven't been wounded in battle so there isn't anything like – like *that* to deal with.' She tried to spare her friend's feelings by not mentioning war wounds. 'They all suffer from what you might call ordinary conditions – things like influenza and epilepsy. I think some may have been at the Front but they don't talk about it.'

'And are they easy to deal with?'

'Yes, they're good as gold. After the male environment of the army they appreciate our feminine touch. One man asked me to talk to him. I said, what about? He said it didn't matter, he just wanted to hear a woman's voice. So I prattled on about my hens. I've no idea why. It was the first thing that came into my head. They like to tease me, though, particularly when I'm washing them. I'm sure I blush but I just ignore them and get on with the job.'

'My dear!'

'I know. Who'd have thought a year ago that I'd be bathing

naked men or fetching and carrying bedpans for them? I would never have believed it. I try to imagine that it's Edmund lying there, but my imagination fails me. I simply can't envisage him calling for a bedpan and "hurry please, nurse".'

They both laughed.

The smile faded from Lilian's face.

'I've learned some very basic lessons too, like how important it is to have a pair of comfortable, well-fitting shoes. I'm on my feet all the time. In all my life I haven't walked so much. In spite of my flat, comfortable shoes, which are my pride and joy, my feet are always sore and swollen by the end of each day. I've lost count of the blisters I've had. And my hands. Just look at them! And this is my day off.' She held her normally elegant hands towards Dolly. They were red and puffy. Dolly took hold of them and turned them over.

'What on earth have you been doing for them to get in this state?'

'Washing. Washing everything – bodies, dishes, floors. It's the lot of the junior VAD, I'm afraid. Most of the regular nursing staff just see me as a dogsbody. It's opened my eyes as to what it's like to be a servant, I can tell you.'

'Are they all like that? Haven't you made any friends?' Dolly asked sympathetically.

'Sister's a bit of a Tartar but underneath her starch I think she has a kind heart. The hospital's only small so there aren't many nurses. There are a couple of other VADs but they're on other wards and there isn't much opportunity to talk to them. They're friendly enough, though.'

'Well, I take my hat off to you, Lilian. It sounds a tough life. I'll make a confession. When you told us you were contemplating nursing I really didn't believe you'd do it.'

Lilian's eyes filled with tears, provoked by tiredness more than anything else.

'It's hard. Very hard. Much more so than I expected. You

know me, Dolly – I think I'd glamorised it in my mind. The bedside angel. But I'm going to persevere.'

They fell silent as they ate their meal. Lilian covertly looked at Dolly. She was paler and had lost weight since Leo's death but still carried an aura of serenity.

'We've talked about me, Dolly. How are you? You so rarely mention yourself.'

Dolly sighed. 'I miss Leo every minute of every day. Not in the big things so much, but little things. Thinking how he liked the newspaper folded just so, seeing his favourite armchair. The smell of his clothes in the wardrobe. The things that catch one out when one thinks one's starting to get one's life under control.'

Lilian squeezed her hand. 'I wish there was something I could say to comfort you.'

'Dear Lilian. Thank you. Everyone is so kind. It's funny, when Leo was alive but away on service he still seemed to have a presence at home. Now it feels empty and desolate sometimes, even with the children running around. I may think differently when they reach school age but at the moment I'm inclined to send them to school locally. My big fear is that I'll turn into one of those clingy mothers who swamp their children. I shall have to find a balance.'

'Dolly, you're a saint. This shouldn't have happened to you. How are Basil and Patricia?

'They're too young to take in the permanence of death. They still thinks Daddy will come home when the war's over.'

They reflected silently for a minute.

'I visited Violet last week,' said Dolly. 'She's still devastated about Piers but she seemed a fraction less distraught. I hope she'll rally soon for Christopher's and Molly's sakes, as well as her own.'

Lilian shook her head, unable to imagine fully what bereavement must feel like. Not only the loss of Leo, which was dreadful, but how was Dolly placed financially? Although they had been friends since childhood, money was a subject they never discussed. Embarrassed because of this, she asked for the bill, insisted on paying, and they soon went their separate ways.

Seven

July 25th 1915

My dearest Lily,

Here I am at last in France. It was a strange sensation to see the cliffs of England receding as we steamed away. I still can't quite believe it. The men are in high spirits and are singing as I write this. Farewell to endless training, marching and musketry drill.

France is looming larger all the time. I'll post this as soon as I can after we disembark.

With all my love,
Edmund

August 6th

My darlingest Lily,

Thank you so much for your news and the parcel. The men loved the fruitcake and have made good use of the cigarettes – they can't smoke enough. The cheese was perfect too. Please don't send any more peaches. I love them but they had become rather a mess by the time they got here. Parcels can get tossed around a bit.

I'm glad you're settling into your nursing routine now. Promise me you'll take care of yourself. I ought to be jealous of you washing the patients but somehow I'm not. I'm just proud of you.

We're settling in over here and have joined a top Division – I can't tell you which. There are some Regular battalions in it, so it's a bit of luck for us. My fellow officers are all very amicable so I've well and truly landed on my feet. Beaumont, my company commander, is 22 yet has a wise head on his shoulders. I like him. He's as keen on Hardy as I am and we've had a number of happy conversations.

We had a long march yesterday. The men were cheerful and sang lustily all the way. I was lucky to have a horse. I inspect the men's feet regularly – it's my most important job. The country around here is very different from Devon – bleak, scarred, mining country. The weather's good at the moment. I wonder what it will be like under rain. Quite desolate, I imagine.

You mustn't worry about me. I'm quite safe, though the nearer we get to the line the more evidence there is of the war – shattered equipment, limbers (the detachable front of gun carriages), and dead horses, I'm sorry to say. I can't help but think of my poor Claudius, wondering about his fate. Lots of shell-holes. It's rather exciting trying to find one's way about in the dark with so many obstacles. One quickly learns to distinguish the sounds of the different Jerry shells, which ones to ignore and which ones to duck. When Jerry's intent on annoying us I think of you and know that nothing he can do will harm me. Your photograph is always with me. It's my dearest possession.

All my love as ever,
Edmund

August 20th

My dearest Lily,

It may be August but the weather's unpredictable — sometimes sunshine, sometimes rain and thunderstorms. Consequently we've had our first experience of the stuff every soldier who's come to France dreads so much — MUD. Forget the Germans, I believe this is the true enemy. My darling girl, you can't begin to imagine it. It only takes a shower of rain and the ground becomes a morass of oozing, squelchy mud. It sucks at your boots as you try to walk through it. It gets in your food and your tea and — horror upon horror — it gets in your clothes and worse than everything, inside your pyjamas and your sleeping-bag. It dominates your life. Add to that the itching of lice, and it can be a challenge to keep bright and cheerful. At least we're able to wash when we're out of the line but of course our clothes still harbour the little beasts. I expected all sorts of things when I came out but I have to confess that the universal squalor and ugliness have surprised me somewhat. I find them sorely trying. The greatest luxury in these conditions is strip off my clothes and leap into a cold, clear river. It's heaven. I hadn't realised quite how much store I set by cleanliness and beauty.

This sounds very negative. Believe me, I'm all right. I just wanted to get it off my chest. The thing is, it's the same for everyone here so one mustn't moan. So we joke about it instead.

I'm glad Walter's hanging on. I know it's easy to say but try not to worry about him.

Your ever loving,
Edmund

September 11th

My sweetest Lily,

I'm writing this sitting comfortably in an estaminet with a bottle of wine beside me. It's evening and there's a cheerful light in the place, which is in the main square of a village about the size of dear Halberton. The estaminet is busy. You can tell from this that we've come out of the line for a spell – I don't know how long. I'm sorry that I hardly had time to write to you at any length since we moved to our new trenches. I thought our first trenches were bleak but the last ones were in a bizarre landscape of quarries and brickstacks. I've hardly had a spare moment. Apart from the usual trench activities of standing to, rifle cleaning, inspections, trench watch (a subaltern takes his turn at this along with the Tommies), working parties, etc., we've been digging new trenches. There's also been a lot of movement behind the lines. Naturally Jerry has seen all this – he has aeroplanes buzzing around above us and anyway the spoil from the new trenches is chalk and therefore visible for miles – and he has delighted in strafing us. I lost my sergeant and a private soldier to a shell as we were marching away from the line, which cast a gloom over the platoon, as you can imagine.

I've made rather a thing of night-time bombing raids. You may find it hard to believe but life in the trenches can be quite monotonous once one has mastered the arts of placing sentries, stand to, stand down, trench maintenance, which men one has to keep a special eye on – and they aren't necessarily the quiet ones. So the raids give me something to do. It's terrific fun, like taking a high hedge on the hunting field. I've managed to bag a few Jerries, which has pleased my CO. I can see the alarm on your face as you read this but my dearest girl you mustn't worry. I'm convinced that your love will keep me safe for ever. I feel cocooned and inviolable. Leonard Jones told me that Reggie Trenchard, who is 18 and looks about 15 and is our youngest subaltern, rather hero-worships me for my derring-do in no man's land. I mustn't get a swollen head!

Any spare moments that I have – and there aren't many – I fill by reading, particularly Clare at the moment. His rural life couldn't be further from war.

Herbert Clements was shot by a sniper the day before we left the trenches. I'll miss him. He was a good friend from the moment we started training together. Which makes me think of Piers Hawkes. I'm glad Violet is getting stronger now, and getting out a bit. Grief is so unaccountable in the way it takes us.

I'm so glad you're feeling less tired now. It sounds hard work. Sister was a brick to give you a half day off for your birthday. How can I thank you for sharing your birthday cake with me? You can't have eaten much of it yourself. It was scrumptious. Tell Mrs Barton that it transported some of the BEF to a very happy place.

I must sign off now. Hugh's just arrived and we're going to chew the fat, probably well into the night over several bottles of vin rouge. I'm now going to embarrass him by telling you that he's a fine officer, rock solid, and held in affection by his men and fellow officers. He's an excellent shot and has put that to good use by doing a bit of sniping. It's a dangerous business because if he were to stay in one place for too long Jerry would pinpoint him and try to wipe him out. But you know Hugh, he takes it all in his stride in his usual phlegmatic way. He occupies his spare moments by drawing the war – men, horses, broken buildings. In short, anything and everything.

He sends you his best wishes.

I must scribble quickly as Hugh's just left the table for a moment. It's his birthday on the 21st – please will you ask Mrs Barton to bake him a cake and send it with other treats. He hasn't anyone to send him parcels and it would be a nice surprise for him.

    Your ever loving
Edmund

September 23rd

Darlingest Lily,
I've only time to scribble a brief note to tell you not to expect to hear from me for a few days as I expect to be working hard.

    Your ever loving,
Edmund

Eight

*E*dmund turned over and tried to sleep. He found it impossible even though he was tired. He had led working parties throughout the previous two nights and had only been able to snatch short periods of sleep in daytime. The guns had been roaring for three days, shells whizzing and screaming overhead like a biblical plague. The ground beneath him vibrated with each firing so that he had the illusion of being at sea instead of on dry land in France. A hammer had been beating inside his head for the last two days. His body seemed to be pulsing to the tune of the guns. If he couldn't stand it, what must it be doing to the Germans? He yawned and turned over again. Occasionally the snores of one of his companions punctuated a rare lull between the guns. Lucky devil. A new sound – thunder. That was all they needed. Rain came swiftly afterwards, torrents of it hammering on the roof of the billet, at least where there were still a few tiles that could be described as roof. Elsewhere it drove relentlessly onto the men beneath. Snoring gave way to a string of curses. Edmund gave up the battle and moved outside. In no time he was soaked to the skin but he found a relatively sheltered nook between two smashed walls, cupped his hands and lit a cigarette.

For a few minutes his brain was dormant, only taking in the sound of the rainwater spattering and gurgling in counterpoint to the shell-fire. His mind began to clear. He thought back to the briefing three hours earlier. They were going to take part in the attack. It was a signal honour for the battalion. They were to move up to the front line tomorrow night ready to attack at dawn the following day. They were to capture two German trench systems about a mile apart, the second of which ran through Hulluch, Cité St Elie and Haisnes. Their first objective was a quarry called The Slit, south-west of The Quarries, then they were to take Breslau Avenue, which ran back from Breslau Trench to the intermediate German line about halfway to Cité St Elie.

The second-in-command of each company was to remain behind with the transports. There had been rolling of eyes and cheerful banter at that news. Reggie Trenchard's face caught his eye. It had drained of colour. Embarrassed, Edmund looked away. He was glad he was only a junior officer. This was the first big Show and he was going to play his part.

The rain eased slightly. He lit another cigarette. He wondered what he would feel like when he went over the top. Nervous? Exhilarated? Scared? He didn't doubt for a moment that he would cut the mustard. The artillery were making things easy for them. Destroying the enemy wire and obliterating their trenches. He pitied the German infantry. He had no argument with them. It was their warmongers who needed putting in their place.

The storm moved away and slowly the sky streaked with a soft grey light. Edmund went in search of breakfast, wondering vaguely where he'd be eating his next one. He had no time for further reflection in the bustle of preparation. Men handed in their packs and greatcoats. Extra rations and ammunition were drawn. Edmund inspected his men's feet and rifles. Rifles had been issued shortly before the battalion came out to France and the Tommies still considered them a novelty and were eager to use them.

He wrote a letter to Lilian to be sent in the event of his death.

One of the men said he had toothache. Edmund wondered if the man was windy but he could see that the swollen jaw was real enough.

'You'd better go to the Regimental Aid Post and get it looked at,' he said.

'Yes, sir. Thank you, sir.' The man smiled gratefully with half his mouth.

'It'll be more than your tooth that's hurting tomorrow,' joked one of his mates. They all laughed.

Night came and they made their way to the trenches. It was a fine night with intermittent moonlight and little wind. Before long, roads and communication trenches were clogged with men, slithering in mud from yesterday's storm, knocking into each other, falling against trench walls. Each Tommy had a tool pushed down behind his haversack which restricted his movement further if it was not positioned correctly. The noise of the British artillery was so loud that it was impossible to hear the German shells as they came over, and explosions took them by surprise. Edmund was relieved when his platoon reached their assembly point without loss. It had taken two hours longer than it ought.

He looked over no-man's-land with the aid of a periscope. From their starting point the ground sloped gently upwards for two hundred yards to Breslau Trench. The length of two football pitches. How difficult could that be? But if any Germans had survived the shelling they would have a clear view of the attack from the moment the British left their trenches unless the advance was obscured by gas and smoke. In the CO's last briefing Edmund had learned that there were two options for the attack, depending on the wind. If the wind was favourable it would take place at 6.30 a.m. preceded by gas, but if the wind showed no sign of changing, zero hour would be at 3 a.m. so that they had cover of darkness, or what passed for it with moonlight and flares. Watches were synchronised.

At midnight the message came through that the attack would be at 6.30.

Edmund tried to get some sleep. Around him, men had contrived all sorts of positions for sleeping, an extraordinary feat considering the din. Just before dawn two sergeants arrived with the rum ration. No two human beings could have been more welcome. At once faces looked less grey as the rum warmed them. Some joked about where they might be at the same time tomorrow. Sergeant Howell went round the platoon checking their equipment for the umpteenth time. He was an affable man, a father of seven boys, the oldest of whom was also in the army. He had an encouraging word for each man as he passed among them.

As the sky was starting to streak with light the guns opened up with an intensity greater than anything that had gone before. Edmund could not distinguish one gun from another. What had been going on during the previous four days seem almost negligible in comparison. Using sign language since it was impossible to make himself heard above the noise, he led his platoon into the front trench. When they had squeezed into place, Corporal Minster indicated that those with smoke bombs should be ready to throw them.

Edmund tried to assess the wind direction. As far as he could tell it was very light from the south-west but varying considerably in direction. Surely gas would not be released in these conditions – there would be too great a risk of it blowing back over the British advance and trenches. Nevertheless he mimed to Minster to make sure that the men had their gas helmets at the ready, just in case. He was glad to have done so because soon afterwards gas was let loose. At the same time men threw the smoke bombs over the parapet.

The bombardment ceased. Edmund was aware of a loud ringing in his ears. He wondered what it had done to the artillerymen. Were they all deaf? In the growing daylight he could see that little clouds of smoke were coalescing into one long cloud. He looked at his watch. Five minutes to zero. He walked among his men and spoke to each of them, giving an encouraging pat on the shoulder.

'Anyone would think we was going out to play a ruddy football match,' Private Dickens said to his mate.

'Ar,' said Private Diggle. 'He's a good skipper, no doubt about that.'

'Doesn't turn a hair,' agreed Private Bicton.

One minute to zero. Edmund was aware that his hands were cold and clammy but he did not want to wipe them or his men would think he was nervous. He took out his whistle and placed it in his mouth. His hand trembled slightly. Thirty seconds. He mounted the ladder.

Zero.

He blew as hard as he could. At the same time other whistles blew along the length of the trench. He quickly climbed the ladder and launched himself over the top.

He made straight for the nearest gap in the wire, as did many other men. As he reached it he was aware of Dickens crumpling beside him. He got through the wire. He had put away his whistle and was brandishing his pistol above his head, cheering his men on as though he was on the hunting field. He felt completely detached, almost as though he was floating. At first there had been almost silence but then a machine gun started up, then another and another, followed by German artillery. Some German infantry had somehow survived the bombardment and were now manning the fire-step of the trench, picking off the advancing infantry with rifle fire. He heard the whisper of a bullet as it passed close to his head. He tripped on a piece of shrapnel and fell into a shell-hole. He looked cautiously around to see how the attack was going. Behind him he saw that there had been bunching at the gaps in the wire and a number of men had been caught by German fire as they waited to get through. This had not been helped by the fact that a support company had moved forward too soon and become mixed up with his company, adding to the congestion at the wire. The cloud of gas had turned and was rolling slowly back towards the British line. Cursing, he rolled onto his back and put on his respirator.

Two other men followed him into the shell-hole. One was Corporal Minster, the other Private Diggle, who was bleeding freely from a shoulder wound. They put on their respirators, then Edmund applied a field dressing to Diggle's wound while Minster cautiously surveyed the German line.

'You stay here and keep your head down, Diggle, and make your way back to our line when you can. Corporal, what does it look like over there?' Edmund's voice came squeakily through his respirator.

'From what I can see through the gas, Jerry's manning his parapet, curse him,' squeaked Minster in reply.

'How's their wire?'

'Hard to tell. Cut in some places, I think.'

'Let's push on while there's still some gas around, otherwise we'll be completely exposed. Keep as low to the ground as you can and follow me.'

'Yes, sir.'

Edmund counted to five and leapt out of the hole. He dared not look round for Minster and had to assume that he was just behind. He ran in a zigzag, doubled low to the ground. He reached the German wire. It was still mainly intact, curse it, but at least the gas was partially obscuring them from the trench. His eyes stung. He cursed his respirator: it must be leaking. He made out that some men had found a way through the wire, and dived through after them. As he did so he bowled a Mills bomb into the trench. The explosion was satisfactory. The men quickly followed his example. They jumped into the trench. Minster joined them.

Edmund tore off his respirator. 'Right, men, we must stop Jerry coming into this bay. Corporal, you go left, Halesworth, you go that way. Pick up any bombs and ammo that you see but don't hang around doing it. Use your bayonets if you have to. You two go with Minster and you three with Private Halesworth. I don't know who you are but I'm glad you're here.'

They took up position just in time to repel a small German counter-attack on their right. Edmund lobbed German grenades into the next bay. He peered round the corner, pistol in one hand and a grenade in the other. Dead Germans lay around. He ran towards the next bay, leaping over a body as he neared the corner. He felt no emotion when he noticed in passing that the top of the man's head had sheared clean away, his brains tumbled out onto the trench floor.

They worked their way along the trench throwing Mills bombs into the deep dugouts as they went. After half an hour, as they were approaching another bay they heard voices approaching. One of the men, a Devon from a different company, prepared to prime another bomb. Edmund stopped him just in time.

'Wait.' I think they're speaking English.' They listened in silence, creeping nearer the corner. Edmund prepared to fire his revolver.

'Hello there,' he shouted. 'Identify yourselves.'

He heard mumbling from around the corner then someone shouted, 'Gordons. Who are you?'

'Devons.'

'Thank God for that.'

Edmund peered cautiously around the corner, wondering if it was Jerry playing tricks. Half a dozen men in kilts approached him, smiling broadly.

'How many of you are there?' Edmund asked a tall captain, their only officer.

'About twenty in all. Myself, Sergeant McMurdo and a handful of Tommies. How about you?'

'Eight, including myself. I've no idea about the rest of the battalion. Lots were caught at our wire. I left three men securing our little patch from the other direction. I need to get back and help them.'

He hurried back with two of the Tommies until he found Minster. One of the men who had gone with Minster had been killed by shrapnel but half a dozen others had joined them. He knew Jerry must try to drive them out soon.

'Stevens, run back to our trench and tell them our situation. Say we're holding on but need reinforcements before Jerry makes a counter-attack. Quick now.'

Private Stevens, an apple-cheeked twenty-two-year-old, peered cautiously above the parapet and climbed out. Edmund watched him as he dived through the German wire and ran until he dropped into a shell-hole and out of sight.

'Behind you, sir,' shouted a Tommy.

Edmund turned in time to see a frightened German face in the doorway of a dugout. In an instant he fell back as a Mills bomb exploded. Minster threw two more into the dugout to be sure of finishing the job.

'That's enough, Corporal,' said Edmund.

'Yes, sir. Damn,' said Minster. 'We searched that dugout an' all. He must have been hidden.'

'That's a warning to us.' He looked around, as though seeing the trench for the first time. 'Jerry does himself well, doesn't he? It's luxurious in here.' He turned and looked over the parapet. There was clear sight of the British trenches and back area. 'My, he certainly had a grand view of us.'

He watched, oddly detached, as another wave of men left the British front line. Machine guns spat out their fire. Few men got as far as half way across no-man's-land. The ground was wormy with khaki bodies.

'Where are the rest, Corporal? Don't say we're on our own here.' Edmund asked rhetorically, knowing the answer but not wanting to acknowledge it.

'There they are, down there,' replied Minster, with a nod in the direction of no-man's-land. 'Just look at our wire. The poor sods never even got past there.'

Reassured by the fact that the Jocks were to their right, Edmund concentrated on securing their line of trench. Some men had made it through to his left and it seemed that the Devons held a good stretch of trench but at a heavy cost. A recent arrival brought the unwelcome news that the CO had been hit and killed. Minster had also seen Sergeant Howell go down in no-man's-land. Edmund wondered how many of his platoon had survived. He was sure only of seven. But this wasn't time to mourn. He was pleased to find Captain Vernon, whom he knew from a different company, in the trench. Vernon gave the order to push on to their objective.

The two most troublesome machine guns fell silent. A new wave of support left the British line but they suffered from German artillery fire as they crossed no-man's-land; some were hit before they left the assault trench. However, more were able to make it across than previously.

Later, Edmund was unable to remember much of the next few hours. They left Breslau Trench and moved forward in a storm of shell-fire from both the Germans and the British bombardment. Shell-holes pitted the ground. Dead Germans and horses lay everywhere. Some Germans fled from the advance; others offered stiffer resistance.

As the assault progressed men continued to be wounded or killed but the remainder did not flinch and kept driving forward. After what seemed an eternity they reached the place where the road from Lens to La Bassée crossed the Vermelles-Hulluch road. The German second line was a quarter of a mile ahead. By now the advance was down to seventy men.

Captain Vernon was dead, obliterated by shell-fire as he led them forward. Reggie Trenchard was the only other officer. Edmund found himself in command. They took stock of their position. Their left flank was completely exposed and they appeared to have reached the limit of the bombardment. To advance further would be suicide. They must either dig in and hold on or retreat.

Retreat was unthinkable.

He set the men digging. Realising the precariousness of their position, the men didn't need asking twice. Edmund tried to bolster them by congratulating them on exceeding their objective. It was a marvellous feat.

In mid-afternoon a message arrived from Battalion HQ. They were to hold their position until relieved the following night. A day and a half! Edmund sent back an acknowledgement and a scribbled report of their situation.

He told the men not to expect rations until they were relieved. They must therefore be careful with their food and water. He organised sentry duty. He was relieved in one way when night came but it brought a new fear of attack. No one slept. The new terrain brought its own sounds, sounds with which they were unfamiliar, and more than once a rifle shot rang out along the British position. Edmund went to and fro along the line, trying to calm the men so that they did not waste ammunition. It was only now when there was no barbed wire that Edmund realised how safe it had made him feel. Although it was night, the ground was continually illuminated by German flares.

Eventually fingers of grey began to probe the sky. It was cold and damp. The men stamped their feet in an effort to bring some life back into them. They readied themselves for a dawn attack but it failed to materialise. Edmund wished that Jerry would get on with it. Anything would be better than this waiting. They endured a torrent of shell-fire all day long but the German guns had not quite got their range and by a miracle only half a dozen men were hit and only two killed.

When Edmund had seen Reggie Trenchard blanch at the briefing before the attack he had wondered how the boy would cope in battle. He need not have feared. He might have come straight from school but he was as calm as an officer could be. He earned the respect of the men twenty times over that day, reassuring them, checking their rifles and equipment, tending to the wounded. He took some of the pressure off Edmund, to Edmund's relief.

At last the day grew dark. Edmund wondered if the longed-for relief would materialise. It seemed a lifetime since they had gone over the top yesterday morning. He had not thought of Lilian since the night before the attack. There was no place for her here, even in his thoughts. He wondered if Hugh had survived. Probably not. So few of them had.

While men took it in turns to sleep – one hour on, one hour off – Edmund remained alert. He had not slept for forty-eight hours and wondered if he ever would again. He hoped he'd have enough energy to fight if Jerry attacked. Trenchard, who seemed able to drop off anywhere at a moment's notice, encouraged him to sleep. Edmund was on the point of giving in when the longed-for relief arrived. The senior officer looked apprehensive. Edmund explained the situation, wished them luck and pulled his men out as quickly and silently as they could go. The last thing he wanted was for them to draw attention to themselves by banging and clattering.

They stumbled their way back to their old assembly trench. Edmund did not recognise any landmarks on the way, the ground was so scarred and covered with the debris of battle. More than once he inadvertently stepped on a corpse.

Dawn was approaching as they passed back to the support lines. They were unutterably weary. No one spoke. Fresh men waiting to go up the line stood aside to let them pass, expressions of wonder on their faces as they watched the ghostly column. Later, when roll-call was taken, Edmund learned that the battalion had lost six hundred and thirty-nine men – more than sixty per cent of its strength – either killed, missing, wounded or gassed. The acting CO congratulated them on having taken and held their objectives. They should be proud of themselves. The battalion had experienced its first test and come through with credit.

Edmund felt no elation at survival. No emotion at all. Complete emptiness.

After having slept for the best part of twelve hours and tucked into a hot meal he felt more human. His servant was delighted to see him again, which also lifted his spirit. But he could not help thinking of all the men trapped by the wire, and the corpses, so many corpses. Sergeant Howell and all the others. He hoped the battalion would go back to the rear to rebuild but he was disappointed. They were to remain where they were in support for three days.

At last they were taken out of the line and moved back to billets at Beuvry. New men were drafted in straight from England to make up the losses. Edmund had to get to know his platoon and fellow officers all over again. He observed that those who seen action and the fresh young recruits seemed like two different races.

Edmund was overjoyed to discover that Hugh had survived. His company had lost all its officers except himself and another subaltern. While Edmund had pushed forward to the crossroads Hugh had been further to the left, but the defence had been fearsome and they had not been able to break through.

The battle ground on but the division received orders to move further left in order to relieve the 2nd Division in Cuinchy and Cambrin. This sector was quieter and gave the battalion some much-needed time to recover.

It was here that Edmund first became aware of his nerves.

He could not say precisely when they began to play up. It happened imperceptibly. The first sign was an attack of nausea every time he contemplated going back into the line. He had seen other men break down and recognised the symptom for what it was; characteristically, he drove himself harder in compensation. He patrolled in no-man's-land every night that he was in the line. Then one night towards the end of October, as they were making their way out of the line, the Germans started shelling. They often did that in the hope – or perhaps with the knowledge – that they would catch a relief in progress. In a split second Edmund saw Reggie Trenchard take the full blast, then the world went black and he found himself entombed under soil and debris.

He did not feel any particular pain and hoped he had not been hit. All he knew was that he had to get himself out of there. He held his breath and struggled to prise his arms free. If only he could free a space around his face. Still unbreathing, he pushed with all his might. He was in luck. He wasn't buried deeply and the earth was loose. As he pushed and shoved he could hear voices.

'Mr Potter's under here. I can see movement. Quick, boys.' It was Minster, God bless him! Between them they uncovered his face. He drew in huge lungfuls of air. The men freed the rest of his body. He rolled onto his side and vomited copiously, then lay on his back sobbing. Minster called for stretcher-bearers.

He was barely aware of the jolting progress to the field ambulance. A doctor with a tired face examined him.

'I can't find any physical injuries. I don't have to tell you you're an extremely lucky man, Lieutenant.'

'Couldn't breathe. I couldn't breathe. Trenchard blown up,' Edmund said.

'You've had a severe shock. It won't do you or your platoon any good if go back into the line while you're like this, so I'm sending you to the CCS. They'll take care of you. You'll go there in the morning.' The doctor smiled and moved on to his next patient.

Edmund slept on the stretcher. In the morning he was able to stand and walk. Any slight noise made him shake violently and he found it hard to talk. But as he had no physical wounds he was denied the relative luxury of being transported by wagon and had to walk the three miles to the casualty clearing station.

Word spread quickly that Edmund had been buried alive and it soon reached Hugh. As soon as he could, he visited his friend. Edmund was lying in bed staring vacantly at the ceiling when he arrived.

'Hello, Edmund. I heard what happened. How are you feeling?'

'Alive, I th-think. I'm so tired but every time I fall asleep I get f-flashbacks. Better to stay awake.' His hands picked fretfully at the sheet.

He saw Hugh look at his hands and tried without success to keep them still.

'Are you going back to England?' Hugh asked.

'Yes, I th-think so.'

'Some people have all the luck.'

Edmund tried to smile but only managed a twisted frown.

'Does Lilian know? Have you written to her?'

'No. She's so far away. How can I tell her that I've b-broken down? She wants me to b-be a hero.'

'You haven't broken down, you juggins. You were buried alive and naturally enough are suffering from shock. It could happen to anyone.'

'I can't write to her. I don't know what to say. I d-don't want her to know what it's like here.' His voice rose hysterically.

They sat in silence for a few minutes.

'Edmund, Lilian has to know. I'd offer to write for you but it would be more reassuring for her if she received a letter in your hand. She'd know that you aren't badly wounded.'

'I c–can't. I d–don't know what to say.'

'Could you write if I dictate something? It only need be a few lines. Enough to let her know you're safe.'

Edmund resisted but by slow degrees Hugh talked him round. Edmund wrote his words and Hugh took the letter to send it back to England.

The following day Edmund began the long haul to England. Rumbling trains full of groaning wounded, transfer to the hospital ship, the fresh tang of salt air and brief revival, yet another train, and to sanctuary in a small hospital on the south coast.

Nine

---

*T*hat he would be 'working hard' was a code Edmund had agreed with Lilian to inform her that he would be going into action. By the time she received his note the newspapers were already full of news from Loos. She waited anxiously for several days and was glad to be busy at the hospital to keep her mind occupied. On October 1st she received a hurried, muddy note to tell her that he had been in action but was now back in billets. '*My guardian angel was surely watching over me, or it was an answer to your prayers.*'

His next letter, written the following day, was little longer but he could not describe the battle. '*It was the worst 48 hours of my – until now – blessed and innocent existence,*' he wrote. '*But have no fear. I am now safe and well.*'

Lilian's images of battle were drawn mainly from Malory's *Tales of King Arthur*, and Edmund's letters did little to alter her view. Of course he had mentioned trenches and shell-holes and dead horses and night sorties in no-man's-land but of the actual battle he told her nothing.

He wrote as often as he could during the next four weeks, then one stormy day towards the end of October a letter arrived from the casualty clearing station.

Lilian tore open the envelope and extracted a single sheet of paper. She was almost too nervous to read what Edmund had written. That he himself had been well enough to write was a good sign. He could not be badly hurt – perhaps he would be home soon with a tidy bullet wound in his left arm (although shaky, the handwriting indicated that he had been able to use his right arm to write the letter). Her eyes skimmed over the letter so quickly that at first she was hardly able to absorb its news. She took a deep breath and read it again, this time more slowly. He had been buried alive following the nearby explosion of a shell. *'I'm not feeling too bad but I think I might be sent across to England for a short while. Fingers crossed that I can be near you.'*

He must be wounded or he would not be evacuated to England, Lilian reasoned. It was exactly what she had wanted ever since he went to France: a becoming battle-scar but not enough to incapacitate him. She was impatient for further news.

She did not have long to wait. By the end of the week Edmund had been transferred to a hospital for officers on the south coast. This was the next best thing to his being at home. She immediately obtained two days' leave from her understanding matron and set out early the following morning. The journey was long and tedious, the more so because of her impatience to see Edmund. Two changes of train were required and in the final train two women were seated near her. One of them talked incessantly, the other making occasional interjections when the first paused for breath. Their constant drone irritated Lilian, and worse, she discovered that their destination was the same as hers. There was to be no respite from them. At last they reached the town and the train slowed down before pulling thankfully into the station. It was out of season and she was able to obtain a room in the Majestic, the grandest hotel on the seafront. Her room was on the first floor. She was delighted to discover that it had a balcony overlooking the sea.

Before unpacking her few belongings she opened the window and stepped outside. She had been feeling travel-weary, but a salty breeze enlivened her immediately. The sea was still grey and disturbed following recent gales. She remembered the day when she and Edmund and Hugh had picnicked at Sidmouth. Was that really little more than a year ago? Already the memory seemed to belong to another life, Life Before The War. Is it possible that so much can have happened in that time? she wondered. And now there seems no sign of it ending.

Leaving the window open, she went back inside and prepared to go and see Edmund. After refreshing her hair and face and changing her clothes, she set out for the hospital as a nearby church clock struck four.

The hospital, a white Georgian house, stood in extensive grounds. It had the air of being a private home converted to a war hospital, and Lilian found herself thinking more generously towards Hugh for allowing Netherculme to be used as a convalescent home. She wondered where he was and what he was doing.

She had written a hurried note to Edmund informing him when she expected to arrive and thought he might be looking out for her. She pushed open the wide, heavy door and stepped into the warmth of an oak-panelled hall. Five minutes later a middle-aged nurse bristling with efficiency escorted her to Edmund's room. He evidently had one all to himself – a luxury not wholly deserved if the nurse's demeanour was anything to go by.

'What exactly is wrong with my husband, nurse?' Lilian asked.

'Neurasthenia,' the nurse said. She offered nothing more and Lilian sensed that she did not want to engage in conversation.

She followed the nurse down a long corridor, the oak floorboards looking lighter along the centre where a carpet had lain until the house was converted to a hospital, and its careful owners had lifted and stored it for safe-keeping. Occasionally a board creaked as it was stepped on. Lilian noticed that pictures had been removed from the walls as well: darker rectangular patches were evident at intervals on the faded wallpaper. Yet it was not an unwelcoming house. She thought it must have been a much-loved home, and wondered if its owner, like Hugh, was in the army, or if the owners were older and had sons at the front. Or if they were simply altruistic. She was pulled back abruptly from her speculations as they arrived at a white-painted door which the nurse threw open.

'Your wife to see you, Lieutenant Potter.'

She stood back, allowing Lilian to enter the room, then left, closing the door behind her. Edmund was sitting on a wooden chair the far side of the bed, huddled in a blue dressing-gown with a rug across his knees. He seemed diminished, somehow – smaller than he used to be. She could see no sign of any physical wound but he was shuddering as though he was deathly cold. His face was almost greenish-grey. He lifted his eyes towards her, twin pools of hazel in black sockets. She crossed the room and sat down in a chair beside him. He winced at the rustle of her skirt.

He read her questioning eyes.

'Sorry, old g-g-girl. B-b-bit nervous today,' he whispered, and lowered his eyes.

'That's all right, Edmund darling,' she replied softly. 'I'm so glad to see you again.'

They sat in silence. She noticed that he repeatedly clasped and unclasped his hands as though each was trying to pluck something indefinable from the other. She took each of his hands in hers. That way she succeeded in stopping the kneading but not the underlying tremor, the force of which alarmed her. She had never seen anyone in this state before and was at a loss to know what to say or do.

She looked around, taking in the room's graceful proportions – the high ceiling, a large sash window, open three inches at the top, curtains the colour of buttercups moving gently in the current of air. They must have been left in place by the owner.

The narrow bed, the single plumped pillow, the white sheet neatly turned over a blanket the colour of blood.

He interrupted their silence. '*Video meliora, proboque; deteriora sequor.*'

'Hush, darling. What are you saying?'

'"I see the b-b-better way, and approve it; I follow the worse." Ovid captured it p-p-perfectly.'

Lilian smiled and released his hands. Neither of them spoke.

After having been stifled for several hours in railway carriages Lilian soon began to feel the need for exercise. She stood up and started to pace around the room. Seeing that her movement was disturbing him she sat down again, only to bounce to her feet a few minutes later, unable to keep still any longer. She crossed to the window in a swirl of silk. Although she avoided watching Edmund she sensed his reaction. She looked out into the gathering dusk.

'W-wish you were more relaxed,' Edmund said, with a great effort of control.

Through the window she caught sight of a pair of pigeons flapping in a cedar tree. The shrill mew of gulls could be heard in the distance – perhaps a fishing boat was coming into harbour.

With an effort Edmund turned towards Lilian and studied her back. A memory stirred in his mind: he had entirely forgotten that there was beauty on this earth as well as hell. Lilian's dress was the colour of midsummer sky and her hair was gilded by the electric light overhead. He wished to tell her that he loved her but his voice would not come.

'I simply must open this window a bit more. It's so stuffy in here. You don't mind, do you, darling? I've been sitting in the stuffiest and smelliest railway carriages all the way here and I simply have to clear my head.' There was no reply so she pulled down the top window a couple more inches.

The gulls screeched nearer.

'No, no. I can't stand it,' Edmund shouted. 'Shut the window. Shut it!'

Lilian was too startled to argue. Edmund had never shouted at her before. Who did he think she was, a private soldier? She closed the window with a thump, drew the curtains and turned round.

'I'm sorry. I didn't realise it would upset you. I've never known you like this before.' She paused. 'What's *wrong* with you, Edmund? The nurse who showed me to your room said you had neurasthenia but aren't you wounded as well? I was expecting to find you swathed in bandages.'

'Sorry if I d-d-disappoint you.' He lowered his eyes again. He hated his stammer, was ashamed of it.

'Don't be ridiculous,' she said, too lightly. 'I'm not disappointed at all. It's just that, well, you aren't as I expected to find you.'

'My nerves are all in p-p-pieces.'

'But aren't you wounded at all?'

'Not in the sense that you mean, no.'

'You have been ill, I can see that.'

'I b-b-believe I am still.'

'Yes, I see.'

Tears started to trickle down Edmund's face.

Lilian watched with alarm, not just because he was so obviously suffering but because she was bewildered. This was completely outside her sphere of experience. She had never known him cry before.

'Thank you for c-coming, d-d-dear. You had b-b-better go now,' he mumbled, turning his head away from her.

'Oh, but I can't leave –'

'Please g-go. Now. It's best for b-b-both of us.'

'If that's what you want, of course I'll go, but can't I do something?'

'No. Thank you.'

She walked quietly towards him, bent down and kissed the top of his head, which was half turned away from her. His forehead was moist with sweat. She straightened up, crossed as quietly as she could to the door and paused. Her heart lurched at his misery.

'Are you sure there isn't anything I can do? Call a nurse or anyone?'

'No, thank you. G-g-goodbye.'

She retraced her steps along the corridor, tears welling in her eyes against her will. By the time she left the building they were coursing down her face and she could do nothing to stop them.

Ten

---

*L*ilian walked along the drive until she was out of sight of any prying eyes, then stopped and tried to compose herself. She was more distressed than she had ever been in her life. To see darling Edmund in such a state was unbelievable. She tried to remember what she had heard people say about neurasthenia. Scum, who were too 'windy' to face their duty. Shirkers. Malingerers. Ought to be court-martialled. Not Edmund, surely, who was bold and brave and had been so keen to go to France and fight the Germans. It didn't make sense.

Personal thoughts intruded. Why hadn't he been pleased to see her after their long separation? Hadn't she undertaken a tedious, dirty journey expressly to be with him? He ought to have shown at least a modicum of pleasure and yes, gratitude. She had little tolerance for displays of naked emotion but what upset her most was that he wanted her to leave. How could he be so mean? The war must have disturbed his values.

Did he still love her?

She wiped her face, dried her eyes, blew her nose, then continued on her way. Her feet tapped sharply on the pavement as she walked erect and proud down the slight hill that took her towards the sea and her hotel. In the harbour gulls circled above an incoming vessel. She caught a glimpse of fish glistening on its deck and hoped they were mackerel – she suddenly fancied a mackerel for dinner. Almost parenthetically she wondered what Edmund would be eating, and whether he was hungry.

She walked more slowly and sighed, trying to fathom Edmund's breakdown. Her life had been sheltered until now. Halberton was a village which afforded the usual gamut of human existence. Its thousand or so inhabitants encompassed the rich, the poor, the strong, the weak, the dull, the witty, the healthy, the sick. Nevertheless, it was not difficult to avoid what one would rather ignore and Lilian was skilled in the cultivation of ignorance where it suited. She knew Potty Blundell, of course, but he was just a bit wanting, not all of a state like Edmund. No, mental breakdown was altogether more sinister. It did not belong to her world. And particularly when the sufferer happened to be Edmund, her own adored husband. It was alien and it frightened her. He had actually cried in front of her. The war must have softened him, there could be no other explanation, she thought with shame. Shame for him. Now if it had been Hugh Brodrick she could have understood. It would be just like him to fall apart. But not Edmund – he was so *strong* and *successful*. It was unaccountable.

A little voice whispered in her mind that she was ashamed because she had absolutely no idea how to help him, and in her helplessness she had become angry with him. Her faced burned at the realisation.

Restless, contrary thoughts criss-crossed her mind through the evening. When she finished her dinner – mackerel was on the menu – she was too agitated to sit quietly in the lounge and decided to walk along the promenade. The night was clear but not too chilly. She was surprised at the large number of people still about: sweethearts, men in khaki, no doubt on embarkation leave, their womenfolk happy or anxious. A music-hall door opened, loosing a shaft of smoky yellow light and a noisy burst of gaiety before it was shut again and quiet returned. Waves tumbled and splashed. The sea sparkled silver in the moonlight. Nothing could be more peaceful.

As she wandered along, looking at the people milling around her, she reflected on her own courtship and how her every move with Edmund had been chaperoned. She had never been allowed so much as to go to Tiverton by herself. Now girls and their sweethearts were so much freer – another difference from Life Before The War. Even if the war ended tomorrow she doubted that people could ever return to the old ways. Unmarried girls were becoming nurses, or worked in munitions factories, in shops or increasingly on farms, though she had heard that Devonshire farmers were reluctant to take them on. They were experiencing unparalleled responsibility and freedom. She wondered what she would be doing now if she was still unmarried. That thought brought her back to Edmund. Their courtship was as short as they could make it, both of them hating to be chaperoned all the time. The sunny day of their wedding three years ago, the joyous, wonderful honeymoon in France and Italy, travelling by train first to Paris, then to Provence and the Riviera before crossing into Italy and down to Florence. The colours and sounds and smells of the south, but most of all the discovery of passionate physical love. Then the return to Devon and settling into the routine of their new lives. Happiness. Then war.

She reasoned that Edmund would not be like this if he could help it, therefore he must really be ill. She would try, would force herself to understand. She consoled herself with the thought that she would not be so unprepared next time she saw him.

She rose early the next day. There was a slight sea-mist but there was no doubt that the day would be fine. She made good time to the hospital and was the first visitor to arrive. Few patients appeared to be up and about yet. This time she made her own way to Edmund's room, accurately negotiating the stairs and passages. When she reached his room the door stood ajar. She knocked self-consciously and entered.

Edmund was sitting on the same chair as before. She wondered fleetingly if he had spent the night there. His face was pale but had lost the greenish hue of yesterday. His eyes were still fretful but when he looked up his mouth made an effort to smile. She smiled back and went to sit down beside him. Her blouse and skirt were made of soft material and did not rustle.

'Dearest Edmund, you're looking a good deal better today,' she heard herself say gushingly, as though she was making a courtesy visit to a distant acquaintance.

'G-g-good to see you, my d-dear. I feel a bit b-b-better.' Edmund tried to be cheerful but he only succeeded in sounding false. 'How about a stroll? Nice d-d-day, I think.'

'Do you feel up to it? It's clear out but quite fresh still.'

'I'll be all right.'

'You'll have to get dressed,' she said looking at his dressing-gown. 'You can't go outside like that.'

'I am d-dressed underneath. Only have my jacket to p-put on.'

With an effort he hauled himself to his feet. Lilian was afraid he would fall, he trembled so violently. She stood quickly to support him but he brushed her away.

'I'm a b-b-bit wobbly at the moment. It's worst in the morning. It'll get b-better.'

'Are you sure about going out? It's a long way downstairs, you know.'

'I'm all right, dear. Hate b-being an invalid.'

'Yes, I can see that.'

He exchanged his dressing-gown for a jacket. He was wearing the uniform issued to the sick – blue suit, white shirt and red tie. It was strange to see him dressed like that.

Lilian linked her arm through his as they left his room. This

71

time he accepted it. They walked slowly along the corridor and down the stairs. In the hall a fresh-faced orderly pointed out the most direct way to the garden. They followed his directions and found themselves on the shady side of the house. A flagged terrace led round to the front of the building, which faced due south. A short distance away on the smooth lawn they found a wooden bench. They sat down and made themselves comfortable. Edmund had carried down the rug that had been over his knees. He placed it carefully on the bench then caught sight of their footprints on the dewy grass.

'Are your feet all right, my d–dear? C–c–can't have them getting wet.'

'Don't worry,' Lilian laughed, feeling more like her old self. 'Look – I'm wearing my stoutest shoes. I need them for the walk up here from the hotel.'

'Is it far? Hadn't you better get a cab?'

'No, it's quite near. And I enjoy the walk. It's good to stretch my legs and breathe the sea air.'

'Yes, the air is good,' he murmured as though he had rediscovered a lost jewel.

They sat in silence. Lilian could see from the way Edmund closed his eyes and lifted his face that he was savouring the sight and smell of this quintessential English autumn day. He had started off sitting bolt upright but muscle by muscle he unconsciously relaxed.

She debated in her mind whether to ask him what had happened to affect him like this. She dreaded saying anything that might upset him, but she was human and curious enough to want to know.

While she deliberated what to say, she studied him.

He was leaning forward, his lower arms resting on his thighs, his fingers still plucking one another unceasingly. The half of his face that she could see was utterly familiar but she realised with a shock that she had been unable to visualise it while he was away. She had thought of him only as an entity, a *soul*. Now she saw details as though for the first time. The hair close-cropped at back and side but long enough on the crown to show signs of curling. Brown newly tending to grey at the temple. Gold where the sun caught it. The lowish, slightly indented forehead, faintly lined. The laughter lines at the corner of the eye. The lazily drooping eyelid with long, curling lashes. The scar that extended from the corner of the eye to below the prominent cheekbone, the result of over-exuberant horsemanship in his youth. The straight, wide nose. The officer's moustache, trim and brown, which failed to hide beads of sweat on the upper lip. The full, sensitive mouth which used to smile so readily but which was now drawn and tense, compressing the lips. The firm, square jaw, closely shaved (had an orderly shaved him or had it been achieved with his own shaking hand?). The skin, bronzed from outdoor living but which could not mask an underlying pallor.

He looked round. A pang of conscience engulfed her lest he thought she had been scrutinising him critically and she reddened.

'D-do I pass muster?'

'How could you ask that? I haven't set eyes on you for months so I intend to feast them now. You look divine, as you always did.'

'D-divine is what I am not, my d-d-dearest Lily. Did Adonis have grey hairs?'

'I expect so, if we could but have seen him. A slight greyness at the temples is said to lend distinction.'

'P-p-perhaps. But you are the one who has to look at them, not me.'

'Then there is no problem.'

She paused, then added, 'Are you feeling strong enough to walk a little? It might do you good.'

He said nothing but stood up. Lilian was pleased to notice

that he moved more easily than he had done earlier. They strolled along a gravel path which was drier than the grass. It crunched beneath their feet. Visitors straggled up the long curve of the drive in ones and twos, some looking happy, others apprehensive, others sombre. It was not difficult to guess their thoughts and fears. Other patients drifted into the garden either alone, with fellow sufferers or with visitors, but Edmund and Lilian just wanted their own company and kept apart from them.

'Edmund, dearest, can you tell me what happened? I should like to know so that I might understand.'

Edmund kept his eyes straight ahead.

'If I were to t-t-tell you, you'd think it of little consequence.'

'No, I should not. But you needn't tell me if you would rather not. I'd hate to upset you again.'

'Like yesterday?'

'Yes.'

'You d-d-didn't upset me with anything you said. When one expects never to see someone d-dear again such a reunion can b-b-be emotional. Traumatic.'

'I felt beastly after I left you.'

He turned and looked at her. 'Dearest Lily. You c-c-couldn't have g-guessed that I'd be like this. You must find me changed b-beyond recognition.'

'I was surprised, I admit. I was naïve. In my mind I associated hospital with – with *physical* wounds. I know better now. I suppose one lives such a sheltered life in this country, not seeing what it is like at the Front.'

'I wouldn't have it any other way. Who was to g-g-guess that this would happen.' He waved his arm in an all-embracing gesture. 'It's b-beyond comprehension. No one this side of the Ch-Channel can ever understand.'

'We can try. *I* can try. I want to help you, Edmund. Please let me.'

'V-very well.'

They turned and retraced their steps past the house. A blackbird hopped a few feet away, ignoring them in its search for food. Somewhere at sea a ship's horn sounded. Nearer, a train whistled as it approached the town and white puffs of smoke rose above a tree-lined cutting. Edmund started so violently at the sound of the whistle that Lilian feared he was going to have some kind of fit. He did not, but he stood rooted to the spot until the panic subsided. His face had blanched.

'Wh-where was I?'

'You were going to tell me what happened – possibly.' Lilian hoped he had not noticed the alarm his panic had caused her.

'Yes, you must know. I should like you to know so that you d-d-don't imagine wrongly.'

'You told me much in your letters,' she said, trying to give him a starting point.

'And I omitted so much more.'

She gave him a quizzical look but remained silent.

After what seemed an age, Edmund started speaking in a slightly stronger voice.

I suppose it was the sh-shells that got to me. The *noise*, always the noise. And the universal *ugliness*. You can have no idea. I'm glad you'll never know the ugliness that's just p-part of life there. It's so hard to b-bear.

'Then at the end of last month we went over the t-top for the first time at L-L-Loos. It was the first t-time we'd been tested and I think we came through well, those who d-did come through that is. We weren't many.' He paused, breathing deeply.

'Well, at least we t-took our first objective. Had to wait two d-d-days for relief. I won't talk about that, if you d-don't mind. Or the gas.'

'Gas!' Lilian was horrified. He hadn't mentioned gas in his letters.

Edmund ignored her remark and carried on.

'We didn't go back to rest but were held in support. B-before I was aware of any material change in myself I started to feel nauseous every time I had to go b-back up the line. I think now it must have started before the b-b-battle. When I b-became aware of it I was ashamed. I had seen other men b-break down. I *would not* get like that. I fought it d-d-day and night. I can't tell you how hard I f-fought it. One night as we were coming out of the line — it was after the most b-beautiful sunset I'd seen in France — a shell came over and exploded no more than t-ten yards away. Reggie Trenchard took m-most of the impact, which saved me. I was b-buried c-completely and survived by sheer will to live. Reggie is buried for ever — or rather, scattered to the four winds. The earth and other stuff covering me was quite loose and my corporal and a couple of Tommies dug me out. I was suffering from shock and was taken to a d-dressing-station, where the d-doctor decided that I should go back to the c-casualty clearing station, or CCS as we call it.

'They tell me I'm n-neurasthenic. I'm not the f-first, and regrettably I won't be the last. I'm sorry I don't have a nice, clean heroic wound to show off. You can't be p-p-proud of me as I am.'

'Nonsense, darling. I *am* proud of you. I admit that yesterday I was puzzled, but I thought things over last night and I realised that something awful must have happened to you. To go through what you did — to see your friend — and to be buried alive. How dreadful. It must have been terrifying.'

'The medic tells me I'm likely to make a c-complete recovery. If I do well, I could b-be home within a month.' He twisted his mouth into a smile.

'But that's wonderful. You must and shall do well. It will be marvellous to have you home. I rattle around without you.'

'My poor dear.' He squeezed her hand. 'How long d-do we have now? You haven't said how long you c-can stay.'

'I must go home later today. I'm on duty again tomorrow

but I'll come back next week, if I can persuade Matron to allow me two more days together. She was very kind about this leave.'

'So soon! B-but it can't be helped, I suppose. Your Matron sounds a reasonable woman. P-perhaps she'll give you three days next time.'

'That is more than I dare hope for.'

'I can't wait to be in D-D Devon again. What's the news?'

'I think I've told you everything in my letters. Violet's bearing up better now, thank goodness. Dolly's a rock. I don't know how she does it. We've all been so worried about Walter. I want to say that he's hanging on but the news from Gallipoli has been so bad that I don't want to tempt fate. Apart from that, there are even fewer men around now, and more of those who went will not be coming back. Jimmy Biggle is the latest but I expect you knew that.'

'No, I hadn't heard.'

They had been walking in no particular direction and were surprised to find themselves back by the bench. It was unoccupied save for the rug they had left there, so they sat down.

'You haven't mentioned Hugh,' Lilian declared suddenly. 'How is he? Does he know you're here?'

'Dear Hugh. He heard what happened and visited me in the CCS while I was waiting to be transferred over here. He's well, and has been mentioned in d-d-dispatches. One of the few who came through unscathed. He'll probably be p-p-promoted soon. We lost so many men at Loos and besides, he's a good officer. His nerves are g-good too.'

Lilian did not know what whim had prompted her to ask after Hugh. Why, she wondered, should Edmund be the one to suffer? How dare Hugh be promoted ahead of him? It was so *wrong*. The world was turning upside down and she could not make sense of it.

Eleven

*W*ithin a fortnight Lilian handed in her notice at the hospital. She had needed little incentive, rapidly losing enthusiasm for nursing once Edmund was in England, arguing with herself that her first duty was to him. Her conscience occasionally chided her for her lack of application but she repressed such thoughts with the idea that she could always carry on where she left off when he had recovered and gone away again. It was as well that she was unable to read the minds of her matron, sister and fellow volunteers, who were less charitable. The professionals took gloomy pride in having been confirmed in their belief that volunteers were an unmitigated nuisance and more trouble than they were worth, and the other VADs felt that she was letting them down.

After having been in hospital for a month Edmund was considered well enough to convalesce at home. His stammer had improved and his fingers were not so busy. He still winced at every unexpected sound, but less markedly.

Against Lilian's wishes he insisted on making the train journey alone.

Full of impatient energy, she walked briskly to the Halt and was standing on the bridge to get the first possible glimpse of the train as it approached. She was well wrapped up against the cold. Her shadow was long on the ground and her breath hung in the November air. For once in these chaotic days the train ran to time and she watched with pleasure as the familiar plumes of smoke coursed between the fields. She hurried down to the platform as the train drew in.

Edmund was the only passenger to alight. The train began to pull away with a lurch and a whistle. He winced. Lilian hugged him until it had disappeared from view. They climbed hand in hand to the road, where Edmund dropped his valise on the ground and gazed silently about, drinking in the fields and trees that he thought he had left behind for good. Still he did not speak as they walked home, nor when he entered the house. By now Lilian had grown accustomed to these silences, knowing them to result from deep thought rather than deliberate avoidance of conversation. He walked around the house, looking, touching, smiling. Remembering.

'It's so good to be home, Lily,' he said at last.

'It's been empty without you. I missed you dreadfully.'

'It's queer, but I never realised until I stepped off the train just how much Halberton is a part of me.'

'Didn't you?'

He looked at her and smiled.

They were standing in the hall. He crossed to the front door and announced, 'I can't hang around here. I have to see the dogs.'

He stepped out and walked round the house to the stable-yard. Lilian followed him and watched him greet his beloved animals. The black greyhound, Pollux, and the grey, Castor, yelped madly with excitement; they had missed their master and were beside themselves with joy.

★

Edmund missed Claudius badly during those winter days. Instead of riding he would set out after breakfast on long solitary walks, crossing the canal, its reeds brown and bent, before striding across the rolling hills. He walked efficiently and rhythmically and found that hours could pass without a conscious thought entering his head. There was an occasional awakening when one of the dogs picked up an exciting scent but on the whole these outings were calm and therapeutic. For a change he sometimes went out on foot with the local beagles but they met less frequently now. Evenings were quiet and peaceful. Lilian, a talented pianist, played Chopin while Edmund would either read or contemplate the flames dancing in the fire. It was still difficult sometimes for him to keep his hands from fidgeting but he made sure that this went unobserved by Lilian from her seat at her piano.

They led a quiet life. The invitations they received were politely refused and they issued none. The last thing either of them wanted was to parade his neurasthenia even though he had improved so much. They both felt that the fewer people who met him at this time the better. The only people they visited were their families, who tried to understand Edmund's breakdown but were obviously embarrassed by it.

One dismal Sunday they had dinner at the Grange with Lilian's parents. Vicky, Walter's wife, was also present. She studiously avoided talking to Edmund or catching his eye throughout the meal.

'I hear Walter's to be congratulated on yet another promotion. He'll make a fine sergeant,' Edmund said at last to break the deadlock.

'Yes, he will. He deserves it for what he's going through.'

'Quite so.'

'After all, he's only been living through hell for the last six months while officers in France come home as soon as they get windy.' She flung down her napkin, left the table and went out, slamming the door behind her.

'I'm sorry, Edmund. I shouldn't have invited both of you together,' said Mrs Franklin, after a few seconds of stunned silence.

'There's nothing for you to apologise for. I understand why

she resents me. I should too, in her position. Lily, my dear, I think we should go.'

'There's no need to do that. Take some coffee first,' said Mrs Franklin.

'Edmund's right, Mama. We ought to go. We've trampled on Vicky's feelings long enough,' said Lilian.

As they were leaving the house Vicky reappeared and walked up to Edmund.

Edmund, please forgive me. I'm sure you've really been ill, but I've been so worried about Walter and seeing you like this – it seems so unfair.'

She held out her hand and Edmund took it gently between both of his.

'It is unfair, Vicky. I can't explain it. Walter's a good man – the best.'

Lilian kissed her sister-in-law on the cheek. 'He'll be home soon, have no fear, Vicky dear.'

'I don't think we should go out again,' Edmund said when they were back in their own drawing room. 'Are you as ashamed of me as I am of myself?'

'I'm not ashamed of you, and you mustn't be either. Neurasthenia is something one doesn't come across as a rule. But no one who saw you in hospital can doubt how dreadfully ill you were.'

'It must be hard for those who've lost loved ones or who are worried to bits like Vicky. I hadn't realised it would be so difficult. Come, play some Mozart. That'll cheer us up.'

She went to the piano and played while Edmund gazed into the fire.

★

When Edmund had first come home Lilian observed that, as in hospital, he was subtly distanced from her. She thought it might just be his illness and, as was her habit when something unpleasant threatened her, she tried to ignore it. It was hard to define: he loved her as much as ever, she was certain, but whenever she attempted to talk about France there was a pulling back, the closing of a shutter, and she could not see behind it.

'Edmund, darling, you hardly ever talk about France, yet you were so keen to go there,' she said to him one morning when a gale kept him indoors.

'Yes, I was keen.'

'Can we talk about it?'

'There's nothing to add over what I've already said in my letters. There are things – the sights and sounds that one takes for granted there that would appal any right-thinking person in England. The gulf is too big to cross. I want to spare you those things – not just because of your sweetness and innocence but because they are beyond the comprehension of anyone who hasn't witnessed them.'

'We used to share everything but now I feel shut out, that there's part of you that's a stranger to me. I know you don't mean it but that's how I feel.'

'I'm sorry, deeply sorry that you feel like that. Please believe me, it's nothing to do with you – or us. It's the war. I'd rather not dwell on it while I'm here with you.'

Lilian went over to him and bent down to kiss him on the top of his head. 'Forgive me, darling. I want so much to understand but I can see that it agitates you. I won't mention it again.'

He said nothing but fumbled in his breast pocket, retrieving a small, slim packet the size of an envelope. He held it in his hand and looked at it as though weighing it up.

I have here – ' he began in a quiet voice.

'Yes? What is it?'

He weighed it again, reached a decision and put the packet back in his pocket. 'No, it's better that you don't see them. It's nothing, my dear. I misled you.'

'What is it, Edmund? A letter?'

'No, not a letter. Mementoes of some people I knew out there, that's all. They would mean nothing to you.'

'I'd like to see them. Do show me.'

'No. No, I can't. I made a mistake. I shouldn't have mentioned it.'

'Really darling, you're being very tiresome. Why can't you show me?'

'I made a mistake, that's all. Please excuse me, Lily. I have some letters to write which can't wait.'

He jumped to his feet and strode out of the room, shutting the door loudly. Lilian could only wonder at his swift change of mood and his strange reluctance to show her the mysterious mementoes. She imagined them to be photographs of posed groups of officers, stern and soldierly, but none so handsome as Edmund. The packet did indeed contain photographs but she could not have imagined that, like a number of officers, he had acquired photographs of dismembered bodies and other signs of carnage to jolt those at home who still believed the war was jolly good fun.

★

The following day Hugh arrived to spend his leave with the Potters. As Netherculme was inaccessible to him except as a patient he said he would rather not go home.

Lilian remained at home while Edmund walked to the Halt in the approaching dusk to meet his friend, the one man who, to Edmund, remained a rock in the changing world. Lilian heard their returning footsteps on the gravel drive and stood waiting at the open door, dark against the hall light. The naked branches of the elms were etched black against the sky. It was almost impossible to distinguish the silhouettes of the two men although Hugh was slightly broader in the shoulder than Edmund. They were exactly the same height.

Lilian greeted Hugh more warmly than she had ever done in the past. She would rather he was not staying with them but as his own house was denied him it would have been churlish not to have him at Sydling. Besides, she nursed the hope that his undemanding company would help restore Edmund to his former self.

'My dear Lilian, as beautiful as ever,' he said, with rare lack of reserve, as he clasped her hands between his.

'Thank you. You must be cold. Do come in by the fire. It will soon warm you.'

'I'm used to being out in all weathers, you know.'

'I don't care. You must pamper yourself while you're here. Your leave is so short.'

'That's true enough but one has to be philosophical – it's better than having no leave at all.'

'That's scant consolation, I'm sure.'

'Far from it, I assure you. Many a time during the last few months I would gladly have exchanged a year's pay for an hour in Devon.'

'Then you would have sold yourself mighty cheap,' said Edmund. 'A year's army pay is a pittance.'

'Perhaps, but you understand the sentiment.'

'Yes, I do. By the way, my dear, you must congratulate Hugh. His promotion's come through. He's now a full lieutenant.'

'Oh. Yes. Congratulations. Edmund said it might happen. We should have some champagne this evening.'

'Of course we shall,' said Edmund.

★

Hugh was a shade tense at first, so great was the contrast between army life and domestic comfort but the following day he was, at least superficially, his usual self-sufficient being, unruffled and unhurried. But his position *vis-à-vis* Edmund had undergone a subtle transformation. Now Hugh was calm, authoritative, while Edmund was insecure and dependent.

On the third day of his visit, when the friends had crossed the canal and strolled to the top of the highest hill in the neighbourhood, Hugh said, 'Life's rum, isn't it.'

Edmund looked at him quizzically. 'Rum in any particular way?'

'No. Generally, I mean to say. You and me, for example. Before we went out I – anyone – would have sworn that I'd be the one to – be affected.'

'Break down, you mean. You might as well come right out and say it.'

'All right. Break down.'

Edmund sighed. 'It might have been easier for you – I mean that in the kindest way. You'd have coped so much better. It's a beastly business. And made ten times worse by people telling one how surprised they are. How they hadn't expected it of me. It was – still is – hateful. I pray that it won't happen to you.'

'It ought to have been me. Nobody would have been surprised and therefore I should have been left to get better in my own good time.'

'Oh Hugh, you never had high enough expectation of yourself. Not at school, at Oxford, at the Slade, nor since. Your humility is your greatest virtue and your greatest fault.'

Hugh shrugged and smiled. 'Perhaps I'm simply a realist. That would explain the resilience of my nerves. They do wobble, of course they do, quite a lot at times. But I never had your heroic expectations. I don't strive to be the best officer or to be covered in glory. All I want is to do as well as I am able, to look after my men and not to let the side down. My men seem tolerably confident in me, which means more to me than I can say. At times I think it's a jolly good thing that they can't see inside my head. I dread letting them down, or going to pieces in front of them.'

'At least I was spared that humiliation. Being buried alive precipitated my breakdown but make no mistake it was already on the way. Any little spark would have set it off before very much longer.'

They were leaning on a dilapidated wooden gate, smoking. Hugh cleared his throat and said, looking into the distance, 'Forgive the impertinence, old soul, but how did Lilian, er, react? Tell me to mind my own business if you like.'

Edmund drew on his pipe before answering. 'You know Lilian. She'd never seen a mental case before. Naturally enough she didn't know what to make of it at first. She always expected me to collect a nice, tidy bullet wound if anything. That was probably my fault for persuading her that's what would happen. But she rallied well and has been unstintingly caring.'

He sighed and continued, 'But there's no doubt that she was disappointed.'

'Not for long, surely.'

'Perhaps not, but I do feel that I let her down. She had such great expectations of me.'

'You're as unrealistic as each other.'

'The perfect couple. Isn't that what people call us?'

'You know it. Tell me, have you told her what it's really like over there?'

'No. We had a bit of a row about it the other day. She naturally wants to understand but I simply can't tell her. Partly because I want to spare her but also I find it impossible to talk about it. She's hurt because I haven't shared it with her. I have some photographs – thought they'd come in useful during conversations with drawing-room warriors. You know the sort of thing. Mutilated corpses and the like. I even have one of a leg dangling from a tree like a flag. I took them out of my pocket to show her, but found that I couldn't after all. She's innocent. Why add her nightmares to mine?'

'You did right.'

They stood in contemplative silence, still leaning on the gate. Sheep, startled away by their arrival, wandered back and stared inquisitively, chewing. Starlings twittered in a nearby thicket.

'It's too bad,' Hugh said at length. 'Look at this landscape. Instead of appreciating its beauty I find myself plotting and scheming and thinking of strategies and positions and objectives.'

Edmund turned to look at him. 'So it *has* got to you.'

They threw back their heads and laughed madly, the sheep backing away before turning tail and cantering out of sight into a dip in the field.

Twelve

*T*he day before Hugh's departure arrived. He had exchanged little conversation with Lilian other than uncontroversial small talk between guest and hostess. He had spent the larger part of every day out walking with Edmund, and had avoided any *tête-à-tête* with her because he dreaded betraying his feelings. As the end of his leave approached he felt that he could not say goodbye without talking to her alone. He told himself that he wanted to ease his mind about her attitude to Edmund's neurasthenia but he knew the real reason was that he wanted something – anything – to cheer him through the weeks and months until he was killed, which he assumed would happen sooner or later. He was writing letters in the morning room when, glancing up at the window, he caught sight of Edmund going down to the village with the dogs. He added a couple of lines to a letter, blotted it, folded the neatly written sheets and inserted them carefully into an envelope which he sealed and addressed with a clear, bold direction. Placing it in his breast pocket, he pushed back his chair and went in search of Lilian.

He found her after a short search, arranging sprigs of wintersweet and holly in a buff-coloured vase in the dining room, but having found his objective he realised that he had no idea what to say. Lilian was always so critical. She looked up, smiled, and continued snipping a woody stem.

'There you are. I was looking for you,' he began lamely.

'Here I am, as you said.'

She waited for him to continue but he remained silent.

'Is there anything the matter. Hugh?'

'No, not at all.'

He felt awkward, as he invariably did in her company. If only he had Edmund's quick-wittedness. Yet he never had a problem talking to other women.

'Um. I thought I'd hunt you out. After all, we haven't had much opportunity to chat since I've been here.' He felt his face redden, and, thankful that Lilian seemed absorbed in arranging the branches, he moved to the window and looked out into the garden. If he had had an inkling of the comparison she was mentally making between his face and the holly berries in her hand he would have tried to walk through the wall.

'Edmund's been keeping you occupied.'

'Talking of whom,' he said, seizing the opening, 'I can't tell you what a relief it was to find him so well.'

'Well? He is much better, certainly. However, he still can't totally control the fidgeting with his hands.'

'That will disappear with time. It's a great healer,' he said, wondering why he churned out that banal cliché.

'What is – time?'

'Yes.'

'I suppose it is.'

'It has been in his case.'

'I may have helped.'

'Oh, indubitably. I didn't mean to imply that you weren't helping him.'

'No, you probably didn't. But you put things so awkwardly, Hugh, that sometimes a conversation with you is mostly guesswork.'

She shoved an obstinate piece of wintersweet into the vase.

The shot hit home but Hugh felt that he had gone too far

now to stop. 'He's an excellent officer, you know, Lilian. First rate.'

'But –'

'But what?' He turned round and looked at her.

She raised her eyes to his.

'*You* were mentioned in dispatches, *you* have been promoted, *you* were not in a lunatic asylum.'

'Steady on, Lilian. The hospital wasn't a lunatic asylum, nothing like.'

'How do you know? You didn't see it. They were crazy, the whole miserable lot of them, as far as I could tell.'

'Some of the patients were temporarily neurasthenic. Do keep it in proportion. Have you any idea how men get that way?'

'Edmund's told me what happened, of course. I'm not entirely heartless, Hugh. What happened to him must have been dreadful. But he's so withdrawn and secretive. He's ashamed of himself. He's – well if you must know – he's embarrassing.'

During this exchange Hugh face drained from crimson to white, as though he had been bled dry. His every muscle was tense. Lilian couldn't possibly understand what it was like at the front but he was shocked, appalled by the disappointment in her voice, the lack of compassion. He fought in his mind to find excuses for her but years of pent-up feelings got the better of him and burst in an explosion of anger. He stepped nearer and faced her across the table.

'You wouldn't say that if you had any idea of what it's like over there. The wonder is that it doesn't happen to all of us. How can you dare to criticise anyone? Take a good look at yourself. You made a half-hearted attempt to do some nursing, probably because you thought it looked good, and gave it up as soon as you got bored with it. You carry on in your selfish little way while every good man is going through Armageddon. When Edmund needs you – really needs you for the first time

– you despise him and treat his illness with contempt. Can you really be so unfeeling?'

Lilian looked stunned. She had a branch of wintersweet in her hand which she placed on the table before replying. When she spoke her voice was trembling.

'How *dare* you even think to suggest that I despise Edmund? Since we seem to be speaking frankly let me tell you this. It should have been *you*. If ever there was a candidate for neurasthenia, you are it. Edmund's ten times better than you – at everything. *He* shouldn't have gone to pieces. *He* should have been promoted before you. And you have the gall to come here and strut around and boast of your success. My God! I suppose you think you'd better make the most of it because it's the only chance you'll ever have to feel superior to him. Well, I can tell you that I for one am not impressed. As far as I'm concerned you've never been able to hold a candle to him and never shall.'

Hugh looked at her with an expression of intermingled anger and pity. He was used to her veiled hostility but the lacerations his sensibility had endured since July made her remarks as painful as vinegar on an open wound. Rather than risk further speech he turned and walked towards the door. It was ajar and he pulled it open but instead of the empty hall he found himself face to face with Edmund. Their eyes locked.

'Excuse me,' Hugh mumbled. 'I need some air.'

He strode past the motionless figure of his friend and went to retrieve his trench coat and, still fumbling to pull it on, let himself out of the house.

Thirteen

---

*T*he gravel of the drive crunched loudly as Hugh strode down it. Without conscious thought he went through the lower village. When he passed the last house he turned off to the right and was soon scrambling down beside a narrow bridge over the canal. The towpath was still hard with frost except for places where the low sun had penetrated or where it had been sheltered by overhanging trees.

'I shall get over her, I shall,' he repeated over and over in time with his step.

He thought of the day he first met her. After Oxford he had gone to the Slade with a view to pursuing a career in art. Towards the end of the summer vacation in 1911 he was invited to a tennis party. He wasn't particularly keen on the sport but went along as he had nothing better to do. A girl of nineteen or twenty dressed in white was standing to one side surrounded by a constellation of admirers including Charles Luttrell, their host. Hugh joined them and Charles introduced him to Lilian. She was slim, of medium height and devastatingly beautiful. Her hair reflected the gold of the sun. She took Hugh's hand and smiled up at him with laughter in her eyes. Her voice was a pleasing contralto. He noticed a few delicate freckles on her fair skin and thought they had never become a girl so well. His heart turned over. His emotion was so intense that he did not take in what she was saying. When he came down to earth she was sharing a joke with someone else and his moment had passed. As the afternoon wore on he realised that the only way to get her attention was to cut her out from whoever she was talking to. It was out of the question. He was far too shy to attempt anything so bold.

Two weeks later he returned to his studies in London which were less successful than they ought to have been as half his mind never strayed far from Lilian. He must see her again. He would engineer an opportunity to meet her when he was home for Christmas. As a starting point he'd confide in Edmund and ask his advice since his friend was so much more confident and experienced in these matters. After a day's hunting shortly after his return the friends were sitting over tea and muffins in front of a roaring fire at Bradcombe Rogus when Hugh saw his opportunity. He was delicately building up to the subject of Lilian when Edmund interrupted him.

'Sorry to butt in, Hugh, but I'm simply bursting to tell you my news.'

'Well, I can see that you're looking pretty pleased about something. You have been all day, come to that. Out with it.'

'While you've been pretending to study in the fleshpots I haven't been idle here. I've met the most wonderful girl in the world and have asked her to marry me. For some reason she accepted. We're engaged.'

'My heartiest congratulations. Who's the lucky girl? Do I know her?'

'Her name's Lilian – Lilian Franklin. She lives at Compton Grange. I asked her if she knew you and she said not. Aren't you pleased for me? It goes without saying that you'll be my best man.'

The bottom dropped out of Hugh's world. Somehow he found words to congratulate his friend. Fortunately Edmund was so busy being pleased with himself and extolling Lilian's virtues that he failed to notice Hugh's reaction. Engaged to

Edmund! Not only that but she had even forgotten she'd met him. He'd made that little impact on her. He never had any illusions – for as long as they had known each other he had never been anything other than runner-up to Edmund but this was the bitterest blow.

As soon as he could he made his excuses and left.

His first thought was to go back to London and quietly drop Edmund from his life but he soon realised he could not do that. Ever since they became friends at their preparatory school they had been like brothers. Besides, without knowing what he was doing he had agreed to be Edmund's best man. He was sure Edmund had not guessed his feelings and he determined to keep it that way, like the current in the depths of a river whose surface flowed smooth and unruffled. No – his feelings would pass. He would get over Lilian in time and meet her as a friend.

He was deeply self-conscious when Edmund introduced them at Maud and Arthur Potter's traditional New Year's Eve party but at least he was prepared for the meeting. Lilian was radiant. She beamed her smile on him. He refrained from mentioning the tennis party and merely congratulated her on her engagement, praising Edmund and wishing her joy. Embarrassment made him awkward and she quickly moved on. At every subsequent meeting he convinced himself that he was relaxing more in her company. He regretted that he had lost her before he even tried to win her but he was not made for jealousy and his innate humility was pleased that if he should lose her to anyone it should be Edmund.

Perversely, as he began to feel more comfortable with Lilian he could sense her growing resentment towards him. And now the war had – thus far – treated him more kindly than it had Edmund. She would not forgive him for that.

He walked on and cursed himself for his weakness in hoping that she might have said something that he could hold in his memory to ease the loneliness of the trenches. When he was busy, which was most of the time, it did not matter but there were occasional quiet periods when he was bitterly lonely, having no wife or sweetheart or close family to write and cheer him. Were a few kind words too much to hope for?

The combined effect of crisp air and regular movement eventually calmed him. His mind began to clear. It would take half an hour to walk around the loop of canal that made a broad sweep around three sides of the village. That would be too soon to go back to the house. He had better push on to the next village. Then, by the time he returned across the fields, emotions might be forgotten. He debated with himself whether he ought to leave immediately instead of tomorrow. If it were just Lilian to be considered he would have gone at once but he did not want to leave Edmund under a cloud. Besides, who was to say if they would ever see each other again? No, there was nothing for it but to endure the rest of the day as best he could.

He did not have an unhappy disposition. He might have lacked Edmund's brilliance and vivacity but he possessed a sound natural philosophy, a willingness to see the best of all situations while placing life's bleaker moments in proper perspective. Edmund had reached heights that Hugh could only dream of but he had also discovered greater depths. For the first time in the twenty years of their friendship it occurred to Hugh that he had an advantage over his friend. It had taken a war to reveal it. The thought insinuated itself into his conscious mind so tentatively that at first he did not believe it but when he gave it greater consideration the impact was enough to stop him in full stride. He stared unseeing at a group of mallard, then muttering in surprise he continued on his way, rolling the idea around his mind as though it were a new wine on the palate. He would not have been human if he had not felt a rush of pride but he had too much humility to savour it for long.

Edmund had experienced dreadful torment and he would not wish that on anyone. He felt deeply for his friend, knowing now the full extent of Lilian's lack of empathy and how it must add to Edmund's suffering. If only Lilian was more understanding. She and Edmund were both ridiculous perfectionists but her view of the war did not seem to have moved on since 1914 – God, that was only last year – of heroics and glory. His own promotion while Edmund was neurasthenic must have profoundly disturbed the neat order into which people and objects were compartmentalised in her mind. Oh, Lilian! He was no longer angry with her. Instead he felt a profound pity.

Edmund had set out to visit Tom Vincent, an elderly neighbour, but when he arrived he found Mr Vincent about to depart for Tiverton. They talked briefly, then Edmund made his way home again. After giving his coat to the maid he was attracted by the sound of voices in the dining room: Hugh's quiet baritone alternating with his wife's incisive contralto. He had intended to go into the drawing room and read the newspaper when the mention of his own name arrested him. It is the most natural feeling in the world to want to know what others are saying about us and Edmund was not immune from curiosity. At first Hugh's voice had been indistinct, then it suddenly became louder – he must have turned to face the door. Lilian's reply was clear enough. When Edmund realised what was being said the muscles of his face set from jaw to temple. The kneading of his fingers that he had come so close to conquering started up aggressively. Surely his own dearest Lily was not saying these things. He moved closer to the door and was about to go in when it was wrenched open and he stood face to face with Hugh. Their eyes met and Hugh was gone before Edmund had time to speak. He stood still for a moment then entered the room, closing the door behind him.

Lilian was once again bent over her task but he could see that she was flushed and angry.

'I thought you'd gone,' she said crossly without looking up.

'Hugh has gone.'

Lilian jerked up and nearly knocked the vase off the table.

'Why are you looking at me like that? You look as though you've never seen me before.'

'I don't think I knew you until now.'

She tried to laugh. 'What on earth do you mean? Everyone is determined to cross me today.'

'Determined to cross you! Are you really as selfish and heartless as you're trying to make out?'

'What do you mean?' she asked again but this time there was a tremor in her voice.

'I mean I heard some of what you said to Hugh. I can't believe your callousness. Don't you realise that he leaves here tomorrow and will be back at the Front in a few days? This time next week he might be dead for all you know, or worse, maimed for life. And his consolation will be your words ringing in his ears and the thought of me living comfortably and idly in my own home. He has no loving wife to comfort him and yet you abuse him in that way.'

They glared at each other.

'I said nothing that was untrue,' she said at last.

'Nothing that might not break a man's spirit when he's most in need of it. Apart from any other consideration, how could you be so vile to someone who's not only a dear friend but also a guest under our roof?'

'I didn't mean to say those things but he's so bumbling and awkward he tried my patience.'

'Your patience! Good God. You play around here day in, day out, without so much as a glimpse of the real world, and you complain that your patience is tried and – what was it you said before? – that we seem determined to cross you. I can't believe anyone can be so naïve and ignorant and self-absorbed. I used to think of you as being tender and generous. Now I know I was a blind fool.'

'No.'

Edmund said nothing.

'I'll apologise to Hugh. He'll forgive me even if you don't.'

'I daresay he will, but how much better if there were nothing to forgive.'

He moved stiffly towards the door where he turned and announced, 'By the way, my Medical Board is on Tuesday. I intend to have myself passed fit for service again. My breakdown won't cause you much more embarrassment.'

He called Castor and Pollux, grabbed his coat and went out to the stables. He stood in Claudius's empty stall, where a horsey smell still lingered, and reflected on the constancy of animal compared with human love.

He then collected some tools and busied himself with pruning and sweeping up leaves, burning them on a comforting bonfire. While his hands were busy he reflected on his marriage. Until now he had taken it for granted. There had been no need to examine it. It just was, and they were happy. Now he realised that it had shifted like sands after a storm. Neither of them had altered intrinsically; rather the war had accentuated both their blessings and their blemishes. Until Loos he had always been self-reliant, confident. His personality radiated out to others. Lilian was his polar opposite, reflecting back the warmth that she received. In company she sparkled like a diamond, alone she could be as dull as an uncut stone. Until now this basic difference in character had not mattered, indeed they had complemented one another. Now he knew they would have to adjust if they were to survive. Perhaps part of the problem was that his life and his concept of Life had changed but Lilian's had remained essentially the same. There were minor hardships for those who were left behind: less petrol for the car, the garden going to weed for lack of gardeners, fewer servants indoors, but on the whole they had little to worry about. And yet – and yet – they felt put upon.

Edmund was not the only soldier who found this hard to understand.

★

Hugh returned two hours later. He was glowing from his walk. He abhorred emotional scenes and fervently hoped that the storm had blown over. He entered the garden by the wicket-gate near the church. His artist's eye noted a scattering of autumn crocuses and, although it was December, primroses were flowering in sheltered spots. As he followed the curve of the shrub-lined path around the perimeter of the garden he passed without noticing a leafless shrub seven feet high with small, pale yellow, waxy flowers. Suddenly he caught its perfume which filled the air. Wintersweet. Mental association with smell was so powerful that he was immediately back in the dining room facing Lilian's contempt. He knew he would never be able to tolerate the smell again, and he hurried past it.

Ten yards further on he heard the crackle and hiss of a bonfire and smelt burning applewood, altogether more pleasant and cheering. He turned along a narrow path which led to the kitchen garden. He found Edmund tossing wood onto a fire which was burning furiously. He turned at the sound of Hugh's approach.

'Had a good walk?' he asked lightly.

'Wonderful. Needed to clear my head a bit. What a glorious day.'

A comfortable silence fell on them as they stood and watched the flames.

'Haven't you left that a little late?' Hugh asked with a nod towards the bonfire.

'Yes, I suppose so. Losing Watts has made us all behind.

Jacks keeps the worst of it in check but he can't do everything. Besides, I dare not ask him to go up a ladder with the pruning-hook. He's shaky enough as it is.'

'Any more need doing? There's nothing I like more than pruning.'

'The William pear. I haven't touched it yet. You can do the nipping if you like, and I'll hold the ladder.'

They crossed to where the tree stood in isolation on the lawn, leaving a trail of dark footprints on the grass. The only sounds to be heard were the snip of the pruning-hook and the playful scuttling of Castor and Pollux. An inquisitive robin perched on a nearby buddleia, alternately singing and cocking his head sometimes this way, to watch the dogs, and sometimes that, to watch the men. Their task complete, they carried the twigs in their arms back to the bonfire, which had died down since they left it. Edmund stirred the embers with a fork and teased it into flame again. Soon it had devoured their prunings. Job complete, they returned their tools to the potting-shed and went indoors for lunch.

★

Lilian's instinct was to plead a headache and avoid seeing Hugh again but she knew that would be cowardly. She dabbed lavender water on her face to try to reduce the puffiness that always followed crying, and determined to put on a bold front. She did not need to worry about making conversation. Hugh was determined not to speak unless spoken to for fear of precipitating another outburst and he assiduously avoided catching her eye. Edmund was still too angry with her to contemplate conversation. Hugh noticed that the vase of wintersweet had been removed to the hall but the scent still lingered like a ghost. With nothing else to do but eat, and none was particularly successful at that, the ordeal was soon over. Announcing as she rose from the table that she was going to spend the afternoon with Dolly Tranter, Lilian thrust her head high and left the room. She returned just in time to change for dinner.

Happily for all of them Edmund's parents had been invited for the evening so the trio were spared the embarrassment of another awkward meal. The Potters had known Hugh since he was a young boy at school with Edmund so conversation flowed readily and easily. If they did notice that Edmund or Hugh lapsed into silence they attributed it to the war and tactfully talked of neutral topics. As soon as it was polite to do so Lilian seated herself at the piano and occupied herself until the evening broke up. Maud Potter observed her flushed face and strange mood and smiled indulgently, hoping she had started a baby.

Hugh and Edmund said goodbye to the Potters in the drawing room. While Lilian escorted them to the front door Edmund went over and poked the fire. Hugh waited until he heard the front door close then went into the hall where Lilian was still standing. He closed the drawing room door carefully behind him.

'Lilian, I'll be leaving before anyone is up in the morning. I want to thank you for allowing me to stay here. It's meant so much to me.'

He walked over to her and offered her his hand.

She took it awkwardly. He lifted her hand to his lips and kissed it lightly.

'We both said things today that are best forgotten,' he said gently, releasing her hand. 'Please forgive me. I hope we can part as friends.'

'Thank you, but there is nothing for me to forgive, just the opposite. I acted abominably. You didn't say anything I didn't deserve. What you said stung me, I admit, but that's because I knew it was true. It's painful to realise that one has such glaring faults. I hope I didn't ruin your leave.'

He shook his head.

'And I'm glad you haven't been wounded – or anything. Long may that continue.'

'Thank you. I hope so too. And no, you didn't ruin my leave.'

There was an awkward pause.

'I'll say goodnight then,' he said, and moved away.

'Hugh,' she called out urgently.

He turned round.

'Hugh – please look out for Edmund when he's out there. He has a Medical Board on Tuesday – I expect he told you. He wants to go back as soon as he can.'

'Of course I shall. There's no need to ask.'

'And will you promise to write to me if anything –'

'Yes, I promise.' He longed to ask her to write to him – even a few lines would be worth the earth. But he knew he could never ask her to. His friendship for Edmund and his scrupulous principles would always stop him.

'Thank you. You're a true friend.' She smiled again. Without saying anything else she crossed to the stairs and went up to her room.

★

The following morning Hugh was up at five o'clock to give himself time to walk to Tiverton Junction since the earliest connection from the Halt would be too late for his train to London. Before leaving he placed two neatly wrapped parcels on the breakfast table and propped a Christmas card against each. Snow had been falling for an hour when he left the house. As he walked along the silent road he wondered if he would see either of them again.

Fourteen

Edmund was sitting at the breakfast table when Lilian joined him. They had not spoken since before Hugh left. She had gone straight up to bed and feigned sleep when Edmund eventually joined her, and he rose early.

As she entered the room Lilian felt shy, unsure if he was still angry with her. She saw immediately that his anger had passed, and stooped to peck him on the cheek before sitting down.

'Good morning, my dear. I hope I didn't disturb you too much during the night. I dreamed a lot, which always makes me toss and turn,' he said.

'No, I didn't notice.' She did not want to upset him by telling him that his fretfulness and calling out in his sleep had woken her more than once. She noticed the present and card left by Hugh and lowered her eyes.

She felt Edmund's gaze on her and looked up.

'This is so kind of Hugh. It's more than I deserve.'

'Lily —'

'No. Please darling, let me speak. I was a beast to Hugh, and to you. You were right in everything you said to me. I'm sorry. I apologised to him last night after your parents left. He was charity itself, which made me more ashamed than if he'd sworn at me, as he had every right to do.'

'My dear.'

'Can you forgive me now?'

'How can you ask that? Of course I can, and have done. I said things to you too which I would do anything to take back. This war is turning us all inside out. We mustn't let it, Lily. We must hold onto what we had, and if we do wobble occasionally we should make allowances from the depths of our hearts. We can't let it come between us.'

'You're right. I was desperately unhappy yesterday. I thought you'd stopped caring for me – that you despised me. See – I'm being egoistic again. But oh, Edmund, I couldn't bear it if you did stop loving me. The war has taken you to another world, a world that's utterly remote from anything I've experienced. I wanted you to tell me all about it and resented the fact that you didn't. It took what happened yesterday to make me realise that there are some things you simply have to keep to yourself.'

He stood up and walked around the table, pulled out a chair and sat beside her.

'I did a lot of thinking yesterday too. Maybe in a few years, when it's all over, it will be easier for me to tell you about it. I don't know. When other fellows have come back from leave or after having been wounded they've all said the same thing – they found it impossible to talk about the war with their loved ones. It's too deep. So you see, it isn't just me being a so-and-so.'

She smiled and hugged him.

'Shall you forgive me if I go back? I meant what I said about getting myself passed fit, but not to hurt you or to get away from you. I feel that I let myself, my men and the regiment down. I have to go back to do the best I can for them and to prove something to myself. It would mean so much if I had your blessing.'

'Of course you have my blessing. I'll miss you dreadfully, but I do understand.'

'Thank you. And now you'd better get on with your breakfast. It must be cold by now.'

A weight lifted from both of them after this conversation

and the few days before Edmund's Board were among the happiest of their lives.

The day of the Medical Board arrived. Lilian tried sewing and kept pricking her fingers. She tried reading but soon put the book aside, realising that she had not taken in a word. She was playing the piano when she heard the car outside. She stopped at once and ran out to meet Edmund.

'Well? How did it go?'

Edmund took her hands in his. 'They've passed me for light duties. If all goes well I could be back on active service within three or four months. I have to go tomorrow. I'll miss Christmas – I'm sorry.'

'Oh, darling. I'm so happy for you. You must be so relieved. Never mind about Christmas – it's very overrated. I'll spend it with Mama and Papa.'

They hugged each other for what seemed like an hour.

★

Edmund considered that the best way to keep his nerves under control was to indulge in frenetic activity, both physical and mental. He put all his energy into his service life and when he was exhausted he sought and found deeper reserves to drive himself still harder. Life in barracks was easy compared with that at the front. He was amused to find himself considered an old hand. Although there was still something lacking to those who knew him well, he gave shallower acquaintances an impression of easy confidence.

Their spirits were lifted in January when news came that Walter Franklin had been safely evacuated from Gallipoli.

One day in March Edmund was sitting in his barracks reading *The Times* when he yelped with surprise. Hugh had been awarded the Military Cross. How like him not to write and tell me, he thought. He probably didn't think it was worth mentioning or that he didn't deserve it. Or that he's embarrassed because I was always the one who was going to get a medal. He wrote to Hugh demanding all the details. Hugh's reply was exactly as Edmund expected. The battalion had been moved to the Somme, a quiet sector, in February. That much Edmund knew already. Hugh could not say exactly where he was but he had been leading a raiding party on the German front line when all hell broke loose. Most men made it back safely but one was killed and half a dozen wounded. Hugh had got all the wounded men back. For some reason his CO thought he should be awarded the MC. Edmund knew enough to know how Hugh must have risked his life over and again that night.

In his next letter to Lilian he told her about Hugh's bravery. When she replied she asked him to pass on her congratulations.

He was posted back to France at the beginning of May. Before leaving England he managed to snatch a day at home thanks to his sympathetic commanding officer. Hedgerows frothed white with may and cow parsley and the air was rich with the scent of orchards. The whole country was alive with the sound of bees and birdsong. Edmund felt alive, full of joy. He smiled ruefully to think that only a few months ago he had wondered if he would ever be able to appreciate these things again. He was philosophical about the fact that he would probably be killed sooner or later – most officers were. That awareness made every good moment, no matter how trivial, worth more than rubies.

By a rare stroke of good fortune he found himself heading homewards again in mid-June, this time for a week. He was pleased – June in Devon was perfection to him. His nerves had remained steady. At last he felt that he could hold his head high again. Of course there was the matter of the Big Push which was on everybody's mind, but he would not let that spoil his leave. Lessons would have been learned from Ypres and Loos; preparations would be better this time. The wire would be cut and the German forward trenches destroyed by the artillery bombardment. He would have the chance to see a proper battle, almost two years after enlisting – he did not count the shambles at Loos.

The train chugged to a stop and Edmund opened the door and stepped down onto the familiar platform. Lilian was on the bridge, looking down and waving. He waved back and bounded up the steep path. They kissed longingly.

'You're looking wonderful,' he whispered.

'I can't look as well as you do. You're glowing with health.'

'I feel well. My nerves have been steady as anything. Look.' He released her from his arms and held out his hands. 'Completely still. No tremor at all.'

'I'm so glad.'

'Let's walk. How's everything at home? It's only a few weeks since I was last here but I'm impatient to see it again.'

'Everything is splendid – the dogs can sense that you're coming, I'm certain. They've been acting oddly all day. They'll go berserk when they see you.'

'Ha! Just like them.'

I hope you're prepared to eat strawberries until you're sick. There's such a glut. The sunshine of the last few days has brought them along quicker than usual. I've been making a valiant effort but more seem to ripen as soon as I've pick them. I go on a tour of the village every day giving them to all and sundry. And I've had summer pudding so often that I've grown quite tired of it.'

'And the garden generally – is it completely overgrown now? How sad that makes me.'

'At least you're expecting it so it won't be too much of a shock when you see it.'

'Is it that bad?'

'Weeds grow so fast. You won't believe this but I'm out there working on it most days myself now. I try to keep the beds near the house in something approaching order. It's dispiriting to see them untended.'

'Good girl.'

'I pay for it with my hands. I wear thick gloves but my hands have still managed to become quite coarse.'

Edmund glanced down at the small hand on his arm but it was elegantly gloved. He tried hard to imagine Lilian with coarse hands but failed. He stopped, drew off her glove and made as though to examine her hand in detail.

'Ah yes. Very coarse. It doesn't look to me as though you've ever been near a garden. Your skin is as soft as it ever was.'

'Apart from when I was nursing. My hands were in a dreadful state then,' Lilian laughed.

It was approaching midday when they arrived at the house but the drive was shaded darkly by elms overhead and shrubs below. The leafy coolness was refreshing after their walk. Edmund noticed that Lilian no longer carried a parasol, an object that would have been indispensable before the war.

Already those days were an evanescent dream. Had they ever been real? Once as a boy he chased a rainbow across a field. He never found its end and felt cheated somehow, but at the same time thrilled that he had witnessed something magical. The summers of his youth were glorious – they were filled with sunshine and galloping and leaping hedges and bathing in rivers and picnics and laughter. Now they seemed no more real than the rainbow. That was what made it so vital to seize the present, to stand at dusk by the open window of his study and breathe the night air heavy with the scent of honeysuckle and stocks and dewy earth and grass. Every evening he would stand there motionless until shadows merged and moths fluttered around the lamp on his desk and an owl stole across the sky.

★

One morning Edmund told Lilian he was going to walk to the village, leaving her snipping flowers in what she liked to think of as her Arts and Crafts border. It was her week to do the church flowers, a duty she undertook with pleasure. Few of the local women could match her skill at teasing flowers into deceptively effortless arrangements, nor were many able to draw on such a depth of variety and colour as she had cultivated in her garden. When she judged that she had enough flowers she carefully placed her secateurs with the stems in a trug and set off humming for the church. Although she had been shaded by a wide-brimmed straw hat the sun was hot and she was looking forward to the coolness inside.

She closed the wicket-gate carefully behind her and soon passed the yews of the churchyard. She put down the trug on the ancient stone bench that ran along the inside wall of the porch so that she could apply both hands to the tricky task of raising the latch on the door, which she achieved with a push and a grunt, making a mental note to remind the rector that it needed oiling again. Inside it was dark and cool with that smell all churches seem to have. She pushed the door shut but did not bother to wrestle with the latch again. She glided towards the chancel, locked in thought, when she noticed her husband sitting in a pew.

'Edmund, what are you doing here?'

'I had an urge to commune with my Maker.'

'That's most unlike you. To come in here during the week, I mean.'

He smiled. 'I must have changed. I feel at peace here. It's so restful.'

'You aren't ill, are you?'

She was standing in the nave, looking down on him. He reached out and touched her hand. 'No, dearest, I'm not ill. It's so rare to find peace and quiet these days that I take every opportunity. One of the things I find hardest to bear is having no privacy, no time to myself.'

'I can understand that. You always have needed your own company for a little while every day. Is it really that bad?'

He slid along the pew and motioned her to sit beside him.

'One can be in the middle of a crowd and still be alone. It's like that sometimes but that isn't the same as having time to oneself – with nobody else within sight or sound. Within sound of human voices, I mean. I don't count the general background noise of war – artillery, rifle fire, machine guns. When I'm not in the trenches, I'm in billets. There's always something going on – drill, working parties, sports sometimes. Always people. Even in no-man's-land one has company, although it's often the dead.'

'But you sometimes manage to steal away with a book, you told me.'

'Yes, I manage it occasionally when we're resting. It was pleasant last week, in fact, the best time I've known in France. We camped not far from a river which must be a swamp after rain but which was fairly low when we were there. I'd rush through my duties then sneak off there. I wish you could have heard the clamour of larks and frogs, and seen the butterflies.'

'You sound wistful.'

'Do I? Perhaps I am. Do you know, dear, the strangest thing about the war is that a couple of miles from the barbed wire and trenches you might not know of their existence. It never ceases to amaze me. Ugliness and beauty so close to each other.'

'It sounds very odd.'

'Yes, it is.'

I find it hard to imagine but I do try, Edmund. Really I do.'

'I know that, my dear. But on the whole I'd rather you didn't know the ugliness. There's no reason why you should know hell.'

'I agree there are some things one would rather ignore, if one could, but in this case I like to think of you and to visualise you being a soldier, where you are and what you're doing.'

Edmund sighed. 'It's mainly humdrum. The same old thing day after day. Sometimes in the line, sometimes out of it. It's all routine. If I were to list my duties in every letter you'd soon toss them onto the fire without bothering to open them. I couldn't bear that.'

'I'd never do that. How could you imagine such a thing? Your letters mean the world to me.'

'All right, perhaps I exaggerated.'

'And my letters, full as they are of domestic detail, do you toss them away?'

'What do you think? I read them over and again until they're crumpled, stained with mud, and rain has made the ink run. Your domesticity and gossip are what I love to hear about most of all. They transport me back here, at least for the time it takes me to read them. I couldn't survive without them.'

'It's the same for me. I couldn't survive without yours. Listen to us. This isn't the place for this sort of talk.' Lilian had strong views of what was and what was not appropriate for conversation inside a church. 'And my flowers will wilt if I don't get them into water soon.'

'Will it put you off if I stay and watch?'

'You may go one better and help, if you like.'

'I wouldn't be so cruel as to ruin your reputation with the flowers. I'd be more of a hindrance than a help.'

Lilian stood up and moved to the chancel step, where she put down the trug, knelt down and set to work, sorting blooms and foliage. That finished, she got to her feet and went to the vestry to fetch vases and water and started building her arrangements. When she was satisfied she placed them around the church.

★

The days of his leave passed quickly and as usual Edmund felt that he never had enough time to do everything he wanted.

As he had told Lilian, since his first tour in France he found himself needing his own company more than he had ever done before. Being alone was not the same as being lonely – it was a welcome antidote to the constant herding of men and the clamour and muddle of war. But it was always the same when a man came home on leave – the round of visits and even people stopping him in the street, all of them ignorant of what the war was really like. Sometimes they were old men, guilty that they were unable to play their part; sometimes giggly girls ready to hero-worship (and frequently to offer more prosaic comfort, even in the backwater of Tiverton) to any man dressed in khaki; sometimes middle-aged women, tongues clacking as furiously as their knitting needles, hoping to hear of horrors which made them feel faint but which they repeated with relish as soon as they could; sometimes drawing-room warriors or men in reserved occupations who were as distant from the reality of the front as were the women.

This social vortex was all the more frustrating on this occasion because of rumours of a Big Push. As far as Edmund knew before he came home, the subject was top secret and certainly not to be discussed, even with one's closest family. So when the grocer hailed him on his first day home and asked in his stentorian tone when the Big Push was to start, Edmund was naturally taken aback.

'Hush, Trudgett. Do you want the whole world to hear?'

'Why on earth shouldn't they? It's common knowledge.'

'Nonsense. It can't possibly be. I don't know about it and I've just returned from France,' Edmund lied.

Trudgett tipped his hat forward and scratched the back of his round head, 'Well, Mr Potter, you must be the only one who don't know. You just ask anyone hereabouts, them'll soon put you in the picture.'

The grocer clicked his tongue and his horse ambled off leaving Edmund, hands on hips, watching the retreating wagon.

He swished a moody stick at some errant nettles and marched home.

He supposed that every person he came across would ask the same question. Most of them did. He responded to all of them with patience and humour but he breathed many sighs of relief when he escaped from them. At times like this the front positively beckoned. Rarely he found a sensible companion with whom he could converse frankly and sincerely, usually a fellow soldier on leave.

'Really, Father, it's disgraceful,' he complained when he and Lilian spent the day at Bradcombe Rogus towards the end of his leave. 'The German High Command are probably well acquainted with the plans for the Push. Don't people realise that all this loose talk could cost goodness knows how many lives? I'd never have believed it possible until I heard it for myself.'

'I couldn't agree more, my boy,' said his father, knocking out his pipe. 'But that depends on two things. One, that there are German spies around, and two, that the facts are as everyone assumes.'

'There's going to be a Push, right enough. As for spies in England, who knows?' Edmund said glumly.

'No need to ask if you'll be in it. I take it that's the reason for your leave now.'

'Yes. I don't mind admitting there are times when I almost wish I wasn't on leave, with everyone asking me about it.'

'And Lilian? How does she feel about it?'

'She's the one person who hasn't mentioned it. I'll tell her before I go back but I don't want to spoil this week for her until I have to. I fear that she'll think I'll have a repetition of – of what happened after Loos. *I* know my nerves are perfectly well now but I understand if others are concerned.'

'Your mother will be concerned too.'

'I know. I've tried to convince her that I'm perfectly well and will remain so. I've been tested with plenty of shell-fire recently and have been rock solid.' He held out his hands to demonstrate their steadiness. 'It would be good if you could reassure her as well, though.'

'Of course.' He paused. 'We know that Noel's in France, but we have no idea if he'll be involved. He hasn't said anything about it. Has he said anything to you?'

'No, he hasn't.'

★

The final day of his leave was warm and sunny. Armed with the picnic hamper and the lively companionship of Castor and Pollux, they set off for Exmoor. The road, lined so thickly with trees that the sun only occasionally succeeded in piercing through, wound peacefully alongside the Exe until they turned off to Dulverton, where it was market day. Edmund inched the car through the crowds and soon the waters of the Barle sparkled alongside them. They left the river behind and climbed out of the valley. Within a few minutes the landscape changed to heather and gorse and trees bent low by fierce westerlies. The climb nearly overheated the engine so Edmund pulled in to the side of the road and switched it off. When it he judged that it had cooled down sufficiently they motored on towards the wambarrows at the top of Winsford Hill. Moorland stretched for miles in every direction. A group of ponies, stocky and shaggy, grazed near the road. Curlew and plover called nearby. The air smelt of heather and warm earth.

After another stop to admire the view and expand their lungs with vigorous Atlantic air Edmund turned the car and they retraced the road until they came to a narrow lane that led to Tarr Steps. Edmund turned down it. They had not seen a soul since they left Dulverton.

He parked near the bridge and helped Lilian out. While she carried the rug and cushions he took the hamper and they made their way along the narrow strip of meadow that separated the river from woodland, the dogs frisking around them. They did not have to walk far before the river meandered westward and the trees thinned out before opening into a perfectly situated pasture, heaven-sent for picnicking. The drive and unaccustomed air had made them both hungry and thirsty, and for a while they thought of nothing but the meal. The only sounds were the hum of insects and the dogs frolicking in the water.

'This sun will bring out my freckles,' Lilian mused, sipping a glass of wine when she had finished eating. 'You see if it doesn't.'

'I don't know why you worry about freckles. They suit you.' Edmund lay back and propped himself on one arm.

'They do nothing of the sort. Anyway, if I'm not careful I'll end up nut-brown like you.'

'Don't worry, dear. Besides, when we finish here we can walk in the shade.'

'Across the Steps?'

'Yes. From what I remember that's the best walk.'

They lapsed into silence, Edmund reflecting on all the things he would do if only his leave were longer. Lilian watched him, and guessed his thoughts.

'How much longer will the war go on, do you think?'

'I don't know. Nobody does. Perhaps the breakthrough we need will come soon.'

'The Big Push?'

'You've heard of it then?'

'Yes. Who hasn't? I didn't mentioned it before because I didn't want to remind you of the war while you were away from it.'

He took her hand and rolled onto his back. The sun disappeared fleetingly behind a cloud. Three buzzards circled on a current of air high above the wood on the far side of the river.

'Thank you. I appreciate that, more than I can tell you. I thought you must have heard the talk − in fact, it's being spoken of so freely that I should be immensely surprised if the Germans don't know every detail.'

'You can't mean that.'

'Why not? If it's common knowledge across every hill and combe in Devon, why shouldn't it be known in Germany? Their spies don't need to be up to scratch to know what people are saying.'

'But that's horrendous, preposterous.'

'Is it? I don't think so. Tell me, how did you first hear of it?'

She pursed her lips and tried to remember. 'I haven't the faintest idea. Somehow one just got to know. There were rumours, then more rumours, then certainty. I can't say when I first heard of it or from whom. The idea insinuated itself into the conscious mind so that one simply *knew*.'

'Well, I can't begin to tell you how angry it makes me, Lily. What may be a titillating item of gossip to people here could make the difference between life and death to thousands of men. Their lives may depend on how much the Germans know.'

'You're frightening me.'

'I'm sorry, dear. I don't mean to. I'm frightened for the men on the front line, though. Senseless, senseless gossip.'

Lilian thought for a moment. 'The rumour must have started with the government or the army. They would have been the only people with the knowledge, wouldn't they?'

'Yes. Whoever spread it should be court-martialled.'

'Darling, will you be involved? Madge Eliot said you were home on leave only because you were bound to be in the thick of it.'

'Did she indeed? What a true friend you have there. I never did like that woman.'

'Madge is all right. She's just a bit tactless, that's all.'

'She makes a hobby of tactlessness to see people's reactions, you mean.'

'Darling, that's too harsh.' She paused. 'You can have no idea what it's like to live in a society of women who are either in mourning or who live in dread of a telegram. You can't imagine the bitchiness, the jealousy, the bitterness. And the grief. Women have changed as much as men have, in our own way. Of course, our experiences are different from yours but I can't describe the numbing awfulness of an unexpected ring of the doorbell in case it's a telegram-boy, or the sound of the telephone when one isn't expecting a call.'

Edmund looked at her with astonishment. 'I've never heard you talk like this before. I had no idea.'

She toyed with a thoughtful buttercup. 'It's only dawned on me recently. I carry on living in the same house, in the same village. My life hasn't been completely dislocated like yours, yet I feel I've changed beyond all knowledge. And not just me, everyone is different. It alarms me sometimes.'

'You're right. The world we grew up in has gone for ever, even if the war were to stop tomorrow.'

'Do you think it will be better or worse, afterwards?'

'Who can say? That will depend very much on the outcome of this summer's efforts. If the artillery do their job well enough, who knows, we might soon be in Berlin.'

'Is that really possible?'

'Between you and me, I very much doubt it. But that's what we're fighting for, so that is what I must believe.'

'Why do you doubt it?'

'Because all along the line where we're to attack the Germans have the advantage of the ground. Hence the importance of the preparatory work with the artillery. If any Germans are left alive we'll be sitting ducks.'

Lilian sucked her lower lip. 'What about the particular place where you'll be? Do they have the advantage there?'

Edmund wanted to dissemble, to allay her fears but instinct told him this was the time for truth. 'Yes, they do. I believe it will be very difficult for us if the artillery fail to obliterate the

German line or if they fail to cut sufficient gaps in the wire. If they do their job well it will be easier for us. I'm inclined to be optimistic.'

'I'll remember that while I wait for news.'

'Good girl.'

'When will it happen?'

'That I'm not at liberty to disclose even to you, my dear. It depends on the weather as much as anything else. You mustn't be alarmed if you don't hear from me for days at a time. I expect I'll be too busy to sit down and write, even if I have paper and pen with me.'

'I'll look forward to reading of the success of the Big Push, as well as your own.'

'You want me to come back with a chestful of medals, you mean?'

'Not *want* exactly, but it would become you, darling.'

'You're incorrigible. My ambitions have changed since I first went out to France. As you know, there was a time when I'd have liked to pick up a medal but now my ambition is to do the best for my men and come back to you in one piece.'

'Without any medals! Is this Edmund Potter speaking?'

'It is.'

They laughed.

Soon they stood up and brushed the crumbs from their clothes, packed the remains of the meal into the hamper, folded the rug, picked up the cushions, and retraced their steps back to the car. The dogs, thrilled at the prospect of movement, raced ahead, black and grey blurs shooting in and out of the shadows that dappled the path.

They deposited their belongings in the car and walked the short distance to the ancient clapper bridge. Like most people who come to that mysterious place they stopped halfway across to admire the river first in one direction, then the other. The water was low and more rocks than usual broke the surface.

They continued across and made their way upstream along the far bank. Instead of keeping low beside the river the path soon took them high along the densely wooded hill, which rose steeply to join the moor. From time to time they were able to catch a silvery glimpse of water below. When they found themselves opposite a hamlet they reluctantly decided that it was time to think of going home, and before long they were driving back over the moor.

The next day Edmund rose at dawn and was fifty miles away by the time Lilian awoke.

Fifteen

*E*dmund looked around, as much as the packed assembly point and the inkiness of the night would allow. It had taken four hours for his company to make its way here from their bivouacs, in a journey that brought back not altogether pleasant memories of the plodding progress to the assembly trench at Loos. The same cratered roads and trenches packed with jostling men. The same shellbursts illuminating the darkness. All that was missing was their innocence.

Four hundred yards ahead of them, the Ninth Devons were waiting to lead the attack. They were near a village – or what had once been a village – called Mametz. Like everywhere else on this front, it was now a heap of rubble. It had been a Jerry strong-point but surely few, if any, could have survived the bombardment that had been falling on them for the last seven days.

A few hours earlier Edmund had written a last letter to be sent to Lilian, and one to be retained in case he did not survive. He had no particular premonition one way or the other, unlike some men who seemed to know they would die. How did they know? Perhaps they were simply pessimists, he reflected, or perhaps their pessimism guided their actions so that they brought death on themselves. No, that could not be true as most were simply the victims of random mechanical fire, either bullet or shell.

He shrugged and lit a cigarette, offering one to his company commander, Guy Christie, who happened to be passing.

'Everything all right?' asked Christie.

'Yes, fine. One or two of the men are a bit jittery but most are cheerful enough.'

'I wish they'd stop this infernal bombardment. It's giving me a headache.'

Edmund smiled. He liked Christie, who was a classicist and writer of poetry.

'Me too. We should write to *The Times* about it when we get back.'

Christie laughed and moved on.

Edmund was pleased that his nerves were holding well. If they were going to give way it surely would have been when the date of the attack was suddenly postponed. But they remained steady and it gave him confidence.

Two hours later Christie reappeared. He had been to look at the front line but was unable to reach it.

'Here we go again. Another bloody shambles,' he said.

'What is it this time?' Edmund asked, with a rueful grin.

'Our front line's been smashed to bits. The Ninth can't even wait in the support line. Twenty-second Brigade have dug a makeshift trench two hundred and fifty yards behind Mansel Copse as their parting gift.'

'For goodness' sake!'

'That's one way of putting it. The Ninth are expressing it more forcibly, I can tell you.'

They laughed.

'I also ran into an old pal, Giles Maddox. He's been in this area for months and knows it inside out. He's made a close study of the terrain. He believes the area just in front of Mansel Copse will be an excellent killing ground if the machine guns around Mametz haven't been knocked out, particularly in an emplacement in the cemetery called the Shrine. Ah well, it's all in a day's work.'

'Quite so. No point worrying.'

They laughed again and Christie moved on.

Dawn broke at last. The day promised to be hot once the early mist cleared. The attack would take place in broad daylight. At 6.25 a.m. an uproar surged along the front, one that Edmund could never have imagined and would never be able to describe. It continued without abating until suddenly falling silent at 7.30. Two minutes before the end he heard mines blow near Fricourt. 'Poor buggers,' he thought. An eerie silence descended, leaving his ears ringing with the noise. Ahead, whistles sounded as the Ninth went over the top.

The Eighth moved forward ready to follow the Ninth. In spite of the ringing in his ears from the gunfire, Edmund was alert for the sound of machine-gun fire for that would indicate how effective the bombardment had really been against the strong-points ahead. He soon heard the ominous sound. The machine-gunners were very much alive and well and their weapons intact, as were plenty of other Germans, though how they survived the bombardment God alone knew.

Maddox was right. The Ninth were being mown down exactly where he predicted.

Edmund's company was in position in the reserve trench by 9.00 a.m. He tried to empty his mind of everything except his training. It was not easy because he was angry, not with the Germans but with the failure of the British bombardment. The optimism that he had tried to nurture like a delicate seedling withered and died as soon as he heard the machine guns.

After what seemed an interminable wait but which in reality was about an hour and a half, the order came to advance and fill the gap between the Ninth and the Gordons, who had both suffered heavily. As he had done at Loos, Edmund launched himself forward, shouting to his men to follow.

At first they were sheltered by a small hill but as soon as they were in sight of Mametz the machine guns blazed. Men were dropping like corn under the scythe onto ground that was already littered with wounded and dead.

Edmund barely had time to take in the scene when he felt something stab him in the top of his left arm. At the same time there was a loud crack from his right leg. He pitched forward onto the ground beside a dead Tommy. Before he had time to gather his thoughts a shell exploded nearby, adding one more to the craters that pocked the ground and sending shrapnel in all directions. Edmund's left leg suddenly felt itchy. He reached down with his right hand to scratch it.

It wasn't there.

There was nothing below mid-thigh except a great deal of blood spurting out. He did not panic. Instead he thought quite calmly: *so this is what it feels like to lose a leg.* He looked cautiously around and realised he had had one significant piece of luck – the shell had thrown up earth in such a way that he was out of sight of the machine-gunner. It wasn't much of a barrier but it was enough. He set to applying a tourniquet using his good arm but it was clumsy work and seemed to take an age. Although he could not feel the severed leg the other one was badly broken and he had to fight the urge to scream with pain every time he moved. Sweat poured down his face.

'Hold on Mr Potter, sir. I'm coming to help you.'

Edmund looked up. Private Halesworth, one of his men, was crawling carefully towards him. Good man.

'Bless you, Halesworth.'

Halesworth inched closer to Edmund but when he was five feet away the machine gun found him. He died instantly.

Edmund pulled the tourniquet as tight as he could and lay back exhausted. It was still mid-morning. He knew there was no hope of rescue until dark, if then. He did not know if he could last that long, and wondered when the severed leg would start to hurt, as it surely would.

He lay still with his eyes shut as the sun moved slowly overhead.

'Edmund. Edmund – can you hear me?'

It was the most welcome voice in the world. His first thought was that he was unconscious and dreaming.

'Hugh – is it really you?'

'Yes. I can't see you. If I call you from time to time just answer in one word.'

'All right.'

'I can't rush. They're shooting anything that moves.'

'For God's sake be careful.'

Hugh's reply was lost in a shell-burst. Edmund sobbed involuntarily, thinking that he had been blown up.

'Edmund.'

'Yes.'

'Not far now, I think.'

★

It was only a few yards but it took Hugh another half hour to reach Edmund. After he'd slithered behind the earth screen he shut his eyes for a few seconds and breathed heavily. Then, carefully checking that he was sheltered from the machine gun, he turned to look at his friend. Edmund's face could have been sculpted by Canova, it was so pale, except where a splinter had seared the skin; his uniform was soaked in blood. Part of one leg was missing, the earth stained around it. The right leg was twisted at an ungainly angle.

'Good God, Edmund. What have you been up to?'

'Target practice. I'm a wreck, Hugh.'

'I'd better check that tourniquet. Don't move.'

'No danger of that.'

Quickly and deftly Hugh retied the tourniquet and applied a field dressing to Edmund's arm. That done, he turned his attention to Edmund's right leg. First he dressed the open wound then he took the dead Tommy's rifle and used it as a splint, securing it with the man's puttees.

To stop himself screaming Edmund bit on the knuckle of his good hand.

'I'm sorry if I'm hurting you, but it has to be done. Have you taken morphine?'

'No. I don't want to. I've lost a lot of blood. I thought it might finish me off,' Edmund said between his clenched teeth.

'I doubt it. Let me give you some.'

'No, I don't want it.'

'Stubborn as ever. In that case scream away if it helps.'

Working as sensitively as he could, he completed attaching the makeshift splint. When he finished he noticed that Edmund's water bottle had been smashed, and opened his own. He pressed it to Edmund's lips. 'Here, drink some of this. You must have a raging thirst.'

Edmund drank thankfully.

'What about you?'

'I've had plenty,' he lied.

Hugh lay back beside Edmund. He winced as he did so and for the first time Edmund realised he was wounded.

'What happened to you, and how in hell's name did you know I was here?'

'I started out on your left and a little behind. I was hit in the thigh almost as soon as I came into sight of that bloody machine gun. It didn't seem too bad so I got up again to carry on but my leg buckled and I went down. Sheer good luck that I wasn't hit again. I tried again but the same thing happened, so I lay doggo. That was when I saw you go down. I saw you stay down and then the shell, so I decided to look for you as my contribution to the battle seemed to be over.'

'I can't tell you how glad I am to see you.'

Edmund drifted off for a few minutes. The sun was high in the sky. Hugh placed Edmund's helmet over his eyes to shield them from the glare. He looked at his watch – it was only 12.30. He was thirsty but knew that Edmund needed water more than he did. He looked at the corpse beside them – perhaps his water bottle was still intact. He turned the body over and was in luck. He took a few sips. When Edmund came to, Hugh gave him some more water, encouraging him to drink plenty.

'Well, old soul, your war's over now. All you have to do is hang on until stretcher-bearers arrive. I'm afraid it might be a long wait.'

'Mm. Do you know what's going on ahead?'

'No idea at all, but we can take it that it isn't the glorious victory that we were told to expect.'

'You should try to get yourself back to our line. You'll make it all right.'

'Go to blazes. I'm not leaving you.'

Edmund closed his eyes again. He dreamed of his mother, of her warm, comforting, safe love, cradling him in her arms. Twice he cried out for her.

The machine gun fell silent. In its place an eerie wailing filled the air – the sound of hundreds of wounded men in their agony. The more able fired their rifles at the German trench from the shelter of shell-holes. However, this brought unwelcome retaliation from the German artillery who concentrated their fire on no-man's-land. At last the battlefield grew quieter and Hugh carefully ventured to look around. He could see men of the Devons and Gordons in the German line and others moving more freely over the wasteland between. *Our boys must be in Mametz. Thank God.* Help might come sooner than he had dared hope.

'Stretcher-bearer. Stretcher-bearer,' he called with all his might.

He heard similar shouts all around. He shouted again and again.

The water that Hugh had husbanded so carefully ran out.

He had given it all to Edmund except a few sips. His throat was parched and his shouts for stretcher-bearers became hoarser. Several corpses were lying within crawling distance and as it now seemed safe to move he retrieved water bottles from the three nearest. He drank copiously from the first one he found and brought two more back to Edmund. He noticed that the groans had diminished as the wounded men either lost consciousness or died. Perhaps some lucky ones had been able to crawl back to the British line.

Stretcher-bearers found them in late afternoon. They already looked beyond tiredness and they would be working all through the night ahead. They carefully eased Edmund onto the stretcher.

'Will you be all right to get back under your own steam, sir?' one asked Hugh.

'I don't know. If you could pass me a couple of rifles I can try using them as crutches,' he replied.

The stretcher-bearer did as requested and handed the rifles to Hugh, who unloaded them and removed the bayonets. The stretcher-bearer helped him to his feet. Hugh tested his makeshift crutches with a few steps.

'Thank you. It isn't ideal but I think it will just about do the job. I'll follow you back.'

'Right ho, sir.'

Progress was slow. The ground of no-man's-land was a tumult of craters and everywhere there were bodies. Occasionally a hand would reach out from one who was clinging onto life and try to catch their ankles as the procession passed. The stretcher-bearers promised to return.

Tears ran unchecked down Hugh's face.

When they reached the aid post they laid Edmund on the ground among scores of badly wounded men. He screamed as the men lifted him off the stretcher.

'Sorry, sir, but we need the stretcher, see.'

Hugh was glad that from his position on the ground Edmund was unable to see the MO, who was working at a trestle table in his vest. He was covered in blood, as were all the nurses and orderlies.

'Edmund, I have to go now. They're kicking me up the line as I can more or less walk with crutches and I'll only be in the way if I stay here. You're in good hands now. I'll make sure I'm kept informed about where you are.'

Edmund managed a weak smile.

'You saved my life.'

'Go to blazes. Your own strength saved you.'

'We'll argue about it later. Hugh —'

'Yes?'

'In case I don't come through. Will you tell Lilian —' His eyes shut.

'Yes, of course I will.' He squeezed Edmund's hand. 'I'll see you in Blighty.'

Hugh was ushered away and merged with the tide of walking wounded on their trek to the dressing-station.

★

An hour later Edmund regained consciousness. In one of those instances when the sense of hearing is working perfectly but the body appears to be unconscious he heard the voice of one of his men, 'Old Potty's copped it all right.'

Edmund determined to prove him wrong.

At last his turn came for treatment. He was one big mass of agony by this time as the numbness had worn off his severed leg. Then came a bumping, jolting motor ambulance ride to the dressing-station. An interminable journey by ambulance train to Rouen. At Rouen there was chaos. In the normal run of things he would not have been moved further in his state but they were so overwhelmed that they were only able to patch people up before transferring them to England. From the

Somme it took four days to reach his final destination. Time and place had long since lost all meaning for him.

Sixteen

*L*ilian's patriotism was fervent enough to hope that the Big Push would herald the beginning of the end of German aggression and the war. She did not contemplate failure – it had to succeed. The bombardment must have destroyed everything beneath it. It was said that it could even be heard on the south coast. As for Edmund, although part of her was fearful for him she kept telling herself that he would survive, and inwardly she still hoped for a medal and promotion. She hesitated when she thought of his nerves but dismissed the thought: he had recovered from his neurasthenia and surely it could not strike the same man twice – in her mind it was rather like measles or chickenpox, something one caught and was subsequently immune from. It was convenient to think of it like this. The alternative was too painful to contemplate. If he were to suffer an injury she believed it would be a clean bullet wound that would soon heal. Reassuring herself with these thoughts, on the morning of June 30th 1916 she sat at her writing desk and scribbled a short letter, hoping it would reach him before the start of the battle. She quickly sealed it and hurried to the postbox.

Madge Eliot had invited her to a tea party that afternoon but, feeling unequal to drawing-room chatter about the Big Push, she telephoned her excuses and took the dogs for a walk along the canal towpath. Edmund was constantly in her thoughts and she regretted her aloofness while he was recovering from neurasthenia. If only she had shown more compassion he might have revealed more about the reality of his life at the Front and she would now be better able to imagine where he was and what he was doing. Self-knowledge can be painful and she was more uncomfortable with herself than she had ever been in her life. Instead of lingering over her walk she hurried home and sat down again at her desk, this time to write a long letter in which she confessed her regret at her selfishness, during the period of Edmund's illness in particular. When she had blotted her signature she stopped for a moment and looked at the photograph of him that was always on the desk, handsome in his officer's uniform, a hint of a smile softening his face. She sealed the envelope. She felt cleansed as though she had bathed in a moorland river on a scorching day. She had never before in her life made such an admission of fallibility, and she was uncertain that she would ever do so again, but she knew that if Edmund had a chance to read it before the Big Push it would be worth the world to him. For the second time she rushed to the postbox.

The next day, Jacks drove her to Exeter – ostensibly to do some shopping but really because she could not bear to remain idly at home, and there would be only one topic of conversation if she visited family or friends.

Her purchases were soon made and she found herself absent-mindedly in the Cathedral Close. She entered the cathedral. It was another hot day and the coolness inside was refreshing. She was preoccupied and hardly noticed that she was by no means the only person to seek tranquillity there. There was no service in progress but the organ swelled and ebbed in practice, filling the building with its sound. She recognised Bach's Passacaglia and Fugue in C minor and immediately lines of Milton suggested themselves to her:

With antique pillars massy proof,
And storied windows richly dight,
Casting a dim religious light.
There let the pealing organ blow,
To the full-voiced quire below,
In service high, and anthem clear
As may, with sweetness, through mine ear,
Dissolve into ecstasies,
And bring all Heaven before mine eyes.

She walked further along the nave and sat down a few seats away from a woman dressed in black.

Lilian was a dutiful rather than a devout Christian. She believed in God, that He favoured the English above all others, and some of them more than the rest. She knew right from wrong, goodness from sin; she attended church unfailingly every Sunday and was responsible for the flowers every fourth week; she gave time, energy and money to parochial events; she gave alms to the needy. But the virtues of humility and compassion were not intrinsic to her nature.

She sat unmoving for as long as the music sounded. It was not until some minutes after the last note had been absorbed into the gothic stone that she stirred. Her contemplation had been so profound that she was almost in a trance: she had the sensation of waking after a deep sleep. She gathered her thoughts, rose to her feet and walked slowly to the door. When she stepped outside the sunlight made her flinch. Its warmth seemed hard, dessicating. She crossed the Close towards a tea shop. Near it a crowd had gathered and a newspaper boy was shouting stridently, 'Great British offensive begins – official.' Another competed with him from a few yards away, 'Front line broken over sixteen miles.'

Lilian suddenly felt hot, her throat dry. She purchased a copy of each paper, entered the tea shop and flung herself down in the last available chair. Having ordered a large pot of tea and an iced bun she tentatively unfolded the first newspaper: the British offensive had started at 7.30 a.m. over a front of about twenty miles north of the River Somme. It was preceded by a terrific bombardment, lasting about an hour and a half. It was too early to give anything but the barest details but British troops had already occupied the German front lines.

So, she thought, the news is good. The artillery have destroyed the wire and killed all the Germans in their front lines. Edmund needn't have worried. She ordered a second bun in her relief, and noticed for the first time that the room was a crescendo of noise from shrill women's voices as the offensive was digested. Each woman seemed to be proudly proclaiming to have a husband, or a son, or a cousin, who was there. Her relief at the apparently good news was delusive. She could feel the little hairs prickling on her neck and her back felt as though it had a column of ants marching down it. She glanced down at her right hand – the knuckle was white as it gripped the teacup. She picked up the second paper and read the front page: it said much the same as the other, differing essentially in its selection of epithets. Realising she was not going to learn anything else, she finished her tea, paid her bill, went outside and made her way through the growing throng towards the car.

When she reached home the letter Edmund had written on June 30th was waiting for her. She tore it open and read it avidly, a smile lighting her face – in her mind she heard him speaking the loving words.

For the next three days Lilian lived in dread of a telegram but none came. There was no further word from Edmund either but he had warned her not to expect it.

On Wednesday, when she had still heard nothing, she relaxed for the first time since she heard the cries of the news-vendors. She felt that she needed to get out and decided to take the train into Taunton for a change of scene, do some shopping and eat lunch there. To think was to act and she was soon seated in a train pulling into Taunton station. It came to a halt and she stepped down onto the platform.

She was walking towards the underpass that would take her to the ticket-hall and exit when her train pulled away to reveal another, stationary alongside a down platform. She barely gave it a second glance. She reached the underpass. Her mind, which had been occupied with shopping lists, became suddenly aware of a bizarre noise. It was like nothing she had ever heard before, a cacophony of groans which merged into a single, hideous wail. It seemed to be coming from the underpass. Odd. She slowed her pace and walked on hesitantly. She reached the bottom and turned the corner into the gloom of the passage. She had expected to see a sick animal, perhaps. Nothing had prepared her for what she found. The passage was lined on both sides with stretchers, scores of them, and on each one lay a soldier.

These were not upright, khaki-clad, clean young men but wan, dirty spectres. It was their groans echoing off the tiled walls and stone floor that blended to form the unnatural sound. They could not have been there long but the air was foul. Even as Lilian stood there, transfixed with horror, more stretchers were brought down from what must be an ambulance train. To her right other stretchers, the first down, were being lifted gingerly and carried to a waiting fleet of ambulances. She lowered her eyes to a man at her feet. How strange he looks with that black cloth on his face, she thought. She looked a bit harder and the bile rose in her throat: the soldier was so odd-looking because half his face was missing. She fumbled for her handkerchief and, not a moment too soon, held it to her mouth with a shaking hand.

Finding some energy, she dashed along the aisle between the wounded, fumbled again for her ticket and hurried into the air outside. How sweet it smelt. She walked just far enough to separate herself from the bustle of the ambulances before she stopped and sagged against a wall. 'Oh, my goodness. Oh, my goodness,' she uttered over and over again.

For some minutes she channelled all her effort into avoiding the spectacle of being sick or fainting in a public street. Her cursory nursing experience had not prepared her for this – she had only seen whole-bodied men, neatly pyjamaed in clean wards.

The nausea subsided. Coherent thought returned but it was not pleasant. *They must have been wounded in the Big Push.* How dreadful. She wondered what they were doing here; they were in such a bad way. They ought not to have been moved, surely. It was madness to move them all the way here. What a journey they must have had.

She became aware that a small crowd of onlookers, mainly boys, were gawping with pleasurable horror at the men as they were transferred to the ambulances. It shocked her, unable as she was to comprehend why anyone would want to look at such a spectacle. Feeling a bit stronger, she started to walk slowly towards the town centre. She was bewildered. She remembered Dolly telling the knitting circle about Leo, how he had been shot in the face. She realised that she had never fully taken it in. Was it because they were in Violet's comfortable home that English April day, so far from the war? And then there was the increasing number of disabled ex-servicemen that one saw nowadays. But although their disabilities were obvious they were clean and presentable, not soiled and groaning in pain. She had never stopped to consider what they had gone through.

Her mind flew to Edmund and the fact that he must have witnessed scenes which she knew would be abhorrent to him. Was that why he had been so reluctant to talk about his experiences? Was that why he had broken down? Nevertheless, in spite of what she had just seen, her imagination balked at the idea that he could be wounded like that, or soil himself as many of the wounded at the station had done, judging from the smell. They were the sorts of things that happened to other people. She fervently hoped that she would never know anyone who had been wounded like that.

Lilian had no appetite but felt that food would be beneficial; her legs were weak and her head felt light. It was still early and she was relieved to find the restaurant half-empty, which meant that she would be served all the quicker. Although she was not hungry she ate ravenously and drank two glasses of wine. When she had finished she felt a good deal more like her old self. She contemplated what to do to while away the afternoon. The shops had lost their charm. She would have liked to go straight home but she dreaded returning to the station before all the wounded had been removed. No, she would do some shopping – perhaps it would divert her. Anything to drive the morning from her mind.

The next two hours passed more easily than she could have supposed, although unpleasant thoughts would intrude. Armed with her packages, she threaded her way back to the station. She need not have feared a repetition of the morning's drama: the station was as she had always known it, apart from the pale and unsmiling faces of the porters. The blues and reds and yellows of the flowers in their tubs on the platforms were as bright and gay as ever, suggesting that the morning might never have happened.

Seventeen

*F*our days later Lilian was writing her daily letter to Edmund, though she still had heard nothing from him since before the Big Push, when Lieutenant Brodrick was announced. She sprang to her feet.

'Hugh, what a surprise! I thought you were in France.'

She stopped speaking as she took in his appearance. His face was pale beneath its tan and he supported himself on the doorknob with his right hand and on a walking-stick with his left. He was wearing blue hospital uniform.

'Are you wounded?' she asked, unnecessarily.

''Fraid so,' he said. Bullet in the leg. Just a flesh wound, fortunately.'

'I'm so sorry.'

'Please don't be. I'm lucky, very lucky.'

'Yes, I suppose you are, in a way,' she said, thinking of Taunton. 'Please sit down. It's unforgiveable of me to keep you standing.'

Lilian stood up and crossed the room towards him. She took his right hand and helped him to the nearest chair. She seated herself near him.

'Poor Hugh. You ought not to have come here if it's causing you pain, as I can see it is. You belong in hospital.'

'Never mind me, Lilian. How are *you*?'

'I'm much the same as usual, thank you for asking. Impatient as ever to hear from Edmund. He must have been in the thick of it not to have had time to send even a postcard but he warned me that I might not hear from him for several days.'

Hugh gaped at her.

'Have you brought a letter from him?' she asked. 'You found me in the middle of writing to him.'

'I – excuse me – I thought you would have had a – a communication.'

Lilian's throat tightened. The tension spread up her face and her eyes welled up. She felt her chin wobble beyond her control, as though it belonged to someone else.

'He's dead,' she whispered.

'No, Lilian. No, he isn't dead. He's wounded. What a muddle. What an infernal muddle.'

'Tell me, Hugh. Please.'

He took her hand gently in his own. 'Of course I will, but first you must have some brandy. This has been a shock to you. I'm so sorry. You ought to have been informed through the proper channels days ago.'

'Days ago?'

'Yes.'

He rose stiffly to his feet and crossed to the bell. Lilian had forgotten his wound.

'We were both wounded at more or less the same time, on July the first.'

'July the first,' she repeated. A vision of cathedrals and tea shops and newspapers swam inside her head.

The maid came and Hugh ordered brandy. He sat down and, without thinking, Lilian let him take her hand again. Neither of them spoke until after the brandy had been brought and she had taken a few sips.

'Better?' he asked.

'Yes, thank you. It was such a shock. Because I hadn't heard anything I allowed myself to believe that he was safe and well.' She shrugged her shoulders in a gesture of despair.

'I am truly sorry.'

'What's happened to Edmund?'

'He's been wounded, Lilian, but let me start at the beginning. It won't take long. We were positioned near a village called Mametz, which was a German strong-point. There had been an almighty artillery barrage on the German front line for a week, which I expect you know all about, with the aim of flattening the first German trenches and breaking their wire so that we would have an easy passage. That was the theory. In practice, enough of them survived to put up a fight. We weren't in the first wave – our job was to wait and go in support when needed. When it was clear that the first wave had failed we received the order to advance. We left our position and started to cross no-man's-land. First of all we had to go down a slope strewn with barbed wire. At the bottom dead and wounded from the first wave were all over the place. It didn't take long to work out why. As we reached the foot of the slope a machine gun that had survived the bombardment opened fire and simply mowed us down.'

He closed his eyes as if to compose himself.

'And Edmund? Why won't you tell me about Edmund?'

'I'm coming to him. I was caught by the machine gun and went down. I was looking around and by pure chance happened to see him. He was leading his men bravely, Lilian. You can be very proud of him. Then I saw him fall. I patched up my leg as best I could and then started to crawl over to him, inch by inch. I couldn't go any faster. The Germans were shooting at anything that moved, wounded or otherwise. It took about two hours to reach him. When I finally got to him I did everything I could to make him comfortable. Luckily, he was in a shell-hole out of sight of the machine gun.'

He shifted position.

'The machine gun was silenced by early afternoon, thank God, and the attack could move forward. When movement was safer I started calling for stretcher-bearers. They eventually found us in late afternoon. They got him back to the aid post as quickly as they could.'

Lilian clenched and unclenched her hands.

'I tried to keep tabs on him through an old friend who's involved in that side of things. First he was sent to a hospital in Rouen but that was overflowing by then so they sent him back here. He should never have been moved but there was no alternative. Inundated.'

'You mean he's in England?'

'Yes, at Exeter.'

'Exeter! I must go there at once. Why didn't you say so before?' She leapt to her feet as she spoke.

'Wait, Lilian. Just a few minutes. You don't – you don't know the nature of his wounds. You should know before you see him.'

She looked at him, frightened, and sat down on the edge of the chair.

'It isn't good, I'm afraid. You must have guessed that much already.'

'Is it his face?'

'No, not that, thank God. As I said, we were caught in machine-gun fire as well as having shells dropping all around. He was shot in the arm and leg, and when he was down a shell splinter caught his other leg. His face was scratched a bit too, but that's of minor significance.'

Lilian silently held out her glass with a shaking hand. Hugh poured some more brandy.

'You are telling me the truth, aren't you, Hugh? You wouldn't jest with me.'

'My dear Lilian, do you imagine I'd tell you this for fun? I wish to God it were untrue.'

'I know. Forgive me. It can't be easy for you. I was clutching for a straw. You see, last week I went to Taunton anticipating a nice, pleasant day out. It could not have been more different.

At the station a hospital train was being unloaded; the patients – soldiers – were all badly injured. I saw one man with half his face missing. When you said that Edmund was wounded I immediately thought of that poor soul. Thank God he doesn't have to suffer like that.'

'I'm deeply sorry you had to see that. Edmund's luckier than some in that respect.'

'You haven't said whether his life is in danger – his being moved while so badly wounded can't have helped him.'

'No. He's ill, seriously ill, but not in danger, I believe.'

'How are his nerves – he hasn't broken down again?'

'No. He's been spared that.'

'Good. That's something.'

'Yes.'

'What am I doing here talking? I must go to him at once.'

'It's as well for you to be prepared. For his sake as much as yours, you know.'

'Yes, I understand. I must order the car.' She looked hesitantly at him. 'I should prefer to go alone, if you don't mind, Hugh, but please don't think me ungrateful. You will stay here, won't you?'

'Thank you, that's very kind, but I can't. I need to get back – I escaped to come here only after a good deal of bribery and string-pulling. The joke is that I'm in hospital in my own home.'

'At Netherculme! Good heavens, how did you manage that?'

'Pure fluke. Some people at the War Office aren't entirely without humour, even at a time like this. But I mustn't keep you.'

'May I visit you?' she asked, remembering his lack of family.

'I should welcome it, if Edmund could spare you for a few minutes.'

'He wouldn't forgive me if I didn't, particularly after all you've done for him. I know you well enough to know that you've been modest about how much you helped him.'

Hugh pinkened slightly. 'I can't claim any credit. I did no more for him than any decent person would have done.'

Fifteen minutes later they set out together, he to return to Netherculme and Lilian on a nervous journey to Exeter. Three-quarters of an hour after saying goodbye to Hugh she entered the hospital.

Part Two

Eighteen

*L*ilian entered a long, low ward that was crammed with beds. She felt nervous. The first thing she noticed was the smell: although windows were open along the length of one wall, there was the same odour of suppurating wounds and incontinence that had almost overcome her at Taunton station. Now it was mingled with that aroma of ether and carbolic which was unique to hospitals. If anything, that made it worse. She looked around. Every bed was occupied and most of the occupants appeared to be swathed in bandages. Nurses, VADs and orderlies moved about at lightning speed. One bed was curtained off. She wondered for an anxious moment whether Edmund lay behind the screen but the VAD who was directing her led her past it. The VAD, who could not have been older than twenty, read Lilian's fear.

'Don't worry about him, Mrs Potter. They're changing his dressings, that's all.'

A loud groan came from behind the screen.

'Poor soul,' whispered Lilian.

'Yes, he's in great pain, I'm afraid.' She stopped at the foot of a bed. 'Here's your husband.'

'Thank you, nurse.'

The VAD bustled off and disappeared through a side door at the end of the ward.

Edmund lay still. His eyes were shut. She was pleased to

see that his breathing was regular. She thought he was asleep and decided against waking him, but as she stood looking at him his eyelids flickered open until, with an obvious effort of will, he pulled them fully open. His eyes were dark pools in his wan face, like pebbles in snow. They took several seconds to focus on her face and when they recognised her they lit up with surprise and delight.

Lilian stooped over and kissed him gently on the lips.

'Don't try to speak,' she said in a low voice. 'I can see that I've startled you.'

He nodded his head and Lilian saw a spasm of pain pass through him. She opened her reticule and extracted a cologne-scented handkerchief which she dabbed carefully on his face. Every muscle was bunched and taut. The cheek and jaw on the left side had been badly cut but she was relieved to see that it looked to be healing cleanly.

A muffled scream issued from behind the screen. She felt nauseous at the sound, but not quite as badly as she had in Taunton. Nevertheless she held the handkerchief over Edmund's eyes so that he was unable to see her weakness. She closed her own eyes and counted to ten, breathing deeply – she *could not* disgrace herself here, in the midst of these sick men. She counted on to twenty and began to feel more composed. It was insufferably warm in the ward even though a fresh breeze from the south cooled the lucky men nearest the windows. Unfortunately Edmund was on the other side.

She withdrew the handkerchief and Edmund turned his head towards her. She reached out for his hand but for the first time noticed that the left sleeve of his blue pyjamas was empty, his arm in a sling across his chest. She withdrew her hand, embarrassed.

'My poor darling, how long have you been here?' she asked.

He looked at the water jug beside a small vase of pale pink roses on the little bedside cupboard. Lilian poured out half a beaker of tepid water and held it to his lips. He was propped up with several pillows so was able to drink without much water being spilt. She poured another measure, which he drank equally greedily.

'Thank you,' he said hoarsely. 'Always seem to be thirsty and the poor nurses are so busy I don't like to bother them.'

'More?'

'No thank you, not now.'

An orderly brought a chair for her and placed it beside the bed.

'How did you know where to find me – did you have a telegram?'

'No, I did not,' she said crossly. 'I had nothing. Oh, Edmund, you must have been cursing me for not having come sooner but until three hours ago I believed you to be fit and healthy in France. You must have thought I'd deserted you.'

'Complete muddle. So many killed and wounded, they can't cope. How did you find out?'

'Hugh came to see me. He's a patient at Netherculme, of all places. I was in the middle of writing to you when he arrived. He thought I knew.'

'Did he tell you that he saved my life?'

'Not in so many words.'

'No, he wouldn't. But I should have died without his help.'

'He only said that he dressed your wounds and gave you water.'

He was silent for a minute. 'No medal, I'm afraid, my dear.'

'Who's thinking of medals?'

'You would have liked to see me wear one.'

'Yes, at one time. But that's long since. All I care about is to have you safe and well.'

'Not sure when I'll get home from here. My war's over now, anyway.'

'I can see that your arm is hurt. Hugh told me that your legs are wounded as well.'

'Was that all he said?'

'Yes. Why?'

He looked away. 'I'm afraid I left half my left leg behind.'

'Oh!' she said, stunned, then without knowing what she was saying, added 'Never mind.'

'Never mind,' he almost shouted. 'You're quite right, it could be worse. There are worse things than having half a leg.'

'Don't disturb yourself, darling. It will do no good. The first thing is to get better, then you can worry about your leg.'

'And that I'm not perfect. We both know that you care only for perfection.' His voice was bitter.

She pulled back as though he had struck her.

'You don't know what you're saying. I love you. I always shall, no matter what. Don't ever forget that.'

'I know. I'm sorry. Not myself today – rather a lot of pain. *Ira furor brevis est.*'

'What?'

'Anger is a short madness. Sometimes in our pain we say things we don't mean. Forgive me.'

'Is the pain very bad?'

'Yes.'

'Your leg?'

'Everywhere.'

'More water?' she asked, not knowing what else to say. All the words that came to mind seemed banal and shallow.

'Please.'

Lilian poured another beakerful, which again she held to his lips. He drank it all. She wiped away a trickle that had escaped the corner of his mouth and was running down his chin.

'Hate being an invalid. It's only been a few days and I've got a lifetime of it to look forward to.'

'I should hate it too, but it may not be as bad as that. You're bound to see things at their worst at the moment, before your wounds heal.' After a pause she added, 'You haven't told me

148

how long you've been here.'

'Can't remember properly. Time ebbs and flows and stands still. I think I've been here for a couple of days. Yes, a couple of days, probably.'

'And before that?'

'Trains, boats, hospitals, all in a blur.'

She poured him another beaker of water. He drank it all.

She replaced the glass on top of the cupboard and eventually managed to catch the eye of a passing VAD. 'May we have some more water please, nurse?' she said, holding out the empty jug. The girl nodded and took it away.

Lilian wiped beads of sweat from Edmund's forehead and upper lip.

'I'll bring you in some lemonade tomorrow, darling. I know you like that. And strawberries and raspberries.'

'Can't wait.'

She was caught between a longing to fold him in her arms and comfort him and embarrassment at public display of emotion so she contented herself with stroking his cheek and hair. A smile twitched on his lips and within a minute he was asleep.

Nineteen

*L*ilian wrote a note, folded it, and placed it between the water jug and the beaker, which she had filled ready for Edmund. She suspected that he would sleep for some time and, seeing that it was getting late, she left him to return home.

While Jacks guided the vehicle along the dusty road she sat back, preoccupied with thoughts of Edmund. Could it only have been a few hours since Hugh broke the news to her? It seemed like an eternity. Her half-written letter, so full of love and encouragement, must still be lying on the writing desk where she left it.

The tears she had conquered while she was with Edmund flowed unchecked.

They pulled up outside the house as dusk was falling. Jacks held the door open for her and tactfully looked at the ground as she got out. Indoors, she went straight into the drawing room and, without pausing to switch on the electric light, flung herself down in an armchair. She stopped crying at last. Now all she could feel was a tightening of the stomach as though it was being wrung out like washing. She leaned forward and folded her arms, pressing them against her belly to ease the pain.

She had changed, as so many had been forced to do, with the passage of the war. She had come to believe that she could cope with anything it could throw at her, even though she had found Edmund's neurasthenia distasteful and embarrassing. Seeing the wounded at Taunton had been a watershed. That day she came face to face with reality. She saw the world for what it was for the first time, but even then her mind had been unable to grasp the enormity of her knowledge, the knowledge that severe wounds could be experienced by all flesh and blood, not just those whom one talked about in the abstract – nameless faces. She was realistic enough to know that the Big Push might result in Edmund's death. She had been preparing herself for a telegram from the time she had sat listening to Bach in the cathedral. But no telegram came and she had relaxed her guard.

Anger welled up in her.

'How dare they not send me a telegram to say that he was wounded. How could they be so callous? What are they playing at, for goodness' sake?' she said aloud.

She stood up and paced about the room. She remembered what both Hugh and Edmund had told her. *Chaos. Shambles. Muddle*. How could they play around with men's lives in that fashion? They must be imbeciles.

She did not know who 'they' were, apart from the fact that they were the organisers of the war, the people responsible for evacuation and care of the wounded, the senders of telegrams.

A new thought struck her. Good heavens. If Hugh had not helped Edmund, if chance had not sent him to Netherculme, she would still be in ignorance. She thought more kindly of Hugh Brodrick at that moment than she had ever been disposed to do in the past. But, as always with Hugh, there was a flaw.

Why hadn't he told her about Edmund's leg? He should have warned her. It wasn't fair, Edmund taking her by surprise like that. Thank goodness he wasn't watching her face; she was sure it would have betrayed her. Anyone would have been shocked, horrified. Oh, how ghastly, how ghastly. Then a more generous thought occurred to her. It had been kind of Hugh, extremely kind, to come and see her when he was so obviously in pain. And he had saved Edmund's life. She owed him so much.

She told herself that she was grieving over Edmund's wounds and the pain and distress he had suffered but she was not able to shut out abhorrence of the fact that he was maimed for life. She tried to imagine him with a leg missing but was unequal to it. She would face the sight when the time came – no need to dwell on it while he was in hospital. She relived the moment when he had broken it to her – how her eyes involuntarily slid down the bed. But the cradle under the bedclothes kept its secret well.

She felt sick and, still clutching her stomach, stumbled to her feet, crossed to the window and opened it wide. Balmy air enfolded her. She closed her eyes, threw back her head and breathed deeply. Unpleasant thoughts jumbled together in her mind. She remembered the smell, the awful smell, of the hospital. She would have to get used to it. There was no choice. It would be there whenever she visited Edmund, or at least until the soldiers' wounds started to heal. From the odour of wounds her mind made a terrifying leap – gangrene. So many men with infected wounds in one ward, what were the chances that he would escape it? Her eyes darted wildly in the darkness as though it would provide an answer to her question.

'He can't get gangrene. He must not. He *must not*,' she repeated, over and again. The shock, the sights and smells of the hospital, a long hot day with little food and drink, were beginning to make Lilian light-headed.

A knock sounded on the door, which opened to reveal the homely figure of the cook.

'Are you in here, ma'am?' she asked.

'Yes, Mrs Barton.'

'Forgive me if I'm speaking out of turn, ma'am, but Jacks tells us that the master's wounded and is in hospital in Exeter. Is it true, ma'am?'

'Yes, it's true. Mr Brodrick brought me the news this afternoon. I ought to have received a telegram days ago but

I didn't. There have been so many casualties, the system can't cope, it seems.' She struggled to keep her voice under control.

'These are sorry times, ma'am,' Mrs Barton said kindly in her soft Devonshire burr. 'How is the master?'

'He's ill, very ill. We must all pray for him. He should have been kept in hospital in France but it seems that so many men were injured in the attack that the hospitals there can't cope. All but the direst emergencies are being evacuated to England. He shouldn't have had to travel. It has knocked him up badly on top of his wounds.'

'Poor master.' Mrs Barton shook her head in sympathy.

'Yes. He was in action at the beginning of the Big Push. In spite of the artillery bombardment enough Germans survived and used a machine gun on them. He was hit by bullets in his arm and leg and – and –' She stopped to compose herself.

'Don't say if you'd rather not, ma'am. Don't distress yourself.'

'I would much rather not, Mrs Barton, but you'll have to know sooner or later. He has lost part of his other leg – a fragment from a shell hit him, while he was lying injured.'

'Oh no. Poor master. Poor, poor master. And him so handsome and brave and such a keen sportsman. It's wicked what this war is doing to all the young men.' She clucked liked a mother hen. She was fond of Edmund and, like everyone who knew him, held him in the highest esteem. Then her mind turned to practical matters. 'You must be worn to a ravelling, ma'am, what with the shock and everything. Did you eat anything while you were out?'

'No, but I'm not hungry. I couldn't eat a thing.'

'People always say that when they've had a shock but you'd be surprised how easily a nourishing bowl of broth will slip down. Take my word for it, you'll feel much better after a light supper and a glass of Madeira. Let me go and prepare something for you. I can have it ready in quarter of an hour.'

Lilian did not have the strength to argue and she knew that

Mrs Barton was probably right. The cook went out, moving surprisingly lightly for such a large woman.

Lilian did not want the servants to see her in her washed-out state so she wearily made her way upstairs to the bathroom where she bathed her face in cold water. She then went into her bedroom to rearrange her hair, all the time avoiding looking at her face in the glass – it always became blotchy after she had been crying and she could not bear the sight. Five minutes later, feeling more composed than she had done for many hours, she went down to the dining room, to her bowl of broth and inquisitive but compassionate glances from Mary. Mrs Barton was right. Lilian felt much better after she had eaten. She returned to the drawing room and opened the piano. After abortive attempts to play something cheerful she found solace in a Chopin nocturne but her fingers, which usually moved with an easy grace, were awkward and stiff and she soon gave up and went up to bed, though she did not expect to find sleep.

Twenty

---

*H*ow is Lieutenant Potter today, Sister?' Lilian asked the following afternoon. They were sitting in a small, cluttered room which opened onto the ward.

'You are his wife?'

'Yes.'

She was finding the nurse rather formidable and could not help but recall her time as a VAD, when she was the most junior nurse on the ward and completely in awe of Sister Pearce.

'He's a very sick man, Mrs Potter, as you doubtless saw for yourself yesterday. We are naturally doing all we can for him.'

'Yes' I know, and I'm very grateful. I also understand that ordinarily he wouldn't have been transferred to England so soon. Will that be harmful to his recovery?'

'It would be wrong for me to lie to you. It cannot have done him any good. As you seem to be aware, Mrs Potter, the hospitals in France, as well as those in London and Southampton, are overcrowded in the extreme. Otherwise they would not turn sick men away, believe me.'

Lilian nodded. 'Yes, that's what I've heard.'

'Your husband is – was – a strong, healthy young man. That helped him survive the journey. Perhaps I ought not to be telling you this, but many of the severely injured, and quite a number less badly wounded than your husband, failed to reach their destination. That he has survived thus far is a good sign – he has a powerful will to live. The next two weeks will be critical. As well as our nursing skills, which are second to none, and those of the doctors who are also first rate, what he needs most are nourishment and sleep.'

'He was terribly thirsty when I saw him yesterday. He didn't seem able to drink enough water.'

'The men are all thirsty for a few days after they're first admitted. The journey is dreadful for them, over and above their wounds, and they are very dehydrated. You should find that he is less thirsty today.'

'I hope so. I've brought him some lemonade, and soft fruit from the garden,' Lilian said, indicating the basket she was holding. 'I hope that's all right. He's very fond of them.'

'That's quite all right, Mrs Potter. As I said, he needs food and sleep, but above all, no emotional distress. The knowledge that he has lost a limb is a severe blow to a man in the prime of life. Was your husband a sportsman?'

'Yes, he was.' Lilian was uncomfortably aware of the past tense. 'He rode and hunted and walked and swam, played cricket and tennis – anything and everything, in fact. He loves – loved – to be outside, doing something active.'

'I'm sorry. All I can say is that since the war began great improvements have been made in the design and development of artificial limbs. I'm hopeful that he will be able to get about and still be physically active, if not quite in the style of old.'

Lilian smiled wanly.

'May I see him now please, Sister?'

'Of course. Do you know where to find him?'

'Yes, unless he's been moved since I saw him yesterday.'

He had not. Lilian stepped into the ward and saw a pyjamaed arm wave at her. She was soon by his side. She bent down and kissed him.

'How are you feeling today, darling?' she asked, sitting down. 'You look a little better.'

'I'm all right,' Edmund said. 'It comes and goes. It helped to know that you were on your way here. As soon as I saw that hat I knew it had to be you. Why the veil?'

'To keep the dreadful freckles away,' she lied. She did not want him to see the puffy reminder of yesterday's tears. 'The sun is scorching today. Aren't you warm?'

'Not really. I'm more cold than anything.'

Lilian looked at him more rationally than she had yesterday. His face was white except for the livid red line on his left cheek where shrapnel had brushed dangerously close to his skull. His hair, now matted and darkened with sweat, contrasted with the whiteness of his face and the pillow. He had been shaved and his face was clean, except where a trickle of saliva had coursed down his chin from the corner of his mouth. Lilian wiped it away with her handkerchief. A muffled 'Sorry' came from beneath it. She wondered with distaste how he could allow himself to dribble.

'Which am I more like, a baby or an old man?'

'Which do you feel like?' Lilian was evasive.

'An old man. About a hundred and fifty years old, give or take a few years.'

She looked at lines provoked by pain that were eating into his youthful skin. *Oh God*, she thought, *he does look old, ten years older than he did when he was on leave last month. My poor lamb.*

'Why don't you remove that silly veil? You know I can't stand them.'

'You're getting back to your old self,' Lilian laughed. Hesitantly, she lifted it over the brim of her hat, glad that Edmund was on the darker side of the ward and that she was sitting with her back to the light.

★

He noticed that she had been crying as soon as she approached his bed. Did she really think she could fool him?

He said nothing. What could he say that would make any difference? He had once been perfect, but that was in another world. Now he was wounded and disfigured and they must put up with it.

In so far as he had been able to gather his thoughts after Lilian left him yesterday he wished that she did not always set such store by appearance, superficiality. His fractured body must be anathema to her.

His mind went back to yesterday, when he told her about his leg. He heard her sharp intake of breath and stared hard through the window. It took courage to go into battle. It took a different kind of courage to turn his eyes back to his wife's face. He hoped he had given her sufficient time to compose herself. Her oval face was smooth. He traced its line from the elegant, slightly pointed chin, past the serious red-lipped mouth, the straight nose, to the perfectly arched eyebrows, darker than her hair but nevertheless fair. Then his eyes, with an effort, looked into the speedwell-blue pools of hers like a diver plunging off some high rock into unknown water. He'd seen enough of suffering and shock to know that it was one thing to compose the body, another to mask the windows of the mind. He read the turmoil within her — horror, shock and disbelief.

When he woke this morning his headache was better and he felt stronger. He had counted the minutes until she would appear in the doorway, an image of radiance and beauty. Then he noticed the veil and the traces of her grief. A hammer started up inside his head and he wished she hadn't come. He could not tell her this so he acted the cheery invalid instead. 'Something I'm going to have to get used to,' he said to himself. Lilian was being gentleness itself. He could not ask her to leave yet.

'What's in the basket?'

'As I promised yesterday — strawberries and raspberries which I picked for you this morning. And I didn't forget to bring some cream — not too much though, as it won't keep.

And also some fresh lemonade that Mrs Barton made last night.'

'Wonderful. I'll be in heaven when I eat them. You're an angel.'

'I telephoned to your mother this morning, to tell them you're here. They didn't know, of course. They're going to come and see you later.' Lilian paused. 'And they've had a letter from Noel. He's been in action on the Somme too but he's back behind the lines again now.'

'Is he all right?'

'Yes. His battalion is resting. He said it had been – bloody.'

'Poor blighter. But at least he's as safe as he can be for a few days.' He frowned and bit his lip.

He listened in silence while Lilian related inconsequential village news. She mentioned a book that she was reading.

'Next time you come, will you bring me some books, please. Fiction and poetry. I need to read. My mind needs some exercise.'

'Of course, darling. If I'd have thought, I'd have brought some today.'

'Doesn't matter. I'm not quite up to reading today anyway. I'm very tired, my dear. If I drop off to sleep, don't stay here. I might be out for the day. Better for you not to hang around.'

She squeezed his good hand. 'I don't mind sitting here while you sleep. It's no hardship.'

Soon Edmund's eyes closed and he breathed deeply to give the appearance of sleep. Lilian stayed with him for several minutes, gently stroking his hand. Then her hand was withdrawn, and with a rustle of her skirt and a waft of perfume she was gone. Edmund groaned, and two minutes later fell into a deep sleep.

★

She walked briskly away from the ward. The fetid smell of the previous day had lessened slightly but she still found it unbearable. Only when she was out in the sunshine did she slackened her pace. She paused on the white stone step that marked the entrance to the hospital and breathed the warm air that was heavy with pleasanter smells of summer. She thought she would never again have the power to force herself through the door into the foul ward, not even to comfort Edmund, but as she stood there the sun warmed her upturned face and the panic wore off. She adjusted her veil down over her eyes and returned to the car, where Jacks was waiting to drive her home.

When she reached home Lilian ought to have written to Edmund's numerous friends and relatives, informing them of his wounds and his whereabouts. She had not been able to face talking to his parents yesterday and put off telephoning them until this morning. His mother took the call. As Lilian had expected she was deeply upset to hear of his wounds, though this was tempered by the fact that he had survived and was in hospital within easy reach.

She went so far as to sit down at her writing desk and take out some notepaper but she could not write. She tidied away paper and pen and walked to Edmund's study and out through the French window. She was overwrought and miserable and wished she could be transported somewhere else, be someone different.

She paced around the garden. It was another warm day and the dogs lay stretched out in the shade, following her with their eyes. Every now and then she stopped absent-mindedly and stooped to snap off a dead flower. She thought of their gardener, Watts, who had gone to the Front. He would not be coming back. She wondered who would return, and when. Would they all be maimed? Hugh Brodrick would survive, she reflected bitterly – he had a charmed existence. She found herself contemplating him with ambivalent thoughts. On the one hand he had saved Edmund's life and, in spite of his own wound, had come to Lilian as a friend, to console her. On the other hand he had kept Edmund alive – for what? At best, a life with an awkward prosthesis, at worst, confined to a wheelchair. What good would either of those be to him? What good would they be to *her*? She had the grace to feel ashamed of these treacherous thoughts. Edmund's needs were paramount. No, she was glad he was alive but wished he was not in pain and confined to that dreadful ward with its sunlight and its flowers and its cheerful curtains and its agony and its smell. She tried to imagine the future positively but she broke down when she thought of his leg. That would never get better. It would be like that always. It would not correct itself when the war was over. His face might be scarred too. Funny how she had not really noticed it when she first saw him – it had seemed so trivial beside his other wounds, which of course it was.

'What does deformity matter,' she asked herself, 'when the person, the *soul*, is intact?' She was unable to find the answer that she knew to be correct.

She thought again of Hugh. It was so dreadfully unfair. Now he wore an MC ribbon while Edmund's chest was bare. He was whole to Edmund's deformity. He who laughs last laughs loudest. Was he laughing now? Had he saved Edmund so that he could walk into Sydling on his own two feet and crow over him? Hugh was totally unlike her in character, therefore he had to be discounted and despised. She ignored the different characteristics and strengths that Edmund saw in him. Loath as she was to admit it, she was jealous of the friendship between the two men. Buried deep within her was an even greater resentment: he had never danced attendance on her. He was the only man of her acquaintance who had not done so – in fact, he seemed deliberately to avoid her – and she felt scorned. And now Edmund owed Hugh his life and she would always have to be grateful to him. She was beholden to him and she hated him for it.

When Hugh had broken the news to Lilian, and she was

suffering from shock, she had promised to visit him. Now she regretted it but a promise was a promise. She had no idea how she would be able to force herself to be pleasant to him. What made it worse was that Edmund would not ask her to visit Hugh, he would take it for granted. She remembered the scene in the dining room last December and Edmund's anger and disappointment with her. She could not let that happen again. She *must* swallow her antipathy and show some kindness to Hugh, no matter how much it cost her pride.

She found Jacks and told him to have the car ready in half an hour. Then, after fetching two punnets from the greenhouse, she went first to the strawberry bed to fill one then to the raspberry canes to fill the other. When she had fetched some clotted cream from the pantry she was ready to leave on her unpleasant errand.

She had not been to Netherculme since the outbreak of war and it was strange to find it transformed into a hospital. She eventually found Hugh alone in his old library, sitting in an armchair reading a newspaper, his leg propped up off the ground. The room was still recognisably a library but more chairs had been squeezed in and a cheap table was covered with a broader range of newspapers and periodicals than he would have taken for himself. That he was both surprised and pleased to see her was evident by the warmth of his greeting but she was determined to be nothing other than coldly civil. He sensed her mood straight away and struggled to his feet.

'Please don't try to get up, Hugh. I don't want to inconvenience you.'

'That's quite all right,' he said, subsiding back into the chair. 'As you can see, I'm not exactly busy. Please, take a seat.'

She remained standing.

'I'm not sure I can stay. I've brought you some fruit from the garden.'

'Thank you.'

He took the punnets and the bowl of cream with a beam of delight. 'A kind person would bring fruit but only a most thoughtful friend would bring cream as well. It's very generous of you.'

'Not at all. It was the least I could do.'

She was aware that she was being ungracious but he was not to think he could get round her by flattery. She decided to carry the fight to him straight away.

'Why didn't you tell me about Edmund's leg? It was horrible and embarrassing finding out about it from him. I consider it most cowardly of you.'

'I should have, I know, but you'd had enough of a shock already. I didn't want to cause you any more pain.' He turned his gaze towards the bookshelves. 'You'd rather it had happened to me, I know. I should too, in your place.'

Lilian's sting was drawn by his forthrightness. She felt trapped. To answer truthfully would be despicable.

'Life seems to play cruel tricks nowadays,' she said evasively. 'To everyone. Look at Netherculme. It's your house but you're a visitor here.'

'Just so,' he said, still avoiding her eye.

'I'm grateful that you came to see me and told me about Edmund, please don't think I'm not,' Lilian heard herself saying. 'It's just that to see him like that –'

She groped for her handkerchief.

Hugh fished his own from his jacket pocket. 'Take this, please. It's clean. Much more use than your little lace thingumajig. Why don't you sit down? It's rather imposing, you standing over me like that, you know.'

She took the handkerchief and dabbed her eyes, then sat down on the edge of an armchair opposite him. 'I seem to be doing a lot of this at the moment.'

'That's perfectly understandable and natural. Do you feel up to talking about Edmund?'

Lilian nodded. Her anger had subsided without her realising it and Hugh was someone who knew Edmund both at home and as a soldier. It might be a relief to talk to him after all.

'It's awful, Hugh. The hospital, I mean. The ward he's in is packed and stuffy, and the smell is indescribable. I'm not sure I can bear to go back there, even to see Edmund. Is that so dreadful of me?'

'It does create a difficulty, to be sure. But surely as the men's wounds recover, the smell will go away. And you've had some experience of nursing, after all.'

'Yes, a bit. But nothing like this. Not open wounds. And they look so ill. It's heart-breaking. And Edmund tries so hard to be cheerful when I know he's miserable as sin inside, and he can see that I'm miserable too, only pretending to be cheerful as well. It's all so beastly.' Tears trickled down her cheeks again. She wiped them away.

'He's lucky, Lilian. So many men didn't make it back from no-man's-land, let alone to hospital. He's suffered – must still be suffering a great deal, but his wounds at least will heal. The greatest challenge will be in adapting to a new life, to being more restricted than he's been used to.'

'That's what's so awful. When one sees disfigured soldiers in the street one wants to avoid them. That's how people are. That's how I am,' she confessed in a whisper.

'You're right, of course. It seems to be a natural instinct in us – that is, for civilians who haven't experienced the war – to turn away from those who no longer have the privilege of being whole. Being in hospital will be the easy part because everyone there is in more or less the same boat. Everyone understands. The men can laugh and joke about it and cheer each other up if they get down. But when he comes out he'll find himself alone and he'll need you to be strong for him, stronger than you can imagine. He'll be at home but at the same time in a foreign land.'

'I don't know if I can do that,' she said, looking down. She could scarcely believe she was admitting this to Hugh, of all people. She hardly dared articulate the thought to herself.

'I find the prospect of him being permanently like that so – so repulsive.' Saying the last word was like pulling a cork from a bottle. The sound seemed to resonate around the room. 'What must you think of me?'

'Self-knowledge is more than half the battle. You've done a very courageous thing in admitting it to yourself – and even more courageous to say it to me. It will take time but I have no doubt that you'll come to terms with it when you've got more used to it. It's early days now – you only knew about him yesterday, after all.'

She twisted the handkerchief round and round in her hand, looking at the floor. She could not look Hugh in the face. 'I don't know. I simply don't know if I can.'

'Lilian, I'm going to ask you something that you may find impertinent. Tell me to go and boil my head if you like. Do you still love Edmund?'

She looked up with a jerk. 'Yes. Yes, of course I do. And you're right – it was impertinent and unworthy of you.'

'Then you can and will help him, be there for him. You can do it. I'm sure you can.'

She shook her head.

'I don't know. I simply don't know.'

She rose to her feet and went over to the window. She said nothing for a full five minutes, just twisting and twisting the handkerchief. At last she turned round. She wanted to go – get away from Hugh and above all from herself – but she did not have the energy to do anything but sit down. She still could not bring herself to look directly at him. Not knowing what else to do, he tried to coax her into conversation about neutral matters, her family and Edmund's and other mutual friends. Without knowing how it had happened, given her black mood when she approached Netherculme, Lilian realised that she had been with Hugh for over an hour and had failed to quarrel with him. Just the opposite – she had imparted her deepest fear. Instead of scolding her for her confession he was gentle and understanding. Comforting. It must be the effect of his wound. When she got up to leave she felt better than she had done since he first gave her the news of Edmund and she found herself promising to visit him again soon.

Lilian's lighter spirits were not destined to last long. As soon as she reached home Mary informed her that Edmund's belongings had arrived from France. As she sorted through them she found the unopened letter in which she had poured out her heart.

★

Although Lilian would rather not visit Hugh again she felt duty-bound to do so, and two weeks later she returned to Netherculme. To her surprise, she again found comfort. When Hugh was on his own she felt less need to compare him with Edmund and began to appreciate the qualities that Edmund valued in him. He would never have Edmund's liveliness but his calmness, wisdom and integrity demanded respect.

'I've been to see Edmund every day since I saw you last,' she told him. 'I still find the hospital deeply unpleasant but I try to ignore it. The only thing that matters is seeing Edmund. He's still bedridden so I haven't seen it – his leg – yet. I still don't know how I'll cope with it. I mean seeing it every day when he's home.'

'I'm glad, very glad, that you've felt able to go. That's brave of you. Is it getting easier now?'

'Yes – a little. The ward is a bit less busy than it was and the men are either recovering – or they've died.'

They were silent for a few moments.

'I hope to get along to see him soon too.'

'He'll be happy to see you.'

She asked after his wound.

'It's on the mend. I've a feeling I'll probably be back in France before the battle finally ends. They're so short of officers now.' He shook his head glumly.

'Do you think so? Surely it will be over soon, won't it?'

'I doubt it. We've made some small gains, I believe, but that's all. And the cost – it doesn't bear thinking about. We can only hope that the sacrifice made by people like Edmund is worth it in the long run.'

Lilian bit her lip and nodded. She wondered if anything was worth that price.

Twenty-one

*I*n September Edmund's family received news they had been dreading. Noel had been killed as the fighting on the Somme dragged on. Arthur Potter telephoned to Lilian to tell her and asked her to break the news to Edmund. Maud was prostrated with grief and he did not want to leave her. Edmund took the news stoically – he had been expecting it for as long as he had known Noel was at the Somme although he hoped it would not happen. Privately, though he would miss his brother badly, he thought Noel was the luckier of the two.

Edmund's wounds did not become gangrenous and the threat to his life diminished. He started to regain weight, ounce by ounce, and some of his former colour returned. The pain receded from his amputated limb. He had known for some time that the wound to his right leg was as serious as the amputation but he wanted to spare Lilian that knowledge for as long as possible.

At the beginning of October he knew he would have to break it to her. The ward, which had been stifling in summer, was now draughty and cold. He waited for her in a wheelchair near a window through which he could look at half-naked trees under a sky the colour of battleships.

'I have some wonderful news, Lily,' he said when she had made herself comfortable on a chair beside him. His once warm, intimate smile was contorted by the fading scar on his cheek.

Lilian waited expectantly.

'They've done all they can for me here. I'm being sent to convalesce at Netherculme. Isn't that too marvellous. I'll be nearer home. It will make it a lot easier for you and my folks to visit.'

'Darling, that's wonderful. Do you know when you'll go there?'

'This week sometime. You'd better not come here after today in case I'm transferred tomorrow. I'll write as soon as I know anything definite.'

'I suppose you'll soon be fitted with your artificial leg.'

Edmund hesitated. 'It isn't going to be that easy, I'm afraid.'

'Why not?'

'Well, to walk with an artificial limb one good leg is required. It seems that this thing,' he pointed to his right leg, 'isn't up to much.'

'Isn't up to much? I don't understand. It's getting better, isn't it?'

'It's nearly as well as it will get, I'm told. It got rather smashed, you know. There will be physiotherapy, of course, but it seems I'm going to be a regular cripple.'

'No! That's impossible.'

'I wish to God it wasn't true but it has to be faced. I shall live in a wheelchair.'

'But you can't! Not you. It's so infernally wrong.' She fumbled for her handkerchief and blew her nose. 'You won't necessarily be in a wheelchair,' she continued. 'You can use crutches. Like other men do on the ward. They take some effort but you're strong.'

'If only.'

'What's that supposed to mean?'

'It means that crutches are out of the question too.'

'Why?'

'Because I need one tolerably good leg to be able to do that and that's what I don't have. At least my arm has healed well. I have that to be thankful for.' He tried to smile but failed.

'You're lying. You must be. You're jesting with me.'

The sharpness of her voice caused several patients to look up but they quickly turned their heads away: they knew only too well the sort of conversation that was taking place between Edmund and his wife.

'How on earth do you suppose I could jest about a thing like this? I'd give anything for it not to be true.'

'How long have you known about this?'

'I think I've always known in a way but while the doctors held out some hope I wanted to spare you unnecessary worry.'

'You needn't have "spared me", as you put it. What difference does a week or two make if you're going to be like this for the rest of your life? Is there really nothing to be done?'

'I'll have physiotherapy, as I mentioned. They're pretty good at that these days. But it *will* be a wheelchair, not crutches.'

'Oh Edmund, how could you? How *could* you?'

Without waiting for a reply, if there had been any to give, Lilian scooped up her belongings and marched out of the ward.

Edmund turned his head to the side and clenched his teeth. He had no idea how he would manage until lights-out, when he would be able to give in to his despair. He bit into his knuckle in an attempt to stifle the sobs that would insist on forcing their way up from his throat. Eventually the taste of blood in his mouth sobered him and he calmed down.

He prayed. He prayed that he would have the courage to bear the pain inside his head that had started up again. He prayed that Lilian would not loathe him. He prayed for a miracle to happen to his crippled leg so that he would have at least a measure of independence. But miracles do not happen. He was grateful for one thing: the ward was so busy that the nurses did not have time to notice his wretched state. He thought that if anyone were to show even the slightest sympathy he would break down altogether. If only his head would cease its continuous hammering he would be better able to come to terms with his physical wounds and Lilian's disgust. As it was, he felt as though his whole being had been smashed into a thousand fragments, tossed into the air, then stuck back together like a cubist painting. And she, who alone had power to soothe, seemed to touch every exposed nerve. The fact that she did it unconsciously added to his misery. If she deliberately tried to hurt him he would at least have something to fight against.

His memory rolled back to his Oxford days. Carefree days. Days of happiness and laughter when the worst hardship was to be chastised for over-exuberance. Days of Aristotle and poetry and rowing and cricket. He began to mumble the lines he loved best from that time, from Euripides' *Hippolytus*:

> *O for a deep and dewy spring,*
> *With runlets cold to draw and drink,*
> *And a great meadow blossoming,*
> *Long-grassed, and poplars in ring,*
> *To rest me by the brink.*

In those days he was independent and prided himself on it. People tried to draw him into their sets but none succeeded. His greatest friend had always been Hugh, another solitary spirit, one who knew the value of self-sufficiency and who therefore made no demands.

Then he met Lilian and fell in love. It was a novel experience for him to need someone and to be needed. His life was enriched. He still found pleasure in solitary rides and walks but he now knew there was a different, deeper kind of happiness as well. And now he would be tied forever to a wheelchair, to one or two square miles, to a life of dependence, to a wife who would probably stop loving him soon if she had not done so already.

He groaned and bit his knuckle again.

★

Following her outburst Lilian returned home full of remorse. She knew full well how much her reaction had hurt Edmund but he caught her unawares and she was stunned by what he told her. It was bad enough having to come to terms with his amputated leg but over time she had become used to the idea of him walking with a prosthetic limb, perhaps using a stick as well. But to be confined to a wheelchair! The thought appalled her. He would be almost as helpless as a child. What would they do? How could they cope? Would he be able to dress himself? What about the more intimate necessities? They would have to engage a nurse, that much was obvious. Thank goodness they could afford it. Then she reflected again on her reaction and how it must have hurt him. She would have to find a way of coping with his condition, for both their sakes. So she returned to him early the next day even though he had said not to come in case he was being transferred to Netherculme.

'I'm glad I haven't missed you.'

Edmund smiled and reached for her hand.

'I behaved atrociously yesterday. It was unforgiveable. I'm sorry.'

He squeezed her hand. 'It was a nasty shock for you. There wasn't an easy way to break it.'

'I've been thinking. We must engage a nurse to help you.'

'There's plenty of time to sort that out. I probably won't be home for months yet.'

They held hands in silence.

'Edmund,' Lilian said some time later.

'Yes?'

'When your things were sent back from France I found a letter I sent you just before the battle but you didn't receive it in time. I've brought it for you.' She retrieved it from her bag and handed it to him.

Edmund opened the envelope and pulled out three closely written sheets. He looked up at her from time to time as he read but said nothing. She noticed his hands trembling as he folded it and placed it back in the envelope.

'Dearest, I don't know what to say.'

'Don't say anything. I'm sorry that I didn't have the courage to say those things to your face. I don't find confession easy.'

'You're too hard on yourself. You must have found me a stranger in the state I was in. I was absorbed in myself – I didn't think how difficult it must have been for you. I'm sorry too.' He looked down at his legs. 'This is hard for you too, I know.'

'Yes, it is. But I – we – will get through it together.'

Lilian stayed with Edmund until a nurse asked her to leave. Neither had any illusion about the challenges they faced but they were both happier than they could have imagined twenty-four hours earlier.

Two days later Edmund was transferred by motor ambulance to Netherculme. Hugh was no longer a patient but was staying, on post-convalescent leave, with Edgar and Clarice James, old family friends who lived nearby. He visited Edmund frequently. Edmund now had the luxury of a room to himself – it was heaven after the crowded ward. Now he could talk to his visitors in private and when they had gone home he was at liberty to find what solace he could in uninterrupted thought or in his books. Here the nurses seemed kinder because they were less rushed than they had been in Exeter. His fellow patients were good men too. To a man they had found their way there from the Somme and, after recovering from the initial trauma of their wounds, were thankful to be alive and out of the war, at least for the time being. Some would return to the front but a number, like Edmund, had finished fighting. The more able-bodied officers produced a satirical magazine, gave concerts, staged plays, and generally cheered the spirits of their less fortunate colleagues. Edmund enjoyed the entertainment; he roared with laughter at the jokes and applauded by thumping the arm of his chair but, like everyone else, he knew that these were mere digressions from the main business of life which was to conquer black moods and to come to terms with his new existence. Nevertheless, the digressions were not unwelcome.

Hugh would soon have to go back: his leave had already been extended by a month. He joked with Edmund that he, Edmund, was the lucky one – he knew his destiny and would not be obliged to face another winter covered with lice in a rat-infested, waterlogged trench. They laughed about their respective fates but more often they talked from the heart. Edmund was deeply grateful for Hugh's company – he was the one person in whom he could confide his hatred of his mangled body and his dread of the future. Self-sufficiency is an admirable virtue when a man is fit and in his prime; it is quite another when he is an invalid. He had once been warned by an old hunting friend that if everything was built on a single keystone, and that keystone became defective, the whole building was likely to crumble. It had taken the Somme for him to understand the truth of that warning. Now, when he needed help – both moral and physical – for the first time in his life, he discovered that it was not forthcoming. This was not through the deliberate fault of his friends and family but it came from their perception of him: he had never needed help before, therefore he would be able to manage all right now. Hadn't he always been robust? Thank goodness it had happened to Edmund and not to someone less able to cope, they said.

As days shortened bad weather settled over the country, with rain falling from a leaden sky for days at a time. At the same time this Edmund's depression grew steadily worse. He could talk about it with nobody, not even Hugh. Instead, he hitched a smile onto his face and acted the part of an officer proud to have been wounded for such a noble cause. It was the expected attitude among non-combatants and it therefore passed unquestioned by them. Loos had destroyed his faith in the conduct of the war. If anyone had troubled to look closely into his eyes they might have seen the truth, but very few did. He had not been long in a wheelchair before he realised that the eyes of the healthy rarely seek out those of an invalid, and if there should be accidental contact the other party quickly looked away embarrassed. At such times such Edmund would appear the essence of his old self, witty, laughing, talking nonsense. His visitors would go home and tell their friends how wonderfully he was bearing up, not the least bit troubled by what he had been through. He was simply too marvellous.

He was at his most charming and vigorous and cheerful when Lilian was with him.

One overcast afternoon when his depression was at its worst she was sitting with him. He was on the verge of telling her about it when she looked him in the eye and said, 'You know, darling, I prefer you as you are now than how you were last year with your neurasthenia. You were frightfully difficult to talk to then.'

What was his reply? – 'Good' or 'I'm so glad' or something equally platitudinous. His headache returned that evening and three days followed when he was unable to lift his head off the pillow. While he lay still in the darkened room, refusing to see all visitors, he wished he still had his revolver. He did not know whether he would use it but its presence would have offered some comfort.

It was after this that Hugh broached the subject. 'You're in the dumps, aren't you, old soul.'

He had taken advantage of a lull in the bad weather to wheel Edmund in the fresh air. Edmund had been up for two days. There was still a throb between his temples but his nerves were quieter. He shut his eyes and lifted his head to feel the full force of the westerly wind on his face.

'Why do you ask that?' he said after a pause.

'It was a statement rather than a question. It's written all over you.'

'Ha! And I was congratulating myself on my performance as the frightfully jolly invalid.'

'You had me fooled for a while, but not for long.'

Hugh stationed the chair alongside a wooden bench that had started to green with moss. Heedless of his trench coat, he sat down. They both stared ahead, where mallard were flapping along the valley.

'Why didn't you say something before, if you knew?' Edmund said after a while.

'I've been waiting for you to bring it up but you haven't. Do you want to talk about it?'

'I suppose so.'

'Is it like it was last year?'

'Worse. At least, I think it's worse. That was bad, the more so because I'd never experienced anything like it before. But I always knew I'd get better eventually and be myself again. This time I can't see an end. It isn't as though I'm in pain or anything, although my leg bothers me in this sort of weather – perhaps it's getting rheumaticky.'

'Is it just your disability that's getting you down?'

'Yes,' said Edmund, too quickly. 'What else could it be?'

'Forgive my impertinence but I was wondering if you were looking forward to going home.'

'Yes, you are being bloody impertinent, Hugh Brodrick, but that's what friends are for. I know you mean well. The answer is probably not, on the whole. It will be grand to be at Sydling again but I can't abide the thought of needing a nurse, of not being able to ride or to go tramping across the fields with the dogs. I shall have to do a great deal of reading.'

'You always did enjoy books.'

'I still do. But I also enjoy freedom. Being my own master. You know that. I'm dreading it, Hugh, and the worst of it is that most of my friends are either dead or dying – except you, of course. You're indestructible, and long may it last. God, who'd be a survivor?'

'The dead would rather have survived.'

'Not like this. No one would prefer to live like this, if you can dignify this existence with the name of living.'

'Doubtless you've heard the platitude about Time, the great healer,' Hugh said with an embarrassed laugh.

'What do you think? I can't think of one person who hasn't said that to me. Don't you start on about it – it's humbuggery,' Edmund said angrily.

'I shouldn't dare. I take it back.'

They fell silent again. A cock pheasant, disturbed by some unseen object, rocketed out of a distant hedge. They watched it with the alert, trained eye of sportsmen as it disappeared behind a copse.

'I seem to have lost my appetite for shooting,' said Hugh.

Edmund threw back his head and roared with laughter. Hugh was startled at first but soon caught the mood. Their laughter, loud and maniacal, brought concerned faces to several windows, then with a shrug and a smile the faces turned away again and went back to the business of the moment.

Both men wiped away the tears that had started from their eyes.

'Well, that did us some good,' said Edmund.

'You can say that again. One of my men sent me the latest copy of the *Wipers Times*, which is now calling itself the *Somme-Times* for the obvious reason. It'd be right up your street – I'll bring it along next time I come.'

'Thank you,' said Edmund, then the smile passed from his face as quickly as it had come. 'After sunshine, the deluge,' he added, gazing into the distance.

Hugh caught his change of mood. 'True, but surely that's all the more reason to appreciate the sun when we see it. Without a sprinkling of sadness we'd never know the meaning of joy.'

'Ah. The philosophy of the trenches: without living like rats we'd never appreciate normality.'

'There is something behind that twisted philosophy, you know. Let's face it, did we – you or I or anybody – appreciate the life we led before the war? It was life, existence, normality, but we were blind to it until we were deprived of it. We took the good things for granted. On the other side of the coin we were surrounded by superficiality and humbug, and we didn't know that either. Or very few people could see it. I certainly can't claim to be one of them. Having said that, what we've gone through to open our eyes has been inexcusable and cruel.'

'You're right, and I fell into the trap as much as anyone could have done. I used to pride myself on my intelligence. I was a fool.' Edmund spoke with such vehemence that Hugh turned and looked directly at him for the first time during their conversation. Edmund could feel his friend's gaze upon his face but avoided his eye.

'Why are you looking at me like that?'

'I was wondering what you meant, that's all. You sounded so bitter.'

'I didn't mean to. I was merely reflecting on the fact that beauty is only skin deep. It has taken a war to make me discover that simple fact.'

Hugh lit two cigarettes and passed one to Edmund. They smoked in silence.

When he had stubbed his out, he spoke again, carefully looking at the horizon. 'Is it possible that you're over-reacting, d'you think, what with your wounds and being in hospital all this time?'

'I've no idea. I only know –'

'Yes?'

'Nothing.'

'Perhaps you'll see things differently when you're home.'

'Yes, probably. Good. That's all fixed. Anyway, that's enough about me. Tell me about this exhibition of yours.'

'Well, as you know, since I enlisted I spent most of what little spare time I had sketching. Simply trying to capture anything I saw. Nothing fancy. When my leg was on the mend and I found time on my hands I started painting again. I didn't have anything in particular in mind – I just let the paints take over. I found that I was painting scenes from Loos and the Somme, as well as daily life in and out of the line.'

He lit another cigarette and drew on it before continuing.

'After I left the Slade I tried several different styles. I turned up my nose at classical representation and experimented with colour and perspective as far as the downright abstract but nothing felt right. All my efforts felt insincere and it showed. No truthful personal voice, and that's the worst criticism that can damn any artist.'

He leaned forward, resting his arms on his thighs.

'The strange thing is my war paintings are realistic and truthful in the extreme. I want to get the message across without ambiguity. Nash and Nevinson are doing the same. The subject's too important to mess with. And I suppose it's cathartic too.'

He drew on his cigarette again.

'Do you remember my mentioning Max Hubert, a friend of mine from the Slade?'

Edmund nodded.

'He was invalided out when he lost an arm two years ago and now he deals and owns a gallery in Mayfair. He came down to see me a couple of weeks ago and was bowled over for some strange reason. His enthusiasm survived his return to London and he's asked me to contribute to an exhibition he's putting on next year. He hasn't fixed a date yet but it'll probably be in the spring. There'll be three or four of us in the show. It's madness, but there you are.'

'If Max Hubert thinks you're worth it, you must be. Congratulations, Hugh. I'm more pleased for you than I can say. I only wish I could get up to see it.'

'I wish you could too. It goes without saying that you can have your pick of the paintings.'

'Thank you. I tell you what, I'll ask Lilian to go. She likes going to Town. I'll ask her to pick one, if that's all right with you.'

Hugh looked away.

'Yes, of course it is. I expect I'll be in France so I won't be there, unfortunately. I'll drop Max a line. I warn you, Lilian probably won't like them. They're not comfortable viewing.'

'I'll tell her it's for my study so she won't have to look at it. I'm getting cold. Let's go in.'

Edmund shivered to match his words. He looked up at the sky and noticed bigger, blacker clouds gathering to the south-west. Hugh rose to his feet without saying anything more and pushed the wheelchair back to the house.

Twenty-two

*L*ilian watched them through a window as they returned to the house. As they approached, all her old resentment of Hugh came surging back. How soldierly he looked with his upright bearing and confidence that had grown through the war. How easily he handled the awkward chair. His black hair and dark eyes were suited to this dismal season. His usually pale skin was tanned by two years of outdoor living. His face was set and expressionless, his eyes wandering neither right nor left, neither up nor down. Her eyes slid down to the invalid. Edmund's brown and gold colouring now looked tarnished. He was sitting motionless, a scowl searing his unnaturally pale face, a vivid plaid blanket covering his hands and legs.

She could not fault Hugh's kindness and consideration to both herself and Edmund but there was the rub. She always felt guilty in his company. When she had visited him at Netherculme and he asked her if she still loved Edmund she reacted defensively, like a child caught with its hand in the biscuit tin. She had said that of course she did but as she spoke the words she knew she did not. What had started as a tiny doubt crystallised to full knowledge in that instant. She had no idea how or when she stopped loving him, it had happened so gradually. She had wondered many times since if Hugh had noticed her lie, but rather than apportion guilt in the proper place it was easier to blame Hugh for asking the question. Now

Hugh was the leader and Edmund was a broken man. It was galling. His health was galling. The MC ribbon on his chest was galling. His serenity was galling.

He had to be curbed.

She went into the hall to meet them.

'Why, darling, how cold you look,' she said, walking up to them. 'How could you take him outside on a day like this, Hugh? What were you thinking of?'

Before Hugh could reply Edmund said sharply, 'Don't blame Hugh. I asked to go out. You know how I hate being cooped up. This has been the first dry day for a week. I couldn't stand being indoors any longer.'

Lilian opened her mouth to say something then thought better of it. She followed in silence while Hugh pushed Edmund into the room she had just left – his drawing room in better times – where he parked Edmund near the fire which crackled cheerfully. They were the only people in the room.

'A fire like this makes me long for muffins and jam,' Hugh declared after he sat down. Lilian distanced herself from him on the other side of Edmund.

'After a long day in the saddle,' Edmund said.

'There's so little hunting nowadays you really aren't missing anything,' Lilian said.

Firelight played on their faces. Many things might alter in a changing world, might be lost for ever or be irrevocably transmuted, but a blazing fire on a dismal autumn day will never lose the power to warm and comfort. They each turned towards it like a flower to the sun.

The spell was broken by Lilian.

'Darling, you won't believe it but we have a scandal in the village.'

Edmund looked at her. 'Oh, what?'

'Phyllis Lynch is going to have what is termed a War Baby.'

'Is she, by George? Who's the father?'

'Nobody knows. She's been asked, of course, but she persists in being unnaturally reticent. You know what she's like – normally one can't stop her talking. Mr Ambrose gave her a sermon on eternal damnation and Mrs Ambrose tried more subtle arts but she persists in remaining silent.'

'Has she been courting anyone in particular?'

'Not since 1914 when that dubious young man from the butcher's shop joined up. You know – Wally Jones. It can't be him because he died last year. She hasn't been seeing any particular boy since then, as far as anyone knows.'

Edmund shrugged. 'Well, whoever he is, he's probably dead by now anyway.'

'Is that all you can say?' snapped Lilian. She felt cheated and jealous because the unfortunate girl had been able to conceive this fatherless child while she and Edmund had no children and were now unlikely to have any.

Falling into an old habit, Edmund said, '*Parturient montes, nascetur ridiculus mus.*'

Lilian's colour heightened with her inability to understand the Latin – something to do with mountains and ridiculous mice.

Hugh turned to Lilian and said, '"Mountains will heave in childbirth, and a silly little mouse will be born".'

'Thank you, Hugh,' she said pointedly, glaring at Edmund. 'Really Edmund,' she continued, 'you're so annoying at times. Don't you *care* what goes on in the village?'

'I do care, my dear, but it would seem that in this case there is nothing to be done. The girl refuses to reveal her lover's name and if he were still alive he would probably deny all knowledge of the child. It isn't the first fatherless child of the war and I'm certain it won't be the last.'

'But you *disapprove*, surely?'

'Naturally I do. But neither my disapproval nor Ambrose's nor anybody else's is going to undo what's already been done.'

'Sometimes I despair of you.'

Hugh attempted to steer the conversation to more uncontroversial topics but Edmund barely spoke and Lilian took advantage of her distance from Hugh to speak to him as little as possible without crossing into outright rudeness.

She watched Hugh fetch a newspaper from the table in the middle of the room and start to leaf through it. She was determined not to leave before him. For some obscure reason she thought he might not think well of her if she left so soon. She stared grumpily into the fire.

After twenty minutes, during which the only sound was Hugh turning the pages of the paper, he placed it on the table beside his chair, pulled himself to his feet and went over to build up the fire. That done, he turned to Edmund.

'I can see you've had enough company for one day, old man. I'll leave you in peace,' he said.

A barely audible 'thank you' came from Edmund.

'I must go too,' Lilian said, getting to her feet.

'You'll probably get too hot if you stay here,' Hugh said, indicating the fire with a sweep of his hand. 'Where would you like to sit?'

'I'm fine here. I'll move myself if when I need to. Thanks all the same.'

Lilian bent to kiss Edmund goodbye and walked away. Hugh followed her out.

She was about to pass through the front door when she turned to him.

'Goodbye, Hugh.'

'I must talk to you, Lilian. Please. It's important.'

Something in his voice, a steeliness she had not heard before, the authority of an officer who was used to being obeyed, made her stop and stare at him.

'Is it really necessary?'

'Yes, I believe it is.'

'Very well. I'll give you a lift to where you're staying. We can talk in the car.'

Three minutes later they glided smoothly away from Netherculme.

'You had something to say,' she stated without interest, her head turned towards the window.

'It would best be said in private,' replied Hugh, nodding towards the back of Jacks. 'There's rather a pretty lane where I'm staying. If you don't mind we could walk there for a few minutes.'

'I'm not dressed for muddy lanes.'

'I can see that. You'll find that it's reasonably dry.'

They continued their short journey in silence, looking out of opposite windows. The car laboured up a steep, twisting lane then purred down the far side of the hill into a long, narrow combe in the centre of which was a hamlet of half a dozen houses, a church and an inn. Here the road widened and Hugh instructed Jacks to pull in and park by the inn.

Hugh handed Lilian down from the vehicle, not before she made a show of scrutinising the ground carefully.

'Do you know this area?' he asked.

'No, I don't believe I do. Where's this lane of yours?'

'Just around this corner.'

They followed the bend in the road and soon came to a crossroads and turned right. Almost immediately they found themselves walking up a slight gradient. On one side was a high-banked hedge that towered above them. A trickle of water ran along its foot but the remainder of the road surface was dry. The hedge on their left was lower and soon gave way to neat, white palings through which Lilian saw a perfectly manicured lawn and a high-chimneyed manor house, obviously Elizabethan. Its brick walls were warm and inviting even on this blustery day.

'I presume this is where you're staying,' said Lilian. She looked at the house with grudging admiration.

'Yes, it is. I'm lucky in my friends. Although I don't regret it at all, it can be awkward having one's home turned into a hospital.'

'Yes, I suppose it must be.'

She heard him draw a deep breath but kept her eyes fixed on the lane ahead.

'Lilian, I know you respect frankness. I trust that if I speak frankly now you'll take it in the right spirit.'

'You're being mysterious. What do you want to say that's so important?' She had an uncomfortable feeling that she was about to be told off, and braced herself. The resentment that had bubbled up while she was watching him through the window was still only just below the surface.

'Lilian, when Edmund was first wounded you told me – perhaps against your better judgement – that you found his injuries very difficult to deal with. I was wondering how you feel about them now? I mean now that you know the long-term prognosis. How do you feel about his coming home to Sydling?'

She was immediately defensive. 'Naturally it will be wonderful for him to be at home again. He's been looking forward to it for weeks, after all.'

'I'm asking about you. Forgive me, but how do *you* feel about him being at home with you?'

'How dare you ask that? When we talked in July I said some things while I was still in a state of shock that were better left unsaid. If you have any consideration you'll forget that entire conversation.'

'I apologise. I'll forget the conversation immediately, if you wish it. Tell me, how do you find Edmund's morale?'

'Why do you ask? You've seen him yourself.'

'Quite so, but people can see the same thing in different ways. I'm interested to know what you think.'

'Very well, though I have absolutely no idea where all this

is leading, apart from a morbid desire on your part to interfere in lives that don't concern you. Edmund's in fine spirits. He is coping admirably. There are days when he's low, naturally enough, but they are rare. You'll have seen all this for yourself, though.'

'It's almost inconceivable that we could see him so differently.'

'What are you talking about? I do wish you'd come to the point. I need to get home.' This was untrue but she wanted to end the conversation.

'The point is, Lilian, that you're mistaken. Edmund's morale is as low as it's ever been. For weeks he's been suffering from the deepest melancholy, worse even than he experienced last year.'

She stared at him in amazement. 'Don't be ridiculous. He's perfectly cheerful.'

'It's easy to overlook the mind when a man has such serious physical injuries. He's been acting the cheerful invalid, can't you see that? He's been acting *for you* because he can remember how you spurned him last year when he most needed your help. Forgive me for saying this and wounding you but I believe he's dreading the day when he must go home.'

They stood facing each other in the middle of the lane, their eyes locked. Lilian, taken completely by surprise, turned alternately red and white and red again, breathing heavily.

'I'm so sorry to have to say these things,' Hugh said gently. 'Ask yourself why Edmund's so dreadfully unhappy. It's partly because of his wounds, yes, but it goes much deeper than that. Why couldn't he bring himself to tell you the true extent of the injuries? It wasn't to spare you, as he flattered you and as you doubtless flatter yourself, it was to spare himself the pain of seeing your reaction. That is God's truth.'

'Did he tell you this?'

'Not in so many words. He'd never be disloyal to you. The

point is he didn't need to. It's what he hasn't said, rather than what he has. It's written all over him.'

'You're wrong. You're just leaping to conclusions for some meddlesome design of your own. You're jealous because he has a wife to care for him and you haven't. My God, you call yourself a friend of ours when all you do is scheme behind Edmund's back to insult me. You disgust me. The sooner you go back to the war and get yourself killed the better.'

Hugh flinched. As soon as the words left her mouth Lilian regretted them. It was a deplorable thing to say to anyone, let alone to Hugh. But she was proud and angry, and her pride would not let her apologise even though her conscience told her she should.

'I probably shall be killed as soon as I get back to the Front. But it isn't my life that concerns me at the moment. Edmund is alive and out of the war and has the awful prospect of living the rest of his days in a wheelchair. There is only one person who has the power to make his life even barely tolerable and that person is you. Tell me that you'll do everything you can for him no matter how distasteful you find it.'

'I can't do more than I'm doing already. Edmund's perfectly happy with me. I will say this, however, since we're speaking frankly. I'll never understand why it was Edmund who was wounded and not you. He's the better man, always has been and always will be. And he has me. Who'd care if you lost your limbs? Life is very unfair.'

It was said to wound, but the only sign of his emotion was a paling of his face.

'I've wondered about it myself, many times. I never thought I'd be obliged to hold a conversation like this with anyone, least of all with you whom I respect and care for in spite of our differences. I'm not accusing you of malice towards Edmund – heaven forbid – but I sincerely believe you've misunderstood him. You know how self-contained and independent he always was. Try to put yourself in his position and imagine what prospect life now holds for him.'

'You're forgetting that there are two people in our marriage. You seem to think that my life, my needs are nothing. I know you're incapable of it but just try to imagine what it will be like for me with an invalid for a husband.'

Before Hugh could reply she continued, 'When do you rejoin your battalion?'

'I expect to be passed fit for general service at my next Board in a couple of weeks.'

'Good. It will be a happy day for us when you go. For some reason we're only really happy when you aren't around. I never want to see you again.'

'You probably won't. For Edmund's sake, Lilian, and for your own – please think about what I've said. Don't dismiss it out of hand just because I said it.'

'As far as I'm concerned this conversation never took place. I won't think of it, or of you, any time henceforth. You needn't accompany me back to the car.'

Hugh watched her until she was out of sight, then turned and marched up the hill until he came to the brow where, slightly out of breath, he stopped and leaned on a gate. He looked at the rolling hills and naked trees and ribbon-like streams that he loved so much and resolved that he would not come back while the war lasted, by the end of which he would probably be dead anyway, so what would it matter. What did anything matter?

The following day he was surprised to receive a letter with a Halberton postmark.

Dear Hugh,

I'm writing to you because I owe you an apology. However, don't think I in any way acknowledge the truth of what you said about Edmund – I still consider it impertinent of you to have raised the subject at all, and you could not have been more wrong. Having said that, in the heat of the moment I said some things to you which I regret. I mean about your fate in the war. I am truly sorry to have said it. I don't want you to go away with my words hanging over you.

It will be best if we don't meet again. I therefore propose to visit Edmund in afternoons and trust that you will adjust your visits accordingly.

Yours sincerely,
Lilian

As a first letter from someone one loved, it left a lot to be desired. However, he would not have been human if he had not treasured it, particularly for her apology. Given her antipathy to him it must have cost her dear to write it. That she was still defensive about Edmund was obvious. She was angry, to be sure, but he knew that her anger was probably prompted by embarrassment as much as anything. He hoped – wished – that once she calmed down she would acknowledge at least some truth in what he had said.

He continued to visit Edmund until the day before he had to leave and he honoured Lilian's wish not to meet. He did not see her again. He never mentioned her to Edmund, though he was curious to know whether she had reflected on what he had said to her. Edmund, for his part, rarely talked of her. If he did it was usually in the context of a more general subject. So Hugh contented himself with observing his friend's morale. He fervently wished to see an improvement but was disappointed.

Edmund was still subject to bouts of acute melancholy. Hugh himself became dejected at the thought of what could only be described as wanton indifference on Lilian's part. He was convinced that she no longer loved Edmund. He wondered when it had started to wane and suspected that it was at the time of Edmund's neurasthenia. Any flames that still lingered after that must have been extinguished by the Somme. There was no place in her life for a failed hero, particularly one whose deformities nauseated her. Hugh loved her but was under no illusions. Before the war a woman was not expected to be worldly and Lilian had not been tested. Now, faced with the darker side of the war that Edmund had embraced so cheerfully, she was unable to face unpalatable facts. He was saddened by the way she tortured Edmund, who still loved her deeply. As for himself, it was clear. She wished him out of her life, if not actually dead. It would be best for everyone if he went away. She was probably right – he had meddled in something that was none of his business. What a mess he'd made of it.

Twenty-three

*J*anuary 1917 was colder than anyone could remember. The canal froze deep enough for skating, the ground was rock hard, and indoors ice lined the windows in spite of fires in every room.

Lilian hired a nurse. She was a local girl, small, plain and freckled with straight black hair and the docile eyes of a spaniel. She had, she told Lilian during her interview for the post, been nursing since 1912 and had qualified in London but she was finding hospital duties too much for her – her health had started to suffer in the autumn. A position such as that under advisement would suit her admirably. Lilian was concerned that the nurse would not be able to lift Edmund. He had lost weight but was still a large man. She was assured that it was not musculature so much as technique that mattered. It was settled. A room was prepared at the top of the house for Nurse Dale and she arrived with her suitcase the day before Edmund's return.

A little-used room downstairs was converted to a bedroom for Edmund. Lilian had good taste for furnishings and chose some that were cheerful without being overpowering, and ensured that the room was as light and airy as possible. It was unfortunate that it had a poor outlook, giving as it did onto the entrance to the stables and garage, but that could not be helped. Two large windows faced north-west but the evening sun, which might have cheered the room, was obscured by the line of elms. Importantly, there was plenty of space in which to manoeuvre the wheelchair. She was proud of the meticulous detail she showed in finding a bed that was exactly the same height as the wheelchair, which would facilitate Edmund's transfer from one to the other. Although coal was becoming scarcer there was plenty of local firewood and she had a fire lit to remove the chill for several days before his return.

As she was going about her preparations for Edmund Lilian thought of Hugh more often than she would have liked – which was not at all – and wondered what he would think if he could see her. Then she would stamp her foot and make a determined effort to think of something else. It was too bad that he kept popping unbidden into her mind like this. And why should she care if he approved of what she was doing or not? Yet perversely his approval seemed important. What happened between herself and Edmund was none of his business, though he had the arrogance to think it was. She never for a moment considered that he might have been right in what he said about Edmund's dread of going home – the prospect was too awful. She was no longer in love with Edmund but she was determined to keep that secret to herself. How dare Hugh guess it. Or – horrible thought – was she that transparent? She was determined to remain a loyal and dutiful wife.

It was a perfect winter's day, crisp and bright, when Lilian and Nurse Dale accompanied Edmund on the journey from Netherculme to Halberton. He only winced a couple of times as he was eased into the car, where Jacks welcomed him with a toothless smile. Lilian took her place beside Edmund and the nurse sat in front beside Jacks. Edmund did not speak during the journey, merely grunting with pleasure when he was reminded of a forgotten village or view. Fields and hedgerows sparkled with frost as they were caught by the sun. Wintering fieldfares and redwings occasionally took to the sky, startled into flight by the car.

The staff stood in welcome outside the house when the car drew up. Their cheeks glowed with the cold but they smiled cheerily. Edmund was delighted with his reception but also embarrassed.

'Was this your idea?' he asked Lilian.

'No, they wanted to welcome you. They are all so fond of you. I hope you don't mind.'

'Not at all. It's very kind of them but I'll be glad if they don't watch me getting out of the car. It will be awkward enough without an audience. Please thank them and ask them to go back into the warm.'

Llilian got out of the vehicle and did as Edmund asked. She alone watched while Jacks and Nurse Dale helped him. Castor and Pollux barked and gambolled around the car, overjoyed to see their master again.

''Tis an awkward business to be sure, sir,' said Jacks. 'Reckon we need a bit of practice.'

'You'll have plenty of that before I've finished,' Edmund replied with a smile.

'Anyways, I reckon ye've shed a good bit o' weight since ye've bin away.'

'Yes, I have, thankfully for you.'

'Be careful, you two,' said Lilian.

'It's all right, dear,' said Edmund, 'there's no need to fuss. We're managing splendidly. Thank you both.'

Jacks had constructed a wooden ramp over the single step to the front door. Now that his wounded arm had recovered Edmund was becoming practised in manoeuvring the wheelchair but he did not resist when Jacks pushed it up the ramp.

'Thoughtful of you to sand the ramp, Jacks. I'd hate to come a smeller on the ice.'

'Don't ye worry, sir. I've thought of everything.'

Once inside, Edmund insisted on looking around the entire

ground floor before joining Lilian in the drawing room. He stationed himself to one side of the fireplace, facing the window.

'I've asked Mary to bring tea,' said Lilian.

Edmund looked around the room. 'It's funny how one forgets so very much. The details that make up the fabric of one's life. Or perhaps one doesn't allow oneself to remember them as the memory would be too exquisite. Like you. I can never picture your face when we're apart. Oh my dear, it's good to be home at last.'

Lilian smiled. 'It's wonderful to have you home. How is your bedroom? Will it be comfortable enough?'

'It's perfect. You've gone to a great deal of trouble and I'm truly grateful. I can't tell you what heaven it will be after hospital life. I feel like a king.'

'You were happy at Netherculme,' Lilian ventured.

'Yes – at least it was an improvement on the Exeter hospital. I still preferred Netherculme when it was Hugh's home though.'

'If there's anything you want – anything at all – you must say. Don't wait to be asked.'

Edmund laughed. 'You make me feel like a visitor. Of course I'll say. Before long, when I get in the swing of things, you'll probably wish wholeheartedly that I wouldn't say what I want.'

'Nonsense, darling. That's not possible.'

Mary brought in tea and muffins. Tucking into them in front of the fire, his dogs beside him and Lilian at her most gentle, Edmund felt almost happy.

The following afternoon he was in his study trying to organise it so that as many objects as possible were within reach when he heard voices in the hall. A minute later Lilian popped her head around the door. He was at his desk facing the window, and craned his neck to look at her.

'Mr and Mrs Ambrose have called to see you. Will you come into the drawing room?'

'Yes, of course,' Edmund said, adding silently to himself, 'Here we go. I wondered who'd be first to come and gawp at me.'

He manoeuvred himself slowly towards the drawing room.

The rector and his wife were standing in the centre of the room, waiting for Edmund. Nathaniel Ambrose was a tall, ascetic-looking man in his mid-sixties. He was much loved in the parish and great allowance was made for his inveterate scattiness. While he was academic and rejoiced in obscure points of theology, his wife was the administrator of the parish. No detail escaped her, to the extent that some parishioners wished she was not quite so noticing.

They both smiled benignly at Edmund. He smiled up at them and quickly asked them to sit. He felt prickly and uncomfortable when people towered over him.

'Well, padre, this is an unexpected pleasure,' he said when they had made themselves comfortable. 'What can I do for you? Are you collecting for the bells?'

Mrs Ambrose continued to smile, observing him acutely, her head cocked on one side like a robin.

'Tut, tut,' clucked the rector. 'Not at all, my dear sir, not at all. Ours is purely a courtesy call. You must have so much to do with having been away for so long, so we won't detain you for many minutes. As your representative of the cloth I determined to waste no time in coming to see you now that you are once again in our midst. Your absence left an irreparable lacuna in our little community. Indeed it did. I can assure you we prayed constantly for your safe restoration.'

'You flatter me, sir. But there are others who need your prayers more than I. I mean the men who are still out there.'

'My dear sir, they are always in our thoughts. We pray that they may conduct themselves as worthily as your good self to the ennoblement of their Great Cause. Your achievement was truly wonderful, everybody says so. They –'

'Excuse me, rector,' interrupted Edmund with icy calm. 'I

don't understand you. What achievement do you mean? I can't think of any.'

The rector was startled. 'Why, I'm speaking of your great wounds. I have told your good lady,' here he nodded with a smile towards Lilian, 'on occasions too numerous to mention how proud she must be. Indeed, if the sin of pride can ever be justified, this is that occasion. We are all so grateful, sir.'

Edmund's knuckles whitened. 'I had no idea how unpopular I'd made myself,' he said. 'To think that all my friends and neighbours rejoice at my mutilation. Thank you for enlightening me. From now on I'll be on my guard.'

'Edmund,' gasped Lilian. 'I'm sure Mr Ambrose didn't mean you to put that interpretation on his *very kind* words.'

'Goodness gracious! No, I did not mean that at all, my dear man. Complete misunderstanding. Dear me. I express myself so awkwardly sometimes. Agnes is always telling me so, aren't you, my dear.' He turned, flustered, in appeal to his wife.

'The rector perhaps expressed himself a trifle awkwardly,' she agreed. 'Nathaniel is so unworldly. He did not mean that we are grateful that you are wounded, my dear Mr Potter, although of course no suffering can be too great for such a Noble Cause, but he – we wished to *thank* you.'

This was the very attitude on the part of civilians that Edmund held in greatest contempt.

'Hmph. Well, in that case thank *you* for your thanks. Now, having got that off our chests I would rather not talk about that subject again, if you don't mind. Not with anyone.'

'You are naturally modest,' said Mr Ambrose, reviving. 'If I may be so bold, and if you are really determined, I shall take it upon myself to warn our good neighbours that your modesty prevents you talking about your heroics.'

'Thank you. I'd be grateful if you would do that. I don't mean to be rude but the subject is a very tender one,' Edmund said more kindly.

A not entirely comfortable pause followed. Edmund was conscious that he was lacking in his duties as a host but he was still seething at the prospect of being treated like an exhibit in a zoo. He decided that his best defence would be to fight back.

'Lilian tells me that there's a girl, Phyllis Lynch, who finds herself in unfortunate circumstances. Are you making a collection for her, Mrs Ambrose?'

'My dear Mr Potter, you are quite mistaken. It has been the sad duty of the rector and myself to point out the error of her behaviour. We have forgiven her as Christians, that is our duty, but as for a collection. Well! That would only encourage that sort of behaviour.'

'Is she going to marry the man?'

'She *says* that he is dead,' said the rector sadly with a disbelieving shake of the head. 'I fear that morals have become lax, very lax indeed. It makes me so terribly sad.'

'That is the peril of war, sir. Look at me, I used to be an upright member of the community and yet I have spent the better part of the last two years in trying to kill men like myself in cold blood, just as they have tried to kill me.'

'That's totally different, Edmund,' said Lilian, with a sideways glance at the horrified clergyman, 'as you well know.'

'Do I? I don't think I know anything any more. A simple girl is hounded and outcast for creating life and I'm thanked by the representative of the Church for taking not one life but hundreds. I wish you could see it from my point of view, Lily.'

'Well, I can't. Please excuse my husband, my dear rector. He's reacting after his journey of yesterday. He has very little strength yet and he gets overwrought. Oh, must you leave so soon? You've only just arrived.'

'We must not tire your husband any more. To return home after a long time away can be a great strain to a sensitive spirit, particularly when he has been through so much.' Mr Ambrose pulled himself to his feet while he was speaking and smiled down at Edmund.

'Forgive me, padre. My wife is right. I am a bit strung up. No hard feelings I hope,' Edmund said, holding out his hand.

Mr Ambrose took Edmund's hand and gave it a limp shake. 'Not at all, my dear man. It's quite understandable. We should have been more considerate and given you more time to settle in before we called. But let us not forget *Dulce et decorum est* – '

'*Pro patria mori.* Yes, I know those words well. Goodbye, sir. Please excuse my not getting up,' said Edmund with a forced smile.

'Ha, ha, ha. You have not lost your sense of humour, at any rate.'

Edmund offered his hand to Mrs Ambrose. 'Goodbye. I am grateful that you called. Really.'

She touched his hand. 'It was our pleasure, dear Mr Potter. Thank you again.'

Casting a savage glance over her shoulder at Edmund, Lilian escorted the rector and his wife to the front door. When she had shown them out she returned to the drawing room. Edmund had his back to the door and was unable to see her but he felt her displeasure roll over him like a wave.

'Really, Edmund, how could you be so rude? I can't tell you how embarrassed I was.'

As Lilian stood over him Edmund was reminded of nursery days, long forgotten, when Nanny would stand just like that, he in his sailor suit, with a wagging finger and a lecture on how young gentlemen ought to behave. The memory was so vivid that it temporarily non-plussed him and he hovered between an urge to roar with laughter and a child's impulse to defend himself.

'Please don't lecture me, Lily,' he said, quietly but firmly.

'I shall, if you persist in insulting our friends. Mr Ambrose, of all people. He's so harmless. You may have been joking but the Ambroses wouldn't begin to understand your barrack humour.'

'Ambrose is a fool and his wife a greater one. Decent enough in peacetime, I grant you, but the war has exposed people like them for what they are. I won't be gawped at like a monkey in a zoo, the Village Exhibit, and I most certainly don't want to be thanked. Their minds are shallower than Potty Blundell's.'

'Have you any idea how kind and generous they were while you were in hospital? What can you possibly hope to gain by abusing them?'

'Less interference and a great deal more peace of mind. They both abuse their position to insinuate their way into the confidence of – people like you, and then they interfere to their hearts' content. I'm telling you, Lily, I don't intend to stand for it. If anyone else comes to thank me, kindly tell them I'm indisposed.'

'I can see that you might have found it irritating to be thanked like that, but it doesn't alter the fact that you were downright rude. The Ambroses were only trying to be kind and neighbourly. I should have thought you'd need every friend you can get.'

Edmund flushed scarlet.

'I – I'm sorry,' Lilian said. 'I should have learned by now to think before I speak. My tongue seems to have a mind of its own sometimes.'

'Better that you speak the truth than lie to me. I can't bear lies.'

'You must admit that you've been extremely provocative this afternoon. You're not at all yourself.'

'My old self is dead. You'll have to get used to the person I am now. Sorry if I'm a disappointment.'

'No, you're not that.'

'Kind of you to say so but I know the truth. It's writ large. I've got the devil of a headache and my temper is never of the best when I have one of those. I was rude to the Ambroses and I'll prostrate myself next time I see them. In future, if anyone says inane banalities I'll grit my teeth and turn on the charm. All right?'

'Yes, all right,' she said doubtfully.

'Now, please will you call Nurse. I'd like to get out of this chair for a while.'

Twenty-four

*L*ife at Halberton settled into a routine. At first numerous visitors called to see the invalid but although Edmund managed to restrain himself from overt rudeness they sensed that they were not entirely welcome. They would have been surprised by his ingratitude for their friendliness if the Ambroses had not warned them that Edmund was not himself yet. He was invited to return their visits but usually with the rider, 'though of course it will be difficult to manoeuvre your chair up the steps – perhaps it would be better if we were to visit you here.' Edmund did not argue. The novelty of having an amputee in the village soon wore off and these generally unwelcome interruptions petered out. There were a few exceptions, those who were regular visitors and whom Edmund visited in spite of the inconvenience. These were old hunting friends who had wide experience of the world and were beyond fighting age. They were able to read Edmund's moods and made no demands. If he wanted to pass an evening smoking his pipe and staring into the fire, that was all right. But on the whole he spent his days alone in his study if wet, and sitting in the garden if dry.

His parents were always welcome visitors but he was grieved to see the impact on them of Noel's death. His father had aged ten years and was worried about the estate. His anxieties were almost a physical weight and he now stooped where he had once stood tall.

'The question is,' said Arthur Potter one afternoon as they sat in Edmund's study smoking their pipes, 'whether you still want to take it on. And now that Noel's gone – '

Edmund had already made up his mind but he wanted to let the old man down gently. 'I don't know, Father. It was my dearest wish before the war, as you know. Now my horizon and my wishes are different. Jennings was a good manager – the best, and if he was still there or indeed likely to return I daresay it could be done. But it will be hard to find a suitable replacement. There's no question that my legs are a great handicap. I can't see the point of doing it if I can't get about. I'd go mad with frustration.'

'I'm not asking for an answer today, my boy. Think about it and let me know when you're ready.'

'What will you do if I don't feel able to take it on?'

'I'll have to sell. It will break my heart after its being in the family for two hundred years but one can't be sentimental. The trouble is so many other families are in the same position. Did you know that the Morchards have put Loxworthy on the market? With Jolyon and Rupert dead Harry has lost the will to carry on. It's the same story across the county. It isn't a good time to sell and the longer I wait the worse the situation will become, I fear.'

Edmund pitied him. The war should not be breaking the spirit of men like his father and Harry Morchard who had given their all to build a solid future for their sons. Having worked hard all their lives they should now be at peace and taking it easy. Instead they found themselves alone and bewildered.

'I'll think about it and give you my decision as soon as I can, Father.'

Arthur Potter cleared his throat. 'You needn't worry – that is, if you decide against taking on Bradcombe – about money. If I sell there will be enough to make sure you're comfortable and can afford all the help you need.'

'Thank you. You're too generous. Now, tell be about Mama. She isn't still trying to contact Noel, is she?'

Edmund's mother, like so many other bereaved women, was unable to accept the loss of her son and had started holding seances to try and contact him.

'Poor Maud. I've tried to talk her out of it but she won't give it up. She's deaf to reason. I confess I find the bangs and movements in the night quite distressing. It's reached the point where I lie awake in suspense waiting for her to leave the bed. Then the creak of floorboards as she makes her way to Noel's room. I can't sleep for waiting to hear her come back. She's usually crying because she hasn't been able to contact him.'

'Poor Mama. Perhaps you should take her to a hotel for a while, somewhere tranquil like Weymouth.'

'I'd like that but I can't leave Bradcombe now there's so little help.' He sucked on his pipe for a minute. 'I could ask your Aunt Dorothea to invite her to stay. Mevagissey is very quiet and peaceful. Yes, that's what I'll do.'

Aunt Dorothea was only too happy to invite Maud to stay though without any knowledge of her night-time activities, which Arthur thought it better not to mention. Maud was reluctant to leave Noel's room because she was sure he would contact her there but eventually Arthur, Edmund and Lilian managed to talk her round.

There was regular news of Walter and John Franklin, who both seemed to lead a charmed existence. After Gallipoli Walter had a long spell in the Salient in 1916 and so avoided the Somme. John was one of the lucky ones who came through the Somme unscathed.

The unfortunate Phyllis Lynch again found herself the centre of gossip when she gave birth to a son and immediately offered him up for adoption. Two weeks later she left for north Devon, where she found work as a dairymaid on a farm near Barnstaple and passed out of their lives.

In spite of his tendency to despondency Edmund nevertheless found much to amuse and console in the private world of his study. He frequently composed long, cheery letters to his surviving friends. Hugh wrote to Edmund whenever he could. As he had predicted, he soon found himself back at the front, where at first the ground was frozen hard and the cold was almost unendurable. Where men froze to death. He was promoted to captain *'not because I've done anything to deserve it except survive. There are so few of the old battalion now, I'm considered quite a relic. The CO proudly shows me off to the new men and tells them this was a man from '14, and they all stare at me as though I'm an exhibit in the British Museum,'* he wrote.

Edmund forgot himself in the world of books. He read Shakespeare in its entirety, Hardy, Gilbert Murray and all the poetry he could lay his hands on, particularly Keats and Clare. He dreamed to the sound of the gramophone. As much as anything he sat at his desk and spent hour after hour doing jigsaw puzzles. The familiar physical activity of matching shape, colour and size freed his mind to wander. He dreamed of a whole-bodied life of riding and walking and independence, not with envy but as something so wildly unattainable that it belonged to a fantasy world.

Lilian was happy to see him settle into a routine and amuse himself, although she struggled to understand his ability to pore over jigsaws and daydream for hours at a time. She had dreaded his homecoming but at first his return seemed to restore something of the vanished world. However, it took only a few days for his presence in the wheelchair to make the house feel even more strange than when he was away. He made few demands but nevertheless he had to be thought of all the time, like a baby. His character had altered too. In place of his former smoothness and easy-going nature there were occasional barbs: not many, but sufficient to keep her on her guard. His headaches did not improve his sociability. He was no longer affectionate. He still loved her deeply but could see from her eyes that his body repelled her so he spared them both any embarrassing scenes. Every night Nurse Dale would help him into bed and then Lilian would go into the comfortable bedroom, kiss him goodnight, and tuck him in. Just like Nanny. He wished they had been able to have children but then he remembered his disability and was glad that none had come along. What sort of a father could he be, after all?

When they expected visitors Lilian was usually at home. She was vain enough to want to be seen as the perfect wife and she also feared that Edmund would be tactless and embarrass the visitors. Her self-designated role was to smooth over any little difficulties if Edmund was in one of his moods. The rector and Mrs Ambrose called once a week, either together or separately, having put Edmund's initial outburst down to the stress of his journey home.

When the number of callers slackened and Edmund spent more and more time in his study it gave Lilian the opportunity to pick up the threads of the life she had enjoyed while he had been away. Dolly, Madge and Violet came to tea – sometimes together, sometimes separately – their laughter filtering through the wall to Edmund in his study next door, and she often went out to see them. At first her absences from home were brief because she felt obliged to hurry back to him but when he made it clear that he wanted her to enjoy herself and not be constrained by him she sometimes stayed out for the whole day. He was not acting entirely disinterestedly when he suggested that Lilian continued her life as she had done in his absence – her presence weighed on him like a guilty secret. He knew she was getting a bad deal with him, that his necessity for solitude hurt her, that he was unable to conjure up the husband, lover and friend that he used to be. It gave him genuine pleasure when she returned from a lunch party or from an afternoon following her latest pursuit, golf. They developed an unwritten rule that no matter how they spent their days they would always dine together in the evening, after which they would repair to the drawing room where Edmund would sit contentedly with the dogs beside him while Lilian played the piano. Sometimes they simply chatted or she would knit garments for the Tommies while he read to her. At these moments he was almost happy.

His headaches became less brutal and less frequent.

Twenty-five

*I*n early April 1917 Edmund received an invitation to a private viewing at the Cranbourn Gallery, Bond Street, of 'War Paintings by Four Soldier Artists'. He was completely ignorant of Lilian's quarrel with Hugh and handed her the invitation with a beaming smile when she returned from the golf course.

'What is it?'

'Read it and see.'

She read it, and saw Hugh's name first in the alphabetical list of artists. She gasped.

'Isn't it wonderful. Hugh told me about it before he went back. It's a great feather in his cap. I can't go, of course, but I'd like you to go for me.'

'He's done well. I had no idea. As for my going, I'm not sure – '

'Please do, Lily. For me. We must support Hugh. Anyway, you like going to Town. You haven't been for an age.'

'Will he be there?'

'No, he's in France. He wants me to have one of the paintings. As I can't go he's instructed Hubert, the man who's organising the exhibition, to let you pick one. You see, I rather assumed you'd be happy to go.'

'In that case, how can I refuse? But I do wish you'd consulted me first.'

Three weeks later Lilian made her way to the Cranbourn

Gallery. She had travelled up the day before, having decided to make an occasion of the trip, and was staying for a few days with her Uncle Victor and Aunt Marigold in Eaton Square. Edmund had reassured her that Hugh was in France but her mouth felt dry and her stomach was turning over – it would be just like Hugh to spring a nasty surprise on her. She found the gallery and went in. It was already thronging with a fashionable crowd, some of them obviously artists and others friends or patrons. Someone handed her a catalogue. She wandered further into the room and was offered a glass of champagne by a passing waiter.

She sipped the champagne as she moved around looking for Hugh's name. Since the arrival of the invitation she had contemplated Hugh as an artist. She had never been interested enough to talk to him about it. He had kept that part of his life totally private, at least from her. And now he was exhibiting in a prestigious gallery.

A crowd was gathered around a large canvas depicting a doctor in a bloody vest and apron operating on a conscious soldier with a green face and terrified eyes while wounded men on stretchers lay jostled together all around as though the artist had wanted to cram as much suffering into the canvas as he could. It was ghastly. The pain on the man's face as the scalpel probed was palpable. It was as live and real as the wounded men in Taunton. She had never seen a painting like this before. The crowd shifted and separated. Lilian moved closer. She read the label beside the painting – 'Wounded' by Hugh Brodrick. Hugh painted *that* – surely not! Edmund had told her that there would be paintings of the war but whatever she had been expecting, it certainly wasn't this.

She drained her glass, handed it to a waiter and looked for Hugh's other paintings. Another large canvas was called 'Battle'. It showed a pitted and cratered landscape with tangles of barbed wire and bodies everywhere, some horribly mutilated, the air thick with smoke and bursting shells. It was painted as seen through the eyes of someone lying on the ground. She studied it in horror, thinking of Edmund, when a man spoke beside her.

'Magnificent, isn't it. So raw and truthful.'

She looked at him. 'It's certainly ... different.'

'You look shocked, but that, dear madam, is the whole point – to stir those of us at home out of our complacency. Allow me to introduce myself – Max Hubert. Welcome to my humble gallery.' His eyes twinkled as he offered her his hand. As she took it Lilian noticed that his left sleeve was empty.

'How do you do. I'm Mrs Potter. Hugh Brodrick is a particular friend of my husband. My husband asked me to look out for you.'

'I'm delighted to make your acquaintance, my dear Mrs Potter. I have particular instructions from Hugh for you to select one of his paintings for your husband.'

'Thank you. I haven't seen them all yet. I think it will be difficult to decide.' Where on earth could one put a painting like this? Either in Edmund's bedroom or his study. He had warned her that they were realistic but even so! It was out of the question for it to hang in any of their reception rooms. But would Edmund really want to be reminded of the war like this? Presumably Hugh had told him what the paintings were like, so it must be all right.

'Allow me to show you the others.'

Max Hubert escorted Lilian around Hugh's remaining half dozen paintings. There were also some drawings in pencil, chalk and charcoal. These were more to Lilian's taste, being of scenes behind the lines or of camp in England before the battalion went to France. She decided to buy one of them and give it to Edmund for his birthday. As for a painting, she chose what she considered to be the least disturbing – a group of three Tommies and an officer standing around a brazier in the shelter of a ruined building at night. At least it didn't have any corpses. She studied the features of the officer for any likeness of Edmund, but he was a stranger.

'I congratulate you, Mrs Potter. You've made an excellent choice,' said the dealer, when he had placed 'Sold' notices beside the painting and drawing.

'Thank you. Have you known Hugh for long?'

'We studied together at the Slade. He's a fine artist. It's a pity his father died when he did and Hugh chose to concentrate on Netherculme. I and others tried to persuade him – bully him, even – to sell up, move to London and devote himself to art but he dug in his heels. A sad neglect of a fine talent. He didn't give it up altogether but he needed to work on it without distraction to enable him to find his true style. I thought we'd lost him, if the truth be told. However, it's an ill wind, as they say, and he's found his voice all right with the war. These paintings are a *tour de force.*'

'Yes, they're certainly very powerful. But more suited to a gallery, I think, rather than a private house. They're so – so strong.'

Max Hubert laughed expansively.

'They're certainly that.'

Lilian thanked him for his time, looked around the other artists' works, which were of a similar nature, then made her way to the Green Park where she sat on a bench and contemplated the exhibition. The scene in Taunton and Edmund's wounds had long since opened her eyes about the brutality of the war but the paintings reinforced it with a vigour that leapt off the canvas. She could not doubt that Edmund had participated in such scenes. She almost sobbed when she thought of 'Wounded'. Was that how it had been for him?

Her mind then passed to Hugh. She was bewildered. How could such a mild man paint these things? It was incomprehensible. And Max Hubert, who must know what he was talking about if he was an art dealer, was singing his praises.

She had always thought Hugh shallow and easy to understand. Now she realised she barely knew him at all. It was mortifying.

Twenty-six

*H*ugh's painting arrived safely after the exhibition closed. Edmund was delighted with it and had it hung in his study. Although the exhibition received good reviews, only one painting had sold, by an artist called Evans. The subject matter was too disturbing to grace anyone's walls, it seemed.

Lilian was subdued when she returned home.

'I wish I could describe the paintings,' she said.

'I did warn you they'd be realistic.'

'Realistic! They were brutal. I thought I had an idea of what the war was like but, oh, Edmund, how you must have suffered. I used to resent the fact that you didn't talk about it much. It's only now that I understand why. You must have thought I was silly and ignorant.'

'No, dearest, never that. I couldn't talk about it. It was too deep. Still is. I knew I was cutting you out but I couldn't do anything else. I needed the tonic of normal life at home. Why make you worry about me even more than you did already, as you surely would have done?'

Lilian lit a cigarette and offered him one.

'I had no idea about Hugh's talent. I knew he was at the Slade, of course, but I suppose I thought that was a time-filler after Oxford. When I was looking at the paintings I felt that he was a complete stranger.'

Edmund smiled.

'He always was rather private. One has to know him well to get his full measure. And let's be honest, my dear, you've always rather avoided him.'

Lilian chose to ignore that remark.

'The dealer, Max Hubert, said that Hugh's friends tried to persuade him to sell Netherculme and make his living as an artist after his father died.'

'Did they, by George? He never told me that. Of course, it's clear as day that Netherculme's in his blood. He's wedded to the place.'

★

The days of 1917 grew longer. Meadows and orchards, untended, grew high and wild. Bees and butterflies filled the air. Every day Edmund studied the casualty list published in *The Times* and shook his head over the accounts filed by war correspondents. Their words might contain a hint of the truth, he supposed, but not much more.

A week after their conversation about the estate Edmund told his father that he did not want to take it on. Arthur Potter had expected as much but was nevertheless disappointed. He intended to sell up but couldn't quite bring himself to do it so he carried on, doing just enough to keep it going. Maud Potter returned from a lengthy stay in Mevagissey, at last able to accept that Noel had gone for good.

Edmund resumed his friendship with an old hunting acquaintance who had also been invalided out of the army. George Bonner was a pleasant, cultured man of twenty-five with a lively sense of humour. Edmund pitied him profoundly – he had lost part of his jaw to a shell at Beaumont Hamel. The two men had much in common, and in spite of the disadvantage of his voice having been reduced to little more than a whisper through injury to his vocal cords, George provided the easy, impersonal conversation that Edmund enjoyed.

Food was becoming scarce but the Potters were luckier than many because of their large kitchen garden and orchard. They gave away most of their produce, so much so that Mr Ambrose again felt it incumbent on himself to heap thanks on Edmund. This time Edmund received the thanks more graciously since he felt that he had actually earned them.

The Third Battle of Ypres was a source of great anxiety. Luckily Edmund had never experienced the Salient but George Bonner had been there in 1915 and his tales had made Edmund blench. And now it was happening again, even worse than before, from what he could gather. Hugh had managed to convey in his letters that he was near Ypres. Edmund dreaded the news that he expected daily. Likewise, he believed that Walter Franklin was there. Their letters stopped coming – a sign either of battle or serious wounds or death. He did his best not to think about either of them but it was impossible to keep them out of his mind. It was a happy day when Passchendaele, as the battle was now called, ground to a halt. By a miracle both men survived.

Hugh returned to England on leave but turned down Edmund's invitation to stay. Instead he took himself walking in the Lake District.

'Can you believe it?' Edmund said to Lilian one evening in early December, as they sat in front of the drawing-room fire. He was holding a letter in his hand. 'Hugh's on leave and has decided to spend it walking in the wettest part of England, where the days are even shorter than they are here, instead of coming to stay in our nice comfortable house. He doesn't even want to stay with the Jameses. You'd have thought he'd had enough of rain and mud.'

'Did you invite him?

'He's welcome here any time he's in England. He knows that. It's strange. That's twice this year he's been on leave and hasn't been to see us. I hope he hasn't got bored with me.'

'Don't be ridiculous, darling. You're like brothers. I expect he simply doesn't want to impose and is taking the opportunity to have a change of scene. Netherculme being out of bounds has given him the opportunity to see more of the country.'

'He doesn't impose. Anyway, I could understand it in the summer, but now … I hope he's all right.'

He could not share it with Lilian but he feared that Hugh was becoming neurasthenic.

Christmas came and went. It was not joyously celebrated. Nobody drank a toast to the end of the war. Edmund found he was no longer alone in his belief that the war would carry on until there was not a single man of fighting age left whole.

At Sydling 1918 passed in much the same pattern as the previous year. Edmund spent much of the winter and spring in his study, slotting piece after piece into a jigsaw while his mind roamed here and there, his pipe sometimes clenched between his teeth, sometimes lying forgotten in an ashtray. When the weather improved he would sit in a new summerhouse in the garden, smoking his pipe and reading. Castor and Pollux remained his inseparable companions. Edmund loved his dogs: their affection was absolute and undemanding.

The German offensive in March upset Edmund deeply as he thought of the ground they seemed to cross so easily, ground that had been soaked with his blood and that of so many others. But then the attack was held and the Germans were pushed back. Could it really be that the war would be decided soon? He dared not think so.

In the summer Hugh, now Major Brodrick, wrote from hospital in London. He had been shot in the neck by a sniper. Somehow it had missed a vital artery and vein and he was recovering nicely. He had been in Italy, facing the Austrians. He wrote,

'Of all the God-forsaken places to die this is the forsakenest – high up a mountain rock-face miles from anywhere. Even worse than the Salient in some respects. At least that was relatively near civilisation. Here there's nothing. We can only create dugouts by blowing holes in the rock. All the time there's either the danger of being blown to bits or missing one's step and plunging down the mountain. And as we're at altitude the weather is nearly always diabolical. What a place! Anyway I'm out of it for a bit but I'm mending nicely and so will probably have to go back quite soon. Isn't it typical. Those who cling desperately onto life go west and those like me who don't give a damn are still here.'

Lilian entered Edmund's study while he was reading Hugh's letter.

'I'm glad you're here,' he said, handing it to her. 'Read this. It's from Hugh. He's been shot but he says it's only a flesh wound and he's recovering well. He's in hospital in London.'

'Oh.'

Lilian read it through twice and handed it back to Edmund. 'He sounds so sad and bitter,' she said. 'Shall you write and tell him to come here as soon as he can?'

'Yes, of course. I hope he'll come this time. He must have been through hell in the last year.'

'Please will you also say that I'd like him to come.'

'Yes, if you like.'

So once again Edmund wrote, inviting Hugh to Sydling for as long as he liked when he was out of hospital, even if it was only for a couple of days, but again Hugh declined, saying that he wanted to stay in London with Max Hubert. Edmund wondered if the sight of him reminded Hugh too much of his own mortality. That was quite possible. Or he might simply want to spend his precious time in England with people from the art world following the success of the exhibition. Or perhaps he had a sweetheart. That was possible too. Probable even. He was good looking and eligible. He would never be the life and soul but what did that matter? Edmund was puzzled but did not feel slighted.

Twenty-seven

*I*n late August Edmund fell ill with influenza. It was a hot day and he spent most of it reading on the lawn in the shade of a large magnolia. In the early evening he felt shivery and his skin was tender to the touch. Two hours later his temperature had climbed to 103 degrees. Nurse Dale sat up with him all night, sponging perspiration from him and cooling his forehead with a moist cloth. By morning it had risen to 105 degrees and he was delirious. Doctor Lowman was summoned urgently but there was nothing to be done except to keep him in an even temperature and give him as much nourishment as he could be induced to take. Nurse made him Bovril with milk – anything to get food inside him. She wrung out sheets in cold water from a tub at the side of the bed and wrapped him in them but they were soon dry. She repeated the process again and again.

Doctor Lowman advised Lilian to keep out of the sickroom because of the risk of infection. She obeyed, unwillingly, and lived in torment. It was like reliving the time when the Big Push had started on the Somme and she didn't know if Edmund was alive or dead. But now he was here, behind a closed door, and she was forbidden to help him. She thought she would go out of her mind with worry. She might not be in love with him any more but she still cared deeply for him and wanted to do everything possible to help him. But she was superfluous. Nurse Dale was dealing competently with him in the sickroom and Mrs Barton lovingly prepared food and refreshing drinks for him in the kitchen. So she played the piano for comfort, and when she could not bear to sit still any longer she went out and walked aimlessly round and round the garden.

On the second day of his fever she could stand it no longer. She went to Edmund's room and walked in.

'You need a rest, Nurse, You haven't had a break for more than thirty-six hours,' she said. 'Tell me what needs to be done and go and get some sleep.'

'That's very kind of you, Mrs Potter, but I can manage, I assure you. You shouldn't be exposed to it.'

'Don't worry about me. I'm very robust. And I can see how tired you are. It won't do any good if you overtax yourself and become ill yourself.'

'If you really insist, I must confess I could do with some sleep. Let me show you what you need to do.' She demonstrated how to cool Edmund, and how to try to get him to take nourishment.

Lilian stayed at her post until the nurse joined her again near midnight.

'I do apologise, Mrs Potter. I slept so deeply. I shouldn't have left you all this time.'

'Don't worry, Nurse. You clearly needed to rest. My husband's been sleeping fitfully. His mind has been wandering a bit but I don't think he's as delirious as he has been. I managed to get a little Bovril into him.'

The nurse took Edmund's temperature. 'Hm, still very high. You go and get some sleep yourself now, I'll be good for the night. And make sure you wash well.'

Mrs Barton had brought Lilian a light supper earlier in the evening but she did not feel up to eating. Now she suddenly discovered that she was ravenous. She went to the kitchen and found bread and cheese in the larder, which she ate without ceremony at the kitchen table. Then she went up to bed.

Although she was exhausted she was so distressed at Edmund's condition that sleep eluded her. She tossed and turned through the night until she felt it would be the end of her to stay in bed a moment longer. She got up and dressed as the sun was appearing behind the church and went down to Edmund.

During the day his temperature dropped to 103 degrees, where it remained steady for a week. Then half-degree by half-degree it crept down to normal. Edmund engaged once more with the world around him but the fever had left him very weak. He did not even have the strength to philosophise as to why he had been spared when thousands stronger than he were dying like flies. He mainly ate, drank and slept. He slowly gained strength but it was more than a month before he was able to leave his bed. His muscles simply refused to support him when he tried to sit up. Nurse Dale's assiduous attention had not only saved his life but also prevented any other member of the household from contracting the illness. Lilian had willingly risked her own health but she remained well.

Edmund left his sickroom for the first time at the beginning of October. The heat of August had long been chased away by the cool winds of autumn which fingered their way around closed windows, causing curtains to move as though a ghost were passing. The countryside was washed by rain, raising hopes that it was being cleansed of the disease.

Once Edmund was clearly out of danger Lilian resumed her social life. She was out when he finally left his sickroom and Nurse Dale wheeled him into the drawing room. Sitting in front of the fire, Edmund looked around at the familiar room and was surprised to be reminded of how comfortable and cosy it was. Large vases of bronze chrysanthemums were scattered around. Lilian made sure there was something from the garden – flowers or even a few twigs if nothing else was available – in the room every day of the year. The sofas and armchairs were deep and comfortable, with a liberal scattering of cushions. It was furniture to lose oneself in with a good book in one's hand. Edmund's study was lined with books but they had spread and invaded this room too, adding to its feeling of peace and timelessness. Lilian's grand piano stood closed, its top scattered with music. The rattling of the window by a gust of wind merely added to the feeling of security. He was still weak but for the first time in weeks he felt alive; he was human again.

He took *The Woodlanders* from his pocket, found his place and started reading. One or other of Hardy's books had lived in his pocket throughout his life in the army: they provided an umbilical link to the world he was fighting for, the West Country of his youth. Likewise he had never been without Shakespeare's sonnets and his pocket Keats. It was a standing joke among the men of his platoon that the Germans would never be able to kill him because their bullets would be unable to penetrate beyond the books that were dotted about his person. Before the Somme he sought, and found, courage in Shakespeare who, more than any other writer, spoke to every human condition just as Beethoven did with his music. Edmund had no time for those people who refused to countenance Beethoven because he was German. His music transcended earthly squabbles.

The sky dimmed outside and rain pattered in bursts against the window. He was oblivious to it. He lifted his eyes from Hardy and stared unfocused into the fire. He was thinking about the day two years ago when they waited for the Somme offensive to start. The river was dark and mysterious and reeded. The day was warm with a sense of dampness in the air from the rain that had cause a postponement of the attack. He had read the sonnets that afternoon. Now, gazing deep into the fire he recited:

Like as the waves make towards the pebbled shore,
So do our minutes hasten to their end;
Each changing place with that which goes before,
In sequent toil all forward do contend.
Nativity, once in the main of light,
Crawls to maturity, wherewith being crown'd,
Crooked eclipses 'gainst his glory fight,
And Time that gave doth now his gift confound.
Time doth transfix the flourish set on youth,
And delves the parallels in beauty's brow,
Feeds on the rarities of nature's truth,
And nothing stands but for his scythe to mow.

His head hung lower over his chest.

A door slammed shut, waking him abruptly. There was a bustle in the hall. He recognised Lilian's footfall as she approached the drawing room. She flung open the door.

'Darling. I accused Mrs Barton of telling lies when she said you were in here. I had no idea you were planning to get up today. Why didn't you tell me?'

'I decided on the spur of the moment. I'm feeling stronger and thought it was time to get back into circulation. Nurse tried to make me stay in bed but I insisted.' He was straining to look at her over his shoulder. 'Won't you come in and shut the door? I can't see you properly over there. Haven't the strength yet to turn this thing.'

Lilian did as he asked and flung herself down in a deep armchair beside him.

'Nasty day for you to be out. Playing golf?'

'No, I was at Lowgate. Violet had a few people for lunch. Oh Edmund, if I'd known I'd happily have cancelled it.'

'I expect she'd have been offended.'

'Nonsense. She knows you've been ill. Everyone thinks you're terrifically lucky to have pulled through.'

'That's kind of them,' he said with an ironic smile. 'Do you?'

'Do I what?'

'Do you think I'm lucky or that I'd be better off dead?'

Lilian flushed and leapt to her feet. She was close to Edmund and looked down at him. 'How can you even think that, let alone suggest it? You mean more to me than anything. I fought with Nurse to keep you alive. Ask her if you don't believe me.'

'I'm sorry. Forgive me. Must be the weather. That and the fact that I'm rather weak. Doctor Lowman warned me that I might be a bit low for a while.'

Lilian sat down. She took Edmund's hand in hers and stroked it. 'Then please don't waste your precious energy on thoughts like that.'

'Don't worry, my dear. Since my brain's felt a bit less like a mess of porridge I've been doing a lot of thinking, not all of it morbid, I can assure you. I've been thinking about you.'

'About me? In what way?'

'Merely that I see so very little of you these days – before my illness, I mean.'

'But you wanted me to –'

'Yes, yes, I know. I encouraged you to go out as much as possible, and I'm always either in my study or the summerhouse. I'm a damper when your friends come here. You don't have to deny it, it's a fact.'

'But – '

'I don't want you to misunderstand me, my dear. I'm not criticising you. I'm not trying to stop all that. Just the reverse.' He looked her straight in the eye. She stared at him, questioning, doubting. He continued, now addressing the fire, 'I'm no good to you as a husband, there's no pretending otherwise. Why don't you take a lover?'

There was no hiding place – he had said it.

Lilian dropped his hand. '*What?*'

'If you haven't already done so.'

'You want to be rid of me. You're casting me off.'

Edmund thought how odd it was that stress reduced them to talking as though they were in a Victorian melodrama.

Lilian sought his eyes but he refused to turn his head to her.

'I love you. I always shall, but my feelings don't, can't enter into it. I'm a liability and you're a beautiful woman in your prime. You deserve better.'

'Edmund, darling, you're still ill. I think it would be best if we don't talk about this.'

While he lay in bed convalescing Edmund had thought a great deal about Lilian. He would be torn apart with jealousy if she took a lover but the alternative might be even worse. She might feel shackled to someone she despised and even grew to hate. That would be unbearable. But whenever he considered her reaction he didn't anticipate having his generosity flung back at him. He lost his temper and thumped the arm of the chair with his fist. Lilian jumped.

'Perhaps I am ill but we won't pretend this conversation didn't happen. It is happening and it's going to continue until it's finished.'

She glared at him.

'Now I'll finish,' he continued more calmly. 'I don't care what you do with whom, provided you satisfy me on three points. One: you return here at night and we spend our evenings together as we did before I was ill. Two: you don't bring your lover to Sydling. I couldn't bear that. Three: that you're discreet. Gossip wouldn't worry me but it would go badly for you.'

She digested what Edmund had said before replying. 'I think you've overlooked something.'

'What?'

'Two things, actually. One: a small point but not unworthy of consideration. There are no men. They are either in the army or dead or –' She could not say the word 'mutilated'. 'There isn't a decent man for miles.'

She laughed suddenly and Edmund glared at her. 'Sorry,' she said, composing herself. 'I was imagining the scene if a half-decent man appeared – hordes of women chasing him.'

'Hilarious. Besides, there are some men – those who aren't badly wounded, those in reserved occupations and older men, of course. And the war can't last for ever. Perhaps even some whole-bodied men might come back, you never know.'

'The second thing you overlooked,' she continued, ignoring his remarks, 'is that I couldn't do that to you. I may not love you as passionately as I used to but I still care for you very deeply.'

A lump came into Edmund's throat. 'I don't know what to say. I feel so inadequate. I don't want to hold you back.'

'I'd be lying if I said I haven't thought about it but I can't do it. Life has turned out differently from what we expected but I'm no less your wife for all that. After all, what would marriage vows mean if we just toss them aside when we feel like it? Do you think I don't know the pain it would cause you if I were to have an affair, no matter how discreet, even with your blessing? Now, promise me you won't worry about me like this again. Please.'

She kissed Edmund for the first time in months, then knelt on the floor with her head in his lap. Edmund, completely taken aback by her words, screwed up his eyes to hold back ridiculous, joyful tears, his fingers gently running through her hair.

Twenty-eight

*L*ilian's brother John died of influenza in November. Since enlisting in 1914 he had survived long spells in the Salient, including Passchendaele, as well as the Somme and the retreat. It was so unfair that influenza should destroy him now. On November 2nd the sister who was nursing him at a hospital in Rouen wrote to Annie, summoning her urgently. She set off immediately with his parents but arrived three hours after he died. The age gap between them meant that Lilian had always been less close to him than to Walter. Nevertheless she felt his loss acutely, particularly as it seemed that by a miracle both her brothers might survive the war. Edmund had liked his brother-in-law and shared Lilian's grief. In spite of all the death he had witnessed and read about daily in the casualty lists, the loss of John was cruel. Again and again he wondered why he should have survived while stronger men succumbed.

But he had, and life carried on.

'You can't imagine what everyone's saying at the clubhouse,' Lilian announced, bursting into Edmund's study a few days later. She was still wearing her outdoor clothes. It was the first time she had faced going out since the news of John's death, other than to comfort her mother and Annie.

'If I can't imagine, you'd better tell me.' He was sitting at his desk watching rain lash against the window. Although it was midday, daylight scarcely penetrated the sagging clouds.

'They're talking of an end to the war. They say an armistice will be signed tomorrow. Doesn't that surprise you?'

Edmund sighed. 'Only in so far as I should have credited your golfers with more sense. People have been talking like that since '14. I'll believe it when it's actually been signed. I'm not going to waste my time even thinking about it beforehand. There have been too many disappointments.'

'Really, darling, this time it's true. Everybody says so.'

He did not reply but picked up his pipe and clenched it between his teeth. He fumbled in his pocket for matches.

Lilian saw them half-underneath some papers on the desk, picked them up and passed them to him.

'Thank you,' said Edmund. He lit the pipe with a trembling hand.

'They all believe it, you say? Even Harry Wallace?'

'He most of all. He had the news from a friend in Parliament.'

'How about Michaelson, what does he say?'

'He's convinced of it. I know we've heard all this talk before but it really seems to be true this time.'

'Just as it was last time and the time before that. I'm going to keep an open mind, just in case. It's iniquitous the way our hopes are raised only to have them dashed.'

But this time Edmund was not disappointed. At eleven o'clock the following morning a peal of bells rang out from the church tower and carried across village and fields. Alone in his study he was scarcely able to think as the almost-forgotten sound came through the window. He found it impossible to imagine what the world would be like in future. Only two things were certain – it would be unlike anything they had known before, and his own situation was not going to change.

Lilian hurried into the room. 'You see, darling. I was right. It's over. Shall we have some champagne?'

'Later, perhaps. I'm glad it's over but I don't feel particularly like celebrating.'

Soon the telephone rang for Lilian. After taking the call she went back to Edmund.

'That was Madge. She's inviting a few people over to celebrate. If you don't feel like celebrating, would you mind if I go? I know it may seem callous, but being with people helps to stop me thinking about John.'

'If you want to, go ahead. And I know you aren't callous. We all have to find our own way to grieve.'

'Are you sure you don't mind?'

'Yes, dear, I said so.'

'Well in that case, I think I will go for an hour or two.'

Edmund found that it took some time for the enormity of the event to sink in. There was little to cheer. The war was over, finished, napoo, but so too were the lives of the dead and of men like himself. His own war did not end when the church bells rang out; it would carry on until his death. He thought of all those who would not come back, especially Noel and John. The men who ought to be shaping the future in the arts, science, politics: they were almost all dead. The bravest and the boldest, the strongest and most creative, had all gone. And others who were not the strongest and the bravest but who had followed the call of duty and paid the price. Only the second- and third-rate remained to multiply and shape the world. He was not entirely certain that he wanted to be part of it.

When Lilian's 'couple of hours' turned into the whole day Edmund grew increasingly morose.

He thought of parties and merriment and all the things he used to enjoy with Lilian. How dare they celebrate, who know nothing of shells and trenches and lice and rats and mud and bloody, blistered feet and black, bloated, decomposing corpses and swarms of fat flies that did not even wait for death before settling down to gorge themselves? How dare they, with their golf and their gossip and their lunch parties, complaining about petty inconveniences? How dare they, with men who had visited hell sitting helpless and comfortless at home?

Ah. So that was it. Edmund sighed and shrugged his shoulders when he succeeded in rationalising the cause of his mood. He rang the bell and asked Mary to bring him a glass of whisky, something he had not tasted since he had been in the trenches.

So that was it. His nose was out of joint. Lilian had abandoned him, he who had nearly given everything in pursuit of this victory. He knew he was being irrational but the fact that he had encouraged her to go only served to make him crosser with himself. She should have read his mind and stayed. He thought of John, who had only been dead a few days. And the biggest question of all – would Lilian have been so keen to join in the celebrations if he himself had just died?

He rang for another whisky and this time told Mary to leave the bottle.

Outside, night was falling prematurely. Indoors, Edmund had no light except the glow of the fire which cast flickering, elongated shadows like tortured fingers on wall and ceiling. He liked the semi-darkness: it suited his mood. He poured a third whisky, larger than the previous two. He had fallen out of the habit of drinking and his head began to feel muzzy. A turmoil of thoughts plagued his mind. Memories of a picnic on the beach at Sidmouth. Men who innocently followed the call to arms and who gave their all. Women who knew nothing and understood less. Women who were embarrassed by his wounds because they were not neat and tidy. Women whose mouths uttered words of comfort and assurance but whose eyes avoided his. Women who never spoke of love. Yet he was grateful to Lilian for her faithfulness and loyalty. Little could the Germans have suspected how completely they could destroy a man without actually taking his life. Yet he was not able to hate them because many of them must be in a position similar to his own. The PBI on both sides were ruled over by a higher authority. That was the greatest surprise of the war as far as he was concerned – the realisation that the average German was no more nor less than he; they had no quarrel with each other. Quarrels were for home. He did not blame Lilian, after all, hadn't he been unable to share with her all but the most superficial of his experiences? But he detested the profiteers and drawing-room warmongers. That was what rankled most – their unwillingness even to try to understand. The total failure to exert their imagination to envisage life at the front.

He poured another drink.

Although Edmund was railing against people at the home front in general, in his heart he was blaming Lilian. He chuckled at the irony of her remaining at home while he was away at war, and her constantly being out now that he was at home. Why couldn't she understand what he was going through now, when she had seen him suffer so much?

He leaned forward to place the glass on the desk but misjudged his movements in his whisky-haze and it slipped off the edge. He lunged to catch it, too awkwardly and too late. It hit floor with a splintering crash. His rapid, unnatural movement made him overbalance and he toppled out of his chair. Mrs Barton, who happened to be crossing the hall at that moment, heard a military oath followed by a thud and a spinning of wheels. She summoned Nurse Dale at the top of her voice and rushed into the study. Between the pair of them they extricated Edmund, who smelt strongly of whisky, from where he lay half-underneath the desk, and with a certain amount of huffing and puffing they managed to lift him into the wheelchair and push him into his bedroom where they put him to bed. Nurse was inclined to speak severely to him but Mrs Barton had a kind heart and remembered him as he was in better days, and said, 'Poor master. He's a good man and deserves better. He's taken his wounds awful hard. Let him sleep it off in peace, Nurse.'

Twenty-nine

*H*ugh was in Italy when the Armistice was signed. There had been no celebration, just a feeling of release from a massive burden. He was very tired. He found it difficult to believe that he of all people had survived. When he had rejoined his battalion after the Somme he did not care if he lived or died. He simply tried to do his job competently, without heroics and without blame.

He had looked forward to Edmund's letters and wrote back whenever he had time. Did Lilian ever think about him? Probably not, unless it was to blame him for something. In his own letters he assiduously avoided any mention of her except for cursory good wishes for her health, although he did make an exception after he learned that she had been to his exhibition. Edmund wrote that she had been shocked by his paintings but nevertheless chose one for him, which he was now looking at on the wall of his study. He asked Edmund to thank her for going and congratulated her on her choice. When he was recovering from being shot in the neck in 1918 he was gratified that Edmund included her wish that he would stay with them. It moved him, and he cursed her for opening a wound that he hoped was healing.

He had tried various strategies for putting her out of his mind. He visited a blue lamp establishment for the first time after his return to the front in 1917. The place was clean and well decorated, and the prostitute was all one could wish: she even gave him champagne and an omelette afterwards. But he was fastidious and could not rid himself of the fear of venereal disease even though condoms were provided for officers, unlike the unfortunate Tommies in the red lamps. Instead he preferred judicious liaisons with other women – some nurses and WAACs were happy to risk dismissal in order to provide solace for officers returning to the line and probable death.

He held himself to his pledge not to go back to Devon for as long as the war lasted. As he wrote to Edmund, he had discovered the Lake District and spent some leave there. When he was in hospital in London recovering from the sniper's bullet he lied about wanting to stay in London. The bullet had caught him in the neck as he had said, but the wound was little more than a graze and he could have recovered without going back to England. He kept to himself the fact that the doctor at the base hospital recognised that he needed a rest from the line more than anything and kindly marked him down for England. That had probably saved his life. When he wrote to Edmund he was sick of living. As he recovered, he made up his mind to go to the Essex marshes, where he tramped all day under the vast East Anglian sky with only marshland birds for company. He badly needed the break and the bleak landscape suited his mood. After four years of war he could feel his nerve going, and he dreaded having a breakdown like Edmund's or going to pieces in the line. He had seen it happen too often. As it was, he wondered if he would ever be able to hear a telephone again without trembling from head to foot, and the sound of a car or motorcycle backfiring made him fling himself prostrate on the ground, shaking.

He returned to Devon in the primrose season.

Netherculme had already been emptied of patients and nursing paraphernalia and officially returned to him. Before anything, he knew that he had to go home and assess what sort of state the house was in and how much work would be needed to make it at least partly habitable while the rest was being restored. The estate, too, would need a great deal of work. How many of his employees would come back? Where would he get men if he needed them? Oh God, everyone was dead. What on earth could he do? Where to begin? He felt overwhelmed by everything and the need to make decisions. His friends Edgar and Clarice James, who had put him up after the Somme, were only too keen for him to stay with them indefinitely while he tried to make sense of everything. Their three sons had all been killed and they became surrogate parents to him. There was real affection on both sides. They gave him space when he needed it and gentle help when he needed that too. Edgar James counselled Hugh gently and wisely as he tried to make sense of the task at Netherculme. Clarice saw his fragile state and mothered him unashamedly.

At first he was unable to face all but a few people, and put off going to see the Potters for as long as he could. But as weeks passed he began to gain strength and felt that it would be rude if he kept away much longer. It was well over two years – half the war – since he had last seen them and he knew Edmund would have missed him enormously. He wondered if they had changed as much as he had.

On a day when a north-easterly wind made the daffodils bob and mocked the clear blue sky, he drove to Halberton. He was unaccountably nervous and scolded himself for his foolishness. He switched off the engine in front of the familiar red sandstone house. It amazed him that something so homely and familiar could still exist when cataclysmic events had been happening in his world. He got out of the car, but, instead of going to the front door and ringing the bell, he followed the flagstone path through the shrubbery to the terrace on the south-eastern side of the house. Blooms of wisteria were already open against the wall, scenting the air. He noticed the white paintwork peeling in places, something that would never have been allowed to happen before the war. The French window of Edmund's study was directly below the wisteria. Hugh went up to it and rapped loudly.

Peering in, he saw Edmund seated at his desk. He looked up with a start, then a smile spread from ear to ear and transformed his face. He waved, and wheeled his chair over to the window to unfasten it. Hugh stepped in.

'Hello Edmund.'

By all that's good, Hugh, I'm happy to see you. Sit yourself down. This calls for the fatted calf. What would you like – whisky, champagne?'

Hugh subsided into a deep leather armchair. 'Tea and crumpets would be perfect – I can't tell you how I missed them.'

Edmund rang the bell. 'Ah, Mary,' he said when she answered his summons. 'We need to celebrate Mr Brodrick's safe return from Armageddon. Bring every crumpet in the house, toasted to perfection, and lashings of butter and jam. Never mind rationing. And the biggest pot of tea.'

'Very well, sir,' said the startled maid, and turning to Hugh.' Welcome home, sir.'

After Mary left the room Hugh looked around at the familiar study with its smell of tobacco and leather – the walls lined with books, some two deep on the groaning shelves, a couple of his own drawings, one given by him to Edmund and the one bought by Lilian, the exhibition painting, the window with its outlook on the garden framed by velvet curtains the colour of claret, the fire burning in the grate, the comfortable armchairs, the knee-hole desk with its green leather inset half covered by a jigsaw, Edmund sitting in his wheelchair watching him, his face pale and gaunt, his hair longer than it used to be and flecked with grey. His mouth was smiling but his eyes told of pain and sorrow.

He said quietly, 'I can't believe I'm here. I never expected to come through.'

'What was your secret? You must have had one. Do I call you "Major" and bow and scrape, by the way?' Edmund asked.

'Certainly not. I'm plain mister again. And as for survival, I suppose my secret was that I didn't care. I've seen too many men go west who were desperate for life. I could take it or leave it, and here I am.'

'Well, congratulations. You're a rarity. What are your plans now? What about Netherculme?'

'The hospital's cleared out but the house needs quite a bit of work to get it right. Until that's done I'm staying with the Jameses, who are looking after me royally. I don't know if you know but they lost all their boys.'

Edmund shook his head.

'When I'm back at home it will be much the same as before – running the estate. There's a terrific amount to be done, of course. More than enough to keep me occupied for several years. The great problem will be labour.'

'All dead?'

'Most. Some disabled. One or two whole. God, what a shambles.'

Mary returned with a tray laden with the trappings for tea, and buttered crumpets and jam. 'As for my painting,' Hugh continued when they'd polished off the last crumpet, 'I have scores of drawings and sketches that I'd like to work up. I've even been offered a commission for a couple on the back of the Cranbourn exhibition. There's no question about whether I want to or not. No, the problem is time. How to do that as well as everything that needs to be done?'

His voice started trembling and to cover his confusion he took out his pipe. His hands shook as he filled and lit it. Edmund averted his eyes and busied himself with his own pipe. For several minutes they smoked in silence.

Eventually Edmund spoke. 'I won't ask what it was like – I know you'll talk about it if you want.'

'Thank you. Maybe I'll tell you about it some time in the future but at the moment all I want, and need, is to get down to the present.' His voice was firmer now. 'Funnily enough, I'm finding it hard to get used to sleeping in a soft bed again – more often than not I sleep on the floor. Clarice and the housemaid very tactfully avoid mentioning it. And the effect of sudden noises – but you know about that.' He could not tell even Edmund how sometimes when he had a particularly bad nightmare he would crawl under the bed as though it were a dugout.

Edmund nodded.

'But that's enough about me – nerves ragged, bad dreams, all the usual symptoms, apart from which I'm fit and well. Tell me about yourself. The 'flu nearly did for you?'

'Yes. God knows how I got through. Like you, it was the perverse Hand of Fate, I suppose. Plenty of folk stronger than me went under. My brother-in-law John, for one. My temperature was 105 degrees for a couple of days and I had to be wrapped in wet sheets to cool me down, I'm told. I was delirious and don't remember a thing. What I do remember is lying in bed for days on end with less strength than a kitten. I've never known weakness like that, not even after the Somme. It took ages for me to get my strength back. Even turning the pages of a book was a monumental task.'

'You were lucky. Er – and Lilian – she didn't catch it?'

'No, thank God. The doctor advised her to keep out of my sickroom but she insisted on nursing me. She was wonderful, and Nurse was too. Between them they saved me.'

'H-How is Lilian?'

'Very well. We have an understanding which suits us. We follow our own pursuits during the daytime and dine and spend our evenings together. It works well. We've always had different circles although it wasn't so apparent before the war. I'm happy with my own company. I've put her off inviting her crowd here because I can't stand making banal small talk with them and they're embarrassed by me being as I am.'

'She isn't at home now?' Hugh asked, half-hoping, half-dreading that she was.

'No, she's playing golf with Dolly Tranter today. She loves it – hail, rain, shine, there's no stopping her. Funny, when one recalls how a few clouds used to put her off going outside before the war.'

'Well, we all change. The person I used to be wouldn't recognise me now.'

'Same here.'

They drew contemplatively on their pipes again until Hugh thought he ought to keep up the conversation in case Edmund divined his nervousness about Lilian.

'Do you get out much?'

'Outside, or to different places?'

'Both. Either.'

'I go outside if it isn't raining. If my nurse has a fault it's that she will insist on cocooning me in rugs and scarves and mufflers and God knows what. I roast alive and nearly always have to strip them all off. It's a charade we go through every time.'

'Doubtless she means well,' Hugh said with a smile. He could visualise the scene.

'Oh she does, that's the trouble. My fuse is shorter than it used to be and I'm afraid she feels the sharp end of my tongue sometimes. I don't know how she puts up with me. Anyway, apart from that I get Jacks to drive me over to see George Bonner from time to time.'

'Poor George. How is he? Have they been able to do anything for his face?'

Edmund opened his hands expansively. 'He's marvellous. He hasn't let it affect his life one iota. Of course it's a damned nuisance that he can only speak in a whisper, and all the girls look anywhere but at his face, but he pretends not to notice. The medics have done all they can – patched it up, done some plastic surgery at that new unit in Sidcup, but he still looks a sight.'

'Married?'

'No, and I fear no girl will have him now.'

'You say that but they can't afford to be so choosy nowadays. Besides, they can't all be that superficial.'

Edmund looked at him sharply and Hugh regretted his tactlessness.

'Perhaps not all, but most of them are,' Edmund said heavily. 'Believe me, I know. I've been living in the middle of it.'

'I'm sorry. Being in the army so long has roughened me. I'm going to have to learn to be civilised again.'

'Don't worry. I was speaking generally, not of anyone in particular. If one is fighting a war one wants to believe that people at home will rally round if one comes home maimed. It would be intolerable to think anything else. Unhappily, reality is a little different.'

'Just as the war didn't turn out as we expected.' Hugh knocked some ash from his pipe, filled and relit it. 'This old pipe's been everywhere with me. My great comforter. I don't think I could have got through without it yet before the war I could have taken it or left it.'

Silence again.

'So what's the news?' Hugh asked after a while. 'What momentous events have I missed?'

Edmund related the local news of good crops and bad crops, food and coal shortages, village gossip, country news. They had just touched on the subject of profiteers when they heard the front door close and the murmur of voices in the hall. Hugh felt his stomach lurch and he braced himself to face Lilian, but she did not appear. She must have gone upstairs because soon he could hear footsteps overhead.

★

Lilian recognised Hugh's car as soon as she saw it. Since the Armistice she knew that this day must come sooner or later and had felt prepared but now she realised that she had no idea what to say to him. She had long been bitterly ashamed of her words and had prayed that he would survive the war. Had he remembered her anger? He must have, or else why had he so assiduously avoided Halberton when he was in England? Nothing else could explain it. Since that day, not without considerable effort at times, she had trained herself to be more thoughtful, less impulsive and hot-headed. But he would not know that. To him she must still be an angry, petulant, spoilt brat – there were no other words for it.

Mary was crossing the hall when she let herself in the front door.

'Whose car is that, Mary? It looks like Mr Brodrick's.'

'Yes, ma'am, he arrived about an hour ago. He's with the master in the study.'

'Thank you. That will be all.'

She went upstairs to her bedroom to change out of her golfing clothes but in reality she wanted to compose herself. She fussed about, putting on first one dress then another, finding fault with each of them, but the longer she delayed the more nervous she became. Deciding to wear the first one after all – pleated linen in eau de Nil with an embroidered bodice which suited her particularly well – she finished dressing and went downstairs.

★

Conversation within the study had become desultory. Edmund asked Hugh to open the window a crack, which Hugh was glad to do. He was uncomfortably aware of a bead of sweat hovering above his lip, now bare where he had shaved off his moustache. His palms were clammy. A gust of air swirled around

him. It cleared his head and cooled his face. He wondered if
Edmund had guessed about the quarrel. It was unlikely that
Lilian would have told him. He cleared his throat and turned
to face the room. He was annoyed with himself for feeling like
a love-struck teenager. He stuck his hands in his pockets and
tried to look nonchalant.

A light footfall sounded in the hall and the door opened.
Lilian stood in the doorway. Hugh's first impression was that
she looked as beautiful as ever, then he noticed that she seemed
to have acquired an air of maturity that gave her an additional
radiance. He walked slowly towards her, holding out his hand.

'Hello Lilian.'

She crossed the room to meet him, took his hand and smiled.

'Hello Hugh. I'm so glad you're safely home again.'

He looked into her eyes, expecting to read a lie.

'Truly,' she said. She moved away and flung herself down in
an armchair. 'Goodness, I don't know how you two can bear
to be in here with all this smoke. I can hardly see the other
side of the room.'

Hugh sat down again.

'We've been celebrating Hugh's return,' said Edmund.
'Pushing the boat out with tea and crumpets but I'm afraid
we were reckless and ate the lot.'

'Not to worry. I'll ask Mary to bring some more tea, at any
rate.' She rang the bell.

'Are there any crumpets left, Mary?'

The maid looked at Edmund and said, 'No ma'am. Would
you like some Madeira cake instead?'

'Thank you. That will do very well.'

Mary went quietly out.

'I'd ask how you are, Lilian, but I can see you're well,' Hugh
said.

'Yes, I'm very well,' she replied. 'When did you get home?'

'I was demobbed last month,' he said vaguely, hoping to avoid having to explain why he had not been to see them sooner.

'I suppose you have Netherculme to yourself now?'

'Yes and no. The hospital has closed and everyone's gone but there's a great deal of work needed to set it right again. I'm staying with Edgar and Clarice James – the people I stayed with before – until I can move back in.' Hugh flushed as he said this, remembering the last time he saw her. He could see that Lilian was thinking of it too, by the way she kept her eyes down. Neither of them could think of anything to say and they fell into silence.

'Talking of which,' Edmund said, 'you've got some explaining to do, Mr Brodrick. Why didn't you come here when you were on leave or convalescing? I was beginning to feel like a leper.'

Here Hugh had to tell a little white lie. He had always wanted to go to the Lakes, so it seemed as good a time as any. It was marvellous, tramping about on the hills all day, weather permitting, staying a night or two at a village inn and then moving on to another. It could not have been more bracing after the confinement of billets, trenches and dugouts. He particularly liked Ullswater – it was less busy than the more popular southern lakes and was as peaceful as anywhere on earth could be. When the weather was good he made lots of sketches and watercolours. And when he was recovering from the wound to his neck he thought it would be good to do something different again. As he was not feeling strong enough to face the exertion of hill-walking he decided instead to explore the wilderness of the Essex marshes. He had stayed in a small but comfortable inn at Tollesbury which suited him perfectly. Wide open spaces without a soul in sight, only the cries of the many birds there. The contrast with Cumberland and Westmorland couldn't have been greater. Instead of sky completing the canvas after the mountains and lakes had been painted in, here the sky was the subject with land and water the minor constituents. Once you realise that, you can see how beautiful sky can be – ever-changing light and colour. That idea wasn't new, of course, but one had to see it for oneself to get full understanding.

He was babbling – too obviously trying to justify his keeping away. He fell silent.

Luckily for him, Edmund understood only too well the need for solitude and did not labour the point. Lilian focused all her attention on drinking her tea and eating a large slice of Madeira cake, which Mary had brought while Hugh was extolling the virtues of the Lakes.

An overwhelming sense of tiredness came over Hugh. It often happened at this time of day. Soon he rose to his feet and, after arranging to see Edmund again in two days' time, made his way home. As he steered the Daimler along the high-banked lanes he was thankful to have got the meeting with Lilian over at last. Nothing would be so bad again. He was still suspicious of her. Whenever she had been friendly in the past it had invariably been followed by pain, but he told himself he was proof against that now, although he knew he was not. He wished he could be like other men he knew who could dart from woman to woman as easily as sneezing but that simply wasn't in his nature and never would be.

And it had been good – very good, to see Edmund again, but how he had changed. He seemed resigned to his situation but it was clear that the influenza had knocked him badly. The bleak Essex landscape lent itself to philosophy and Hugh was not exempt from its influence. When he had been tramping around there he had asked himself if one of the worst things he had ever done was to save Edmund's life. He knew that he had to do it, and if the circumstances were repeated he would do it again, but he had preserved him for what? A life of frustration and unhappiness, denied all the activities he relished and distanced from Lilian. He asked himself the same question again as he drove home, and still could not find a satisfactory answer.

Back at Sydling, Hugh was being discussed in Edmund's study.

'By God, Lily, I'm so happy he's back. Ever since he went back after the Somme I've dreaded to hear that he'd been killed. What he must have been through in that time.' Edmund shook his head, unable to express his imaginings.

'Yes, I'm glad too. But he looks so frail. He used to be robust – like granite. Now he looks as though a gust of wind would blow him away. I was shocked when I saw him and I'm afraid he noticed my surprise. He looked so tired, so sad, and his clothes are hanging off him.'

'You're right, he doesn't look well at the moment but the main thing is he's home and safe. Now he can concentrate on getting fit again.' Edmund forbore to mention Hugh's trembling hands.

'He must have a big job ahead, getting Netherculme straight again.'

'It will be. It's a heavy load for him, particularly while he's so worn out. He has to get the house straight and engage staff. The good news is that at least some of his old servants stayed on while it was a hospital and so are in place already.'

'That's something. I hope he'll be all right.'

'He's bound to be. As you said, he's made of granite,' Edmund said, adding, 'I wish he could find a good woman to marry. He needs someone to care for him. The war's brought him out of himself a great deal but the right woman is just what he needs.'

Lilian did not agree with Edmund about this. 'Oh, I don't know. Bachelorhood suits him. After all, you'll be seeing a lot of him again, I suppose, and he wouldn't be able to do that so much if he was married. No, he's far better as he is.'

Thirty

*H*ugh moved back into Netherculme at the beginning of June. His housekeeper, cook and housemaid had remained there during the war and were delighted that the master was coming home. Charles Wilson, his estate manager, had returned in early 1918 after losing an arm at Ypres. Hugh had always valeted himself in the past but when Mervyn Aldhelm, his former sergeant, wrote to ask him if he knew of any vacant positions, Hugh took him on as his valet and factotum. He also offered outdoor work to several unemployed ex-servicemen. He knew he was being soft-hearted and did not need so many staff but while his accountant told him he could afford it he was determined to do what he could.

He was regaining strength, and now that he was back in the comfort and familiarity of his own bed he began to sleep more easily. More and more often in the morning he found himself in bed rather than on the floor. He still had nightmares but they became less frequent and only occasionally did he find himself right under the bed when he woke up. The telephone still alarmed him so before he moved back he had it moved to the servants' quarters and made sure he would not be able to hear it.

★

Following Hugh's example, Edmund also appointed an ex-serviceman as his manservant. He had long been conscious of the demands he placed on Nurse Dale, and now he did not need nursing so much as general help. He could not believe his luck when he learned that Thomas Minster, his corporal at Loos who had helped dig him out after he was buried by the shell blast, was looking for work. He was ideal for the job. He had endless patience, had endured many things worse than dealing with an invalid, and above all he had a real affection for Edmund. Also, he had no family to complicate matters.

'I'm glad, darling,' said Lilian when he told her. 'Nurse has been wonderful but it will be easier for a man to lift you, and you'll like the masculine company. I hope he isn't good looking or a lady's man, though. I don't want him unsettling the maids.'

'He's pure as the driven snow,' Edmund replied, keeping to himself certain scenes he had witnessed behind the lines. 'I'll tell him he can cast his eye anywhere but within this house.'

So Nurse Dale left with many thanks and good wishes and a glowing reference, and a promise to come back if ever the master needed nursing again, though God forbid.

While work was in progress at Netherculme Hugh managed his time so that he could spend at least half a day a week with Edmund. Picking up their friendship again provided Edmund's morale with the boost it needed to help him get over the lingering effects of the influenza. He looked and felt healthier than he had done for months. Lilian was pleased to see the effect Hugh's company had on him but found that she still had mixed feelings about Hugh. She had stopped hating – even resenting – him a long time ago but her conscience wasn't so forgiving and it troubled her when he was around. He never said anything or looked at her in a particular way, in fact he rarely looked at her at all. Although she usually contrived to be at home when he visited Edmund, she kept out of the way in a different part of the house as much as politeness would allow.

Soon after Hugh moved back into Netherculme he suggested that Edmund might like to stay there occasionally for a change of scene – he had converted a downstairs room to a spare bedroom for that very purpose. The offer was accepted with alacrity and within a few weeks it became established that Edmund would spend his Saturday nights there. Lilian was invited, of course, but she laughingly said she would inhibit their male chatter. She could quite happily keep herself occupied at home.

Thirty-one

*L*ilian held a tennis party on a balmy Saturday in July. She had hesitated about it for some time but when she raised the subject with Edmund a couple of weeks earlier he'd wanted her to go ahead. However, when the day arrived she was not in the best of moods because Edmund had insisted on her inviting Hugh, who would take him back to Netherculme in the evening. Worse, he had demanded an invitation for George Bonner, that man who had only half a face. She'd have enough to put up with already, with Edmund's wheelchair always being in the wrong place and her friends not knowing what to say to him. Hugh was too serious and George was frightening. Naturally one felt sorry for him and for what he must have suffered, but really!

Although Lilian was familiar with the sight of the wounded and was sympathetic in principle, she could not conquer her aversion to unsightly deformities. She knew this was wrong but this knowledge only made her irritable.

She was at a loss to know who she could prevail upon to partner them. She said as much to Edmund over the breakfast table.

'That's all right,' he replied, a twinkle in his eye as he buttered a slice of toast, 'as hostess you can take turns with them. They will deputise for me.'

She glared at him.

'My dear Lily, since the tennis is going to take place in my garden and I'm obliged to attend, surely you won't begrudge me a couple of friends, particularly since Hugh and George could do with some gaiety.'

'No, of course not. I just wish – '

'What?'

'Nothing. I suppose I'm in a bad mood because I've been thinking about when we used to play together before the war.'

'We won most of our matches, didn't we? I used to be so proud playing with you.'

'You couldn't have been prouder than I was. We had such fun then.'

'And we shall again. There's no reason why you shouldn't enjoy today. After all, it was your idea.'

Lilian's mood softened, although she still harboured a secret hope that Hugh and George would be tactful and decide not to come. She was to be disappointed.

She partnered Hugh in the opening set.

Her embarrassment started before a ball had been played, when she saw his clothes. They were pre-war whites that he must have dug out of store and, although he had put on some of the weight he had lost, they still looked loose and ungainly. She and all her friends, on the other hand, were the height of elegance, dressed as they were in the latest fashions from Wimbledon. Hugh's play was diffident and clumsy. Just like he used to be before the war, she thought. He went for the ball when she clearly called 'mine' and he left it when she called 'yours', and he smashed repeatedly into the net. Their opponents congratulated themselves on an easy victory, six-two. They both walked off the court flushed and silent, thankful it was over. Lilian marched straight over to where Madge and Violet were sitting, threw down her racquet and said too loudly, 'Well, that's half my duty done.'

Hugh, who had strolled across the lawn towards Edmund,

did not hear her, but as soon as she had spoken she glanced towards the house and looked straight into the eyes of George Bonner, who was standing less than six feet away. She had failed to notice him among the gaggle of people around the drinks table. He flushed scarlet as a poppy over his patchwork face, bowed stiffly and threaded his way, drinks in hand, towards Edmund and Hugh. The other guests, mostly friends from Tiverton, were happy to remain apart from Edmund. Their views were similar to Lilian's: wounded soldiers were all right provided they had the right sort of wound, which Edmund and George had not. They found it difficult to hold a conversation with him and when they did condescend to talk to him they found it impossible to look him in the eye.

Lilian was torn between not wanting to let Edmund down in public and getting what enjoyment she could from the afternoon. She accepted that she would have to sacrifice at least some time to Edmund and his friends. She regretted her lapse of manners and temper, which she had mastered so much better since her row with Hugh. Why was she always so temperamental when he was around? And now she had to make amends to George. It was galling. Pausing while Minster poured her some lemonade (that man really was a godsend), she followed George across the lawn to where Edmund was sitting in his wheelchair. He was placed where he could watch tennis and see everything that was going on while maintaining a discreet distance without appearing rude. George was sitting to one side of him. She noticed that the disfigured part of his face was invisible to herself and the other guests and mentally gave him full marks for tact. The other chair near Edmund was empty; Hugh was lounging on the grass examining his racquet. Both Hugh and George stood up as she approached.

'Ah, here you are, dear,' Edmund greeted her. 'Bad luck about that set.'

She swallowed the obvious retort about its having

nothing to do with luck and everything to do with Hugh's incompetence.

'Sorry I let you down, Lilian,' said Hugh before she could reply. 'My game's rather rusty. It must be a good five years since I last played.'

It was impossible to quarrel with that.

'Of course. It's perfectly understandable. It was good of you to have a go anyway,' she said. 'I owe you an apology for being an ungracious partner.'

'Not at all. Please, have a seat,' Hugh indicated his chair.

'Thank you, but I can't stay.'

'I don't think you've met George recently, have you?' said Edmund.

'Hello, Mrs Potter,' George whispered. He smiled over half of his face and she was surprised to observe that seen from a certain angle he appeared quite boyish and handsome. He turned his face a bit more and the illusion vanished. She shook his hand and bestowed her most radiant smile on him.

'George cycled over,' said Edmund.

'Oh. That must have been hot work.'

'Not at all. I enjoy wheeling along under my own steam. Cars are so stuffy, don't you think?'

Lilian did not think so and changed the subject. 'You aren't dressed for tennis, Mr Bonner. I hope this doesn't mean you're going to let us down,' she said, wishing the opposite.

'I'm frightfully sorry, Mrs Potter, but in my haste I seem to have forgotten my kit.'

Lilian always took people at face value and consequently did not realise that he was offering her a way out of playing with him. 'Well, if you have no clothes of your own you can always borrow Edmund's. You don't mind, do you darling?'

'Not at all. You'll find them a trifle old-fashioned,' Edmund said, casting a look at the other guests, 'but they should fit you all right.'

George made some half-hearted objections which Lilian overrode and soon she was ushering him into the house to take his pick of Edmund's sporting wardrobe. As she led him towards the stairs she failed to notice the canvas bag that he had thrown down near the front door. He glanced at it and was horrified to see the initials G.H.F.B. stare boldly back at him. Realising that it was bound to be the first thing she saw when she came back downstairs he resigned himself to looking foolish.

'Oh,' he squeaked.

'Why, Mr Bonner, how you startled me. Is anything the matter?'

'You will think me extremely foolish, dear Mrs Potter, but I've just this moment remembered. How could I have forgotten? It must be the bump on the head I received during the war.'

I'm afraid I don't understand you. What did you forget?'

'Down there by the door. My bag with my tennis kit. How very foolish of me.'

'Well, that's very convenient. Perhaps you'd like to retrieve it and I'll show you where you can change.'

'Yes, thank you. You're very kind.'

'Don't mention it.'

Knowing Lilian's distaste for physical injuries, Edmund usually visited George at his home so Lilian had had little opportunity to get to know him. Now he was turning out to be everything she feared. She showed him into Edmund's bedroom and left him to find his own way out when he was ready.

She stepped out into the sunlight and saw Edmund beckoning to her. She ambled over to him. Hugh had resumed his former position on the grass and was watching the game that was in progress. He seemed not to notice her approach.

'All right?' Edmund asked her.

'All right?' She threw herself into the nearest chair. 'Honestly! I was taking him upstairs to find some clothes in your wardrobe when he suddenly remembered that he had brought his own after all, and there was his bag sitting large as life by the front door.'

'Perhaps he saw how frustrated you were with the way I played and didn't want to let you down too,' offered Hugh, still looking at the tennis.

Lilian could not see his face and was unable to decide if he was being amusing or was ticking her off.

'Nonsense.' she said, confused. 'And you didn't let me down because you played exactly as I expected. Oh, that came out wrong – I mean, as you said yourself, you haven't played since before the war. You're game's bound to be rusty. I'm sorry, Hugh, the sun is rather hot today – I'm a bit tetchy.'

'I've been thinking,' Edmund said, 'why don't we three motor down to Sidmouth for the day? Take a picnic and have a bathe. Minster will come too, of course, to help me. It's a long time since any of us have been to the seaside.'

'Actually, I went there last week.'

'Oh, I didn't know.'

'I thought I mentioned it. I went there with the Jacksons. On Saturday. You were at Netherculme.'

'Oh, yes.' Edmund turned to his friend. 'What do you say, Hugh?'

'I think it's a grand idea. Lilian, you'll be able to show us everything that's changed.'

'When are you thinking of going?' she asked.

'Soon – before the weather breaks. How about Monday? Is your diary empty then?'

'Yes, I believe it is. I'll have to check but I'm almost sure it is.'

'How about you, Hugh? Would Monday be all right?'

'I think so. I have one or two things to see to but I could probably move them to Tuesday. I'll check when I get home.'

'Excellent. I'm looking forward to splashing around in the water.'

'You? Can you? I mean, is it wise, after your illness?'

'Certainly. I don't see why not. Sea bathing has been recommended for invalids for hundreds of years. Minster and Hugh can help me – if you don't mind that is, old man?'

'Happy to.'

Before Lilian had time to argue, George Bonner appeared to claim her for the tennis court.

'Excuse me, here's my partner. I must go.' She jumped to her feet and went to join George, who was now dressed smartly in whites. Happily for Lilian he was an excellent player and they beat all comers. To round off her fun she noticed Hugh watching him enviously from time to time, though he spent most of the afternoon deep in conversation with Edmund.

Thirty-two

The weather held for the trip to Sidmouth. The sky was the colour remembered from childhood but rarely seen, with a sprinkling of cumulus clouds. Minster made sure Edmund was up in good time and when Hugh arrived the Sydling party were ready and waiting. Mrs Barton had prepared a feast for them. There was a slight awkwardness as they prepared to get into the car. Where would be the best place for Edmund to sit? It was undoubtedly easier to lift him onto the front passenger seat but that would leave Lilian in the back with Minster. He had a knack of effacing himself into the background but she might feel left out. So it was agreed that Edmund would travel in the back with Lilian, and Minster would ride in front with Hugh. With a little effort Minster and Hugh manoeuvred Edmund onto the back seat and Lilian took her place beside him. The wheelchair was stowed and soon the Daimler was loaded up and they drove out of the village.

Lilian was alone with her thoughts for most of the journey, Edmund and Hugh being content to exchange news of army friends or tree-felling or crops. She sighed, and wondered why they had to be so boring. If only they knew what a sacrifice she had made to be with them, missing an exploratory ramble on Exmoor with the Jacksons and the Hunts. Julian Hunt had served in the Guards and had had a good war, reaching the rank of lieutenant-colonel. He was such fun, larger than life and deliciously indiscreet, particularly when he described the Guards' opinion of service battalions. He made her laugh until tears ran down her cheeks. She could not remember when she had last laughed like that with Edmund. It was a long time ago. Poor Julian, he had been so disappointed when she telephoned to say that she was unable to take part in the ramble after all.

While these reflections passed through her mind her eyes were fixed on the back of Hugh's head, directly in front of her. At first she was absorbed in her own thoughts and took no notice of him, but after a while she came back to the present and began to observe him. His head was dark and square from behind, in contrast to Edmund's which was chestnut, curly, rounded. Both of them were touched with grey – how sad in men of their age. He was wearing an open-necked shirt under a cream linen jacket and a fading scar was just visible above the collar below his right ear where the sun had not reached. That must be the bullet wound. How close he had come to death. Death that she had wished on him in a most unforgiveable fit of temper. She moved her hand to reach out and touch it but suddenly realised what she was doing and stopped. She had only raised her hand a matter of inches so Edmund could not have known what she was going to do, if he had noticed at all, but nevertheless she crimsoned and turned her head to look out of the window. What on earth had she been thinking?

'Are you all right, my dear?' asked Edmund after she had remained in that position for several minutes. 'I'm afraid we're being rather boring.'

'I'm fine,' she said. She had cooled down and turned towards him and smiled. 'I'm admiring the scenery.'

No one spoke for a while.

'Do you remember our last outing to Sidmouth?' Edmund broke the silence. 'It was almost this very day five years ago. My God, if we'd known then what we know now.'

'I was just thinking of that too,' said Hugh over his shoulder. 'Just as well we didn't know.'

The car pulled smoothly up the long, winding road to Hembury Fort. From the summit they had a perfect view of Honiton lying between folds of rich pastureland. The heat haze of the previous week had diminished and the town was clearly visible. Here and there the sun was reflected brightly as it caught some shiny object or a ribbon of water. After they had all admired the view Hugh drove on and soon they passed through the town towards the coast.

Lilian wondered how they would manage with Edmund's wheelchair on the shingle beach but Hugh had thought of that. He drove to the Esplanade but instead of turning left towards the fishing boats, where they had gone in 1914, he steered to the right. As they tootled along, avoiding the usual holiday-makers who wandered blindly over the road, he addressed her over his shoulder.

'I hope you don't mind, Lilian, but as Edmund's chair can't cope with the shingle I thought we'd go to a nice quiet spot with a view for the picnic. It isn't far.'

'That's very thoughtful of you.'

Hugh said nothing more and concentrated hard on negotiating the hill that climbed steeply away from the resort. The mass of people thinned out and disappeared altogether before they started the climb, such is the desire of human beings to congregate together and avoid strenuous exercise. At the top they found themselves in an enchanted world of trees and sudden clearings and fields and views. Hugh carefully drove off the road and switched off the engine. The sky was vast overhead and far below the sea looked smooth as velvet. In the distance they could see the happily named Smallstones Point, Crab Ledge and Brandy Point before the land curved out of sight. A whistle sounded in the distance, causing Hugh to shudder slightly, and a trail of white smoke indicated the course of a branch line.

Minster spread rugs on the grass, which was baked hard by two weeks of sunshine.

'Would you prefer to sit in your chair or on the ground, sir?'

'On the ground please, Minster. There's nowhere else to sit for a picnic.'

Minster and Hugh duly eased Edmund out of the car and onto a rug. Lilian walked about to stretch her legs while the men busied themselves.

'I insist that you're a fully paid up member of the picnic, Minster,' Edmund said.

'Thank you, sir. I shall enjoy that.'

★

Hugh was stiff after the drive. He stretched luxuriously then threw himself down on a rug. After four years of war he could make himself immediately comfortable on any piece of ground, as could Minster. Lilian arranged herself elegantly on her rug.

'I love it here,' Edmund stated simply. 'I adore the blueness and the greenness of it. It was an excellent idea of your to come up here, Hugh. Don't you think so, dear?'

'Yes, it was. The town can be so crowded.' She looked at her watch: it was too early to eat. 'Shall you mind if I stretch my legs for a few minutes? There's a sort of path over there which looks ripe for exploring.'

'Of course not. But do be careful. It follows the edge of the cliff by the looks of it.'

'You don't need to worry about me, darling,' she said lightly, getting to her feet and brushing imaginary dust from her linen skirt.

Hugh said nothing but indicated goodbye with a wave of the hand.

He lit a cigarette and lay on his back looking up at the sky. An occasional bird flew into his field of vision and out of it again. Treetops swayed when the breeze caught them. Insects hummed. The air was perfumed with the scent of clover and the tang of the sea, even at this height. Few vehicles and no hikers disturbed them. They chatted desultorily until an hour after noon, when they began to feel hungry. Edmund was starting to show signs of agitation.

'I say, Hugh. You couldn't look out for Lilian, could you, and give her a shout?'

'By all means. I hope she won't be long. I'm feeling starved. Must be the sea air.'

'She's usually the first to feel hungry. I wonder where she can have got to.'

'Don't worry. I'll soon find her. Minster, you'd better stay here with Mr Potter.'

'Very well, sir,' replied Minster.

Hugh jumped to his feet as he spoke and ambled to the path that Lilian had taken. He soon found himself looking down on the sea four hundred feet below. He turned left and followed the well-trodden path that led to the town. He was soon lost from view in a world of bracken and brambles, wild roses and butterflies. The path lost height and before long he could see Sidmouth looking insignificant in its valley. The path wound down the hill, sometimes in sight and sometimes hidden. Before long he spotted Lilian, small as an ant in the distance. He was curious as to where she had gone but had not shared Edmund's anxiety. He put her absence down to making a point. It was obvious to him from the moment Edmund proposed the outing that she would rather not be with them.

He lit a cigarette and waited until she was within hailing range. He whistled, and waved when she looked up.

'Food,' he shouted. 'We're hungry.'

'Coming,' she shouted back.

★

The sun was high in the sky and the path was steep. Lilian saw

Hugh waiting and decided that no matter how difficult the ascent, she would under no circumstances ask for his help. It was hard going: she was wearing inappropriate shoes, and brambles would keep clinging at her skirt, but eventually she reached the place where she had seen him. She was out of breath and very hot. She turned to where he had been standing, ready to chide him for thinking she would need assistance but he had gone, a cigarette butt heeled into the ground the only evidence that he had been there. She waited until her breathing was regular again then strolled nonchalantly to join the men.

'There you are, my dear,' said Edmund, unable to keep the relief out of his voice. 'I was wondering where you'd got to. You were gone such an age.'

He squeezed her hand. 'Do sit down. You look warm.'

She lowered herself gratefully onto the rug beside him.

Hugh was helping Minster lay out the picnic and had his back to her. He looked cool and relaxed, bother him.

'I was expecting to find you at the top of the path,' she said to his back.

'I waited for a while,' he said, turning to look at her, 'but I could see you were managing very well so I thought I'd be more use here.'

He turned away again and busied himself with laying cutlery on the crisp white tablecloth that was groaning with food.

'Minster, I don't suppose there's any lemonade, is there? I'm parched.'

'Certainly, ma'am.' He poured a glass and handed it to her.

'Thank you.' She drank thirstily. 'I'm sorry if I worried you, darling. I didn't realise how far I'd gone. You know what it's like. You turn one corner and look at the view and think there's bound to be another marvellous view from around the next corner so you go there, and then the next one, and so on and so forth. When I realised the time I turned straight round but it was steep and slow.'

'And it's hot today. Never mind, what you need is a swim. It will refresh you nicely. I'm certainly looking forward to mine.'

'Surely you aren't serious about bathing, are you?'

'Never more so. You used to think I looked rather dashing in my bathing dress. Don't tell me you were pretending all the while.'

'No, of course I wasn't. You always looked very handsome. But – well – things have changed since then. I don't mind, but won't people stare?'

'They stare at me anyway, so what's the difference? A chap may as well have some fun while he can.'

'Pie?' Hugh offered a plate of veal and ham pie to Edmund. 'I'll leave you to help yourself, Lilian. Just say what you want passed, old man.'

Edmund took a slice of pie with his fingers. 'Thanks. I'd like some salad as well please, and some Chablis.'

Lilian ate some moody salmon mayonnaise and celery, which she crunched loudly. Making any sort of noise while eating was a solecism in her book, so it was obvious that she was worked up.

'Don't worry, Lilian. It isn't as though any of your friends are likely to see us,' Hugh said.

'I'm not at all concerned about that. I just think it's totally ridiculous of Edmund to go out of his way to make an exhibition of himself, that's all.'

Edmund swallowed a mouthful of cucumber salad. 'I have no particular desire to make an exhibition of myself. It's a hot day, the sea is calm and blue, *ergo* I shall take a dip.'

'Don't you care what people think?'

'No, I don't. I happen to believe that the average woman has more interesting things to gossip about than my legs and the average man has seen far worse sights than me. What do you think, Hugh?'

'I should like a swim if I were in your place,' Hugh said

after he had taken a large sip of wine. He looked away again.

'Oh really! You haven't the least idea of style, either of you.'

'You're too hidebound, my dear. You have fun every day of the week – surely you won't begrudge me a little bit.'

'I didn't mean that,' said Lilian, stung. 'It's just that – well, can't you have fun some other way?'

'No, I don't think so, not today. I'd give worlds for a swim, you know.'

'But you won't be able to swim.'

'Well, a dip then. Same thing.'

The men were hungry but Lilian was too tense to eat more than a few mouthfuls. She pushed her plate aside unfinished and lit a cigarette. Hugh had never seen her smoke before and looked at her with surprise. Edmund, seeing his expression, burst out laughing.

'Don't be shocked, Hugh. Lilian's emancipated. She smokes, she bobs her hair, she wears short skirts, and she knows all the latest dances. Times have changed while you've been away.'

This speech hurt Lilian. It was true, all of it, although there had been a time when he had known all the latest dances as well. They had gaily danced them together. She wished he had not expressed it quite as he had. She smiled and held her cigarette case towards him. She noticed Edmund's eyes slide down to the gold case and up again into her own. She flushed scarlet.

'It was a present,' she said, holding his gaze.

'Very nice. Looks like Bond Street. From anyone in particular?'

'Not really – Julian Hunt. As a matter of fact I was invited up on Exmoor with the Hunts and the Jacksons today but I preferred to be with you.'

'Thank you. I appreciate that. Are those his foul-smelling cigarettes or your own?'

'Mine.'

'Then I should like one, thank you.'

Lilian took out a cigarette, lit it, and passed it to him. She offered Hugh one but he preferred his pipe.

'Bully beef and biscuit can't hold a candle to a picnic like this, can they, Minster?' Hugh said to fill an uncomfortable silence.

'You can say that again, sir. I bless the day I turned my back on that army food. Not that we went hungry when we were resting. But it was a happy day when I never had to face another portion of Maconochie's.'

'You're right there, Minster,' said Edmund.

'Lilian, please give the heartfelt thanks of three ex-soldiers to Mrs Barton. We're eternally grateful to her,' said Hugh with a grin.

Lilian smiled back but the smile did not reach her eyes.

Hugh and Minster cleared away the debris, reminiscing blithely about the army until they were ready to help Edmund into the car again.

★

They retraced their route down the hill and into the town. Hugh had no difficulty finding a convenient place to park on the Esplanade. Lilian went straight off to change. Minster and Hugh helped Edmund into his wheelchair, which between them they were able to carry easily over the pebbled beach. Hugh went back to the vehicle to fetch rugs and towels and their bathing clothes. With expert hands Minster helped Edmund change into his pre-war bathing costume while Hugh changed nearby. Minster had demurred at the prospect of going into the water, pleading his inability to swim, so as soon as they were both ready Hugh lifted Edmund and carried him into the water. Although it was late in July the coldness of the water made them both gasp before they were invigorated by its freshness. Given the season the beach was emptier than Edmund had expected – probably because of the absence of men now, he reflected. A few family groups were sitting here and there and watched him flapping in the water with amused interest but he, in his delight, was blind to them.

★

Lilian, having changed into a navy woollen bathing dress which became her well, was about to rejoin the men when she noticed that Edmund was the centre of attention. She was awash with embarrassment, torn between wanting to disown him and the realisation that she could not. If she had been able to read the thoughts of one tired-looking woman onlooker with four young children – 'What a brave man – his wife is so lucky to have him home, even like that. Oh, my poor Bert,' – she might not have been so precious but she was guided by the self-consciousness of the insecure.

Whether it was the heat of the day or the wine they had drunk she did not know, but now they were behaving like schoolboys, yelling and splashing. She slipped unobtrusively into the water some distance from them. Its cold saltiness made her skin tingle. It is impossible for the average human being to maintain a dark mood when the sun is shining from a perfect sky and the sea is caressing one's skin, and Lilian was no exception. Before long she felt herself mellowing. The water made her dress heavy but it did not prevent her floating on her back for a minute or two, eyes scrunched tight against the glare of the sun. A voluminous cap protected her hair but never mind if it got wet. Rotating onto her front, she swam towards where the men had been. Hugh was swimming out to a raft that had been anchored offshore for the amusement of swimmers, his black head bobbing up and down between the waves. He was clearly better at swimming than playing tennis. Edmund was half-sitting, half-lying at the water's edge so that the gentle waves could lap over his legs. It was an ebb tide, not far from low water so there was no danger of his suddenly being submerged. Nevertheless, Minster was standing nearby, bare-footed and trousers rolled up to the knees in case he needed to dash into the water to help Edmund. He melted discreetly away when Lilian drew near.

Edmund waved to Lilian, a smile creasing his face as it used to do, throwing off the care of the last three years. 'Isn't this too wonderful?' he said as she drew near.

'I can see you're thoroughly enjoying yourself,' she replied, trying to smile.

'I know you think me rather an exhibitionist, my dear, but I do love the sea. It's the first real fun I've had for as long as I can remember.' He paused, and continued more seriously, 'Good of you to give up Julian Hunt for today.'

'Please don't say that. You make me feel so awful.'

'Sorry, I didn't mean to. Truly. I'm glad you enjoy yourself, really I am. There's no reason why you shouldn't. I know I'm rotten company.'

'I wish you wouldn't keep saying that.'

She looked out to sea. Hugh was lounging on the raft. He was looking at a group of sailing boats in the distance, their spinnakers bright against the sea like a fauvist painting.

'Am I very selfish?'

'No, of course you're not. Whatever put that idea into your head?'

'Nothing in particular. But I am. I know it.'

Edmund carved circles in the water with his hand.

'Is Colonel Hunt still the pompous ass that he was before the war?'

'I don't know. I didn't know him then. I met him for the first time in January. He's a friend of Freddie Eliot, Madge's husband. He is a bit full of himself sometimes, I admit. How do you know him?'

'I knew him in a distant sort of way before the war. He hunted with us a few times. It didn't take long to see that he was as dumb and pompous as they come, so I rather avoided his company. I didn't see him after the outbreak of war until our paths crossed shortly after I first went out to France. He was in an estaminet, sitting at a table drinking with some friends when I walked in with some other Devon officers. I saw him and saw that he saw me so I went over to say hello. He cut me dead. He was in a swagger regiment – one of the Guards, and only too clearly looked down his nose at mere service battalions. And now he of all people is giving you cigarette cases. I don't like him, Lily. It gives me the shivers to think he's lavishing attention on you.'

Lilian thought of Julian's humour at the expense of service battalions and suddenly it did not seem so funny. She knew Edmund was the better man but she had been flattered by Julian's attentions, and had been gullible. Luckily, she had not let it go too far, though it was clear that he'd like it to. That was one reason why she had come with Edmund today.

Odd that he had never mentioned meeting Edmund in France. On the other hand, if he had cut Edmund …

'I didn't know. But that's all it is, darling. One cigarette case.'

'Gifts like that from a man like Julian Hunt usually lead to one thing. Are you his mistress?'

'Edmund!'

'Why so shocked? He isn't the sort to worry about having an affair, particularly if the husband is conveniently out of the way. Does he know I'm still alive, by the way?'

'Yes, of course he does. I talk about you often. And we are *not* having an affair. He never –'

'Ah. *He* never. What about you? Would you say no?'

'No. That is, yes. I mean, I'm loyal and faithful to you, Edmund. We've had this conversation before, remember? Nothing's changed as far as I'm concerned. I admit I like to have fun but there's a very firm line which I have no intention of crossing.'

Whether it was the effect of the sea air or the sun or the wine, Lilian could not help being provocative. 'Anyway,' she continued after a pause, 'you said I was to take a lover if I liked.'

'Christ, Lily. Have anyone but him. I can't stand the man, never could. But he'd make use of you and toss you aside when he moved on to the next available woman. I know. I've heard him boast of doing just that. And you're worth so much more than that. Anyway, whether he's your lover or not I don't want him at Sydling. Ever.'

'I doubt if he'd come if he had the chance, given what you said about his cutting you in France.' She paused. 'Thank you for telling me about him. I've been a fool.'

Edmund did not say anything but took her hand, breathing heavily.

They both turned their eyes seawards and looked at Hugh, who was stretched out sunbathing on the raft.

'Hugh would do nicely.'

'Do what nicely?'

'For your lover.'

Lilian laughed. 'Now I know you're teasing me.'

'Why? He's a good man and he needs a woman. Besides, you can't possibly dislike him as much as you make out – nobody could.'

'I don't *dislike* him exactly. He's – well, he's everything I'm not. We just don't get along. We never have and never shall. That's all there is to it. And you're forgetting what I said about having a line I won't cross, no matter how much you egg me on.'

'Well, if you ever change your mind you won't find a better man.'

'That's a matter of opinion. I've never thought as highly of him as you do. He isn't my sort of person. I respect him as your friend and for saving your life, of course, but that's all.'

'All right, all right. Anyway, I didn't really mean that about

Hugh. He needs a woman who'd cherish him, bring him out of himself. Smooth his edges. You'd drive him dotty.'

Lilian did not reply. She wondered if she would ever be able to shake off her feeling of guilt. She had no intention of taking a lover but in the unlikely event that she changed her mind Hugh was the one man absolutely denied her.

'I'll drop Julian,' she said after a pause.

'Thank you, my dear. I hope it won't be difficult for you.'

'No, I don't think it will be.'

Hugh did not seem in any hurry to rejoin them so Edmund waved to indicate that he wanted to get out of the water. Hugh saw him, waved back and dived from the platform. In a couple of minutes he emerged splashing from the water. Lilian was looking in the opposite direction and was surprised to see several female heads looking towards them. Curious, she turned to see what had caught their eye. As Hugh walked through the shallow water towards them it dawned on her for the first time what a fine physique he had. No wonder heads turned. Odd that she had never noticed before. And he was wearing a costume that would not have looked out of place on the Riviera.

★

While Edmund and Lilian were talking Hugh kept an eye on them from the raft. He was concerned that Edmund might be feeling cold but was reluctant to make a move until he was summoned. The sight of Lilian in her bathing dress, reposing half-in, half-out of the water like a siren transfixed him. He wished she would go and change before he had to go back but Edmund beckoned him. He dived in. The sun had been hot and the sea was like a cold shower. He swam energetically and soon joined them. Minster was there too and between the two of them they made light work of lifting Edmund onto a towel a few paces up the beach where he could dry himself and dress.

Lilian hovered nearby. Hugh seemed not to notice her. As he

bent down to lift Edmund she saw the full extent of the scar on his neck and the other on his leg from the Somme, and a knot formed in her stomach.

'I'll go and get out of these wet things,' she said to no one in particular.

'Right ho,' said Edmund, drying himself briskly.

When they were all dressed they had a final welcome drink of lemonade before loading the car for the homeward journey. Conversation was sparse, as it so often is after a bracing day at the seaside. Hugh chose a route along winding country lanes and concentrated on his driving, avoiding the occasional pigs and dogs and hens that wandered in the road. Edmund slumped, exhausted from the unaccustomed activity. Lilian was absorbed in her thoughts – her naïvety concerning Julian Hunt and the lunch engagement next Saturday that she would have to break. Did she mind? At first she thought she might, but no, she didn't mind. She had no reason to doubt what Edmund had told her about Julian's cutting him in France and she thought his behaviour iniquitous. He must have been laughing to himself, playing with Edmund's wife, playing Edmund for a fool. She thought of Edmund's astonishing suggestion about Hugh. The natural progression of her thoughts led her to reflect how skilfully Hugh managed to avoid her – how she seemed to be invisible to him. And who could blame him? She'd do the same if he had told her that he hated her and wished her dead. No, that was untrue – she would not. She would be far less charitable than he was. What a true friend he was to Edmund. He had a great deal to do at home and then there was his painting but he always found time to be with Edmund if he was needed. And he put up with her company for Edmund's sake no matter how much he must want to avoid her.

They reached home sooner than Lilian expected. Staying only long enough to help Minster with Edmund and to unload the car, Hugh started up the engine again and headed home.

Thirty-three

Lilian was true to her word: she did see less of Julian Hunt after her conversation with Edmund. It had been awkward, lying to Julian that Edmund was unwell and needed her, but he was probably man of the world enough to understand. She did not think he would regret her for a minute – what would one conquest more or less mean to him, if what Edmund told her was true, and she believed him. That aside, her life continued through August and September much as it had through the previous two months: with tennis until the weather turned, golf, and outings. At weekends she was free to stay with friends or remain quietly at home while Edmund went to Netherculme. She rarely saw Hugh after the outing to Sidmouth. He was busy at home during the week and on Saturday afternoons Minster drove Edmund to Netherculme. It was a nuisance not having the use of the car but she welcomed Edmund's visits there for his sake.

★

Edmund enjoyed his weekends. Hugh's company was peaceful and undemanding. They could spend many hours sitting smoking and reading or playing chess in comfortable silence. Hugh's studio was in a converted outbuilding and sometimes Edmund watched him at work. If the weather was good, they would go for long walks in the nearby lanes, Hugh pushing the wheelchair with practised ease when Edmund tired. The room that Hugh had converted for him was well appointed and thoughtfully planned for the invalid, and an electric bell linked directly to Minster's bedroom.

In contrast, the drive home on Sunday evenings was the bleakest hour of his week. Minster sensed his despondency and at first tried to make cheerful conversation until Edmund said to him one day, 'Thank you for trying to cheer the baby, Minster. It's very thoughtful of you. But I'd rather not chat, if you don't mind.'

'Very well, sir.' After that, he always left Edmund to his thoughts and waited for him to start a conversation, if any.

They usually travelled at the time of day that was neither day nor night. On clear evenings Edmund would insist on having the hood down in spite of the chill that intensified as the days shortened. He would reflect with satisfaction on the weekend before wondering how he was going to survive another week of idleness and solitude, for Lilian was bound to be out most of the time. From there, his mind would turn to her weekend. He imagined gaiety and laughter and good-looking, whole-bodied men paying court to her. Men who had fought their war either at home or on the staff, or self-important survivors like Julian Hunt. He knew his mood always improved when he reached home but that insight singularly failed to lessen the misery of the journey.

One Sunday midway through September Edmund insisted on having the hood down as usual. There was a freshening breeze although the sky was clear. He was well wrapped up in a thick coat and cap. Minster judiciously placed a rug over his legs which he immediately pushed aside.

'I'm not an old woman, you know, Minster.'

'No sir. I wouldn't dream of suggesting such a thing. But if I may be so bold, sir, these autumn evenings can be treacherous even though the days are fine. I'm warmed by the heat of the

engine but sitting in the back here you don't get that benefit.'
He knew better than to suggest raising the hood.

'I promise to pull the rug over me if I feel cold, if that makes
you feel any better.'

'Just make sure you do,' said Hugh, amused by the weekly
battle of wills between the two men.

'Don't you start. You're like a gaggle of mother hens. Right,
Minster. Let's go before it gets completely dark. Bye, Hugh old
man. See you next weekend.'

Hugh waved them off.

On this occasion they were deceived by the clear sky and
before they had been driving for ten minutes heavy clouds had
scuttled across and they felt the first drops of rain.

'I'd better stop and put up the hood, sir,' said Minster.

'It's only a few drops. Carry on as we are,' replied Edmund.

After another quarter of a mile, without warning, the whole
valley was lit up by huge forks of lightning which seemed to
rend the sky from heaven to earth. A clap of thunder sounded
almost directly overhead, making both men jump. At the same
time the deluge started. Visibility was reduced to nothing and
Minster swerved blindly to one side of the road and leapt out
of the car. Already he was soaked through. Edmund helped
him raise the hood and between them it was soon fixed but
not before the inside of the car had become saturated. They
sat shivering as the rain beat down.

'Minster, I owe you an apology. You were right and I was
wrong and we've both got a soaking because of it. I know we're
half drowned but it would be dangerous to drive on while it's
lashing down like this. It will soon pass, I expect. Cigarette?'

He offered his case to Minster, who gratefully took a
cigarette and offered a light to Edmund in return. The master
could be a stubborn blithering so-and-so sometimes but he
was always ready to admit it when he made a mistake. One
could put up with a lot when a man did that. He had known

some officers who would have cut out their tongues rather than acknowledge they were human. More fool them. They smoked in silence, Edmund trying not to dwell on how cold and wet he felt, Minster concerned that being soaked would do Edmund no good, and he ought to get him home and out of his clothes as soon as possible.

Edmund might not have seen the storm coming but he was correct in believing it would soon pass. Fifteen minutes later they were on their way again, carefully negotiating roads that were running with water. He was thankful that Sydling stood on raised ground. When Minster lifted him into his wheelchair he was shivering violently. He had never known such cold, not even in the trenches. Minster quickly wheeled him indoors and asked Mary to fetch hot water bottles while he got Edmund out of his wet clothes and into his pyjamas and put him to bed.

'Please tell my wife I'd like to see her,' Edmund said to Mary when she brought the bottles.

'I'm sorry, sir, but Mrs Potter telephoned a few minutes before you arrived to say that she had set out for home but the road was impassable and she'll be staying the night at Pinham.'

'Damn,' was Edmund's only response.

Minster left the room and returned with a large glass of brandy. 'Drink this, sir. It will help fight off the chill.'

'Used to use whisky for that in the trenches. I never drank so much in my life.'

'Needs must, sir.'

He went out and left Edmund to sleep. When he took in his cup of tea in the morning he found Edmund feverish and immediately summoned Doctor Lowman. A severe chill was diagnosed and Edmund received a stern rebuke for driving in the night air without so much as a rug, never mind the foolhardiness of trusting it not to rain at this time of year. The patient smiled abjectly and tried not to shiver.

Lilian telephoned from Pinham later in the morning. Minster

told her that Edmund had caught a chill and had seen the doctor, who said there was no cause for concern. She had a pang of misgiving but asked him to tell Edmund that Dolly had invited her to stay on until Wednesday, unless he would rather she came straight back. Minster checked with Edmund: although he would dearly have loved her to be nearby he saw no reason to ask her to hurry home.

'Minster,' Lilian said when he passed on Edmund's message. 'Please promise you'll telephone me immediately if there's any change in my husband's condition. I'm relying on you.'

'Yes, ma'am. Of course.'

'Thank you. I'll telephone again tomorrow.'

The doctor was confident that Edmund's temperature would return to normal within forty-eight hours but on Tuesday evening it went up. He was flushed and his breathing became rapid, shallow, and painful and he coughed a good deal. Minster sent for the doctor again.

'Why has my temperature gone up?' Edmund asked him.

'I'm afraid your soaking on Sunday has done you no good at all, my dear Potter. What started out as a regular chill has turned into pneumonia.' The doctor had a rare and laudable habit of being honest with his patients.

'The prognosis?'

'That rather depends on you. You don't need me to tell you that you have a remarkable constitution. Frankly, I didn't expect you to come through your influenza last year. However, I'll be honest with you and say that I don't know how much damage was done to your lungs at that time. We're you ever gassed at all?'

'No, thank God.'

'Well, that's something. We can only keep you warm and do little more than wait and see. If necessary, I'll move you to hospital.'

'No, hospital won't be necessary. Will you promise me something?'

The doctor hedged. 'I never make promises until I know what is being asked of me.'

'Very proper of you,' said Edmund, raising a smile. 'What I ask is simple. If I start sinking I want to be sure that you will give me no treatment whatsoever.'

'Let me be quite clear about this,' said the doctor quietly. 'You're asking me to let the disease take its course.'

'Yes.'

'My dear man, this is a shameful confession for a medical man to have to make but there is precious little that we can do in any case. Be that as it may, I now ask you to repeat what you just said.'

Edmund repeated his request calmly and without hesitation. 'This isn't a spur of the moment thing,' he added. 'I've wanted this opportunity for three years and have been waiting for it. I thought it had come last year but thanks to your good offices and those of Nurse Dale and my wife it didn't happen.'

'I see.' Doctor Lowman had seen too many young men like Edmund. He would probably want the same if their roles were reversed.

'Would you like me to contact Nurse Dale and see if she's able to come and take care of you? It will be a heavy burden on Minster and your wife otherwise.'

'Thank you, but only if she isn't too diligent.'

'As I said, there's very little we can do medically but she will be able to keep you comfortable. There's no need to suffer more than you need, you know.'

'One final thing,' said Edmund as the doctor placed his stethoscope in his bag and closed it. 'I beg you to keep this conversation from my wife. She is to know nothing.'

'Very well. But I insist on sending for Mrs Potter first thing in the morning. Did you say she's due back tomorrow anyway?'

'Yes.'

'Well, I would advise Minster to telephone to her this

evening to let her know that you have pneumonia. She won't thank you for being kept in the dark about that. We don't want her to have a nasty surprise when she gets home.'

After the doctor left Edmund felt more at peace than he had done since the Somme.

Even though Lilian would probably be sitting down to dinner he asked Minster to telephone straight away and ask her to come home first thing in the morning. He did not want to give her an uneasy night but he was concerned that Dolly might persuade her to stay longer and go out for the day tomorrow. He did not want to risk missing her. Minster did as he was bid. As soon as he had spoken to Lilian he rejoined Edmund.

'Mrs Potter was deeply concerned about you, sir. She was all for coming straight home. Given the lateness of the hour I suggested that she remain there overnight and I will drive over and collect her before breakfast. I hope that will suit you.'

'Yes, thank you Minster. There's no need for her to go rushing around the countryside in the middle of the night. I'm not that ill. I'd like you to do something else now – send a telegram to Mr Brodrick. I would ask you to telephone to him but he hates the contraption – has done since the war.'

'That's very understandable, if I may say so,' said Minster. He took down the details.

Soaked in storm on Sunday. Chill now pneumonia. Beastly. Things to say. Come tomorrow if you can. Edmund.

★

Hugh was surprised to receive a telegram so late. He tore it open immediately and was filled with misgivings. Edmund had not been strong since the Somme and by a miracle he had already survived one serious illness. Hugh doubted that he could survive another. That must be why he wanted him. He would be under no illusions.

He went to bed but was unable to find sleep. In the early

hours after tossing and turning and thinking of the Somme he gave up the struggle, dressed and went down to the library where he built up a fire and sat smoking his pipe until morning.

★

Minster also passed a fitful night. He was devoted to Edmund and was deeply concerned about him. He rose before dawn and went to check on the patient, who was sleeping in spite of his laboured breathing. He left the room as silently as he had entered it and went to the kitchen, where Mrs Barton was already bustling about.

'How is the master this morning?' she asked as he walked in.

'His breathing's bad but he's sleeping, which is a good sign.'

'He's such a good man and so hard done by, with the awful war. I said special prayers for him last night.'

Minster had no such consolation, having lost his faith in France.

'He's a strong man, Mrs Barton. You saw him come through the influenza which took off many a healthier body. I've no doubt he'll see this off too. The mistress will be here for breakfast. I'm going to fetch her shortly.'

Mrs Barton pursed her lips meaningfully.

'Now don't go judging her, Mrs Barton. Mrs Potter is fond of company and Mr Potter isn't lively nowadays. He's happy for her to be with her friends.'

'That's as may be, Mr Minster, but it's one thing to say something and another to mean it in your heart. You didn't know them before the war. So happy and in love they were.'

'The war's changed many things,' said Minster with a sigh.

Mary came in and put an end to the conversation.

Minster looked at his watch. 'I'll just look in on him again and then go and fetch Mrs Potter,' he said.

★

Lilian had said her goodbyes before retiring for the night since the household kept late hours and Dolly was unlikely to be up when Lilian left. She too had slept badly and was glad to hear the nearby church strike six at last. She dressed quickly and waited at the landing window to catch the earliest sight of the car.

'How is my husband, Minster? What did the doctor say?' she asked as soon as they were on the way home.

'He was asleep when I left him, ma'am, and also when I looked in on him during the night. I telephoned to you as soon as he'd seen the doctor yesterday. He said we are to keep Mr Potter comfortable. He's also going to see if Nurse Dale can come.'

'Oh, I'm glad about that. She's very capable. I have great faith in her.'

'Mr Potter also instructed me to send a telegram to Mr Brodrick asking him to come and see him today if he can.'

'Oh.'

An hour after leaving Halberton to fetch Lilian, Minster pulled up in front of the house and turned off the engine. Lilian leapt out of the car and rushed indoors. She met the doctor coming out of Edmund's bedroom.

'Ah, my dear Mrs Potter,' he said. 'I thought I'd just look in on the patient before I begin my surgery. You'll find him quite comfortable.' He stood aside for Lilian to enter. He closed the door behind him and left the house.

'Hello, my dear,' said Edmund.

She sat down on the bed and studied his face which was as pale as she had ever known it. 'I'm so sorry I wasn't here for you. I thought you had a simple chill and would be better by now. I shouldn't have dreamed of staying away otherwise.'

'That's all right. It was my fault for insisting on having the hood down when we drove back from Netherculme. Minster had better judgement but I insisted.' He paused to cough. 'My fault entirely. You know what the storm was like. We got drenched. Minster's shrugged it off but I took a chill. That's all it was at first, which is why I didn't ask you to hurry back. But I'm so glad to see you now. I can't tell you how glad.'

He coughed again.

'I gather Doctor Lowman's going to try and get Nurse Dale again. I do hope she can come,' Lilian said when he was quiet again.

'She can. She'll be here later. He told me just now.'

'I'm so glad. She isn't going to stop me nursing you as well, though,' Lilian said, and leant over to kiss him.

Minster entered with Edmund's early morning tea.

'Ah, routine must go on,' said Edmund.

Minster smiled. 'Mrs Barton asked me to inform you that breakfast will be ready in ten minutes, ma'am.'

'Thank you, Minster. I'd better go and sort myself out.' She went out and left Edmund in Minister's care, with a promise to be back as soon as she had breakfasted.

Nurse Dale arrived shortly after eleven o'clock. Mary had prepared her former room for her and as soon as she was settled – which took only a few minutes – she made her way to Edmund's room. Lilian was sitting with him. The room was cosy and a cheerful fire burned in the grate. Edmund was propped up in bed. Lilian was reading to him. They both looked up as she entered, a broad smile on her face.

'Well now. Who'd have thought I'd be seeing you again so soon,' she said as soon as they had welcomed her. 'I hear you've been a silly boy, Mr Potter.'

Lilian laughed.

When she was previously at Sydling Nurse Dale's occasional scolding made Edmund feel that he was back in the nursery. Then it had annoyed him but now it was strangely reassuring. It was as though he had given up responsibility for himself, a feeling that had been growing since his conversation with the doctor the previous evening.

'I'm glad you could come, Nurse, even if you do bully me,' he said. 'Doctor Lowman didn't know if you'd be available at such short notice.'

'I did have to rearrange a couple of things, I don't mind admitting, but it was no real inconvenience to anyone. As luck would have it only two days ago I finished looking after a new mother.'

The nurse, as efficient as ever, soon organised Minster, Mrs Barton and Lilian, seeing to it that no detail of care for Edmund was overlooked.

While she was sitting drinking coffee with Edmund after lunch Lilian heard a car draw up outside.

'I wonder who that can be.'

'I hope it's Hugh. I asked him to come over if he could.'

'Oh yes, of course. Minster mentioned it while he was bringing me back.'

Before they could say any more Minster opened the door and announced Hugh.

'Hello, old man. Sorry to hear about your illness. Good afternoon, Lilian.'

'Hello, Hugh.'

'My dear, do you mind? – there's some business I need to discuss with Hugh.'

'No, of course not. I'll leave you to it. Send Minster if you need me.'

She went out and closed the door.

★

Hugh sat down in the seat Lilian had just vacated. He could feel her warmth, which caused his mind to flutter.

'I got your telegram last night but I waited until now in case you had the doctor and things this morning. I hope I did right. How are you, truthfully?'

'There's no need to look so worried. Thanks for coming.

280

And yes, it was rather busy this morning. Doctor Lowman was here, then Lilian came back, then Nurse arrived. I was done in but I had a bit of a sleep and some medicinal poached fish and I'm not so bad now.'

'I heard the storm on Sunday and knew you must have been caught in it. I should have insisted that you had the hood up. You and your stubbornness.'

'You've nothing to reproach yourself with, neither has Minster. It was my fault entirely. The storm came out of nowhere. I caught a chill. The doctor didn't think anything of it but it suddenly went wrong and here I am with pneumonia.'

He coughed and shifted on the pillow to breathe more easily. 'I asked you to come because I want you to know something.'

Hugh waited while Edmund marshalled his thoughts.

'Can you guess?'

'No.'

'You probably can but you're too infernally tactful to say. I've asked the doctor not to hold me back if he sees that I'm on the way out, and to make sure that Nurse does the same.'

Hugh looked at him in silence.

'You're not surprised?'

'No.'

'Do you propose to argue with me?'

'No. I couldn't. I've often wondered what it would have been like if our positions had been reversed. I don't know that I could have borne it any better than you have – probably a darned sight worse. No, I'm not going to argue, apart from the fact that I'll bloody well miss you after … Still, who knows what will happen.'

'No, old man. I know.'

'Does Lilian know?'

Edmund shook his head, which immediately provoked a fit of coughing.

When he was calm again Hugh said, 'You mentioned about her coming back this morning. Has she been away?'

'She didn't intend to stay away but she was visiting Dolly Tranter on Sunday. Dolly's chauffeur was driving her home when the storm caught them and the road became impassable so they turned back. Then Dolly asked her to stay on until today.'

Hugh looked glum.

'She wasn't to know how it would turn out. I only had a chill, after all. She telephoned on Monday. I asked Minster to say there was no reason for her to hurry back.'

He paused to cough. Hugh offered him some water but he waved it away.

'Then last night Minster telephoned to her as soon as the doctor left,' he continued. 'She wanted to come straight away but I didn't see any point in her rushing around the country in the middle of the night so he fetched her early this morning.'

They lapsed into silence. A carriage clock ticked comfortingly in the background. Edmund looked as though he were falling asleep.

'Hugh,' he said after a while.

'Yes?'

'Afterwards, will you see that she's all right? Keep an eye on her. Make sure she doesn't get in with the wrong crowd, that sort of thing?'

Hugh didn't know what to say. There was as much likelihood of Lilian taking any notice of him as of King Canute holding back the sea.

'I'll do my best but she – I doubt that she'll listen to me. Forgive me for speaking freely.'

'Please do. You know, I've been hoping that after my death you and she would get together.'

'I'm afraid you're wasting your hopes. I'm – fond – of Lilian, very fond, but you know how she feels about me. Complete anathema. Just different types, I suppose. But you can be sure I'll do my best for her.'

'Thank you. She can be rather silly sometimes.' Edmund spoke fondly, not critically. 'The war should never have happened to her. She couldn't adjust to it. I've been a sad disappointment to her.'

What could Hugh say? 'She isn't the only one who struggled to adjust, not by a long way.'

Nurse Dale bustled in and remonstrated with Hugh for tiring the patient. He rose and left Edmund with a promise to come back the following day. He went home with a heavy heart and picked a quarrel with Robbins, his steward.

He arrived early the following morning and was shown into the dining room where Lilian was finishing breakfast.

'How is he today?' he asked.

'Much the same as yesterday, according to Nurse. She rules with an iron hand and hasn't allowed me to see him yet. Won't you have some breakfast?'

'Thank you. I'd welcome a cup of coffee.'

She rang the bell.

'Mary, please bring another cup and some fresh coffee,' she said when the maid appeared. 'Are you sure you won't have something to eat, Hugh?'

'No, thank you. I had breakfast before I set out.'

Mary went out and soon returned with the coffee. Hugh was thankful to have something to do with his hands.

'How are you?'

'Me? I'm well, thank you. Why?'

'It's an anxious time for Edmund. I wondered how you were bearing up.'

She placed her cup carefully on its saucer. 'I am anxious about him. I'm worried sick. He isn't strong nowadays.' She paused. 'Why didn't you make sure the hood was up on the car when he left you?'

'Have you ever tried to make him do something he's set his mind against?'

She smiled. 'Oh yes. He can be stubborn all right.'

'Minster wanted the hood up from the start but Edmund wouldn't hear of it. We'd go through the same performance every week. Unfortunately this time the weather turned against them.'

'He can be a complete idiot sometimes – Edmund, I mean.'

'No, Lilian. I must disagree with you there. He's no fool. He has a reason for everything he does.'

'You don't know him as well as I do.'

'Just so.'

Hugh stirred his coffee. 'Lilian, this isn't the time for us to quarrel. We can do that as much as we like when Edmund's better.'

'For once I agree with you. Truce?'

'Truce.'

'How could he want to get soaked? It doesn't make sense.'

'The storm was very sudden. You were caught in it too, I believe.'

'Yes, I was.'

Hugh finished his coffee. Lilian sat still, looking at nothing in particular.

'I think I'll go and stretch my legs outside for a while if you don't mind,' he said, not being able to think of anything else to talk about. If he remained in the house Lilian would feel obliged to keep him company, which they would both rather avoid. 'Would you mind asking someone to fetch me when I can see Edmund?'

'Of course.'

Edmund's condition had remained stable during the night and soon Hugh was able to join him. He sat with him for an hour, neither of them saying much.

The next few days followed the same pattern.

★

Doctor Lowman expected the crisis to come in the second week and checked on him every day. Seven days after he became ill Edmund's temperature crept higher; he was racked with pain every time he coughed and now he gasped with every breath as though he were fighting for air. Nurse Dale sat with him all night.

The next day, when they were alone, Edmund said to Hugh, 'It won't be long now but I'm worried about Nurse. I hope she doesn't pull out all the stops to keep me going.'

'Hasn't the doctor had a word with her?'

'No. He probably doesn't think it necessary.'

'In that case there's no need to worry. I wish there was something I could do. I feel so helpless.'

'Oh, but you are doing something. Your being here is immensely comforting. We've been brothers, you and I, for so many years.'

Soon Edmund drifted into sleep. Hugh rose quietly to his feet and left him. When she saw him leave Lilian slipped into the room and took his place beside Edmund. She sat with him through the evening, holding his hand. He pressed her fingers to his lips from time to time. He lapsed into sleep again at nine o'clock. Nurse Dale wanted to relieve Lilian but she insisted on staying with Edmund, so the nurse kept vigil from the hall and supplied Lilian with regular cups of tea. Edmund did not wake again and died in that bleak hour around three o'clock when the slender thread uniting body and soul is at its weakest. When his breathing ceased she laid her head on his chest and sobbed.

Part Three

Thirty-four

*F*orgive me for troubling you with a detail at this time, ma'am, but would you like me to telephone to Mr Brodrick in the morning before he leaves home? It would be awkward for him if he were to come here as usual,' Minster said to Lilian after the nurse had laid out Edmund. The entire household was up, moving silently and speaking only when necessary, in hushed voices.

'That's very thoughtful of you, Minster, but I had better tell him. They were so close – it will be a terrible blow to him. I doubt if I can sleep but in case I do drop off, please wake me at seven o'clock.'

'Certainly, ma'am.' Minster turned to leave the room.

'Oh, Minster,' Lilian called out.

'Yes, ma'am.'

'It's rather early to talk of these things but I'm aware of course that my husband's –' Her voice trembled and she paused to control it. 'That you're placed awkwardly. I have no need of a valet as you must realise but I do hope you'll stay with me until after the funeral. Would you like me to ask Mr Brodrick if he can help you find another situation? I'd be more than happy to give you the most fulsome reference. My husband thought so highly of you. You made an enormous difference to his life – to both our lives.'

'That would be exceedingly generous of you, ma'am. Thank you.'

Mrs Barton ushered Lilian to bed with a warm milky drink and a hot water bottle. Lilian complied, grateful that someone had taken over responsibility for her. She felt numb and incapable. In the darkness of her bedroom she lay awake revisiting episodes from her life with Edmund, weeping uncontrollably at the most trivial memories. She did not sleep and was up and dressed by the time Minster called her.

'Excuse me, sir. Mrs Potter is on the telephone and is anxious to speak to you,' Aldhelm said to Hugh as he was coming downstairs to breakfast.

Hugh was expecting it but nevertheless his stomach lurched and he put his hand on the banister to steady himself.

'Thank you, Aldhelm.'

He went to the valet's room where the telephone was located.

'Hello, Lilian. Hugh here.'

'Oh Hugh,' Lilian said and went silent. He thought he heard a sob and stared hard at the wall.

'My dear Lilian. Is it Edmund?'

'Yes. He went just after three o'clock. It was −' she sobbed again − 'very peaceful.'

'I'm more sorry than I can say.'

'Thank you.' A pause and another sob. 'I knew you'd want to know as soon as possible.'

'Yes. I appreciate your calling. Is there anything − anything at all I can do? Would you like me to come over?'

'You're very kind but there's no need. There is one thing you may be able to do, though.'

Hugh waited hopefully.

'I promised Minster I'd ask if you could help him find a new position. Would you be able to do that? I'll give him the very best reference.'

'Of course I shall. It had occurred to me that he would

be out of a position should – should this happen. Please tell him I'd be more than happy to put out feelers, though I can't promise anything.'

'Thank you so much, Hugh.'

They were interrupted by the operator telling them their time was up.

'We've finished,' said Lilian. 'Goodbye, Hugh.'

'Goodbye. Look after yourself.' The line went dead.

Hugh was devastated. It was kind, very kind of Lilian to call him. He longed to comfort her but that was out of the question. He might as well try and fly to the moon. And he'd miss Edmund like hell. Poor soul, his life had been an arid, painful struggle since the Somme. He ought to be glad that Edmund had been released at last, but what a gap there'd be in his own life now.

Later that morning he sat down in his study to compose a letter of condolence. He struggled with it for an hour, by which time the wastepaper basket was overflowing with crumpled drafts, the air was thick with pipe smoke and he had worked himself into a thoroughly bad temper. Nothing he wrote seemed right. Drafts veered wildly from stiff formality to downright obsequiousness. What to say when the last three years had been hell for Edmund and difficult for Lilian? This is ludicrous, he told himself, thinking of the many hundreds of letters he had written to families of soldiers killed in the war. The kind lies telling them what they wanted to hear – 'he died instantly from a single bullet to the head'. Even though each one pained him he could knock them out in a couple of minutes. In the end he decided to put down the truth. Edmund had been the brother he never had. Ever since the Somme he had wondered if he'd done the right thing in helping save Edmund. With the benefit of hindsight should he have let him die? He knew he would have to do the same if they were to go through it again. The instinct to preserve life is so great. He would miss him enormously. He hoped that with time Lilian would remember the good times she and Edmund enjoyed. If there was anything he could do, et cetera, et cetera.

The funeral was arranged for Thursday the following week. In the meantime Hugh busied himself in finding a position for Minster. As luck would have it, a friend from the Devons was looking for someone because his man had recently got married and decided to go and run a public house with his wife in Suffolk. He would be happy to interview Minster. The position would be in London. Would the man mind that? Hugh wrote to Minster with the good news and details.

★

The funeral took place on a blustery day of sunshine and showers in the church where Edmund and Lilian had been married seven years earlier. Although Hugh arrived in good time he found that half the pews were already full. He saw George Bonner signalling to attract his attention and went to sit with him. By the time the service began there was standing room only. The whole of Edmund's life was reflected in the congregation. Hugh looked around and recognised a smattering of school and university friends – the few who were still alive; ex-soldiers, some whole, some disabled – looking serious but not overly distressed. After all, Edmund was just another officer gone west, though he was a good man but then so were most of them. There were hunting friends who were too old to have fought, looking shame-faced; workers from the Potter estate; Minster with moist eyes; Mrs Barton and the maids openly crying; distant relatives; village neighbours; the doctor and his wife looking solemn; Nurse Dale dabbing her eyes; the rector's wife looking around and wondering how everyone would fit into the small church and hoping the rain would hold off until it was all over.

Finally Lilian arrived with Edmund's parents, who looked

bowed and beaten at the loss of their one remaining son. Arthur Potter walked slowly, supported by a stick. His wife leaned heavily on his other arm. The only consolation – scant though it was – was that Edmund would be buried in England, unlike Noel whose grave was in France and which they would probably never see. Lilian was heavily veiled, so Hugh was unable to see her face. He barely took in a word of the service, his mind reliving memories, some fresh, others buried for years under the impedimenta of events. At last they could move outside. His family and a small group of people chosen by Edmund went to the graveside in a distant corner of the churchyard for the burial. Others stood around near the church in small groups, silent or talking with hushed voices. Hugh went to the grave. Lilian frequently wiped her eyes. The rector droned on in his reedy, intellectual voice but finally came to the blessing. It was over. Hugh stayed back while the mourners moved away. He bent his head and offered a silent prayer.

He was invited back to the house afterwards but dawdled in the churchyard, having no desire to make small talk and knowing that Lilian and the family would be some time talking to well-wishers. He heard someone approaching behind him and turned to see Minster.

'This is not the right occasion, I know, sir, but I'd like to thank you for your exceedingly kind help.'

'My pleasure, Minster. It was the least I could do. Mr Potter was sorry he was going to leave you in the lurch. Have you seen Mr Giles?'

'Yes, sir. I went up to Town the day before yesterday. We seemed to like each other and I'm to start with him next week.'

'Excellent. You won't mind being in London, I take it.'

'Not at all. In fact, I'm looking forward to it. To tell you the truth, sir, I've always had a hankering to go there, not but what my position with Mr Potter didn't suit me well. The poor soul.'

'Quite so. But he's gone to a better place now. He was such

an active man, you know. He was never able to get used to his helplessness after he was wounded.'

'No sir. But at least he came home and was able to say his goodbyes, even though it took a long time, unlike many men.' He shook his head. 'He always had a cheerful word for men he could see were a bit despondent in the trenches. More's the pity that he wasn't able to cheer himself.'

'Indeed.'

They stood side by side looking silently at the grave until Minster remembered himself.

'Excuse me, sir. I have to get back to the house to help out. It's my final duty for Mrs Potter.'

'Of course.'

The crowd was thinning out and Hugh felt obliged to go and mingle. Soon the remainder moved away and he walked slowly to Sydling. He had not spoken to Lilian since she told him of Edmund's death. He wondered how she was coping. She was at the other end of the room and he thought the day would finish without his being able to speak to her, apart from a perfunctory greeting when he walked in. After the meal he was talking to Arthur Potter over a whisky in the drawing room when he was aware of someone at his side.

'Excuse me, Father, but do you mind if I borrow Hugh for a few minutes?' said Lilian.

'Go ahead, my dear. We were just chewing the fat.'

Hugh was surprised but not unwilling to follow Lilian into the hall, where she stopped by the window and turned to him. Now that he was near her he could see lines of grief on her face.

'I needed to speak to you away from the crowd,' she said in a low voice. 'I want to thank you for your very kind letter. I should have replied but the truth was, I didn't know how to. I hope you're not offended.'

'Not in the least. I didn't expect a reply.'

'What you said about the Somme – please don't ever think you did wrong in saving Edmund. You did the only thing a decent human being could.'

'Thank you for saying that. It means a lot to me.'

They both looked out of the window.

'How have you been?' he asked, eventually.

'Up and down. We – we had to make a lot of adjustments in the last few years but I'm sorrier than I can say that he's gone. The house is so empty without him. It's silly things like the smell of his pipe or the way he breathed when I played the piano. But enough about me. How are you? He was closer to you than to Noel in many ways. It can't be easy for you.'

'The last few days have been pretty miserable, I admit. He hated being an invalid, as you know better than I. We have to remember that he's free from all that now and try to be happy for him.'

'If only it were that easy. By the way, thank you for helping Minster. I'm glad he has somewhere to go. He's very excited about living in London.'

'I'm pleased I could help.'

The drawing-room door opened and some guests came out to say goodbye to Lilian. Hugh melted away, and soon he too was on his way home.

Thirty-five

*I*n the following months Hugh busied himself at Netherculme: there was still a great deal to be done after more than four years of neglect. Now he threw himself into it with even more energy. From time to time he disappeared into his studio and painted in a frenzy, working out his grief on graphic scenes from the war.

He did not hear from Lilian after the funeral and their circles were so entirely different that the only way he might have news of her was either through chance or from the Potters. But Edmund's death was the last straw for them. They finally closed up the house, put the estate up for sale and moved to Bournemouth. He exchanged cards with them at Christmas but they had merely sent greetings and no news.

The only news he had of Lilian was a letter from Max Hubert informing him that she had asked him to sell Edmund's painting. A new public gallery in London snapped it up for a handsome sum but this did nothing to mitigate his sense of rejection.

His promise to Edmund that he would keep an eye on Lilian never left Hugh's mind and, finding himself in the neighbourhood of Halberton one day in February 1920, he decided to call on her after visiting Edmund's grave.

The churchyard looked dismal and bare under a leaden sky. He was glad he had thought to stop in Cullompton and buy some flowers. He placed them on the grave, wondering how often Lilian did the same. There was no evidence that anyone had been there recently, which surprised and saddened him. He looked across to the upper floors of Sydling, visible beyond the churchyard wall. Smoke was curling from a chimney, a sure sign that someone was in. Leaving his car where he had parked it near the church, he walked the short distance round to the main entrance in case Lilian thought it impertinent if he were to take the usual short cut across the garden. He rang the bell. There was no response and he was about to ring again when the door opened. He was mildly surprised to see a different maid.

'Good afternoon. I've called on the off-chance of finding Mrs Potter at home.'

'Mrs Potter? No sir. Mrs Potter hasn't lived here for a while now. Not since November, I think it were.'

'Oh. Then the house is empty,' said Hugh, taken aback.

'No, sir. Mrs Drake and her sister Miss Pottinger live here. They bought the house from Mrs Potter.'

'Bought it? You're telling me that Mrs Potter sold this house and has moved away permanently?'

'Yes, sir.'

'She moved away in November. And she said nothing.'

'Yes, sir.'

'Well I'm blowed. November. That would be too soon for her to have married again.' This was spoken to himself rather than to the maid but she was a kind girl and took pity on the handsome gentleman. He seemed genuinely upset.

'No sir, she weren't married again. Least, not so far as I know. She went off to live in London. Said she'd had enough of Devon now her husband were dead. She said there were nothing to keep her here.'

Hugh stared at the girl.

''Scuse me if I'm talking out of turn, sir.'

'No, no, that's all right. Did she leave a forwarding address, by any chance?'

This conversation had taken place on the doorstep and before the maid could answer an elderly female voice called from the depths of the hall, 'Who is it, Ellen?'

Ellen turned and faced indoors. 'It's a gentleman, ma'am, inquiring after Mrs Potter as used to live here. He didn't know she'd gone and was asking after her address.'

'I'll speak to him.'

'Yes, ma'am.'

Ellen slipped away. Her place at the door was taken by a tiny old woman who seemed to consist entirely of fluffy wool and fluffier white hair, but her eyes were shrewd and she sized Hugh up with one glance.

'You had better come in, young man,' she said amiably. He followed her through the hall and into the drawing room. He handed her his card and looked around the room while she studied it. She seemed satisfied and invited him to sit down. He continued his mental inventory. It was amazing that a house which he had known so well could have undergone such a transformation, both in its occupants and its furnishings. The shell remained but that was all. The ladies had furnished it in the height of Victorian fashion. He could not imagine how so much furniture could have been fitted into a single room, all of it dark and sombre. Every flat surface was covered with porcelain or brass knick-knacks and masses of sentimental paintings furnished the walls, all of them by indifferent artists. There was even an aspidistra. He felt himself as much a stranger as if he had walked through the door for the first time in his life. While he was looking around the lady had been studying him and uttered a tiny, musical laugh.

'I can see you are very much surprised,' she said with a smile. 'Allow me to introduce myself – I am Miss Pottinger. My sister, Mrs Drake, is out at the moment, arranging flowers in the church. Such a *lovely* church, and the rector and his wife are everything one could hope for.'

'Yes,' said Hugh non-committally, remembering Edmund's views on the Ambroses.

'Now, Mr – Brodrick, what is it you're after?'

'Mr Potter was a friend of mine. I live a little distance away and haven't seen Mrs Potter since his funeral and as I was in the neighbourhood today I thought I'd call in and say hello. I was – am – surprised to hear that she's moved. I was just asking your maid if Mrs Potter had left a forwarding address when you came to the door.'

The old lady, though charming, was rather disposed to chatter but eventually he persuaded her to look in her address book. The address was not there. Oh dear. It might be anywhere. She was sure she had it somewhere. Connie would be able to find it when she returned. Could it be with other papers in a desk, perhaps? What a sensible idea. Yes, she would look there straight away. She could tell that he had a business head on his shoulders, just like Connie's late husband. Gentlemen had such organised minds. Failing that, she could ask Ellen to run down to the church and ask Connie.

Fortunately for Hugh's sanity Miss Pottinger found the address tucked away in a bureau drawer. As soon as he could do so politely he thanked her and left. He could have gone to Lilian's parents, of course, but he was glad he did not have to disturb them. After all, she might have instructed them not to give him her address if she was determined to sever all links with her former life.

After Edmund's death Hugh realised that his path and Lilian's would be unlikely to cross unless either of them went out of their way to seek out the other, but he had never imagined that she would move away without so much as informing him of her change of address. It was clear – she never wanted to see him again. She had said as much on that dreadful day in

1916 but since last summer he had begun to hope that she did not hate him quite so much as she had done then. What a fool he had been. What a complete and utter fool. How could he have allowed himself to hope that she would give him a second thought now? A voice whispered in his head that she might have kept in touch for the sake of Edmund's memory, if not for himself. No. She must have such a low opinion of him that she could not even do that. He arrived home in an agony of self-pity and decided to catch the early train to London. To hell with it, he would be bloody, bold and resolute and go and see her.

Thirty-six

*H*ugh had no difficulty in finding the fashionable block of flats at the Mayfair address, but then his luck ran out. Mrs Potter was holidaying on the Riviera. He did not leave a message. He made his way forlornly back to Paddington and took the first train back to Taunton, where he had left his car. The train was not busy and he had a compartment to himself. He lit his pipe and indulged in a litany of unpleasant thoughts. His first fear on hearing that Lilian had moved was that she had rushed into marriage with someone like Julian Hunt. But the maid said that Lilian had not married again and the concierge at her block of flats knew her as Mrs Potter. That was a relief. Now that the tinder had been lit Hugh knew he could never rest until he saw her again. He was coming up to stay with Max Hubert in a month's time and would call on her then.

He returned as planned – Mrs Potter was still abroad. In April she was out. In May she was in the country. Hugh was beginning to believe he would never see her. He had never given his name so it was unlikely that she was euphemistically 'not at home'. He returned the following week and booked into a hotel in Bloomsbury, prepared to stay for as long as it took. He could think of nothing else.

This time his determination was rewarded. A maid informed him that Mrs Potter was out at present but would be at home in the afternoon. He found a bookshop, bought a book and kicked his heels reading in the Green Park until it was lunchtime, when he found a quiet restaurant in a side street. He had little appetite but it passed the time.

He rang the bell of the flat at two-thirty precisely. The maid opened the door and recognised him.

'Yes, sir. Mrs Potter is at home. What name should I say?'

Hugh handed her his card and waited. Lilian appeared. She was slimmer than he remembered but that might have been the consequence of her fashionable clothes. Her dress looked as though it was made of gossamer and barely disguised her body. He guessed it had cost a great deal.

She smiled warily.

'Hello Lilian.'

'Hello Hugh. I never expected to see you, of all people, in London.'

'I'm thinking about another exhibition at the Cranbourn and had to come up to discuss it with Max. I heard that you'd moved here so I thought I'd look you up. You're looking well, I must say.'

She was, he considered, looking exceptionally beautiful, though her eyes lacked sparkle.

'Thank you.'

She led him into a generously proportioned room decorated in black and orange, and offered him a seat and a cigarette, which he accepted. He lowered himself into an armchair shaped like a box and looked around. The room could not have offered a greater contrast to Sydling. There, furniture was comfortable and paintings and other ornaments conservative. As his eye moved around the room he recognised a pair of Brancusi sculptures and paintings by Augustus John, Picasso and Matisse as well as a couple of Chagalls. Her taste had certainly changed and he mentally applauded her judgement.

Her furniture was a different matter, square and stark and, if this chair was anything to go by, extremely uncomfortable.

It was unaccountable – after all, Lilian had been responsible for furnishing Sydling. Hugh belonged to the tradition of passing furniture down from one generation to the next, not of throwing everything out and starting again whenever the fashion changed. Had her taste altered so dramatically or was this a reaction against the past? Was she unhappy and running away from her home and family and friends in Devon for this? He guessed the answer and pitied her.

She watched, amused, as he took it in.

'I must say it was a shock to discover you'd left Sydling,' he said. 'I was passing one day and called to see you and found two old ladies living there.'

Before she could reply, the doorbell rang. She glanced at a square clock on the mantelpiece.

'That must be Gerry and Claude,' she said by way of explanation though Hugh had never heard of either. 'They're taking me to tea.'

'In that case I'd better push along,' he said, rising to his feet.

'You're welcome to join us.'

It was obvious from the way she avoided his eye that she was only being polite. 'No, thank you. Things to do. Lilian, will you have lunch with me tomorrow?'

'I – yes. All right.'

Gerry and Claude were shown in by the maid. The two of them epitomised everything Hugh loathed in his fellow man – they were all hair oil and unctuous charm. Lounge lizards. Gerry, the shorter of the two, was tending to tubbiness and had a weak chin while Claude had more chin than was absolutely necessary for anyone who did not aspire to boxing or rugby football. They were bragging about themselves even before they were fully in the room, how they had raced up from Richmond and played cat and mouse with a traffic policeman. 'You should have seen his face when we made a U-turn and he couldn't follow us. My bus touched sixty through Putney without a blink. I positively forced at least half a dozen people off the road and scattered goodness knows how many pedestrians. It was terrific fun,' Gerry said to Lilian. Hugh might have been invisible.

He tried not to scowl and said nothing. Indeed, it would have been difficult to interrupt without using a parade-ground voice. He could not imagine what Lilian could see in them apart from their dissimilarity to Edmund. It was all of a piece with décor and the square furniture. She made no attempt to stem their chatter and introduce him so he moved towards the door. She showed him out.

'They aren't as bad as they look. Really.'

'I'm sure they're not. Well, shall we meet at the Ritz at one o'clock?'

'Yes.'

Hugh made his escape and headed to the British Museum, where he filled the remainder of the afternoon. He wandered through many of the rooms but afterwards would have been hard put to describe a single artefact.

The following day he arrived at the Ritz fifteen minutes early. Lilian was half an hour late. She offered no apology and he took it that it was fashionable to arrive late.

'How's your exhibition coming along? What are you going to show?' she asked after they had been shown to their table and ordered cocktails.

'It's likely to be towards the end of the year. Max thinks it would be a good idea for me to have a solo exhibition. It would be quite a feather in my cap if it comes off. As for the content, things are settling down at Netherculme at last, though it still takes most of my time, but I've been able to do some painting.' He refrained from mentioning that he was still working the war out of his system and that he knew she'd sold Edmund's painting.

'That's splendid news. Congratulations. Though it must be tiresome for someone who dislikes London as much as you do.'

'I don't know why you think I don't like it. It isn't my favourite place, I admit, but I don't find it as bad as all that. After all, I was a student here and also spent some time here during the war – a couple of days each time I was on leave and after I was wounded. And you – you like it here?'

'I simply love it.'

They sipped their drinks in silence. Lilian looked around – at fellow diners, the décor, the waiters. Anywhere but at him.

'As I started saying yesterday,' Hugh said eventually. 'I went to see Edmund's grave in February and called at Sydling to say hello. It was something of a shock to find two elderly women living there.'

Lilian laughed. 'How wonderful. Your face must have been a picture.'

'I suppose it was. Anyhow, Miss Pottinger, I think her name was, was so kind as to give me your address.' He could not bring himself to ask why she had not given it to him herself.

'I thought you must have got it from them since my parents haven't mentioned seeing you.'

'Shall you go back to Devon, do you think?'

'Never. For the first time in my life I'm free. I'm not tied to a village with its tiny minds and provincial nothingness, or to an invalid in a mockery of a marriage.'

Hugh looked doubtfully at her.

'I – I didn't mean that. But London is so alive. It's me. I love it here. I could never live anywhere else again. The people here are incredible – so lively and witty and clever. There isn't anyone in Devon who can compare with my friends here.'

That's put me in my place, Hugh mused. Not that I had any other expectation. But the lady doth protest too much. I'm sure it's all reaction to the war. Odd, how it has affected people so differently.

'But you must have some happy memories, surely?'

'No. Memories least of all. I don't want any. Is that so wrong?'

She looked defiantly at him, challenging him to argue, but he remained silent so she continued unprompted. 'The last few years were loathsome. All right, you can tell me I'm cruel but Edmund wasn't the man I married. You only saw him for a few months. I lived with him like that for three years. He changed in character as well as physically. And I couldn't bear his – his infirmity.'

'He couldn't bear it either.'

'Did he tell you he wanted me to take a lover? Doubtless it will surprise you that I didn't. I wasn't the best wife to him but I still cared deeply and was loyal and faithful.'

'Perhaps it would have been better if you had.'

'Why?'

'Because you'd have felt guilty and might consequently have treated him more kindly.'

She toyed with her half-empty cocktail glass before finishing the remainder.

'He thought I'd lied to him,' she said looking into the empty glass. 'After he died, by chance I picked up the book of Shakespeare's sonnets which he always kept beside his bed. I was flicking through it when something he'd underlined caught my eye. '*When my love swears that she is made of truth, I will believe her, though I know she lies*'. He died believing I was unfaithful.' Her eyes filled with tears. 'The last few years weren't easy. Everyone thinks of the wounded hero, not of those who have to live with him.'

'My poor Lilian. You must be so unhappy.'

She lifted her head, stuck out her chin and looked at him defiantly. 'Actually, you're quite mistaken. I'm very happy. I've never been happier. Ah, here's the soup. I'm starving.'

For someone who was starving Lilian ate very little. She sipped a couple of spoonfuls and then played around with her bread roll without eating it. They both took advantage of the food to fall silent.

The plates were removed and the fish brought. Again, Lilian only toyed with it.

'I don't know if I should tell you this,' said Hugh, 'but did you know Edmund wanted to die?'

'What do you mean?'

'He was pleased that he caught pneumonia. He knew it could be fatal and welcomed it. If the expression isn't too fatuous, he had a happy death. That's more than most people achieve.'

Lilian reflected for a moment. 'Yes,' she said. 'I believe you're right. He was at peace in the last few days. Do you blame me for making his life a misery and his wanting a way out?'

'Is your conscience troubling you?'

'No, of course not.'

'Then why do you think I would blame you?'

'Because it would be just like you. You always make out I'm in the wrong. Judging me. You've always hated me.'

'You couldn't be more mistaken. I've never hated you. I've often thought you the most headstrong, silly, spoilt person I know but I don't hate you. In fact, I've loved you from the first moment I met you.'

Lilian dropped her knife in astonishment and burst out laughing. Heads turned and looked at them, hoping for a scene. When nothing happened the other diners returned, mildly disappointed, to their meals.

'That really is a joke,' she giggled. 'You've always been either terrifically formal or gone out of your way to avoid me. You didn't come near Sydling for more than two years after you went back to the war even though you had several spells of leave. Or for an age after you were demobbed. And you're always so – so unemotional.'

'That's right. Made of granite, isn't that how you and Edmund used to describe me? Good God, Lilian, how could I be anything else when you were absolutely denied me? You were Edmund's girl from the beginning. I knew I couldn't hold a candle to him, which you very kindly reminded me of more than once. I had a choice – either grit my teeth or go away and not see either of you again. I was weak enough to choose the former, even though it was agony sometimes, but I stuck it because Edmund was the brother I never had. Or that's what I told myself. My other motive, which I hardly dared acknowledge to myself, was that I couldn't bear not to see you again even though you were out of reach. And as for the war, how do you think I felt knowing that the person who was dearer to me than anything on earth wished me dead? The memory of your words and the expression on your face that day still give me almost physical pain. When I went back I was determined to get killed, and keep clear of Devon until that happened. It was my bad luck that I survived and had to go home. Netherculme never felt such a millstone. I could happily have chucked it. I hoped I'd be over you but I knew as soon as you walked into Edmund's study that I never shall be.'

When he finished, silence hung over them like a shroud.

'I had no idea,' she said at last.

'You weren't meant to know. Your knowing would only have made it even more unbearable.'

'When I said those things to you I – I – as soon as I'd said it I could have cut out my tongue. It was cruel of me and I didn't mean it. I spoke without thinking. I know it won't be any consolation to you and you probably won't believe me, but ever since then I've done my utmost to be different, to be cautious before I speak. I hoped there were other reasons why you stayed away but in my heart I knew it was my fault. Edmund wondered so often why you didn't come and I had to lie to him over and over again. I couldn't tell him. I prayed that you would survive. Please believe me when I say that I was immensely glad when you came home.'

'Thank you.'

They turned their eyes away from each other while the

roast was served. The sommelier poured Hugh a small amount of claret. He agitated it carefully around the bowl of the glass, trying to keep his hand from shaking, watched its legs as it ran back down, smelt it appreciatively and nodded assent. Their glasses were filled and the sommelier melted away. Hugh took a large sip. He was accustomed to keeping his feelings hidden, and baring his soul as he had done had left him limp and ragged. But now that he had started he felt compelled to go on.

'If you don't positively hate me do you think you could get round to marrying me one day?' he asked, trying to sound as though it was all the same to him if Lilian answered one way or the other.

'I'm touched that you feel like that in spite of our differences but it's out of the question.'

'Oh. Any particular reason? Should I change the furniture? Part my hair on the other side? Do I slurp my soup?'

'No, it's nothing like that. It's much deeper. Let me see.' She began to enumerate Hugh's deficiencies with her fingers. 'First and foremost you'd always remind me of Edmund. I couldn't look at you without thinking of him. He belongs to the past and you do too. That's why I didn't let you know my address, in case you were wondering. Secondly, as we discussed earlier, I've cut away from Devon. I belong in London and you'll live and die at Netherculme. It's in your blood. Thirdly, we wouldn't like our respective friends and associates – I saw how you looked at Gerry and Claude yesterday and I as good as heard the thoughts going through your head. Fourthly, you think I'm headstrong, silly and spoilt – your words. You'd be forever judging me just as you always have done. And I think you're – to be truthful, I don't really know what you are these days. You've changed since the war. You've been a stranger since you came back. Fifth, there's the question of love. It's sweet of you to say you love me but I'm afraid I don't and can't love you for the above reasons. Finally, I'm not at all sure that Edmund didn't put you up to this.'

'Edmund! Why?'

'It would be just like one of his bright ideas to tell you to look after me after he'd gone and you, faithful dog that you are, after what you judged an appropriate period of mourning followed me here and asked me to marry you.'

'You're misjudging me, Lilian. Do you honestly think I could sacrifice the rest of my life just to please Edmund? Do you think I'm made of stone? I want you for myself alone or not at all.'

'The answer is no.'

'So I gathered. Sorry if I offended you – I hadn't intended to ask you. It slipped out somehow. Will you mind if I ask you from time to time in future? My mind will never alter.'

'That's kind of you, but don't hang around waiting for me. There are plenty of other women for you to choose from and who'd love to be mistress of Netherculme. You're just the right age, you're good looking, you're wealthy and now you're a famous artist. In other words you're eminently eligible. Haven't I read that there are two million superfluous women in the country now?'

'Yes, I read something like that too. The trouble is there's only one that matters, as I rather thought I made clear. Forgive my mentioning it.'

'Not at all. I am grateful though. Please don't think I'm not.'

Hugh felt numb but determined to show there were no hard feelings on his part. With an effort he remembered that she'd been abroad. 'Tell me about the Riviera. Is it all it's cracked up to be? Would I like it there, do you think?'

They talked resolutely about travel and holidays until coffee had been drunk and the bill paid, and at last they could go their separate ways.

Hugh went back to his hotel, collected his suitcase and took a cab to Paddington where he arrived just in time to catch the

3.50 train. He settled himself into a corner seat in a first-class carriage and took out his pipe. He allowed himself to think, for the first time since he parted from Lilian outside the Ritz. The regular movement of the train and the clunkety-clunk as it moved over the rails were consoling, the more so with every mile that came between them.

He hadn't intended to ask her to marry him but it followed as night follows day once he had spilled his feelings for her. She was blunt but he expected nothing else. He chided himself for his foolish impulse but on the other hand, he who ventures nothing ...

Like Edmund, he was fond of Shakespeare and he silently started to recite the twenty-third sonnet to himself in time with the rhythm of the train:

> *As an unperfect actor on the stage*
> *Who with his fear is put besides his part,*
> *Or some fierce thing replete with too much rage,*
> *Whose strength's abundance weakens his own heart;*
> *So I, for fear of trust, forget to say*
> *The perfect ceremony of love's rite,*
> *And in mine own love's strength seem to decay,*
> *O'ercharg'd with burthen of mine own love's might.*

He could not finish it. His eyes misted up and he quickly fumbled to lift his newspaper so that it hid his face from curious fellow passengers. After he composed himself he made a pretence of reading a few pages and then folded the paper away. He indulged in feverish thoughts for the remainder of the journey, staring unseeing through the window. All things considered, he was glad to have confessed his love to Lilian at last. It was like a sore he had carried silently and alone for almost ten years. Now it had been lanced, and left a strange sensation behind it. Tingly, yet numb. He had caught her off-guard, which was perhaps foolish. His mental agony was not helped by the fact that even more than yesterday he was convinced that she was deeply unhappy and running away from everything she used to hold dear, like a moth fluttering blindly around a light. She was sound at heart, he was certain, but what was she going to do until she found her equilibrium again? He dreaded to think. The worst of it was that he was powerless, completely powerless, to help her.

★

*A*s soon as they said goodbye Hugh turned away from Lilian. She stood unmoving on the pavement, not caring how many pedestrians she inconvenienced, watching him until he disappeared from view. The familiarity of his back somehow affected her as much as his words had done.

I don't believe it, she thought, as she turned and walked slowly back to her flat. I simply cannot believe it. Hugh in love with me. It's impossible. But why would he make it up? – unless Edmund really had put him up to it – and yet he denied that. What did he say? – 'Do you honestly think I could sacrifice the rest of my life just to please Edmund? Do you think I'm made of stone? I want you for myself alone or not at all.'

Oh, Hugh! I simply can't believe it. In love with me ever since you first met me, but then ignoring me more often than not until now. You had a good reason for that – I was married to Edmund, after all. You've got a nerve. You're only man I ever met who ignored me. How must you have felt when I told you I wished you would be killed? I felt bad enough about it before but now, knowing that you loved me … And yet you said you love me in spite of everything and want to marry me. It would be madness, of course. You're very kind. But I could never marry you even if I did love you, which I don't. It would be like living with Edmund again. Oh no, it wouldn't do at all.

Incoherent thoughts darted around her brain until she had

another, mortifying recollection. The things she'd said to him not just once but several times about his not being able to hold a candle to Edmund. How Edmund was and always would be the better man. How could he not hate her, despise her? That must be it – he wanted to marry her so that he could punish her. So confused and irrational had her thinking become that she persuaded herself that this was the real motive for Hugh's proposal. Her conscience and her common sense combined forces and told her she was being unfair to him, that one would have to go a long way to find someone of greater integrity, but her prejudice against him was so profound that she refused to believe them.

When she reached her flat Gerry Cuvelier telephoned to invite her to dinner that evening before going on to the latest nightclub which he assured her was bound to be raided by the police. It would be a scream. She accepted almost before he got the words out.

Thirty-seven

---

*F*our weeks later Hugh was reading *The Times* over breakfast when he saw an announcement of the marriage of Lilian Potter, widow, of London W, and the Hon. Gerald Cuvelier, also of London W, motor-racing driver. He read it half a dozen times in the hope that the words would miraculously change between readings, but it obstinately kept saying the same thing. He threw down the paper, leapt to his feet and summoned Aldhelm. He immediately dispatched the surprised man to buy all the newspapers he could find that were given to gossip. Soon he learned that the marriage had taken place after a whirlwind romance. The bridegroom was excessively rich and enjoyed his passion of motor racing. He would be competing at the recently repaired Brooklands Motor Circuit later in the year (this was accompanied by an indistinct photograph of a man, who could have been anyone, smirking behind the steering wheel of a car). The bride's first husband had been wounded at the Somme in July 1916 and invalided out of the army. He had died in September of last year. This was followed a brief panegyric on fallen heroes.

Hugh shook his head sadly and wondered if this was the same Gerry he had met at Lilian's flat. That tubby chinless oil-slick who was too full of himself. Judging by the photograph he rather thought so, though it was hard to tell. 'Oh, my dear Lilian, what have you done?' he said aloud, but the walls of his study remained silent. There was no doubt in his mind that this was a gesture. A rebound gesture of monumental proportions. His emotions were in turmoil – pity for Lilian jumbled with despair for himself. And he had an awful feeling that he had precipitated it.

---

Thirty-eight

*H*ugh was right. Lilian was not in love with Gerry Cuvelier. She had met him for the first time at a party a few weeks before Hugh encountered him at her flat. The conversation with Hugh, his proposal of marriage, and the painful reminders of her past that he brought with him, served to enhance Gerry's attractions. To be sure he was loud, opinionated and weak-headed but he fed Lilian's craving for parties and fun, and above all for anything and everything that was the opposite of her life in Halberton.

Like Lilian, Gerry loathed the tedium of the country; if he went out of London it was likely to be to a race-track or the Riviera or New York. His one skill was driving motor cars. He adored them, the faster the better, and luckily for him he was rich enough to be able to indulge his passion. He styled himself 'racing driver'. He never spoke to anyone in Latin or shut himself away for hours in his study.

Provided with a good home, wealth and a lively social scene, Lilian considered herself happy.

The Cuveliers spent the winter months in a hired villa on the Riviera where they partied with like-minded people, returning to England in the spring when Gerry would launch into the motor-racing season. Shortly after their return to London in 1923, after a convivial evening with some motoring companions, Gerry tripped on a pavement and damaged ligaments in his shoulder. The news was grave: he would have to miss the first part of the racing season.

Their most intimate friends were Wilbert and Fleur Beer, who, like them, had little more to do with their lives than spend money and enjoy themselves. One day in early April Lilian and Fleur returned to the Beers' house in Kensington after a shopping expedition and found the men poring over maps.

'What's that you're studying, darling? You look engrossed,' Lilian greeted her husband.

'If I've got to be a crock I'll go mad unless I get away, so we thought we – us four, I mean – could take a motoring holiday,' Gerry said, without looking up.

'What a good idea. I can't think where I'd like to go, though. Everywhere seems the same these days. I don't know why,' she said, as though she had drained the cup of all the world had to offer.

'This will be different. We thought we'd try Alsace,' offered Wilbert.

'Alsace. Where's that?' asked Fleur, who had always found geography and history boring and made a point of forgetting everything she had been taught on either subject.

Lilian pulled a face. 'Is it in France or Germany? I never know.'

'France now,' said Wilbert. 'It was Germany before '14. It might be interesting to see what the French have made of it now they've got it back.'

'What's special about it?' asked Fleur. 'Is that the reason you want to go there, because of the war? If so, count me out.'

'No, not at all. The war's by the by,' replied her husband. 'You'll simply love it, angel. It's full to the brim with pretty houses with storks nesting on top. There are mountains and lots of vineyards. It should be fun. Go native. Bit of fresh air for a while. Escape the hordes.'

Lilian suddenly saw a half-finished jigsaw on Edmund's

desk. The memory was so powerful she could almost hear his breathing as he laboured over it. She had ruthlessly suppressed all memories of him but this one somehow slipped her guard and caught her above the solar plexus. She shuddered.

'Cold?' asked Gerry.

'No, no. Alsace sounds all right. As Wilbert said, it will be different. It's a bore to meet the same people wherever one goes. How do we get there?'

'Drive. I'm crocked for racing but I can manage the Rolls all right on normal roads. And anyway, Wilbert can help out with the driving if need be. We could cross from Folkestone to Boulogne, tootle across country stopping for a night or two *en route*, then over the Vosges Mountains into Alsace. What do you think?'

'Fine. I've only ever passed through northern France on the way south, so it will certainly be different.'

'Are there any shops there?' asked Fleur, taking her purchases out of their parcels and examining them. She was bored by details and always left arrangements to Wilbert.

'I expect so, honey,' Wilbert replied absent-mindedly. 'That's settled then. All we have to do now is decide when we're going and find a route across France.'

'I'd like to see Montreuil again,' Gerry volunteered immediately.

'May I see the map?' asked Lilian.

Gerry and Wilbert moved aside for her.

'Here's Boulogne, and we want to go there,' Gerry said, drawing an imaginary line with his stubby finger from the coast to Alsace and then wiggling it north to south and back again over the general area.

Lilian's interest had been aroused by the mention of Montreuil. She bent over the map and found it, then her eyes scanned over the paper until they halted at Mametz, to the south-east. The insignificance of the place astonished her.

She knew at once that she had to go there. She must see it for herself, breathe its air, touch its earth. The very earth that had perhaps absorbed Edmund's blood. It would be different now, of course, but no matter. She would not be able fully to understand him until she had been there herself. It was vitally important.

She expressed a wish to visit the battlefield. It was not well received. Fleur considered the idea of the Somme obscene – so many ghastly corpses there apparently. Supposing they hadn't all been buried yet. Ugh. Wilbert shrugged – he could take it one way or the other. Gerry suspected the idea had something to do with her first husband and vetoed it out of hand. But Lilian was adamant, and when she was adamant she seldom failed to carry the day.

So it was decided, just like that. She, who had not spared Edmund a voluntary thought for three years, was bemused by the turn of events. She would have liked to know exactly where he had been wounded but that would have meant asking Hugh, which was out of the question. There had been no communication between them since their lunch at the Ritz and it was going to stay that way.

★

On a bright Monday in early May a Rolls Royce the colour of ripe cherries bumped over a pot-hole before coming to a halt. They were at a T-junction with the road from Albert to Peronne. To left and right, in front and behind, were the scars of war, now softened by the passage of years but still clearly visible. To the side of the road was a dump of dud shells, this month's harvest, waiting to be removed.

'Now where?' asked Gerry with more than a hint of impatience. He was in a bad mood, as he did not like the thought of what these rough roads might be doing to the car, and what's more, driving had started to make his shoulder ache.

'God knows,' muttered Wilbert from the rear seat. Fleur uttered a sigh of such meaning that it was clear what she thought of the expedition. Lilian, in the front passenger seat, sucked her lower lip in concentration.

'Left, I think,' she said. 'Or no, perhaps right. Hold on a moment, darling.' She looked again at a rather dog-eared map she had been clutching since they set out from their hotel, turning it first this way and then that. She had never been good at reading maps and it invariably irritated Gerry, which made her nervous and even more likely to make a mistake. 'Oh, of course. I was right first time. Left.'

The remark from behind her about women navigators was lost in the revving of the engine as Gerry obediently but disbelievingly steered left.

'Don't go fast – we'll be there in a moment,' said Lilian.

'Where are we going, anyway?' pouted Fleur.

Lilian was concentrating too hard on the map to reply, and both the men were too peevish to do so.

'Stop, Gerry. It must be up there. Oh, it's a farm track. I'm certain it's the right place though. Yes, look – there's a sign.'

'Then I'll park here. It'll be a miracle if we get to Alsace as it is, what with the state of these roads.' Gerry duly parked well into the side of the road, which was not a busy one. There was complete silence when he turned off the engine.

'Well, I'll just wander up and take a look around,' Lilian said lightly. Too lightly. Her voice sounded false, even to herself. 'There's no need for anyone else to come. I shall only be a few minutes.'

Gerry leaned across her to open her door. She stepped onto the road, looked around to take in her surroundings, and turned up the track.

Gerry also climbed out and proceeded to pace up and down smoking a moody cigarette. Wilbert joined him.

'I say, Lilian's a bit testy today, isn't she,' he said.

'Damn fool idea to come here. I don't know why I didn't put my foot down when the idea first came up. God knows what she hopes to get from it.'

'Why did she want to come? I'd have thought the less seen of this godforsaken place the better.'

'I couldn't agree more. But her first husband copped it here in '16.'

'Oh, I see. Killed?' asked Wilbert, who knew nothing about Edmund.

'No, wounded. Rather badly as a matter of fact. He made it home but she couldn't stand the sight of his injuries – amputated leg and all that. He took a deuce of a long time to die too. Three years. Awkward business, hanging around like that when you're not wanted. I can't think why she wanted to come here, especially after all this time. She's hardly ever mentioned him before.'

He drew a final gasp from his cigarette and crushed the end beneath his spotless shoe as though he were crushing Edmund. It would not do to admit it but he was jealous. It had been rather pleasing to marry a woman of experience – made him seem a man of the world – but the other side of the coin was that she must have cared for Edmund, when they were first married at least. She had told him enough for him to know it had been a love-match. Gerry and Lilian got along well enough but neither was under any illusion about love and romance, hence his need to deny being jealous. He had married her because hers was the type of beauty he liked, she was fun and she was not the sort of woman to hang around him the whole time demanding attention. The trouble was, dead men too often became heroic and inviolable – particularly when they had been wounded at one of the big battles – no matter what they had been like in life. It wasn't done to criticise them, which put one at a disadvantage.

Wilbert scanned the devastated landscape. 'God, what a place,' he uttered. 'Were you in it?'

Gerry puffed out his chest.

'As a matter of fact I passed from Sandhurst straight onto the Staff. Quite a good job, though I say it myself. It would have been a whole lot easier without the bungling that went on up the line but what else can you expect during wartime. Bunch of amateurs, most of them.'

'Actually, I was at the Front,' said Wilbert, 'but I couldn't agree more about amateurs. It was easy enough to survive if you had your wits about you. Plenty of medals to be picked up too. I don't want to malign the dead and all that but Lilian's ex must have been something of a part-timer by the sound of it.'

'Quite. Better off out of it, chaps like that. They get in the way of real soldiers and are nothing but a nuisance. There were too many like him.'

'Where's Lilian?' interrupted Fleur from the car. While the men were talking she had been adjusting the toque on her expensively sculpted hair with her perfectly manicured hands.

'She's gone to look at some graves, precious,' replied her husband.

'Graves? Ugh. Don't give me the creeps, Wilby. Lilian would never be so silly. Why on earth would she want to do that?'

Wilbert shrugged in reply and helped Fleur descend from the vehicle.

'I suppose we'd better go and drag her back from her ghoulish pleasure, eh Gerry?' he said.

Hands in pockets, the two men preceded Fleur up the narrow track.

★

Lilian did not known how she would feel when she finally arrived at Mametz but her nervousness surprised her as she walked up the track. She was trembling all over. In spite of what Edmund had told her about the war she was unprepared for the sights that greeted her at Albert and beyond. The war had ended nearly five years earlier. She thought there might still be some sign of it but not this. Fleetingly, she questioned the wisdom of her desire to come here but just as quickly she dismissed the thought. One should not question one's instinct.

The landscape had once been pastoral – gentle hills with farms and villages, fields and woods. Now it was nothing but devastation. The village of Mametz a few hundred yards away looked like a pile of rubble. Where there had been fields there were trenches and shell-holes. Where there had been woods there were sticks and stumps and more shell-holes. Then she looked harder and noticed that it was not quite as bleak as she had at first supposed. Nature was trying to reassert itself, nursing it back to health and peace. Fields were scarred but they were also green. Trees were battered and stunted but new life was sprouting from them. Buildings were damaged but clearance was taking place and new construction was in progress. There was no mud. There was no barbed wire. There were no corpses.

She remembered that the Devons started their assault from a trench at the place known as Mansel Copse. Somewhere between where she was standing and the ruins of Mametz Edmund was wounded and Hugh saved his life. He was also wounded – funny, she had almost forgotten that, overshadowed as it was by Edmund's tragedy.

Fifty yards up the steep track, she found the Devonshire Cemetery. It was bound on two sides by a field and on the other two by regrowth of the copse. It was not large like some of the cemeteries they had passed. Instead its size conferred a pleasing intimacy, in so far as a cemetery can be pleasing. There was a wooden sign by the entrance carved with an inscription:

THE DEVONSHIRES HELD THIS TRENCH
THE DEVONSHIRES HOLD IT STILL

She studied it and went in, walking slowly between the two lines of graves. Edmund must have known these men. He must have lived and laughed and suffered with them.

She closed her eyes and tried to visualise the scene. She tried to hear the guns, the whistle for the attack, the machine gun, but the only sound was skylarks high overhead. She opened her eyes and raised her head to look at the village. To see it better she walked across the cemetery but already the growing vegetation obscured it from view.

'So this was a trench – his trench,' she said to herself. She took a few more steps. 'Why did I come here? Because I had to. I had no choice. Edmund brought me here as surely as if he were still alive.'

She scolded herself for being fanciful but was unable to shrug off the conviction that he was here, at her side, leading her. She had no truck for spiritualism but this feeling was overwhelming. She paced to and fro between the two rows of graves. Looking down she saw her hands folding and unfolding, ironically the trait that had so annoyed her in Edmund when he was neurasthenic.

'Oh Edmund, why did you make me come here? Why churn up old memories? I've managed to put you out of my mind. I'm happy. Gerry adores me and I have everything I could ever want. Why spoil it now? Life's much more fun than it used to be in Devon, after the war started and you went away. It's so much better in London – the shops, the theatre, the parties, the Ritz, More friends than I ever had before, never a minute to be bored. How I hate Devon.'

'Are there you are,' Gerry said behind her, making her start. 'Did you see what you wanted?'

'Yes, I did,' she said, hoping she had not been speaking out loud. That would be too embarrassing – talking to a dead man.

'Good. Let's go back to the car. We need to push on now.'

She linked her arm through his and they made their way back down the track. Soon they were motoring eastwards and left the Somme behind.

Thirty-nine

*T*hey stayed the night in a small hotel at St Quentin, a dismal town which did nothing to mend spirits ruffled by the day's tour of the battlefield. All four travellers were glad to head east again in the morning. They discovered that although they had left the Somme they had not left evidence of the war. Their route took them through Laon, perched above the plain like an acropolis, through Champagne, past Châlons-sur-Marne to Vitry-le-François before following an interminable Roman road to Nancy. All along their route there were constant reminders of the war, where the Germans had swept west in 1914 and their retreat four years later. None of them felt inclined for conversation.

They made their final overnight stop at Nancy. The evening began in a bar in the Place Stanislas where by common consent they put the tribulations of the day to one side. They were awed by the beauty and scale of the baroque square. Fleur declared it was 'sheer' – a sign of great approval. They found a wonderful little restaurant in the old quarter and keenly anticipated Alsace. It was bound to be a good holiday, their best ever, and Wilbert was toasted for suggesting it. They checked out of the hotel early the next morning, Wilbert and Gerry nursing their heads somewhat, and took the road south towards the Vosges. Soon they were following the Meurthe up into the forested mountains which, viewed from a distance, were every tint of blue. Their line was gentler, more hospitable than that of the Alps. The road climbed higher until they reached the Col du Bonhomme where they were surprised to see snow lingering. At the summit Gerry stopped the car and he and Wilbert took photographs. The air was as pure and intense as any Lilian had ever breathed and she made an involuntary comparison with the air of London, to London's disadvantage. They continued to Kaysersberg, which was to be their base for the next two weeks.

Gerry, Wilbert and Fleur were contented enough – although Fleur would have preferred more shops – but Lilian had not experienced a tranquil moment since leaving Folkestone. She sought something elusive, nameless. At first she was not concerned – she believed that once she had seen Mansel Copse and got it off her chest everything would revert to how it was before. She was wrong. The neat cemetery with its peaceful atmosphere and the feeling that Edmund was with her had only heightened her fretfulness. Perhaps she would find what she was looking for in the mountains, she reflected, as she listened to Gerry's snores one night. As she lay there, sleep eluding her, she thought about Mametz. On the whole she was glad she had insisted on going there. She remembered a proverb she had heard as a child: you cannot make an omelette without breaking eggs. Why did she think of that? Was she making an omelette? How? Why? And why had she suddenly started thinking of Edmund nearly four years after he died? Having first felt his presence in the cemetery she felt him beside her in the car and on mountain paths – now even. She felt that he was watching her every move, listening to her every word, and what was worse – reading her thoughts. She hoped she was not having some sort of brainstorm.

Slowly the past she had locked deep inside her mind began to emerge, memory layered upon memory like an onion. She found herself reliving scenes she had shared with him, not the important occasions but insignificant words and actions like chiding him for his obsession with the jigsaw of Alsace which he had put together so many times he could have done it blindfold. How it had annoyed her because jigsaws belonged in the nursery. It should have been beneath his dignity to spend his time on it. But what else did he have to do with his time, after all? She thought of how she had avoided touching his disabled limbs and been embarrassed by his being in a wheelchair. It was *her* pride, *her* dignity that was affronted. Edmund had sacrificed his body and the best part of his life and all she could do was turn her back on him. 'Oh my darling, I'm sorry, I'm sorry,' she said aloud.

Gerry mumbled in his sleep and turned over.

She waited until he was snoring again and continued her agonising. Hugh came into her mind. Poor Hugh. She replayed every scene since the start of the war when she had upbraided him for being inferior to Edmund, how he should have been the one to have neurasthenia or be disabled. It should have been him because there was no one to care for him. Such cruel words. How could anyone in her right mind have said those things to someone at any time, least of all to a soldier returning to the Front? To a friend. And yet she had said them. Once said, words can never be unspoken no matter how much one might regret them. And yet – and yet he not only had forgiven her but he loved her. He wanted to marry her in spite of her prejudice and cruelty. The word prejudice stung her. Why had she always been so prejudiced against him? Was it that she had simply been jealous of his friendship with Edmund?

Another layer of memory peeled away. Late summer in 1911. She was twenty and Hugh was introduced to her at a tennis party. He was shy and awkward so she turned away to her more lively companions. All the other men she knew buzzed around her like bees around a fragrant flower. Four of them proposed to her, including Edmund. Hugh was the only one who ignored her. Her pride was wounded. Yes, it was as simple as that, and for that she repaid him with coldness and humiliation, even pretending she didn't remember having met him. She had thought herself so clever making disparaging remarks about him, always putting him down in comparison with Edmund. She could not have been more foolish. Her only comfort, and it provided scant solace, was that she had been immature and inexperienced in life. She could see clearly now that while Edmund was like champagne – instant sparkle and gratification, Hugh was like a great claret – initially quiet but maturing to a wine whose taste would linger for ever. And she had thought him insignificant. It was mortifying to be so wrong.

She climbed quietly out of bed and moved to the window. She drew back the curtain, opened the window wide and sat on the cushioned window-seat, her arms around her legs. A gentle breeze played about her. Although her reflections were painful she had no choice but to follow them to their conclusion. Having been suppressed for so long memories now surged like a cataract.

1916. She was standing by a window at Netherculme watching Hugh pushing Edmund in his wheelchair. At that moment she realised their roles had been reversed. Hugh was upright and strong, confident. Edmund was diminished, mentally as well as physically. Not long after that she had said, 'You disgust me. The sooner you go back to the war and get yourself killed the better.' How could she ever forget those words? How could he forget? *He hasn't forgotten but he has forgiven me*, she thought. *He must be the most generous spirit alive.* Then she corrected herself and remembered how he used to tell her off. That's why she had said those words: he had said that Edmund dreaded going home to her, that he had been acting the cheerful invalid for her, unable to confide how he was really feeling. Insufferable cheek. Hugh ought to have minded his own business. He can't blame me for reacting when he interfered like that. But in her heart she knew Hugh only tackled her when she deserved it. She was deeply ashamed. He saw through her yet he still loved her. He had been a better friend to Edmund than she ever was. And he seemed to know her better than she knew herself. Her cheeks became hot to think that she had never loved Edmund as Hugh seemed to love her. He recognised that her selling Sydling and moving to London was reaction to Edmund's death and the war. And her marriage to Gerry – she had decided to marry him on another impulse after seeing Hugh that day at the Ritz. What must he have thought of her? Did he ever think of her now? Had he finally given up on her and fallen for someone else? Surely he must have. She experienced a stab of jealousy.

Another memory surfaced: sitting with Edmund in his study after Hugh came to Sydling for the first time after the war. What was it Edmund had said? – that Hugh needed a good woman to take care of him. And she replied that bachelorhood suited him and if he married then Edmund wouldn't see so much of him. So that was it. The final layer had peeled away at last. Hugh must not marry because *she* would lose him. It wasn't about Edmund at all. It never had been. She could not bear the thought of Hugh loving anyone but herself. She loved him. Perhaps she always had, in a way, though she had loved Edmund passionately at first. When did she start loving Hugh? She racked her brains but could find no conclusive answer. She must have loved him when he came back from the war or she would not have minded what Edmund had said about him needing a wife. She understood now why she reached out to touch the scar on his neck when they were motoring to Sidmouth.

What a fool she had been. What an utter, unspeakable fool.

It dawned on her that Edmund's spirit – if that was what it was – had gone. Was this what he had been trying to say to her? Was this why she felt so compelled to visit the Somme?

Gerry stirred and turned over again.

Gerry! She was married to Gerry. What a mess she'd made of her life. She had buried one husband, was married to a man she didn't love and loved a man to whom she had been hateful and who must well and truly have given up on her by now. The plain truth was that she didn't deserve him. It was a bitter reflection. What on earth could she do? There was only one viable answer – to ask Gerry for a divorce. She was under no illusions – he had had liaisons from the beginning of their marriage so he would probably be expecting it sooner or later. But divorce brought stigma. It might be all right in London – people were getting divorced there all the time – but in Devon, which was so provincial? She knew from her life there that a divorced woman could be a social outcast. And would it damn her in Hugh's eyes even if he did still care for her? Did he love her enough? And what if she divorced Gerry only to find that Hugh was no longer interested in her? No, she would have to wait, to find out somehow how Hugh was situated. She would have to be more patient than she had ever been in her life.

★

One day halfway through their holiday Gerry and Lilian drove alone to admire the scenery from the route that ran along the spine of the mountains. When they reached the Col de la Schlucht Gerry parked the car and they got out to admire Hohneck, standing stark against the sky. The air was sultry with unreleased thunder. Looking back along the valley they watched as greenness turn grey as a storm sped towards them. They ran back to the car and dived in, slamming their doors just in time. From sunshine they were suddenly engulfed in a white blanket as thick as fog. Hail crashed onto the roof like the rattle of a hundred machine guns, drowning any attempt at speech. Gerry put his hands over his ears and pulled faces. Lilian took no notice of him. She sat motionless, hands folded in her lap, staring straight ahead at the streaming windscreen.

The storm moved on as suddenly as it had arrived.

The sun reappeared and they saw rivers running down the mountainside where it had been dry before. The only sound was of running water.

'Whew, that was fun. Jolly lucky we weren't caught in it,' Gerry said.

'Yes.'

'I thought I'd go deaf at the very least.'

'Yes.'

'What's up? You're very quiet. Have been ever since we landed in France as a matter of fact.'

'Have I? It's just that coming here has reminded me of things I thought I'd forgotten. Silly things.'

'Like what?'

'Oh, this and that.' She paused. 'Gerry, do you believe in ghosts?'

'Good God, no. Don't tell me you do.'

'Not as a rule no, I don't. But I couldn't help feeling that Edmund was with me when we were at the Somme in particular. I don't believe in ghosts but it was a very strong feeling. I can't explain it. I suppose it's unsettled me. I haven't quite been able to shake it off.'

Gerry looked at her incredulously. 'Now don't go getting silly ideas like that. I won't have it. I always thought you had more sense. He's dead and gone. *Fini*.'

She had hoped Gerry would show some understanding but realised she was not going to get it. 'Yes, you're probably right.'

'I've been thinking,' he said after a tense silence. 'I'm going to start racing again as soon as we get home. My shoulder's getting better all the time. I can't wait to get on the track again.'

'Didn't the doctor say you should wait until later in the summer? You don't want to risk putting it out again.'

Gerry was adamant. Soon after they returned to London he busied himself preparing for his racing comeback. Lilian took advantage of one of his frequent absences to visit her parents. She knew they did not cross paths with Hugh but she hoped to find out by discreet inquiries if they had heard anything of him. She laughingly said it was time he settled down and wondered if he had yet. No, they had heard nothing of him at all and changed the subject. She decided she would ask Walter – he might have heard something. She would go and see him the next day. But before she went she received a telegram. Gerry had overshot a corner and crashed his car. She was to come at once.

Lilian left immediately and reached the hospital in good time. She had not set foot in one since 1916 and had to conquer painful memories before walking through the door. Gerry was seriously injured and she found him swathed in bandages. Doctors and nurses alike wore long faces and spoke in subdued voices. For the second time in four years she stroked the hand of her husband as he lay dying. Gerry passed away four hours later without regaining consciousness.

Forty

Nothing eventful happened in Hugh's life between Lilian's marriage to Gerry and his demise. His daily routine continued more or less the same, depending on the season. As things settled on the estate he had more leisure for art. As well as continuing to paint he became increasingly adept at wood engravings and found himself in demand to illustrate books, which he enjoyed. He worked the war out of his system and turned instead to lyrical representation of the countryside and rural activities, often preferring the softer tones of watercolour instead of the oils he had used in his war paintings. It might be unfashionable but he had found his own voice at last and was comfortable with it.

He had a couple of liaisons with war widows as lonely as himself, which provided sexual gratification on both sides without emotional encumbrance. As an eligible bachelor mindful of the shortage of marriageable men he tactfully made clear at the outset that the lady should have no expectations. He did not invite them to Netherculme.

Convinced that Lilian would never contact him, he subscribed to a press-cutting agency – Gerry was bound to be in the news occasionally for his motor-racing activities if nothing else. He never mentioned this to anyone but he suspected that Aldhelm knew about the cuttings though he was too discreet to allude to them.

Thus his life meandered on until the day after Gerry's death, when the headline screamed out from *The Times*. He wondered about Lilian. Had she really cared for Gerry – learned to love him, even? Was she grief-stricken as she had been over Edmund?

Hugh had not fully recovered yet from the war, and that together with the loss of Edmund and Lilian – he grieved for her as though she were dead – had worn him out. His reaction to the news was an overwhelming feeling of tiredness. He could not even feel relief that she was free again and hope that he might succeed where he had failed so abjectly in the past. It was pointless to speculate – there was no hope. The tiredness persisted and three months later his doctor prescribed a change of scene. He packed his paints and went to Italy, well away from the mountains that held unpleasant memories of war. He enjoyed his month in Venice, Tuscany and Rome. He took each day as it came, absorbing the sights and sounds and smells; tasting food and wine that he had never experienced before, painting and visiting galleries by day and the opera by night. By the time he returned home he felt brighter and more at peace with himself than he had done for years.

He had left the estate in Robbins' capable hands and was soon able to fall back into his daily routine, which carried on as before, only more cheerfully.

★

One autumn morning Aldhelm brought in his post as usual.

'Anything interesting?' he asked.

'Mainly business and a couple of catalogues, sir. And there is one letter in a feminine hand.' He said nothing more. Like a good servant he turned a blind eye to any female intrigue.

'Oh? I wonder who that could be.' Hugh picked up the envelope and did not recognise the writing. 'Thank you, that will be all.'

Aldhelm went out, closing the study door behind him. Hugh

slit open the envelope and pulled out a single folded sheet of thick paper, curious as to who it could be from. He opened it and immediately read Lilian's scrawled signature.

'Good God,' he said, flinging it down as though it was burning his hand. He stood up and went to the window. 'I wonder what she wants.' He did not want to read it, in fact he wanted to tear it into minuscule fragments and flush it away, but curiosity soon got the better of him. He deliberately did not rush. He went back to his desk and sat down, took out his pipe, lit it, smoked for a minute or two in what he fancied was a nonchalant manner, then picked up the letter. The address was Compton Grange, her parents' house.

Dear Hugh,

I expect this letter will come as a surprise. I hope it finds you well.

I was turning out some things from Sydling the other day and found a handkerchief which you so kindly let me use after Edmund was wounded. May I come and return it to you? I am staying with my parents for a few days and could easily drive over to Netherculme.

Best regards,
Lilian

'Well, well,' he said to himself, repeating it several times. He remembered the incident with the handkerchief with perfect clarity, just as he had never forgotten any event with Lilian. It was July 1916. It had been his unpleasant task to tell her that Edmund was badly wounded. She was devastated. After she had seen Edmund she came to see him here at Netherculme where he was convalescing – she had brought him fruit from the garden and cream. She had cried and taken out a flimsy lace handkerchief of her own which was good for nothing except looking pretty, and he had offered her his own. She forgot to give it back – understandable in the circumstances. He had long assumed that she had thrown it away.

His instinct was to pick up his pen at once and ask her to come, but no, he would not let her think he spent his time waiting for her. He steeled himself to wait until the evening and then wrote, thanking her for her letter and stating that he would be at home the day after tomorrow, if that was convenient. Remembering their last meeting when an expensive meal at the Ritz had tasted of ashes, he invited her for mid-morning when he could offer her coffee if any refreshment was required. On re-reading his brief reply he found it stiffly formal but that was too bad. What else could she expect? He wasn't going to agonise over it as he had over his letter of condolence after Edmund's death.

The following day was one of the worst of his life. Worse, he mused, than waiting to go over the top. At least one knew what one was going to face with that. He tried to keep busy but it was impossible to prevent intrusive thoughts. Why had she written after so long? What was the real reason behind her wish to see him? It could not be the handkerchief as she could easily have enclosed it in a letter. No, that was merely a pretext, and a transparent one at that. What was he to say to her? How could he act normally? What if he found he no longer loved her? That would be the best outcome – at long last he would be free to get on with his life untrammelled.

Eventually the day arrived, as all days must. If Hugh had but known, he could have taken solace from the fact that Lilian's night was as disturbed as his own. He rose early, bathed and dressed with rare fussiness, to Aldhelm's consternation. He was not a vain man but he could not help reflecting with satisfaction that at least he still had most of his hair, even though it had lost its blackness in places. He forced down a small breakfast and then drifted aimlessly around his study and the downstairs rooms, puffing furiously on his pipe, before finding indoors too constraining. He went outside and strode about the garden instead. Aldhelm recognised the symptoms and hoped the lady was worth it. He had long since deduced that the mysterious letter was from Mrs Cuvelier. He had only met her twice when she was married to Mr Potter. Mr Potter's man Minster, while not saying anything indiscreet, managed to convey that the lady had rather rejected Mr Potter after he had been wounded. Poor blighter. He was a real gent, he was. Sure, his situation had made him a bit tetchy but who could blame him? Aldhelm hoped Mrs Cuvelier wasn't going to play fast and loose with the major, as he still thought of Hugh sometimes. He deserved the best. He was the kindest, most generous man and it was sad to see him so lonely, burying himself in work or his studio and rattling around this big house. It fair broke the major up when Mrs Potter went and married that motor-racing driver. All glamour and no substance, people like that. While these thoughts turned in his head he was polishing silver, rubbing so hard he was in danger of erasing the hallmarks.

Hugh was still pacing in the garden when he heard a car approaching. He went up to the terrace and walked round the corner of the house just as Lilian was descending from the Rolls Royce, the door held open by a liveried chauffeur. She did not see him.

He studied her. She was dressed more for the country than when he had last seen her in London, which was only to be expected, but he could see that her clothes were expensive. She clearly had not suffered financially through being widowed twice.

★

Lilian looked up at the house as though seeing it for the first time before moving hesitantly towards the door. She stopped and turned at the sound of Hugh's footsteps. Little did she realise it but several pairs of curious eyes were watching her through a downstairs window before Aldhelm shooed them away.

'Hello Lilian,' Hugh said, walking up to her.

'Hello Hugh.' She held out her hand.

He hesitated, clasped it in one hand, then both. She left it there almost carelessly as though it didn't belong to her. She took in at a glance that he was still thinner than before the war and his forehead was more lined than she remembered. He had been looking solemn but suddenly a smile creased his face and lit up his eyes and her heart turned over. 'How on earth could I have thought I hated him?' she wondered.

He still had possession of her hand and released it gently. 'I'm sorry about your husband. I ought to have written, I suppose, but I didn't know what to say.'

'That's all right. Gerry wasn't cut out to make old bones the way he drove those racing cars.'

'And you. Has it been difficult?'

Lilian's colour heightened and she looked away. 'No. No, it hasn't. Gerry was a mistake. I didn't love him – nor did he love me. It was convenient. I suppose you could call it a gesture. Oh Hugh, I've been every kind of idiot.'

They turned and walked towards the garden. After a faltering beginning Lilian told him about France, the feeling that Edmund was with her, guiding her, and how she began to understand her feelings about Hugh. 'I thought you might have forgotten about me completely by now,' she said at the end of her recital, which Hugh listened to in silence but with a wave of joy that grew with every word.

He quickly assured her that that was as far from the case as ever. He had been miserable when he read of her marriage and had sunk so low as to follow her life through press cuttings. If she felt as she did about him, what made her wait before getting in touch with him once she realised the truth? She had wanted to contact him straight away but there was the impediment of her being married to Gerry. She had at last learned to curb her impatience. She was only waiting until she was sure that Hugh was still free before asking Gerry for a divorce, and before she could do that he crashed the racing car. She had no doubts about her own feelings but she had been regrettably impulsive on more than one occasion in the past – here she gave him a sideways look which was answered with a generous smile – and she would not blame him if he had found someone else, given the way she had treated him.

Here she paused and Hugh assured her that he had never stopped loving her and there was no one else in his life. He kissed her to prove it.

At length Lilian continued her recital, saying how she had tried to find out about him. Her parents had no idea, and in the end she had to confide in Walter, who promised to make discreet inquiries. Hugh chuckled to think that he had been under investigation. That was as bad as his press cuttings. She wanted to get in touch with him sooner but heard that he was away. The problem was to find a suitable excuse for contacting him, then she remembered the handkerchief. She had been nervous, very nervous, in case he said he did not want to see her. She would not have blamed him if he sent her away with a flea in her ear.

'And had you really kept the handkerchief? I thought it was just a pretext,' he said.

She opened her handbag and produced it.

'I got rid of almost everything else from my previous life but I kept this without knowing why. I just couldn't let it go. You'll think me silly, but in those dreadful years after I sent you packing I would take it out and hold it, praying for your safe return.'

Hugh's eyes moistened and he was unable to speak. Lilian hugged him. They did not speak or move until a robin began to think they had turned to stone and might make a suitable perch. Eventually they separated and walked on. She had to ask the question that had been troubling her since that day in 1916. 'Can you ever forgive me for how I treated you?'

'I forgave you a long time ago. I felt sorrier for you than I can say. It was so obvious that you were deeply unhappy and struggling to come to terms with Edmund's disabilities.'

'It's taken all this time for me to develop the wisdom of hindsight – any wisdom, in fact. Do you believe that love and hate are different sides of the same coin? I think they must be. You see, no matter what I thought of you I was never indifferent. You always provoked some strong emotion in me.'

'Yes, I believe you're right. I'd have been crushed if you'd been indifferent towards me. You can't feign it, you know. Even when you appeared to be indifferent I could tell that you were seething about something or other that I'd done, or that you thought I was going to do.'

This brought them round to discussing when Lilian had started to love Hugh, from which the next step inevitably was Edmund.

'Is it possible to love two people at once, do you think?' she asked. It was a question that had been vexing her since May.

'I honestly don't know. I know I couldn't. But, my dearest Lilian, perhaps you started to love me after you stopped loving Edmund.'

She stopped in her tracks and nearly remonstrated with him before thinking better of it. 'You're right. I did stop loving him, at least in a passionate sense, but I cared deeply for him until the day he died. Even now, I can barely face up to my coldness towards him. It's a guilt I live with constantly. That's why I ran away. Why I couldn't bear to see you. I believe you always knew me better than I knew myself. You saw what I was unable to admit to myself.'

'I have my share of guilt as well. I was in love with my best friend's wife. I'm not proud of that. Sometimes I felt jealous as hell – particularly when you came back from your honeymoon and all too obviously had a wonderful time and were so much in love. I think that's why I scolded you sometimes – I wanted Edmund to have the happiness that was denied me. I don't blame you for resenting my interference, because that's what it was. It was unforgiveable of me. I've often asked myself if I'd have – I suppose propositioned you is the most appropriate way of putting it – if you'd been someone else's wife. I think I might have done. But I couldn't do that to him. I hope to goodness he never knew how I felt.'

They had been walking randomly around the garden and lost track of time. Hugh consulted his watch and was astonished to see it was twenty past one.

'The last time we ate together was rather fraught,' he said. 'Shall we try again? I have no idea what Mrs Coombe has got lined up for lunch – I hope it will stretch.'

Lilian smiled. 'Thank you, I'd like that, as long as it isn't something awkward like a chop.'

They turned and took the quickest route back to the house.

'Are you still set on living in London?' Hugh asked.

'No. That was all part of my reaction against the war and everything. I've got it out of my system now. It was lively and I enjoyed it but my life there was shallow. No, at last I know where I belong.'

'Then will you marry me?'

'Are you really sure you want that? You haven't forgotten that I've buried two husbands? I might be considered more suitable material for a mistress.'

'If that's your only concern I've had one or two lovers myself, come to that.'

'Do I need to be jealous of anyone?'

'No. No one at all. It was just to pass the time. So is it yes or no?'

'It's yes, with all my heart.'

In the kitchen Mrs Coombe was worried that the master's lunch would spoil – he was punctual to one o'clock as a rule. You could normally set your clock by him but he was all a-twitter today and must have forgot himself. She went to the window to see if he was coming.

'Well I never did!' she exclaimed, looking out at two figures kissing passionately only yards away.

'What's the matter, Mrs Coombe?' Aldhelm asked, moving to join her. He looked out. 'I'll set another place at the table, and you'd better put another plate to warm.'